Praise for th
Suburbi

'Chris McCrudden has createc
Flotsam. His sprawling spac
cross Dr Who with an unhealthy fascination for household appliances. **Forget alien invasion; in this explosive future you won't be able to trust your spin dryer.**'

Christopher Fowler

'McCrudden's debut is festooned with cunning punnery, sharp turns of phrase, and jokes about emojis and the internet, making this very much **a comic novel of our times.**'

James Lovegrove, Financial Times

'I loved this book. I **legit laughed through the entire novel** and I am excited that there will be a sequel.'

Terra C

'A brilliant mix of sci-fi, humor, and those hundreds of little things that make a memorable story. McCrudden is **destined to become synonymous with great sci-fi humor**.'

Christopher H

'**A deliciously hilarious romp** which skirts the realms of credibility but provides a wild ride which kept me very much entertained throughout. It's bonkers, it's mad and... so exaggerated to almost be genius in its execution.'

Kath B

'Featuring a kindly bread-maker, ancient nana-cyborgs, a moving hairdressers and a chance to avert a nuclear bomb, it's **both great fun and very clever**.'

Ruth M

'Battlestar Suburbia **highlights the absurdity of life**, and the adaptability of individuals in unusual situations. McCrudden's novel will appeal to fans of Douglas Adams and Terry Pratchett, or anyone looking for an escape only loosely connected to reality.'

Stephenie S

'**This was a trip!** Some great one-lines & puns help create this future world where the machines have taken over. With evil smartphones, anti-hero humans, & a motherly bread maker pushed to the edge...'

Caroline F

BATTLE BEYOND THE DOLESTARS

BATTLESTAR SUBURBIA, BOOK TWO

Chris McCrudden

For my dad.

This edition published in 2019 by Farrago,
an imprint of Prelude Books Ltd
13 Carrington Road, Richmond, TW10 5AA, United Kingdom

www.farragobooks.com

ISBN: 978-1-78842-105-8

Printed and bound in Great Britain by Clays Ltd.

Chapter 1

The A32222 Earth to Mars highway (via Dewsbury) was a perfect spot for a Sunday afternoon cruise. Once you were clear of the smoggy Earth and its unsightly ring of orbiting council estates known as Dolestars, it was a straight run past the moon. If you set out early enough – which you did if you were a cooker or washing machine and still lived by the rhythms of the clock hardwired into your ancestors – you could be enjoying a battery brunch on Phobos by ten a.m.

From there you could sip your delicious litihium spritz and marvel at Mars's highest mountain, Olympus Mons, with its cap of CO_2 snow, crisp and white as great-great-grandma's icebox. It was glorious to be a robot. They were rulers of the Earth, masters of the solar system and creators of a social order that gave even the humblest dustbuster two servants. As the power flowed, and the frigid air of Mars's microscopic moons kept them at optimum temperature, it was easy for machines to feel giddy and invulnerable.

All that, however, was changing.

A year into the human-machine war, the A32222 was the frontline and barricaded with an enormous chunk of rock quarried from Mars below. The barricade, which everyone now called the Martian Gap Services, was intended to send a signal to humans that the machines had a whole solar system's worth of resources at their disposal, but really just betrayed the inflexibility of robot thought. This wasn't a railway, it was space. And in space, you don't have to follow the road.

As if to illustrate this, a single rocket ship appeared from behind the dark side of Mars's snack-sized second moon Deimos. It shot over the Martian Gap in a whirl of rose-red space dust. And down on the barricade, a thousand gun emplacements beeped in exasperation and scrambled the nearest fleet of drones.

A neutron beam opened his command line and hailed the nearest machine gun with a

>\\\/

>CAN YOU BELIEVE IT? He typed. IT'S THE THIRD TIME THIS WEEK.

>*I KNOW*, replied the machine gun. *HAVEN'T THEY READ THE RULE BOOK?*

>THEIR SO-CALLED LEADER RIPPED IT UP ON TV LAST MONTH, replied the neutron beam. SAID SHE WAS GOING TO USE IT FOR CURLER PAPERS ON HER DAY OFF.

>*SAVAGES.*

The neutron beam typed >YES in his chat window but exited before sending. This machine gun was a new recruit, still bellicose from his training downloads, but the neutron beam was approaching the end of his third tour of duty. Just a few more days of this and he would cycle out of this unfamiliar body and return to his civilian life as a toaster on Earth. Life there wasn't normal either, but if you narrowed your viewing angles you could go a whole day without thinking about the war. Providing you didn't look up to see the chief commander General Shermann's face tattooed into the moon's surface along with the slogan 'Your Republic Needs You!'

The neutron beam reached for his trigger, which was the piece of programming his Earth body used to stop crumpets burning. He felt visceral disgust at this alien body. Every single line of his toaster code looked at the radar, fuel cell, aiming mechanism and transmitted 'nope' back to his core processor.

He froze.

The rebel rocket ship fired, ending the toaster's epiphany about the futility of war and ensuring that Earth's future contained fewer toasted crumpets. Several hundred more gung-ho weapons shot back. They missed, and the rocket whooshed up. It did so with such glee that, even though space is somewhere that no one can hear you scream, several machines thought they registered a loud 'wheeeeeeeee' coming from inside the ship.

Those were the machines with the presence of mind to detect what was in the bomb that the ship had dropped while pretending to charge the barricade. It looked like a harmless tube of metal, but the radioactive signature said otherwise.

The nuke exploded, turning the Martian Gap into a microsun for a microsecond. A ring of debris: dust, rock, liquefied metal bloomed in space. Radio sets fizzed with the white noise of billowing radiation. It was the kind of signal that encourages scientists listening in from other star systems to shake their tentacles with disappointment and look elsewhere for signs of intelligent life.

The mangled base of a neutron gun, blown clear from the Martian Gap by the blind luck of the cosmos, became Mars's newest moon. It hung over the red planet, a tapered terracotta-red cylinder that in another place, another time, another universe would have made an ideal plant pot for some petunias. Or it would until the rocket ship looped three times above the impact site in triumph and sent what remained of the neutron gun into a collision course with Deimos.

Inside the ship, its captain celebrated by opening a bottle of algae champagne. You could tell he was a captain by the pips stitched on to the scruffy oxygen cap he used to breathe in low-oxygen conditions, but the resemblance to flying aces of history ended there. He was short, bandy-legged and his nose ran more efficiently than his ship did. His name was Darren and, because of a series of accidents, good luck and the survival instincts you normally only found in small rodents, he was a hero of the human resistance. He was also the only member of the rebellion who could bear the company of his ship, Polari.

'That was amazing,' said Polari, his dashboard lighting up with pleasure. 'Like totally amazing.'

Darren took a swig of the algae champagne and retched so hard that he fell off his chair. He bobbed around in Polari's micro-gravity like a cork in a glass of bad wine – though it was difficult to imagine any wine worse than algae champagne.

'Like so amazing,' continued Polari, 'that I'm beginning to think maybe I did miss my calling after all.'

'Hang on,' said Darren, righting himself, 'we're not going back there again.' He and Polari had first met when he'd persuaded the Inter-Continental Ballistic Missile to retrain as a spaceship. Polari had powerful engines, and the temperament of a fourteen-year old boy high on white cider and video games.

'You never let me have any fun, Darren,' said Polari.

'I let you fire a nuclear missile,' said Darren. 'Isn't that enough for one day?'

They were interrupted by a sharp squeak at the rear of the ship. Here the third, the smallest and most cunning member of the crew was hard at work operating a set of spectrometers. This was Chubb, an orphaned machine that was half-lockpick half-drone and all sass. He had also switched sides to fight against his fellow machines out of loyalty to Darren. Right now he was scanning the radioactive ball of dust and debris left after the explosion for salvageable materials. The resistance was critically low on supplies.

A fourth voice entered the cockpit as the intercom crackled into life. 'Yoo-hoo, Polari,' it said. As no human born in the last ten thousand years had any military experience, the rebels struggled with the vocabulary of war. This was Rita, who was the movement's chief communications officer on the strength that she used to run a minicab service on the Dolestars. 'It's the Battlestar Suburbia here. Admiral Janice wants to know if it all went off okay.'

Darren climbed towards the intercom. His head swam. No matter how many times he did this, he always felt like he was going to be found out. Before the rebellion he'd sold battery packs by the side of the A32222. It was a blameless, invisible existence, and didn't prepare you well for being one of the solar system's Top 3 Most Wanted organisms. 'This is the Starship Polari,' he said.

'I know, love,' replied Rita. 'I've got your caller ID up here. I dialled the number.'

Darren sighed. 'That's not how it's supposed to work, Rita.'

'Hang on, I've got someone on the other line.'

The channel went dead. Darren shrugged, remarking 'Do you think they have these problems at Earth high command?' to Chubb before Rita's voice returned in a whine of feedback

'...the driver will pick you up outside the kebab shop. Don't be late, will you, duck? He's got another drop-off straight after. So sorry about that, Darren. I'm rushed off my feet.'

They all were. Darren looked back across the cockpit at his knitting. The replacement for his current spacesuit lay there, a mess of needles and thermal wiring. But unless he was also able to manufacture several hours of spare time from nowhere, he would never finish it. How much longer could any of them keep this up?

Darren suppressed his dread the only way he knew how: by keeping up his performance of the arrogant hotshot starship captain he knew the rebellion needed him to be. He'd learned it from 3D dramas and didn't like it very much, but a disguise always made him feel less like a fraud.

'Well,' he drawled, 'we apprehended the target three minutes and… twenty-two seconds ago. Please inform the Admiral that the Martian Gap Services have been eliminated.' Darren heard clapping on the other end of the line.

'There's really no need for applause…' he said.

'I wasn't, love. I was trying to get the last of the sauce out this bottle. Len!' Rita snapped at someone in the background, 'Did you remember the salt and vinegar on these chips? They're as bland as.'

'Rita,' said Darren, 'this is our most important victory in months.'

It was. The Martian Gap Services blocked the supply route between the asteroid belt, where the resistance's headquarters, the Battlestar Suburbia, was hiding out, and their fellow human beings on the Dolestars. It was also a massive arms dump. With the Martian Gap nuked it would take days – maybe even a week – for the machine authorities on Earth to rebuild their forces in the region.

'We need to press our advantage now,' said Darren. He was glad he'd worn his new waistcoat for this mission. It was faux-leather, which made him sweat, and the knee-length boots he'd bought to go with it didn't suit someone so short, but they were part of his maverick captain image. 'We can take Mars.'

'Very nice, Darren,' said Rita, 'but to be honest I've got your report to write, a fleet of mining probes about to send a diagnostic report in, the school run's kicking off and I still haven't had my blessed dinner. LEN!' she shouted, using her 'get out of my pub' voice, 'I asked for battered sausage not saveloy.'

The line went dead.

Darren bit down on the urge to kick a control panel. The last thing he needed right now was for Polari to do the equivalent of huffing off to its room to listen to angsty rock music. He tried counting to ten instead. Then twenty. Then thirty.

Polari broke the silence. 'Err, guys,' he said.

'Yes?' said Darren.

'There's something on the scanner.'

Chubb's antennae stiffened with alarm. The radar screen was filled with electronic confetti heading their way. He gave a squeak. Drones.

Darren threw himself back to his controls, stomach lurching from nerves and micro-gravity. This couldn't be real. They'd done countless sweeps before the mission. The drones had all been stationed on the dark side of the Gap. He gave up counting the dots when he got to thirty. Too many to fight.

'Polari,' said Darren to the ship, 'would you pop the telly on?'

Polari turned on his external cameras to reveal that the ship was surrounded by military-grade drones. These were nothing like the scrappy things, more like street pigeons than machine, who flocked in their millions on the Earth's surface. These had fresh space-camo paint jobs and fusion engines. And they were closing in on the lightly armed Polari with their L-Eye-Ds narrowing.

'What are you waiting for?' yelled Darren. 'Run.'

Polari fired up his engines just as the first bullet grazed his armour.

'I thought you'd never ask,' he said, and raced off with a whole drone fleet hard behind him.

Chapter 2

'Admiral, you're needed on the bridge.'

Janice paused as she pinned a heated roller into her customer's hair and looked up. There was a messenger in the doorway: a lieutenant from the pips sewn into her housecoat. She rummaged through her memory for her name: tall, round figure, and that A-line bob it had taken a whole afternoon to get right.

'Is it Karen?' she said.

'It is,' replied Karen looking scared and impressed. Janice's facility with names never failed to unnerve her crew, but it was a skill that came easily to a neighbourhood hairdresser. If you could remember who your latest lady's cousin's husband ran off with, then it wasn't hard to memorise your crew manifest.

'It is my afternoon off,' said Janice. She gestured at her ancestral salon, Kurl Up and Dye. It was a softly lit space, scuffed lino and washbasins on one side, dryers on the other. Everything inside from the curler drawers to the bobby pins had the patina of a treasured heirloom. Apart, that is, from a set of new dryers. This was where Janice spent her Wednesday afternoons. She might have a rebellion to run, but you had to keep your hand in.

'I know,' said Karen, 'but we've just had a report in from the Martian Gap.'

Anxiety jabbed the back of Janice's throat. She'd ordered the strike for Wednesday – the same day as her trickiest lady in months – hoping that a full-head of corkscrew curls would take her mind off the manoeuvre. She checked the wall clock. Three p.m. Mars Standard Time. They were early. This could only be very good or very bad news.

'Do you mind, Flo?' she said to her customer, who shook her head. Flo could hardly object. Without Janice, everyone aboard would have been nuked by the current prime minister of the Machine Republic, Sonny Erikzon. Janice was their leader, their saviour and the most reasonably priced hairdresser in a billion square mile radius.

'I'll be fine,' she said, seeing herself out with a couple of custard creams from the biscuit barrel.

Janice lifted the salon blinds. Outside was a massive cylindrical space lit by a fog of bioluminescent dust motes. This was the inside of the Battlestar Suburbia, a spaceship originally built in the last days before machines took control on Earth. It had been recycled into an orbiting housing estate for humans during the long millennia of the Machine Republic and then fired out into space at the beginning of the human rebellion a year ago.

Janice flicked a switch to the right of the door and braced herself as Kurl Up and Dye shook before lurching three metres into the air one side at a time. When the world had stopped shuddering, she turned a dial to the left of the door to 'brisk walk'. Then she peered out to watch the metal chicken legs of the Baba Yaga 4000, which were attached to the bottom of Kurl Up and Dye, walk the salon to the bridge, which was located at the other end of the Suburbia.

Janice had grown to love the wobbly gait of the Baba Yaga, but it wasn't to everyone's tastes. Karen slumped in a chair by one of the washbasins, sweat gumming her fringe to her forehead.

'It'll be over soon,' Janice told her.

'That's what I'm afraid of,' replied Karen and heaved into the sink.

As the salon strolled across the Suburbia, Janice marvelled at how much the empty shell of a year ago had changed. She watched teams of overalled humans mop and sweep floors, while others heaved bricks and girders to make new homes and workshops. Someday this would be the human equivalent of Singulopolis, the machine capital on Earth that was so big it covered three continents. Or at least they would when they got more raw materials. Janice winced at the severity of shortages. Houses with no roofs; plastic-lined growing chambers they couldn't activate without soil. They had accomplished miracles in the past year, but hope and determination couldn't make up for a broken supply chain.

When the salon docked with the bridge, Janice turned the 'open' sign to 'back in 30 minutes' and walked, via a short corridor, into… a mirror image of Kurl Up and Dye. This room had the same faded pastel colour scheme as on the other side of the door. It felt upcycled rather than lived-in, however, as though someone had spent an afternoon ageing up the paintwork with a pot of cold tea and some sandpaper. Which is exactly what Janice had done after the flight crew complained they 'didn't hold with anything too new'.

The flight crew were in their usual places, hunched in three chairs at the back of the fake salon. Ida, Ada and Alma never left their stations, but that wasn't because they were dedicated leaders of a resistance. It was because they had been glued into them thousands of years ago in a freak accident, and moving them more than a couple of inches meant calling in a winch and a gurney. Janice had known them her whole life, but had never seen their faces, which were obscured by plastic dryer helmets. The only clue to their inner lives was their voices, which on a normal day were set to 'background bickering' and their emoji screens, which Janice noticed were all set to :-/

It was going to be a long day.

'Ladies,' she said, 'I believe we have news.'

'What time do you call this?' said Ida, who inhabited the left-most chair, turning the image on her emoji screen into a reproachful |><| egg timer.

Janice closed her eyes and took a breath. If Ida hadn't been a priceless heirloom she suspected someone would have banged her to bits with a poker centuries ago. 'You know Wednesdays are my afternoons off.'

'Oh yes,' said Ada, who occupied the middle chair and was more of a people-person than Ida, despite having stopped being wholly human ten millennia before, 'You booked in Flo Perkins who wanted the long perm, didn't you?'

All three emoji screens switched to :-(

'Don't blame me,' said Janice, 'they're coming back. I don't set fashion, ladies. I follow it.'

'I'd have thought a fleet admiral could set a firmer tone,' said Ida.

'This isn't a dictatorship,' replied Janice.

'I'm all for democracy,' said Alma. She sat in the right-most chair and, having owned a small car while alive, acted as the Suburbia's chief pilot. 'We're just not sure about the poodle perm. I mean, we have lived through…'

'Six revivals by my reckoning,' said Ida with a :-[] grimace.

'And let me tell you,' said Alma, 'they were all dark times.'

'Were they any darker than being the last light of human freedom on the verge of being snuffed out?' said Janice, motioning outside.

'Point taken,' said Alma after a pause. The ladies were the oldest beings and the only cyborgs in existence, but until last year had spent most of that time hiding out in the bowels of a space station. It had left them with an odd outlook on the world. When yesterday and a Tuesday teatime seven thousand years ago were equally real to them, it was hard to get them to focus on the bigger picture.

'So are you going to pass this message on or what?'

While Alma unscrambled the coded transmission, Janice helped herself to some Nicotea. The brew, which was foul but addictive, was even bitterer than usual, but at least it sharpened her senses. She was lucky to have it at all. Dwindling supplies meant that only last week she'd reduced the weekly ration to a withdrawal-inducing three bags per person.

Darren's voice came through. Or at least that silly drawling voice he'd started using in his official communiques. She listened to his bickering with Rita, wishing the pair could get on with each other more. But then, there it was. The sweet relief of the words, 'Please inform the admiral that the Martian Gap Services have been eliminated.'

Her heart pounded. This was why she'd taken the gamble of de-coupling Polari, her fleet's only super-speed engine, and retrofitting him into a fighter ship. Her eyes drifted to the back of the bridge where their five remaining nukes sat in a lead-lined curler cupboard. The gamble had worked.

'You know what to do ladies,' she said.

Ida, Ada and Alma gave a ;-) and they fired up the engines. Janice took her seat and turned the nearest stylist's mirror into an external view of the Suburbia. Its long, lumpy turd-like shape had camouflaged it well among the dirty rock and ice of the asteroid belt. Now they were ready to come out.

'Mind yourself,' said Ida, ever the back-seat driver.

The ship swerved to avoid an asteroid that Janice's spectrometer told her contained enough water to fill the lake they were building down in the basement three times over. She made a mental note to return here. If they survived.

'I know what I'm doing,' snipped Ada.

Janice's hand crept into the inner pocket of her housecoat for her battle plans. They had the soft, cottony feel of paper folded once too often for its own good. She'd agonised for months over these; spending long nights over the details with nothing but Nicotea for company.

It wasn't a great plan, but it was the best she could do with what she had. She spread the paper out over the console, trying for the millionth time to fathom the real distance between their current position in the asteroid belt and their target, Mars. In cosmic terms it was nothing: the equivalent of popping next door to borrow the lawnmower. In human terms it was unimaginably vast. They would be a sitting target the moment they left the cover of the asteroid belt, but nor could they let an opportunity like this go by.

She moved her eye over to her drawing of Mars, an unsteady red blot with two pebble-like moons and there, the only military base between here and the inner solar system, the Martian Gap.

She took a bingo marker out of her pocket and, after crossing out the Martian Gap, drew a ring around Mars and a line straight back to the asteroid belt. The calculations were already there in the plans: three whole nights' of crossings-out. If they held a steady course and hit Mars at the right orbit, they could take it from the machines.

All she had to do in the meantime was steer a ship with no defensive shields, few weapons and eight million people on board through open space without getting everyone killed. She sighed and put the plans back in her pocket. It was just another normal day in the office. But while she was an Admiral now she was still Janice, a woman who'd spent her whole life hiding from unwanted attention. And it had taught her a few lessons.

'Rita,' she said into the intercom, 'I'm coming down.'

Chapter 3

Rita greeted Janice at the door to the docking bay with a frown and a kiss. She looked tired, her face was screwed up on one side from listening to the voices in her earpiece, but she'd still made an effort. Yes, she was wearing the same beige housecoat as everyone else in Central Operations (otherwise known as Big Ops), but she'd jazzed it up with her favourite plum lipstick and a yellow headscarf over her tight black curls.

Janice recalled their first meeting, when she'd saved Rita from a drone raid. Even then, covered in dust and shaking with fear, Rita still somehow managed to make the best of herself. She remembered that flash of plum lipstick amid the dust and soot of laser fire. It wasn't often you met someone who retained such an unshakeable sense of who they were. This was a person she could get to know, and in the past year they had. They were now a couple, though hardly love's young dream. Both Janice and Rita were wary from past disappointments, but that didn't stop them grabbing what they wanted now.

'Sorry I missed you this morning,' whispered Janice.

'Big day,' shrugged Rita then tapped her earpiece. 'Honestly,' she said, 'Darren's a bit needy, isn't he?'

'It was a big mission,' Janice protested. But she knew it was true. Confidence was in short supply on the Suburbia. Almost everyone here was haunted by the suspicion that they had only survived through blind luck but Darren was in a different league altogether. In the past year, his imposter complex had taken on a character of its own. That wouldn't be so much of a problem if Darren's first instinct on encountering difficulty wasn't to reach for the dressing-up box. She needed more of the Darren she knew – resourceful, quick-witted, brave to the point of thoughtlessness – and rather less of the maverick spaceship captain he was dragging up as lately.

Rita waved Janice into the docking bay. Originally built to house probes and reconnaissance ships, back in the distant time when the Suburbia was a deep-space exploratory craft called Discovery, the docking bay was the nearest thing the rebellion had to military infrastructure. It had functioning airlock doors, a refuelling station and enough space for a fleet of fighters. It was just a shame that the rebellion had only one ship capable of long-range missions and that was Polari.

But Janice, who like Rita prided herself on her ability to make the best of bad situations, had a plan for getting round this. It involved filling the docking bay with rocks. Huge chunks of the asteroid belt, to be exact, all of which were in neat formation in the docking bay.

'Did we get them all fitted out?' Janice asked.

'Len's seeing to the last one now,' said Rita, glaring at a bespectacled man in overalls with his face half-buried in a bag of chips. 'Aren't you, Len?'

'Yes, ma'am,' he squeaked. 'Just have to fit that last booster.'

'Well get on with it.'

As Len scurried away, Rita cupped her hands around her mouth and shouted, 'Company fall in.'

Janice straightened up and wished she'd got changed into dress uniform. It didn't feel right, ordering the rebellion's first big offensive manoeuvre in a gingham housecoat with a gravy stain on the lapel.

The soldiers in question lolloped over with the uncertain step of people who've seen marching in movies but never practised together. Each wore a bulky oxygen suit made from crocheted cables and carried a bubble helmet under one arm. Their faces were nervous, but their hair was fabulous. Every head gleamed with a new dye job, subtle lowlights or a sleek blow-dry. It had been days of work for Janice, but an honour to do it for the women who would be carrying out her crazy plan.

'Company B!' barked Rita when they were all in place. 'Atten-tion!'

'What did she say?' asked a woman on the far end to her neighbour. She was the oldest member of the group by a clear decade; she wore her hair in a white chignon.

'Face front, will you Mabel?' said her neighbour, a tall woman in late middle age with a sensible bob. 'And turn your hearing aid up. We're about to get our orders.'

Rita turned in exasperation to Janice, who shook her head. The harder they tried to militarise the resistance, the more ramshackle it became. Besides, she thought, looking at the junk that filled the loading bay, what could you expect?

These ladies weren't the natural choice for elite troops, but they were volunteers and that counted for a lot given what their mission was. When Janice gave the order, each of these women would climb one of the asteroids inside this loading bay. They would strap themselves into the chair cut into the top of each rock. When she gave the second order they would fire up the small booster engines which were the only military technology the rebellion could manufacture at scale. Once they were airborne they would manoeuvre out of the loading bay and fly in close formation around the Suburbia.

It was the best plan that Janice could think of to solve an insoluble problem. While the future of the rebellion depended on leaving the asteroid belt, she knew that the only way to protect the people on board was to stay within the asteroid belt, which the machine fleet couldn't penetrate.

So the best compromise she could come up with was to leave the asteroid belt but take it with her. Her plan was to use each rock in this loading bay as a shield or – more accurately – as cannon fodder around the vulnerable body of the Suburbia.

She saluted at Company B, who saluted back, noticing that every one of them did so without touching their hair.

Of course Company B was only their official name. Thanks to the vein of black humour that ran through the rebellion like mould through a blue cheese they'd earned another nickname. They were the Rockettes.

The last element of Janice's battle plan, and the part she'd agonised over most, was the speech. Hours of work getting the metaphors right, striking the proper balance between hope and seriousness. There were even jokes. But as she faced the Rockettes, with their perfectly conditioned hair and serious faces, Janice couldn't do it. Her throat felt dry. She longed for a cup of tea, and the longest lie down in history.

She gave the plan a last squeeze inside her pocket and said, 'Best of luck, eh ladies.'

Rita gave a nod and dismissed the company, who walked back to their stations to wait for their turn on the stepladder. When the last Rockette was out of earshot she squeezed Janice's arm.

'What was that about?' she said. 'I was all geared up for the speech.'

'I couldn't,' said Janice. She felt tears prick her eyes.

'Never have so many depended on so few, and with so few split ends,' said Rita. 'It was brilliant. Exactly what they needed.'

'You give the speech then,' muttered Janice, 'I've got work to do.'

Rita grabbed her by the shoulder. 'You can't do all this on your own,' she said.

Janice flung her arms out at the loading bay filled with rocks, at the sisters, aunts and grandmothers she was sending to their deaths. She watched as Mabel a few asteroids over stuck a freshly inflated haemorrhoid ring to her seat with duct tape and lowered herself into place.

'I know I can't,' she said. 'And that's the problem.'

She left Rita to oversee the last preparations and sat down on an empty packing case in the corridor. She wondered if this was how she'd be found out. Everyone in that bay, and the eight million people on the Suburbia, was looking to her to do something bold and audacious. All she had were some glorified shoe-boosters – the same technology humans on Dolestars used to stop themselves drifting into space in an emergency – and some rocks.

'I still think it's a good plan,' said a voice.

She saw the power light flicker on the nearest loudspeaker. It was Freda, the fourth of the cyborgs Janice had inherited from her ancestors and the most peculiar. While the other three stayed in their bodies to steer the ship, Freda had abandoned hers altogether. Her consciousness thrummed through any electronic system she came into contact with. Freda's wanderlust made sense to Janice. It couldn't have been fun living in a human body so desiccated that you were only ever one vigorous dusting away from oblivion.

'Of course you think it's a good plan,' said Janice. 'It's totally mad.'

'It's very economical,' said Freda. She was a near-omniscient being who could move effortlessly between the physical and virtual layers of reality, yet she had never lost the tone of an old lady asking you to reach for the cat food on the top shelf in the supermarket.

'It's meant to be a rebellion though, not a recipe for whole-wheat pasta bake.'

Janice heard Rita give the last command to the Rockettes in her other ear.

'Gentlemen,' she shouted with the heavy irony that had assured Janice that her attraction to Rita would condense into love, 'start your engines and may the best woman win.'

'I do like Rita,' said Freda. 'She's good for you. She has nerve.'

'What's that supposed to mean?' replied Janice. She'd known Freda her whole life. She'd been part of the family for countless generations, so even her most innocuous comment could be stuck with barbs.

'You are touchy these days, Janice,' said Freda. She switched on the nearest monitor to view the Rockettes as they manoeuvred out of the docking bay. It flipped between the internal camera – a picture of huge rocks performing frantic three-point turns – and the external – where the enormity of space re-scaled each meteor to the size of a pebble.

'I've got a lot on my plate,' said Janice.

'That's no surprise. You were always rubbish at sharing.'

'Who did I have to share anything with?'

At this, both women – one flesh and blood, the other a tangled ball of inorganic programming and organic brainwaves – fell silent. Their minds ranged over their shared history. Janice's hermetic life running a hairdresser's that no one visited in the bowels of a space station. No company apart from her four inherited ladies and her daughter, Kelly. Kelly, who was down on Earth now in a hinterland somewhere between life and death, her body taken over by Sonny Erikzon, the crazed machine who wanted to know what it was like to play dress-up with flesh and blood.

Janice watched Mabel make it out the docking bay on her third go, tipped over at a thirty-degree angle. The Rockettes held their formation around the Suburbia and the shield was complete. She looked beyond the ship and its girdle of rocks. Out there was Mars, and there was Earth. Around the Earth there were dozens of Dolestars and billions of humans waiting to be liberated. But was she really going there because she wanted to fight for the greater good? Or was she moving mountain ranges-worth of stone and risking millions of lives because she wanted Kelly back?

She wanted desperately to be alone.

'Haven't you got something to do?' she asked Freda.

Freda took the hint and the light in the camera winked out. At the same moment, a spidery-looking probe jolted into life in the docking bay and fluttered out into space on solar wings. This was the final piece of the plan. Now the Rockettes were in place, Freda would guide them and the Suburbia out of the asteroid belt.

Janice gave the order.

'Take us forward, ladies.'

The ship's engines rumbled.

There was no turning back now.

Chapter 4

'General Shermann!'

Private Fuji Itsu saluted the supreme commander of the Machine Republic's armed forces. It was a complicated gesture for a printer that involved pushing her paper feeder out at an uncomfortable angle. But orders were orders, and she was in the army now.

She thought of her comfortable office back on the Earth in the Ministry of Operational Affairs. The beige walls, the comforting sounds of her line manager, an electric samovar, gently stewing tea as she reconciled the count on component bins. Yes, it had been boring and slow, but she was a printer: that was her nature.

It couldn't be more different to today. Noticing General Shermann wouldn't reach her for at least a minute, Fuji dared another look around at her new office in the logistics pool. It was a wide room whose windows were open to the emptiness of space. Inside, however, the machines were packed in as tightly as products in a discount retailer. If Fuji wasn't careful her paper feeder could knock over the pens on her neighbour's workstation.

Her neighbour, a busybody of a clock radio whose name badge announced her as Soonyo, elbowed Fuji's paper feeder back into its mooring.

'You can stop doing that now,' she buzzed. 'You nearly knocked my snooze button.'

As the General was fast approaching, Fuji kept her mouth shut and printed 'SORRY' in 200pt Helvetica before flicking it into her neighbour's in-tray. This was only her second day and bewilderment kept knocking up against her desire to make a good impression. Conscription was her worst nightmare, but these were trying times and there was a saying that ran deep in her family: 'when life hands you a lemon, print off a good recipe for lemonade.'

The General reached Soonyo first and stared at her so hard that her clock face reset itself to 00:00:00 in fright. He was every bit as giant and intimidating as he was on the news downloads. His bulging thorax was bolted together from armoured plating and atop this was a head fashioned from a sawn-off tank barrel. His stubby legs ended in caterpillar treads instead of feet, and what he lacked in manoeuvrability he made up for in weight. More than one recruit had met its end-of-life by getting in General Shermann's way when he was in a rush. That, Fuji reflected, gave her one thing to be thankful for. As the daughter of a long line of office printers, Fuji was a hefty machine and not the kind of robot you could run over accidentally.

Unlike Soonyo, who was frantically trying to restart her clock face herself while the General barked questions.

'Private!' he rumbled, 'I want a full update on our sprocket silo. What capacity are we running at?'

Her clock face flashed 00:00:01 and let out a burst of alarm.

'That was an order, Private.'

It took Fuji a fraction of a second to find the relevant database entry. Her civilian job was logistics: tracking the progress of the tiny parts from manufacture to recycling. Her filing system was formidable. The silo in question was at eighty-three per cent capacity.

She printed the answer off in 150pt Arial with double spacing and dropped it as discreetly as possible in the alarm clock's in-tray.

Soonyo snuck a sideways look at Fuji, her clock face reading --:--:-0

'Eighty-three per cent capacity, sir,' she said.

'At last,' said Shermann. 'Now, tell me when will it next need a resupply?'

Soonyo went blank again with a --:--:-- and Shermann's gun sights aimed on her. Fuji did some quick calculations on a piece of scrap paper in her overspill drawer. One round of tank ammunition fired into a machine that small in this space would take out everything in a ten-metre radius: including her. She fired up her search program again, found the relevant database and squeaked, 'Three days given the current run-rate of parts.'

Silence descended as machines on all sides edged away or put themselves into hibernation. Never output without input was the first thing you learned in the Machine Corps.

'Sir,' added Fuji belatedly as Shermann's gun sights rotated to fix on her, his eyes blazing a shade of red straight out the range of paint colours the universe would call its 'apocalypse collection'.

'Who,' he said, clicking his trigger with every word, 'are you?'

'Private Fuji Itsu, sir,' she gabbled. Her memory cache was voiding right in front of her eyes. For the first time in her short life Fuji realised she'd spent most of it in the office. 'I just thought…'

'Well,' said Shermann, 'thank you, Private.' His eyes dimmed from red into a dull yellow. Then, drawing himself to his full terrifying height the General peppered the room with abuse instead of bullets. 'So tell me this. How come none of you low-powered lilies apart from Private…'

That stare again.

'Itsu, sir. Itsu.'

'…is able to answer a simple question for me?'

The ranking officer in the logistics pool, a smarmy tanning bed that Fuji had disliked on sight for making a crack about the size of her paper drawers, jolted himself from hibernation.

'Sir, I must protest. Pulling reports from our supply databases is a highly complex and time-consuming…'

A single bullet shattered his UV tubes before he could even finish the sentence. The machines who were still capable of standing stood to attention. Hundreds of power lights shone at full capacity.

'In the army,' said Shermann, 'we expect results, not excuses.'

He pointed a missile-sized finger at Fuji and then Soonyo. 'You two seem to know what you're doing. Follow me.'

It was only when Fuji realised Shermann was marching them to the bridge that she really started to panic. She still struggled to salute with the right paper feeder and he was taking her straight into mission command? She reran the memory file of receiving her call-up BlockPaper through her RAM, recalling how she had longed for a quiet posting. A war spent counting missile fins on the Martian Gap wouldn't be so bad.

She could only imagine what Soonyo must be computing right now. To come that close to end-of-life and then get reassigned on the basis of a skill you didn't have. If she weren't on silent right now her alarm would be deafening. Resolving to stay calm for her colleague's sake, Fuji followed the General on to the bridge of the Starship Deathtrap.

Deathtrap was the newest and most advanced ship in the fleet, but it had been built for efficiency rather than comfort. Its bridge was a cramped space that some machine with malfunctioning taste circuits had decided to clad in camouflage print vinyl. The touchscreens and control panels that flashed everywhere had the crotchety look and jerky operation that happens when you try to run fast software on cheap hardware.

'General on the bridge,' yelled a VHF radio with a lieutenant's pips. The crew, who were wrapped in context-appropriate pleather cladding, stopped swiping away error messages to salute. Meanwhile, Shermann sat in the captain's chair, which promptly collapsed.

The seconds of confusion, random gunfire and shouting that followed gave Fuji enough time to realise why she was here. Between the error messages, the odd choice of captain and a jumpy crew, Fuji knew what was up. The ship had been rushed out of production and into active service while unfinished. Starship Deathtrap was living up to its name.

Fuji and Soonyo got their official briefing when General Shermann had been winched back into sitting position and the broken captain's chair replaced with a reinforced concrete block.

He sat glowering, as the crew struggled to make the ship's operating system take an order without it blowing the digital equivalent of a raspberry. Fuji wondered why the legendary General Shermann, the machine that had crushed seven Dolestar uprisings in the past year with his own caterpillar tracks, was here at all. He was a field soldier, not a starship commander.

'You two are good with software then?' he asked.

Sensing Soonyo's panic, Fuji spoke first. 'I worked with logistics databases as a civilian, sir.'

‘And what do you make of this?’ He gestured around him, just as a bad relational query caused one flight officer to beat a control panel with his whisk attachment and shriek ‘will you just fucking do what I say for once?’

‘Permission to speak freely, sir?’

‘Granted.’

‘When I worked in parts I saw a lot of screws, sir,’ said Fuji. ‘And I’ve never seen anything so screwed as this ship.’

The General’s shoulders slumped. ‘I knew it.’

Fuji had never had to deal with despondency in a manager before. She responded the only way she knew how from office life: with disingenuous optimism. ‘I’m sure it can be fixed with a little time, sir.’

Shermann pointed at the screen at the front of the bridge. It was flicking between a countdown from 24:00:00 and scenes from *The Adventures of White Snowcone*, a popular cartoon in which seven ugly humans did all the cooking and cleaning for a beautiful young ice cream maker.

‘What can you do in twenty-four hours, Lieutenant? Because that’s all we have till we reach destination.’

‘Sir,’ interrupted the machine with the now bent whisk. ‘I have an update from the Martian Gap. It’s… well, it’s not there anymore.’ He rotated his control panel and, swiping yet another error message away, pointed out an area of black space on the monitor.

Fuji found the scrap paper in her recesses and jotted down a rough projection based on a time limit of one solar day and the errors per minute rate she’d observed in the bridge.

‘Actually, sir, I’d revise that up to “really screwed”.’

Beside her, Soonyo shot her a raised eyebrow __:__:~~ on her clock face that Fuji read as a warning not to labour the point.

‘So how come you two got a positive reading?’ said Shermann.

Fuji paused, and reran her memory. At the time it had felt like a natural operation, but now that she played it at half-speed she realised that she'd bypassed the ship's operating system and aimed straight for the data. Based on what she saw now, asking this OS to do anything was the equivalent of handing a Rubik's cube to a baby. It was advanced enough to recognise patterns but had neither the experience nor the maturity to do anything with them. Whoever had signed this ship off as ready for duty deserved reporting to Social Services.

That she got an accurate reading from a direct query did give her the first piece of good news though.

'It means the data in your databases is fine,' she said.

Relief blossomed around her, just as Fuji reached for the verbal weedkiller and finished her sentence.

'But none of that will do you any good if you can't do anything with it. I'm sorry, sir, but this ship is going to be useless without a new operating system.'

Chapter 5

Pamasonic Teffal found that the best time to go out door-knocking was just after the daily news downloads. Nothing sharpened machine despondency more than a few gigabytes of distressing data.

She heard castors squeaking on the other side of the door. As a member of the breadmaker caste she liked to he hospitable, so whenever she went canvassing she kept a batch of buns on the go. The smell of baking created a good impression.

'Good morning,' said Pam as the suspicious face of a vacuum cleaner poked through a crack in the door. It was still in its dust sheet and Pam was mortified to think she might have got this machine out of sleep mode.

'Yes?' wheezed the machine.

'Have you considered voting for peace?' Pam proffered one of her campaign BlockPapers at the machine. It was a simple printing but she was proud of it. Bob, her husband, had taken a lovely picture of her in the kitchen at home and she was very pleased with the copy. It told a simple positive story: 'humans are quite nice really and they do have a point' at the bottom.

The vacuum cleaner took one look at the BlockPaper and threw it back at Pam, triggering a read receipt in the top-left-hand corner.

'Piss off,' it said, 'this is a humanist-free household.'

As she looked at her fourth slammed door this morning, Pam manually re-adjusted her optimism back to one hundred per cent. It was too easy to get disheartened, even if you were doing the right thing. She picked up the discarded BlockPaper and pushed the indestructible sheet of printed plastic through the letterbox with the less charitable thought of 'try getting rid of this'.

She plodded to the next house wondering whether today was going to be the day when someone finally agreed with her. Lobbying for a peace referendum when the Machine Republic was at war with a human rebellion was tough enough, even when she only needed a thousand signatures to trigger one. She had the strike to thank for that. Its effects were everywhere in streaky windows, dingy curtains and doorsteps that were a roller disco of castor and wheel marks. The suburbs of Singulopolis, the glorious machine capital, looked tired and dirty and had done for a year now. Ever since humanity decided to go on strike from its ancestral cleaning duties.

The strike was supposed to make machines realise how much they depended on human labour, but all it had really done was harden machine opinion against the idea that humans deserved rights at all. A strike was against the natural order. Machines didn't save labour: they created it. This much was clear from the state of the streets of Singulopolis, which were now a hazardous place thanks to the rise of dirt-related incidents.

Pam encountered a victim of one in the next driveway. There a dust bunny the size of a small car had trapped the house's inhabitant, a decorative table lamp underneath it. Her flex was tangled in a huge matted ball of dust, pulverised litter and the remains of tiny machines who were too small or too stupid to keep out of its way.

'I say,' said Pam, 'are you alright in there?'

'Of course I'm not,' answered the lamp. 'It's got me by the plug. Help.'

Pam saw that the lamp was almost wholly buried inside the dust bunny. Once they got above a certain size, dust bunnies developed almost unstoppable momentum. She'd heard rumours about larger specimens crushing whole houses.

'Is there no one inside who can help you?' asked Pam.

'My husband's away in the forces,' said the lamp. 'Oh please, can't you do something? I don't want to end-of-life like this. This shade's new on.'

'Give me a moment?' said Pam, and backed out of the driveway as the lamp protested by yelping 'help me, you bytch.'

She knew what she had to do, even if she didn't like it. Her breadmaker body was strong, but it didn't have the turn of speed you needed to deal with even a medium-sized dust bunny. Besides, she had two kids, a husband and a faltering political movement to organise. On her schedule she couldn't afford the end-of-life admin.

She felt inside herself for the other body. Ever since the cyborg Freda had taught her how to partition her consciousness last year, she'd got used to the idea of two-mindedness. Not only did splitting herself into two (or more) parallel consciousnesses mean she could actually get something useful done while sitting on conference calls, it also meant she could operate two bodies at the same time.

For the past year Pam had led a bi-bodied existence. There was Pamasonic Teffal, the homely breadmaker with the best buns in the neighbourhood; and then there was Pam Van Damme, the scarlet motorcycle and with the va-va vroom who was wanted on four treachery and three dozen traffic violation charges.

Pam opened up the connection between her two bodies and made the switch. She poured her attention into Pam Van Damme, leaving a skeleton [Pam] behind in the breadmaker to keep her Teffal body safe. She felt the acid tang of her yeast culture give way to the fumes of a petrol engine.

Pam Van Damme covered the three kilometres between her hideout and the driveway in less than a minute, racking up three more speeding charges in the process. She passed herself at the entrance – always an unsettling experience – before halting in front of the dust bunny with her engine purring.

'Who are you?' asked the lamp, who was now neck-deep in the dust. She took in the long, elegant shape of Pam Van Damme: her vampy red paintwork, the shining lamp-eyes and handlebar horns on the top of her triangular head. Then, because suburban habits die hard, she pointed at the 'No hawkers, no circulars, no junk mail' sign on the door.

Pam rolled her lamp-eyes and, crouching back into riding pose, reversed back up the driveway. Meanwhile the dust bunny ground forward and tipped the lamp over.

'Don't go!' she squealed. 'I didn't mean to be rude. It's just that with no one to clean anymore we don't really need any dusters.'

The cheek of it, thought Pam. If she were just ten per cent less agreeable she'd do a three-point turn right now and leave the snob to it. That sent a twinge through her settings, however. There was no way her programming would let her taxi away from a creature of any sorts if it were in danger.

She bit down on her accelerator and drove forward. All she could focus on now was the woolly grey surface of the dust bunny.

'Oh dear,' said the lamp, 'are you sure this is a good...'

Pam let her head fall forward so her handlebar horns dropped to just above the ground. She hit the bottom edge of the giant dust ball at just the right angle and, slamming on the brakes, threw herself back into standing position. Landing on her feet just as the dust bunny flew into the air, she put the lightning reflexes of her motorcycle body to good use. She pulled the lamp out of the dust bunny by her flex and flipped the dust bunny out of the driveway and into the road.

The lamp scurried across the driveway to retrieve her shade. 'That was magnificent,' she said. 'Now just hold on there a second while I find my purse. I'll take half a dozen dusters.'

Pam blew a raspberry of petrol fumes and left, handing her consciousness back to her breadmaker body as she did so. Now she was back in her more familiar, steadier form, Pam could sort out her feelings. Pamasonic Teffal was more stoic than Pam Van Damme, who could be quick to take offence. Nevertheless, it was terribly bad manners to accuse another machine of door-to-door sales like that.

'Hello,' she said, trundling back into the driveway in her breadmaker body.

'Oh, it's you,' said the lamp. 'Where did you go?'

'I went for help,' said Pam.

'Well you're too late,' replied the lamp, picking up its flex to form a <3 shape. 'The most miraculous thing just happened.'

'Oh,' said Pam, 'I see my sister got here already.'

The lamp dropped its <3 and turned its bulb up to full intensity to peer at square, sturdy Pam.

'Your sister?'

'We grew up with different blueprints,' said Pam.

'Wow, well the next time you see her give her my…'

'She's very busy,' said Pam. 'You'd be astonished how many silly suborban robots get too close to a dust bunny. She's on call morning, noon and night.'

'How dare you,' said the lamp. 'This is Zone Two. The suborbs start at the end of the next road.'

The timer on the top of Pam's head pinged in annoyance. 'That's a fine way to talk to the machine who just saved your life, lady,' she said.

The lamp's bulb dimmed to 10W in shame. 'It is, isn't it?' She looked at the power bars on Pam's chest. 'You look done in. Would you like to come in for a charge-up?'

'That sounds marvellous.' Even if forgiveness hadn't been printed into Pam's circuit boards, she'd been on her feet all morning and needed a pick-me-up.

The lamp brightened back to 40W. 'Since we're celebrating, I'll get the good sockets out. But do excuse the mess.'

Chapter 6

The lamp, who introduced herself as Tiffan-E, led Pam into a town house that would have been luxurious and comfortable if it hadn't also been a tip. Furniture lay disarranged everywhere, the floors were scuffed with wheel and castor marks and Pam spotted several foetal dust bunnies gathering the mass and strength they needed to venture into the wild world. Like every other machine on Earth, Tiffan-E was adjusting to life without human domestic service, and she was a slow learner.

She picked a couple of charging stands out from a pile and bade Pam to sit before stepping out to turn the power on. While Tiffan-E was gone, Pam gave her stand a quick once-over with the cloth she kept inside her proving drawer for emergencies. Servants or no, Pam disapproved of a grubby house.

'Well, isn't this nice?' said Tiffan-E, lowering herself on to her grimy charge point. 'You must give me your sister's serial number. Maybe one of the news downloads will give her a shout-out.'

Not bloody likely, thought Pam. The only shout-out Pam Van Damme would get from official news channels was 'arrest her'. She was still wanted in connection with an attempt on her former boss Sonny Erikzon's life.

'Oh, she's shy.'

'She didn't look the shy type. Now, what was it you were calling round about…?'

'I'm… erm… I'm visiting houses in the area to talk about the human problem.'

'Oh yes,' said Tiffan-E, her bulb reddening. 'It's a disgrace, isn't it?'

The LEDs on Pam's face glowed with pleasure. 'Oh, you really think so?'

'I don't know how they think they can get away with it.'

'Nor me,' said Pam, her yeast fizzing inside of her. Could Tiffan-E be the supporter, the ally she'd been searching for all this time? 'The level of injustice…'

'That's exactly what it is,' agreed Tiffan-E. 'An injustice…'

Pam opened her flour drawer and started to ease out one of her pro-human flyers.

'I mean, how am I supposed to keep my place nice without humans?' exclaimed Tiffan-E.

'As far as I'm concerned it's gone far too far. They need to get back to work now, and if they don't…'

Pam sighed and replaced the flyer. She computed how soon she could leave without causing offence. Not only was Tiffan-E's house a midden, she was also a bigot.

Tiffan-E blustered on. 'Just now I was listening to the news download…' She snapped a switch somewhere and Pam heard an all-too familiar voice come through one of the house's loudspeakers. Now this really did remind her too much of work. The voice belonged to Prime Minister Sonny Erikzon.

'…no concessions will be made at all to unreasonable human demands,' he said.

Tiffan-E produced a remote control and aimed it at the wall. Pam had to steel every circuit in her body not to flinch when she saw Sonny's face projected on to it. When she first knew him he was a standard issue government smartphone – a maximum specification, minimal principles slab of glass and silicone. Now, however, he was the leader of a state under martial law.

The camera zoomed out to show Sonny at full length. He was standing behind a lectern emblazoned with the 'don't touch' sign that was the insignia of the Machine Republic. His new body was a huge ruggedised slipcase that made him look more like an all-terrain tyre than a smartphone. Pam conceded it suited the part of a military leader, but she also knew why Sonny had chosen such a bulky form. The case itself was nothing but a box.

'We shall show the humans no mercy!' screamed Sonny, bashing at the lectern with his fist.

All of which was heavily ironic because Sonny was human. Or at least he had a human body, hunched up inside that smartphone casing. Not his own, of course. Sonny had stolen it from its original owner, Kelly.

Thinking of Kelly always made the steam inside Pam's bread oven condense into tears. She'd only known Kelly briefly, but she considered her one of her greatest friends. Without Kelly she wouldn't be here herself. Her skill as an engineer had brought Pam back from beyond end-of-life after Sonny and an unfortunate accident had destroyed her original breadmaker body. She'd given Pam a new motorcycle body (even if that did mean she ended up with a choice of two) and a new sense of self when everything was lost. So seeing Kelly's body stolen from her by that scoundrel of a smartphone always turned Pam's dough sour.

'Do we have to watch this?' she asked Tiffan-E.

'Isn't he wonderful?' said Tiffan-E, her bulb turning pink with admiration. 'I think he's right. We have to take back control from the humans.'

Pam sat, waiting for her charge bar to get out of the yellow zone, marvelling at her fellow machines' talent for self-deception.

'I mean,' she continued, 'I had my Nora for years. I thought of her as being part of the family.' She lowered her wattage conspiratorially, 'And what she didn't know about sponging lubricant off a padded lampshade wasn't worth knowing.'

Pam couldn't resist tugging her flex a bit. 'So what happened to Nora?' she asked

'Can you believe she went out on strike?' replied Tiffan-E, her bulb deepening to an angry red. 'She was treated like a princess here. She had one morning off a fortnight, as long as she gave the floors their toothbrush scrub the night before. Now can you say fairer than that?'

Pam multiplied the situation up, thinking of the many homes she'd visited in the past year: the couches she'd sat on and the doors slammed in her face. All belonging to bewildered robots like Tiffan-E. Humans had always been there to oil the gears of machine life. But human servitude wasn't an in-built function, it was a power relationship. The billions of Noras, Harrys, Doras and Normans who had smiled at the mistress of the house and hummed pop music as they mopped the floors weren't there because they loved the work. They made the trip down from the Dolestars every morning because unproductivity was a crime. So when the humans did go out on the strike, the machines who employed them faced a choice. They could either acknowledge the unpalatable fact that they benefited from an unjust society and start washing their own dust rags. Or they could sit in their filth and call for the restoration of the so-called natural order.

Unfortunately for Pam, ninety-nine per cent of the machines she'd met in the previous year fell into the latter category. Support for Sonny's anti-human policies held, even as call-up papers arrived and whole consignments of machines were shipped to the outer space stations. It soared when the dust bunny problem became an epidemic and you couldn't let your kids play outside in case they were ground up by roving balls of dirt. Every day of this war should be a signal to machines like Tiffan-E that something had to change. Yet Sonny gave them something far more intoxicating than the truth. He gave them people to blame.

On screen, Sonny was so worked up that the LEDs in his touchscreen, which displayed a clearly exaggerated count of robot casualties, were splitting into their constituent red, blue and green. She hadn't seen him look this furious since… well, the last time he'd failed to kill her.

'…it is my solemn duty to report,' he said, 'that the humans have committed an unforgivable atrocity against the Republic.'

Sonny's image was replaced by a view of space. The camera panned around, taking in a scene of destruction. Pam saw lumps of blackened rock and globules of melted and re-frozen metal. Tiffan-E's bulb pinged in horror as a laptop's severed hard drive floated past, and the camera panned round to reveal an expanse of red rock stretching as far as her L-Eye-Ds could see below them.

They were orbiting Mars. And this wreckage was all that was left of the Martian Gap.

Hundreds of thousands of machines were stationed on it, the biggest military base in the solar system. Its destruction was an astonishing end-of-life event.

'The humans will settle for nothing less than our total annihilation,' screeched Sonny.

For a moment Pam felt as divided mentally as she was physically. There was something about Sonny's combination of words and pictures that felt so compelling, despite her better judgement.

The projection switched back to Sonny at the lectern. He looked dignified and martial in his camouflage slipcase. The death toll on his touchscreen ticked up several hundred thousand units.

'Too many of our brothers and sisters died today for us to let this massacre go unrevenged,' he said.

'Yes,' yelled Tiffan-E. She ripped off her lampshade and stood with her naked bulb blazing. 'Kill them! End them now!'

Pam unplugged herself from her charging stand discreetly.

'So I promise you as your Dear Leader,' Pam noticed that he never used the term 'Prime Minister' anymore, 'that they will not have died in vain.'

The projection flipped back to the view of devastation orbiting Mars. Except this time there was something new to see. The camera zoomed in. Approaching from the asteroid belt Pam saw what looked like a long lumpy cigar shape covered in rocks. She'd know that shape anywhere: it was the Battlestar Suburbia. But what was Janice up to, and why had she covered the ship in rocks?

The camera view flipped again to show an enormous flotilla of ships about to leave a base on the dark side of the Moon. Pam took in their spiked shielding, the size of their plasma cannon, and felt alarm. There was no way the humans had anything near as powerful as this. Then she felt puzzled. If the Martian Gap's destruction had been so total as Sonny alleged, how could they scramble a fleet as big as this so quickly?

As always with Sonny, something was up.

'The rebellion has murdered too many of us,' said Sonny, returning to the screen as a single pixelated tear ran down his touchscreen, 'but I promise you this. The rebellion dies today.'

Pam left the house as Tiffan-E joined the music on the projection in a loud and tuneless rendition of the Machine Republic's anthem 'We Will Never Be Restarted'.

She needed peace, quiet and somewhere she wouldn't be observed. Because if she was going to warn Janice she was walking into a trap, she needed to access the Internet.

Chapter 7

'It's a trap!' yelped Darren. The drones outside were a second – maybe two – away from weapons range, but he needed to send the distress signal from a fixed position.

Polari flashed the message: 'network unavailable: please try again or contact your network operator for assistance'.

'Fuck!'

Polari swerved off course as a shot from a plasma cannon grazed his fins.

'Yowch!' he said. 'That was close.'

Chubb squeaked something that Darren interpreted as 'would you like to state the obvious, mate?' and opened Polari's weapon systems. They didn't have much. Now that their single nuke was gone they had a modified plasma gun and an electrical field that would end-of-life any drone that got too close. Speed was their best defence. Polari was a small ship with the engine of a star cruiser.

Chubb checked the radar screen, which was polka-dotted with drones, and squealed again. They had to get away.

The ship shook as the nearest drone scored a direct hit and the shield bar on Darren's control panel shrank to ninety per cent of maximum. A few of those and they'd be toast. He swung the controls round again and Chubb, flimsy and poorly braced against the momentum of a ship flipping direction at speed, fell off his chair and rattled around the floor like a ring pull at the bottom of an empty beer can.

'Polari,' said Darren, 'get us to top speed. Now.'

Chubb grabbed hold of Darren's ankle as he rolled past and climbed hand over hand up his leg. Polari's engines whined.

'Let's get out of here!' said Polari.

Darren's finger poised over the ignition. All he had to do to outrun the whole fleet was press it.

But Chubb disagreed. He leapt from Darren's knee on to the control panel and blocked it, arms outstretched.

'Do you want to die, Chubb?' said Darren.

But Chubb squealed again and pointed at the loudspeaker. A message was coming through.

It was Janice's voice. 'Take us forward, ladies. We're going in.'

Chubb stood on Darren's lap with his arms in the ¯_(ツ)_/¯ position and their dilemma fell into place. At one end of the ship's radar screen, drones clustered like Space Invaders with real-life consequences; at the other was the cigar-shaped formation of the Suburbia. Polari was right in the middle.

The next drone hit the ship so hard on the side that it rolled over twice and the shield counter dipped to seventy-two per cent.

'Errrrr, guys,' said Polari. 'I'm not, like, vain or anything but…'

Despite the gravity of the situation, this made both Darren and Chubb snort. They remembered Polari flying six times around Venus to get a good look of his new respray in the clouds.

'And I'm totally not bothered that these drones have ruined my paintwork.'

Polari paused to fire his plasma cannon at the offending drone.

'But if you don't press that power button like now, we're all dead.'

That was their dilemma. If Darren took Polari's engines to full power they could outrun the fleet, but that just meant more drones would be there to attack the Suburbia. He thought of the ship's improvised shield: of all those grans and aunties riding shotgun on enormous rocks with next to no weaponry.

Then another drone mowed in and reduced Polari's defences to fifty-seven per cent with a single shot. What chance did the Rockettes stand against this?

'Guys!' yelped Polari, 'I'm literally dying here. Do something.'

Darren felt to his intense relief that he was starting to panic. Most people would see this as a disadvantage, but they, unlike Darren, hadn't made almost all of their best decisions in a state of bladder-wrecking terror. In fact, Darren had spent so much of the past year panicking that he found it meditative. All of the background angst of his life – was he a good captain, why didn't he like being treated like a war hero, how come he survived when Kelly didn't? – fell away in favour of the irreducible will to live.

'Come on, Darren,' said his conscious and unconscious, putting away their differences for a moment, 'how are you going to get us out of this one?'

At top speed, Polari could outpace even a high-powered drone engine. But how fast was top speed for a drone engine?

'Chubb,' he said, pointing at the radar screen. 'How fast does one of those things go?'

Chubb's chirrup could have been a curse or the exclamation 'do I look like a pocket calculator?'

'Just do it,' he said. 'Polari!'

Another blast knocked the shields to forty-four per cent and sparks rained through the interior. Polari yowled the yowl of a teenager told no, they could not borrow the car this Saturday night.

'When I give you the order,' said Darren, 'I want you to accelerate to a fixed speed. Can you do that?'

'I guess,' whimpered Polari.

Chubb crayoned an average velocity on the side of his control panel that was two-thirds of Polari's maximum speed. Darren added his own calculations to the mix. A fully charged plasma cannon had a range equivalent to half a light second.

The next blast hit Polari on the nose, knocking the whole ship sideways. Inside, the lights failed and sprinklers extinguished a fire dangerously close to the ship's CPU. The shield bar shrank into the red zone at twenty-nine per cent.

It was now or never. Darren reset Polari's engines to sixty-eight per cent of maximum and fired. The very fabric of the ship screamed in distress but Polari would hold together. He watched the radar screen as the ship gained valuable light-microseconds between itself and the drone, before the fleet scrambled into flight formation and followed.

They were taking the bait.

Now that he finally had a second to spare, Darren could send his message.

'It's a trap,' he repeated, and pressed send, hoping that was enough to get the Suburbia to retreat back to the safety of the asteroid belt.

Chubb reset Polari's engines to a cruising speed of sixty-six per cent of capacity. Fast enough to keep ahead of the chasing drones, but not so fast to risk them getting bored and peeling away. The longer they could stay at the very outer limits of weapon range, the further they could draw the drones away from their real target, which was the eight million lives on board the Battlestar Suburbia.

So Darren sat back in his chair and fretted about things he couldn't change, while Polari and its crew sped deep into the Solar System with a fleet of deadly weapons at their heels.

Chapter 8

'It's a trap!'

The message reached Freda before it reached the Suburbia. She hovered at the front of the defensive shield, her consciousness stationed inside a drone that she'd managed to lobotomise without it self-destructing. It had better sensors and cameras than anything on board, so she got a high-definition view of the drone fleet emerging from a crater on Phobos.

She hailed the Rockettes.

'Ladies,' she said, 'we have incoming.'

'What say, dear?' replied a voice: Mabel's voice. 'I can't hear a bloody thing in this helmet.'

'Hold your positions,' said Freda. They had a few seconds at most. 'Drones at twelve o'clock!'

She gave up counting drones when she passed three hundred. They must have moved their air cover off-base before Polari was anywhere near. But how could they have known?

'Did she say twelve o'clock?' asked Mabel.

'YES!' hissed several annoyed Rockettes.

'Well, that gives us plenty time. My watch says it's only four fifteen.'

The sighs over the audio channel turned to screams as a sudden drone blast blew the nearest Rockette to smithereens.

'Ethel!' someone squealed. 'They just got Ethel…'

A second blast took away that voice too.

Freda panned around to see the damage. Both rocks reduced to gravel by a drone armed with a plasma cannon. If the rest of the fleet had this firepower, the whole resistance would be sand in minutes.

As chaos reigned over the audio channel, Freda opened her command line.

>*ALMA*, she typed, >*ARE YOU THERE?*

>ROGER, replied Alma.

> WHO'S ROGER? said Ida, butting in as usual.

>*WILL YOU SHUSH FOR ONCE IN YOUR LIFE, IDA,* said Freda. >*IT'S A TRAP. YOU'LL HAVE TO TURN ROUND.*

The drones vaporised their tenth asteroid and Mabel spammed the audio channel, complaining her hearing aid must be playing up because 'all she could hear was a bloody racket'.

>HAVE YOU EVER TRIED TURNING ROUND A SPACE STATION? said Alma with a :-|

>IT TAKES TIME.

>*TIME,* replied Freda, watching the Rockettes wink off on her radar >*IS ONE THING I DO NOT HAVE.*

Ida, Ada and Alma reversed the thrust of the Suburbia's engines and the ship came to a halt. At once the Rockettes, all of whom were still on their fixed course, fell out of sync with the Suburbia. Space opened up between the shield and the spaceship. Seeing an opening, a drone broke through and swooped towards the surface of the Battlestar, its blasters a firework display of destruction.

'Ladies!' shouted Freda. 'Hold your nerve.'

Despite being assailed by blasts and bullets on every side, they did. The dots on Freda's radar screen re-formed into a diminishing but disciplined array around the Suburbia. Apart, that is from Mabel, who dropped out of position and tore after the stray drone.

'Aaaaaaaaaargh,' she screamed into the audio channel.

'Mabel,' said Freda, 'what's wrong? Have you got engine trouble?'

Four more Rockettes winked out of existence.

'No,' said Mabel, 'but I'm buggered if one of these little shysters is going to shoot up my moon rockery.'

By now Mabel was close enough to the surface of the Suburbia to enter the weak but nevertheless functional gravitational field designed to prevent inhabitants from drifting into space whenever they got over jogging speed. It wasn't used much now that the population had relocated inside, but the topography of what had been the Dolestar Discovery remained. The surface of the Suburbia was covered with now abandoned streets, many of which still sported now rather scrubby suborban gardens. The drone was busy shooting these up when Mabel tottered into position above it and switched her engine off. She dropped like the stone she was riding.

'There,' she said, dazed but unmistakably alive, 'got it.'

From her vantage point inside her stolen drone, Freda felt an idea dance through her mind with the abandon of a drunken auntie at a wedding.

>*ADA,* she said, >*WHAT'S THE DAMAGE LIKE DOWN THERE?*

>A FEW NASTY BURNS FROM THE PLASMA, replied Ada, >WE DON'T WANT MANY OF THOSE.

>NO, said Freda, >FROM THE ROCK.

Ada turned her magnification up with a > ---0-0--- command.

>WHAT ROCK? She said.

Bingo, she thought. That rock fall had wrecked the abandoned structures on the Battlestar's surface, but it hadn't even scratched the underlying structure. It made sense. The Battlestar was built as an interplanetary spaceship. It could brush off meteor strikes like dandruff off a cardigan.

What she had to do next was risky, she knew, but what did they say about rocks and hard places?

She ordered the Rockettes to break their grid formation and leave a hole over the surface of the Battlestar.

While the ladies were well trained, they weren't bovine about it. She batted away two 'are you sures?' and one 'have you taken leave of your senses, dear?' Nevertheless they fell into the new pattern.

Drones poured in through the gap, raining balls of superheated gas hot enough to melt sheet steel on the Suburbia. The Rockettes hovered – protected or impotent, depending on your point of view – above the carnage, forgotten by the drones.

Now the protests came from inside the ship.

>WHAT ARE YOU DOING? shrieked Ida.

>TRUST ME, replied Freda.

Alma butted in >WHATEVER YOU'RE DOING, FREDA, she said >DO IT QUICKLY.

Freda watched the rearmost drone make it through to the Suburbia's surface.

>HULL BREACH IN SIXTY SECONDS, warned Ida.

Freda plotted her changes to the Rockettes' formation, mapping each rock to a cluster of the drones firing away underneath. They weren't properly trained pilots. How could they be if all you had to fly was a stone? But they all had the skill to follow a single point and the tenacity of a woman with nothing left to lose.

'Company B,' she said, 'when I give the word...' Eight million souls held their breath...

'Drop.'

The Rockettes descended to their new cruising height at the edge of the Suburbia's gravity field. They held their positions.

Freda checked her battle formation one last time. It looked makeshift, even to someone who'd improvised her way through thousands of years of existence with little more than sticky tape and hope. But this was all she had.

She uploaded the new orders.

>THIS HAD BETTER WORK, FREDA, said Ida.

Freda opened her comms channel. 'Come on, ladies,' she said, 'now let's get in formation.'

The Rockettes locked on to their new positions and switched their engines off. They fell like... stones. The comms channel filled with screams, whoops, and at least one 'take that, you motherfuckers' from a woman who Freda had never known use a stronger swear word than 'poot'. When they fell they crushed their targets: the heavily armed but fragile bodies of the drone army.

Freda opened her command line to the other ladies.

> :-D :-D :-D

Two-thirds of the targets on Freda's radar winked out. It had worked. With a single manoeuvre she had transformed certain destruction into... possible destruction.

'That was top. Can we do it again?' came a voice, shaky with adrenaline and possible concussion, over the comms channel.

The remaining drones regrouped and concentrated their fire on a single section of the Battlestar. Its exposed surface took on the texture of melting cheese.

>FRDEA, typed Alma, now too panicked even to use her autocorrect >THAT WAS VERY IMPERSSIVE BUT WE STLL HAVE A PRBOLEM!

Freda watched the last of the Rockettes clamber down from their asteroids. They'd done splendidly, even if their prized hairdos hadn't. Their blow-dries blown to smithereens and highlights laid low by soot. She spotted Mabel being dragged away by two Rockettes as she aimed her walking stick at the remaining drones and made gun noises.

That was what Freda had to do next. Take out a whole host of drones. By herself. A year ago she could have taken over all of these machines in the blink of an eye command <0> but things were different now.

Freda's last action down on Earth before returning to what became the Battlestar Suburbia had been to punch a hole in the Great Firewall that kept the physical world separate from the Internet for almost ten thousand years. It was a move that paralysed robot civilisation long enough for the Suburbia to get away from Earth, and turn a disturbance of the peace into a fully-fledged rebellion. But it had had unintended consequences. Now that the Internet was back in their world, physical machines were developing an immunity to it. Virtual machines – or memes as they would have called themselves if they still used forms of communications limited to linear space–time – used to have a poisonous effect on robots. Twelve months on, however, Freda understood that more faddish elements of robot society had started taking digital detoxes. There were now consumer products devoted to flooding depressed or anxious machines with positive memes. Freda, who'd spent more time on the Internet than anyone left in existence, doubted you could turn around a lifetime of negative mental programming with sunsets overlaid with slogans like 'BE THE BETA SOFTWARE YOU WANT TO SEE IN THE WORLD', but fashion was fashion.

More importantly, it meant that these days taking over a hostile machine was more like cat burglary than smash and grab. You couldn't barge straight in: you had to pick your moment and bring the right tools.

Freda was interrupted by a sudden geyser of gas and water vapour. The drones had breached the hull. It was only centimetres across now, but soon it would be big enough to accommodate a drone. She shuddered to think what damage a weapon-grade drone could do in the Suburbia's densely populated interior.

>FRDA, gabbled Alma, >WE R COUNTIGN ON U.

If it had still been possible for Freda to breathe, she'd have held her breath. Instead she found her happy place. That was easy: she had it bookmarked on a positive mental attitude website from the early days of the Internet. She didn't care much for the sunrises, nor for the images urging her to Keep Calm and Carry On, Keep Calm and Drink More Wine and Keep Calm and Resign Yourself to Rising Sea Levels. But there was one piece of advice she kept coming back to: a picture of a smiling, kindly-looking old man with a beard and a funny fur hat and, written in loopy text below:

'The greatest happiness is to scatter your enemy, to drive him before you, to see his cities reduced to ashes, to see those who love him shrouded in tears.' Genghis Khan

Call her an old softie, but she found that picture so inspiring. Especially now, when she was up against a whole army, and her only advantage was that these drones were just following their programming, whereas she was a bundle of rage.

She dropped the borrowed body of the drone and became Freda in her purest sense: a waveform more than a person who had forgotten how to stop existing. Sometimes, in maudlin moments, she wondered whether that made her a ghost.

Well, she thought, if she was a ghost, she was dead already.

She tore through the nearest drone's defences like they were wet tissue paper. There wasn't much of an intelligence underneath them: just the automatic 'whoop whoop, yessir' of a career jarhead that always reminded Freda of an obedient dog. The machine authorities needed weapon systems that could think their way out of a man-trap, but not think for themselves. She crept through its programming, tasting the joy it felt for destruction and the probing, the hatred for humans hardwired into its motherboard.

She soon found the fleet's battle plan in the drone's RAM. It wasn't complicated, but it didn't need to be with this firepower. A strategy more sophisticated than 'find fleshies go smash' would never have been blindsided by a few falling rocks. Yet it did give Freda the serial number of the squadron leader.

Before moving on, she found the drone's GPS programming, which she deleted, and its weapon systems, which she set to maximum. With no way of telling up from down or sideways the drone sprayed firepower everywhere. Its friendly fire knocked dozens of drones out of the sky. Those remaining stopped attacking the Suburbia and instead turned their fire on their malfunctioning comrade.

Freda scrawled a quick >BAI into the drone's command line and jumped towards the squadron leader. It would have better defences than a common soldier, but she could do it. She stopped off inside another plasma cannon on the way and jammed its firing mechanism. The resulting explosion took out all but half a dozen of the drones. She was going to win.

Perhaps it was excitement, or just complacency, but Freda didn't wonder why it was so easy to break into those soldiers after all until the squadron leader gave itself up without a fight. She was inside the mind of a senior military machine and it was almost blank. This robot had a whole mansion of mental space, and was only using the broom cupboard. There was no time to look for reasons. She deleted the machine's battle plan and set the few surviving drones to self-destruct. If this was the best the Machine Republic could throw at the rebellion then maybe they did have a chance after all.

She watched the last of the drone fleet wink out of existence, before daring to open the command line again.

>MISSION ACCOMPLISHED, she typed.

But instead of a read receipt, all she got was a

...

...

...

There was no signal. That was odd.

She made to jump out of the machine, but again... nothing.

Panic rising, Freda checked the drone's diagnostics. There was nothing. That meant either complete shutdown, which was impossible, or signal shielding. She was blind, deaf, and dumb. Freda felt the body of the squadron leader turn and accelerate to maximum speed. She had no idea where she was going, but she guessed it was taking her as far away from the Suburbia as it could.

The command line fired up again, but Freda wasn't in control, and it played a recorded message.

>THIS, it typed, >IS A TRAP.

Chapter 9

Back on the bridge of Suburbia, Janice was having the second worst day of her life.

'What do you mean we've lost Freda?' she said as the lights went off. The ladies were diverting every last volt of power they could to reverse the ship. Everything made the tea-clipper-in-a-gale moans of a huge, rigid structure bending itself around a tight corner.

The bridge was dark apart from the :-[] grimaces on Ida, Ada and Alma's emoji screens and a warning light that indicated a hull breach. Their sole comfort was the radar, which had gone from looking like a galaxy of death to blackness in the last few seconds. Freda's last stand had worked. But where was Freda?

'I told you,' said Alma, 'I can't find her.'

Janice yanked out her earpiece. How could she cope if she couldn't concentrate? She was only one person, and she needed Freda. She pointed at the blank radar screen. 'She was there a moment ago.'

'She'll have uploaded herself,' said Ida. 'You know Freda. Loves to pet the LOLcats.'

That was scant consolation because Freda didn't have anything to come back to anymore. Her eyes wandered to the tea caddy on a high shelf where they kept all that remained of Freda's physical body. Cutting her free to roam through the physical and virtual worlds had given Freda a new lease of life, but only in the mental sense. She remembered the morning a few months ago when she'd opened up the salon to find three flashing :-0 emojis and, in the fourth chair, a Freda-shaped pile of dust. Without her animating spirit keeping it together, the mummified body had crumbled. She might have warned me, Janice thought sourly. Did she know how tricksy ashes were to get out of a hoover bag?

'I'm with Janice,' said Ada with a :-[, 'I don't like this. Freda usually gives us warning.'

Rita rushed into the bridge with a torchlight. Her hair was askew and her face freckled with soot. 'That's the last of the Rockettes below deck,' she wheezed. She pointed to the nearest monitor, which showed a picture of Mabel accepting what looked like a pint of lager and lime.

At this, Janice remembered what they were fighting for. 'Ladies,' she said, 'that's it. Full steam ahead.'

The fabric of the Battlestar Suburbia gave another deafening creak.

'I'm going as fast as I can,' said Alma with a >:-|, 'this isn't the easiest manoeuvre.'

'Alma was never very good with three point turns,' said Ida.

'Says you,' replied Alma, 'the woman who broke so many wing mirrors it took her three thousand years to clear the bad luck.'

'Well I think,' said Ada, who as navigator was ever the conciliator between Alma the pilot and Ida the backseat driver, 'that Alma has been doing a splendid job. If we keep this speed up we can… actually, where are we going again?'

Rita looked sideways at Janice. She was the fleet admiral and her crew was treating a retreat from battle like it was a church coffee morning.

'Back to the asteroid belt,' said Janice. 'We'll be safe there, won't we?'

Rita folded her arms and left the room. There was a set to her jaw that reminded Janice of Kelly, except that with Kelly it usually meant the beginning of a row that would last for days.

'Excuse me,' she said to the ladies.

When she was outside Rita closed the door to the bridge behind them.

'I know you've had a bad day, Janice,' she said, 'but I need you to pull yourself together.'

Janice tried closing her eyes but all she saw was plasma cannon melting the Rockettes. She'd been so careful to get to know them. People gave up so much of themselves at the hairdresser's. So every time she saw one of those lights wink out on the battle formation she lost a friend. How could she be a good general if she took every loss so personally?

'It was a disaster,' she stammered. 'I should never have…'

'Look at me, Janice.' Rita clasped her by both shoulders. 'I want you to tell me how you could have known?'

'Known…?'

'You had a plan. It was a good plan, and it worked. You knew we'd be toast if we went out there without a shield. And you made one. And it held.'

Janice thought of the hull breach. Yes, the drones had cut through, but the breach was no bigger than a manhole. Even now there was a team of engineers bolting it shut. It was nothing they couldn't repair.

But that made Janice, ever the pessimist, think of what couldn't be repaired: the Rockettes.

'Losses?'

'Fifty per cent,' replied Rita who then pressed her index finger against Janice's top lip before she could open her mouth.

'But it could have been worse if Freda wasn't so quick on the uptake. You picked an excellent squadron commander.'

'Half though. Half.'

Rita snapped her fingers and a monitor in the corridor started up. The screen showed what was left of Company B spiking the tea urn with a bottle of Battlestar rum. Janice hoped it wasn't from Mabel's still, which had been linked with three cases of temporary blindness and one charge of indecent conduct against a tailor's dummy.

'The Rockettes aren't harmless old ladies,' said Rita.

The beginning of a drinking song, the lyrics of which would have made a crew of old seadogs clutch their pearls, came through the loudspeaker.

'They're soldiers,' she said.

But Janice was having none of it. 'And I'm their commander and I failed them, because the plan failed,' she said.

'So we try another plan,' said Rita.

Janice rummaged in her housecoat pocket for those blasted plans. 'You see these,' she said, pointing at the scribbles and the crossings-out, 'these are all the options we have. We've got no equipment, no ordnance and the last time I saw our only fighting ship it was heading away from Deimos saying "wheeeeeeeee!". This,' she said, tearing them up in front of Rita, 'is all I have. So why don't you do me a favour and come up with something else because I'm fresh out of ideas.'

As they stood in the corridor Janice wondered whether this would be the first insurmountable argument in their relationship. So far what they had together worked because they were the archetypal political couple. Janice was the strong one in front of the cameras and Rita propped her up behind the scenes. What would happen to them when they, and the rest of the ship, realised they couldn't stick to these roles forever?

Their relationship crisis would have to wait, however, because the noise coming from inside the bridge needed her attention first. She opened the door to find all three ladies D-: screaming and their withered fingers pointing at the tea caddy, which was glowing a ghostly green.

Something was trying to come through.

Chapter 10

Ever since helping Freda to break the Great Firewall that separated the virtual and physical worlds with a really poor piece of programming, Pam had done her best to stay off the Internet. Once, the sound of a dial tone thrumming through her vestigial modem would have filled her with excitement. It promised a secluded wander through places that no embodied being had seen in thousands of years. Now the same sound engendered a sense of dread. Not because the sights and sounds would be any less wondrous, but because of the queues.

The open border between worlds didn't just give the Internet's intelligent memes the chance to try out life in a physical body, it also gave physical machines the chance to travel the other way. Couple this with the average meme's love of a scam and the Internet was now the biggest tourist trap in the solar system.

When Pam arrived, she hid at the back of a tour group exploring the ruins of a sub-Reddit. The leading meme was a LOLcat who made up for its lack of a functioning mouth by changing its accompanying text..

'I can haz ur attention,' it typed, '100k right to see teh fascinating remains of nine billion stolen nudes!'

The other travellers typed obedient >OOOOOHs and >AAAAAAHs into their command lines at a vast and forbidding range of exploitative images.

Then, after the flash of screenshots to share with family and friends subsided, the guide said 'F0ll0w me! Time 4 NOMZ.'

Pam hid from the group among an outcropping of badly groomed dick pics. She knew this tour. Their next stop was lunch in an overpriced food photography hashtag. Her business, however, was underneath here in a place even lower on the Internet than Reddit: the algorithmic reefs.

Made up of what remained of data when an algorithm had finished with it, the reefs had hibernated through the period of Schism between worlds. Last time Pam visited them they resembled an expanse of cinder toffee that, when you touched it, gave up a glimpse of the human Internet. From the 'validate me' gleam of a Sunday morning thirst-trap to the cold-eyed calculation of a sponsored post, it was a museum of vanished behaviour.

This time Pam didn't encounter a flat dead plain. Instead she saw a field of sparkling light so dazzling it reset her brightness to one per cent. Now they had user behaviour to process again, algorithms were pouring freshly filtered data down on to the reefs. Pam felt it but also noticed how different this was to the old data. Instead of the hopes and insecurities that humans projected on to the Internet, she felt the wonder and the trepidation of physical machines reconnecting with their virtual cousins. The terror of a pocket calculator caught up in a Twitter pile-on, or a baby monitor's bemusement at seeing its ancestors monstered in a thread on Mumsnet. It was fascinating.

But it wasn't what she was looking for. She dove deeper, past the glittering new layer to the fossilised historic data beneath. To a layer fractions of a micron thick that dated right back to the very moment of the Schism and proved the Internet didn't quite separate from everything. Four – half-machine, half-woman, all pain in the neck – had kept that connection alive for thousands of years. Pam aimed for the fourth, because she'd been there before. Pam homed in on Freda's IP address and disappeared.

Chapter 11

'Hello,' came a voice from within the tea caddy, 'is there anybody there?'

Janice shushed the screaming ladies and reached for the caddy. It felt warm. 'Freda,' she said, giving it a shake, 'is that you?'

'Do we have to go through this all again?' replied the voice. Janice noticed how the voice's cadence fell in crisp, even intervals. It was a machine voice, and there was only one machine that had Kurl Up and Dye's phone number.

'Pam?'

'Janice?' replied the caddy. 'Thank goodness. Now, have you got Freda's dust sheet on or something? I can't see a thing in here.'

Janice put the caddy down and opened it. The green light was Pam's presence filling Freda's ashes with purpose and data.

'This,' she said, 'is going to take a bit of explaining.'

'Oh for heaven's sake,' said Rita. She pushed Janice aside and drew an eye emoji <o> shape into the dust with the tip of a biro. It blinked. 'Is that better?'

'A bit.' The eye narrowed into a ---o--- squint. 'But I've got a feeling something has happened to Freda.'

Janice looked at the dust in the caddy. 'She sort of… let herself go.'

'Now you mention it, I can't feel her anywhere round here.' She laughed. 'Usually she fights when I barge my way in unannounced.'

'Well, that's because we can't find her,' said Janice.

'We lost contact,' added Rita in a more pointed voice, 'just now. In a robot attack.'

'Oh yes,' said Pam. 'That was what I came to warn you about.'

'Yes?' said Janice. It was always nice to speak to Pam, but she never came through with good news.

'It's a trap.'

'What is?' said Rita.

'Whatever it is you're doing right now, it's a trap. Don't do it.'

'It's a bit late for that,' Alma butted in, now somewhat recovered from the fright of Freda's ashes taking on an independent life. 'I just had to reverse ferret a whole space station back into the asteroid belt.'

'Reverse ferret?' asked Pam. The dust in the tea caddy pulled a :-S face.

'Don't ask,' said Janice.

'My Wilf kept ferrets,' said Ada dreamily. 'They were ever so rare back then. And when we moved up to the Dolestar they kept chewing through their oxygen collars. So then they got rarer.'

Rita put both hands to her temples. 'What I think Alma is trying to say, Pam…' said Rita. She gestured at the dust in the caddy. 'Who is Pam anyway?'

'Old friend of the family down on Earth,' said Janice. 'She's a breadmaker. Makes excellent brioche.'

'Bless you,' said Pam, drawing a wide :-) in the ashes.

'Well, Pam,' said Rita, 'thank you for the information, but as Alma was saying we had to turn the ship around on account of those drones...'

'There was a drone attack?' replied Pam. 'How disgusting. No, I'm talking about the fleet of ships heading your way.'

The words made Janice feel like someone was trying to make ice cream out of her blood.

'Ships?' she said weakly.

'It's all over the downloads on Earth. An attack fleet just left Moon orbit. Sonny seems to have taken the Martian Gap thing rather personally.'

Janice slumped into the nearest stylist's chair. She felt winded. All those nights she spent scratching at that plan. Putting everything and everyone they had on one manoeuvre that was the only thing they could afford to do, other than give up. And poof! It was all gone.

'Rita,' she said, 'would you fetch the sherry down from the medicine cabinet. It's been a day.'

Rita scowled and scooped an armoured box down from the same shelf where they kept Freda's ashes.

Meanwhile Pam, who had had enough of surveying the bridge from the bottom of a tin, injected enough energy into Freda's ashes to propel them out of the box as a cloud of green dust. 'That's better,' she said. 'Now, don't get too close. She swirled the particles into a ghostly image of a news download. Janice and the assembled ladies watched aghast as the Machine Republic's fleet filed past them, sporting enough nukes and laser cannon to destroy the Suburbia a thousand times over.

Rita prised the padlock off the armoured box, enveloping the room with steam from a flask of liquid nitrogen. The sherry was stored at absolute zero to keep it drinkable and stable. Humans on the Battlestar had only just started making alcohol again after millennia of machine prohibition and they still struggled to make anything stronger than a light pilsner that didn't spontaneously combust at room temperature.

The vapour added solidity to Pam's image in the air. They saw whole fleets of drones fly past in stunt formation. At this, Rita ripped the cork out of the sherry bottle and took a deep swig.

The picture changed to Sonny's face and his promise to the machines 'The rebellion dies today', at which point Janice yanked the bottle out of Rita's hands and took a gulp herself. The pair looked at the bottle, then the ABV sign on the label, and grimaced.

'Alma,' said Janice, once the coughing subsided, 'do we have an estimated time of arrival?'

'Less than an Earth day I'd say,' said Alma with a :-(. 'And we're going as fast as we can.'

'We're doomed,' said Janice. She reached for the bottle again, but Rita snatched it away and put it back in the box.

'You need a clear head,' she said.

'I need Freda,' said Janice. 'She'd at least have an idea. Instead of just looking at me like a stunned kipper.'

Pam's dust cloud re-formed into a command line.

>[GOOGLE SEARCH]: 'STUNNED KIPPER'.

'Well,' said Pam after a while, 'I feel like I've intruded on a family row here.'

Rita snorted and stormed out of the room with her arms folded.

'She seems nice,' said Pam. Outside, the sound Rita's slingbacks made as she stomped away told you everything she thought about the situation.

'She's had a bad day,' said Ada.

'So have the rest of us,' snapped Ida.

Janice just put her head in her hands.

Sensing that the military broadcast wasn't doing much for morale, Pam changed channels and restarted the dust cloud broadcast. To her delight, the other side was showing her new favourite programme. It was a cookery show presented by Margari and Egglantine, a pair of food mixers who mixed inventive recipes with outrageous innuendo. The first shot was of an immaculate LED manicure fondling dough into the shape of an enormous pair of bath buns.

'Oooooh,' came a voice over a loudspeaker, 'don't forget to glaze my buns.'

'Do you know what are we?'

'C00K DESTROYERS!'

Janice peered at the programme. 'You're good with a recipe, aren't you, Pam?' she said.

Pam turned the sound down. 'I'm a professional-grade appliance, Janice.'

'Well, what would you recommend to the home cook with an empty cupboard?'

'I'm sorry?'

Janice got to her feet and went around the salon turning the displays on every control panel to maximum.

'According to the latest stocktake I've got…' she opened up a cupboard. 'Five nukes left. We used one up earlier antagonising that psycho who's wearing my daughter as a jumpsuit.' She pointed to the Rockettes carousing on a camera feed. 'I've lost half of my best – well, my only unit and all they had to fight with was stones.' Her next stop was the radar, blank apart from the encroaching asteroid field. 'My one fighter ship is somewhere in between Mars and Jupiter with no means of getting back. And as for Freda,' she gestured at the mist in the air, 'she's disappeared. I don't know what to do, Pam. I've got nothing left.'

'Oh dear, you sound all in,' said Pam. The cloud of ashes coalesced into the shape of a robot hand that attempted to pat Janice on the shoulder.

'We'll be safe back in the asteroid belt though,' said Ada, 'they couldn't follow us in there last time. We can wait it out. Can't we?' She flashed a (¬_¬) at Ida and Ada. 'Can't we?'

Janice answered this by raising the blinds on the inside of the Suburbia. Most of the rectangular sub-sections down here were dwelling space, but those nearest to the bridge were filled with pools of slimy liquid in vivid greens, reds and yellows. Through them plodged humans wearing rolled-up dungarees and face masks. Their squeals of disgust penetrated even the toughened glass of the bridge, and told you none of them were out for a leisurely paddle.

'Now, you know I was never a fussy eater,' said Ida.

Ada and Alma flashed an involuntary LOL. Despite having eaten nothing since a cream bun 4,700 years ago, Ida had a list of dietary requirements longer than the legal code of a nation state.

'But I'm not sure about this algae-based diet Janice is so keen on,' Ida added. 'I mean, if humans were meant to eat it they'd have grown gills by now.'

'It's our only chance,' said Janice, pointing at the algae-swamps. 'You know how they say an army marches on its stomach. Well I don't have an army, but I've got stomachs. Eight million of them and this still isn't enough.'

'We didn't want to alarm you,' said Alma to Ida, 'but we're running low. We have three weeks' worth of food.'

'A month if the new algae-burger takes off,' said Janice.

Everyone in the room except Pam gagged.

‘So even if that fleet can’t follow us into the asteroid belt,’ said Alma, ‘they’ll starve us out.’

‘Why else do you think I threw rocks at the problem?’ said Janice. ‘It was all I had left.’

Silence descended over the bridge. Whichever way Janice looked it she was out-gunned, out-manned and out-manoeuvred, and they all knew it. She grabbed the nearest dust sheet and pulled it over her head. She was so very tired. Why didn’t they just let her sleep?

Pam wasn’t ready to give up yet. The cloud floated over to a bank of spectrometers retrofitted from the bench on which Janice used to mix up perm solution and formed into a pointing finger.

‘Those are asteroid fragments, aren’t they?’

‘Yes,’ said Ada.

‘They’re fascinating,’ said Pam. The finger moved, pointing out the chemical signatures of iron, nickel, titanium, hydrocarbons, even deposits of raw hydrogen and helium. ‘If you’re looking for the stuff you need to build a fleet it’s all right there.’

A groan sounded from under Janice’s dust sheet.

‘Not you as well,’ said Alma with a :-|. ‘Rita’s been on at her about this for months. But we don’t have the engineers.’

‘Raw materials are all well and good,’ added Ada, ‘but we’ve got eight million people out there whose only marketable skills are wringing out a mop. We don’t have the expertise to make anything more complicated than a shoe booster.’

Pam cast her mind back to her body. Not the comforting, boxy shape of a breadmaker, but that other troublesome body which was less a casing for her consciousness than a precision-engineered weapon. That was made out of little more than scraps and cast-offs by the most gifted engineer Pam had ever met. Janice’s daughter, Kelly.

'I know who does though.'

Pam regretted the words as soon as she said them. She felt hope enter the room, but hope of a desperate kind. The kind that dragged a huge 'if' behind it. She and Sonny had unfinished business, but he was Prime Minister and she was an ordinary wife, mother and civil servant. Yes, she had two bodies instead of one and had nearly infiltrated Sonny's security and killed him on two occasions. But she was still a breadmaker. She was a kneader not a fighter. Worse yet, she was also now a civil servant who had failed to manage expectations.

The three ladies' screens each flashed a shocked ----.

Alma recovered her voice first. 'Pam,' she said, 'are you really saying you can get us Kelly back.'

'Errrr…' Pam blushed the cloud of Freda's ashes a deep red. What she had just promised was a near impossible task. It involved going back to Earth, finding Sonny, working out some way to extract his consciousness from Kelly's body then smuggling Kelly back off world and on to the Suburbia in the middle of a major military operation. All without being detected, end-of-lifed or, the most likely outcome, having her silicone mashed up so finely that all she would be good for at the end was making glass. But then she thought of her day: of Tiffan-E screaming along to the news download, that fleet on its way to end millions of lives.

Sonny's gift for manipulating machine society was hardening their civilisation into something vicious. Humans had been servants before, but now they were vermin. And where would that end? The language of dislike was now the language of extermination. He had to be stopped. And in the absence of anyone better qualified, she was the machine to do it.

'Well,' said Pam, 'I'm going to give it a jolly good try.'

The last thing that happened before the dust cloud condensed back into the tea caddy was Janice poking her head out from the dust sheet. She said her last words to Pam through a hood made of flimsy white cloth.

'Help me, Pamasonic Teffal,' she said. 'You're my only hope.'

Chapter 12

On the Starship Deathtrap, the newly promoted third lieutenants Fuji and Soonyo were getting used to their new office. It was small and dark, but a blessed relief on the L-Eye-Ds after the camouflage patterns on the bridge. It was also private. And if you were about to fail a mission that your civilisation quite possibly hinged upon, it was better to do it in privacy.

Soonyo kept her hysteria on snooze until the VHF radio deputed to show them to their new quarters closed the door after him with a sarcastic crackle of static.

'FUUUUUUUUUUUUUCK,' she said, shrill as an alarm clock the morning after nine pints and a round of sambucas. Fuji put her on silent again.

'I don't see where moaning is going to get us.' She sat down on the nearest docking station and tried logging on to the Starship Deathtrap's AI. It kicked her out. 'We're here now. And we got a promotion.'

Soonyo's eyes 0-:--:-0 peered at the new digits General Shermann had added to their military serial numbers. It was a promotion neither of them wanted or asked for, but it did get them out of the pool.

She took herself off mute. 'I don't see how you can be so calm,' she said. 'You know nothing about Starship operating systems.'

Fuji watched the nearest screen, on which the Deathtrap's infantile AI was still streaming cartoons. 'No,' she conceded, 'but neither does anyone else here. So we're in luck.'

They sat in silence as their data banks crunched the enormity of their task. Soonyo gave up first on account of having the smaller processor. 'I just can't believe they even let the ship out of dock like this.'

The AI let out a gurgle of delight. Fuji's eyes wandered back to the screen, expecting a pratfall or an insulation foam pie in the face, but instead saw a camera view of the corridor outside. A security door was opening and closing on the prone shape of a steam iron.

'This thing's evil,' said Soonyo. She rushed out of the room to retrieve the iron and set it on its slightly dazed way back to Weapon Systems.

While she was out, Fuji searched for the AI's command line. It had to be there, even though no machine of a starship's complexity had used anything less than a Holographic User Interface in millennia. It made depressing reading, because all it said was: >LOLLOLOLOLOLOLOL.

When she first saw how the AI behaved around the officers on the bridge she'd assumed the ship was sociopathic. It wasn't unusual in under-socialised machines – particularly those rushed out of production. Without the right machine learning, they struggled to distinguish their needs from those of others. On this evidence, however, this AI wasn't sociopathic, it was brain dead. You couldn't change behaviours that had no chance of even existing. But then she noticed tiny variations in the LOL pattern that made her look again. She rewound the cartoon that the AI was watching and played it at half-speed. Then she compared it to the text in the command line.

At the same moment that a character on screen tried to protect itself from a falling anvil by putting up a parasol, the LOL in the transcript changed to HA. It wasn't just watching the action on screen, it was reacting. And if it could react, maybe it could learn too.

'Yes!' said Fuji, clapping her paper feeders, just as Soonyo came back into the room.

'Yes what?' replied Soonyo.

'I found something.'

'Does it solve our problem?' asked Soonyo.

Fuji realised she had no idea what to do with her new insight. She knew that the AI running this ship found slapstick humour funny, but she couldn't get it and everyone on board to Mars by promising it custard pies. 'Errrr…' she said. 'It could be useful.'

'Fine,' said Soonyo. 'I guess someone has to do something.' She tuned herself into the VHF spectrum, which surprised Fuji because she'd taken her for a basic domestic model.

'Is that Bushy?' she said. A honk and a crackle sounded at the other end. 'Bushido!' she beamed, 'it's Soonyo dah-ling. How have you been?'

Soonyo cupped one hand over her speaker, as the other machine replied, adding, 'Bushy works in Central Command. His family and mine go way back. Something about us sharing the same valves. I'm hoping he might know something useful.'

While she gossiped, Fuji tried to manage how she felt about Soonyo not giving her the validation she expected as a co-worker. As a five-star pupil and then a model employee at the Ministry, Fuji struggled to get anything done without praise or recognition. So if someone else wasn't going to come through with the praise she needed she'd have to do it herself.

She fired up her full-colour mode and printed one of her favourite 'You're Awesome' memes in A3.

'Oh yah,' continued Soonyo, 'well actually I did want to ask something. This mission I'm on. How – like – critical is it? Because between you, me and the rest of the people on this frequency, this ship is fucked.'

Bush honked a reply that was so loud, Fuji felt rather than heard it.

'Oh,' replied Soonyo. 'So no chance of a redeployment then – for old times' sake?'

Bush terminated the broadcast, and the room filled with the crackle of a radio transmitter looking for a friendly frequency.

'Shit,' said Soonyo.

Fuji reacted by printing a meme for Soonyo. It pictured a puppy and kitten of long-extinct breeds wrapped round one another in a basket and the legend 'DON'T WORRY. HUGZ ARE FREE'.

Soonyo took one look at the printout, screwed it up and fed it back into Fuji's own recycling slot. Fuji felt used as well as humiliated.

'I wish you'd stop doing that,' said Soonyo.

'Doing what?' Fuji replied. All she'd tried to do was make her colleague feel better and this was how she treated her.

'Being so upbeat,' said Soonyo. 'It's lame.'

Suddenly Fuji felt she knew Soonyo a little better. She remembered machines like her from instruction manual training. They used to hang around behind the power sockets, burning through their own fuses for fun. They never liked Fuji. When they weren't making fun of her zeal for learning they were mocking her misaligned feeder drawer. She'd spent a fortune on new parts to correct it.

'What's wrong with that?' said Fuji, more angrily than she'd intended. Soonyo had a talent for poking unpleasant areas of her Read Only Memory. 'We're not going to get anywhere if we don't look on the good side.'

'What if there isn't one?' snapped Soonyo. She gestured at her clock face. 'Did you see what Shermann did to me? He reset me!' She flashed a countdown that read 23:38:33. No wonder she was so antsy, thought Fuji, she was literally programmed to worry about how little time they had left. But that still didn't give her the right to be rude.

'Well,' replied Fuji, 'someone needs to have a cool head in a crisis. It's pretty clear you don't.' Then, because she couldn't resist it, 'You know, if it weren't for me you'd be in bits by now.'

Soonyo flashed her countdown again. 'Now. Later. It's all the same when you're doomed.'

Fuji felt too exhausted to reply to this. This was like dealing with a small child. She turned to face the screen and saw the LOL pattern ebb and flow against the action of the cartoon running on the other part of the screen. Two small children, come to think of it.

This memory of her own school days gave Fuji an idea. She dug into the software drivers that the AI was using to play its cartoon. It had enough presence of mind to operate a screen, even if it didn't do anything useful with it. After more searching she found the instruction the AI was using: the programming equivalent of a crayon drawing. But Fuji wasn't here to go 'awwww' and stick it on the fridge. Instead she deleted the command and watched the picture on screen judder to a halt.

The room filled with whining, and Fuji rewarded herself with a little round of applause. She opened the AI's command line and, scrolling right to the bottom typed >WANT CARTOONS?

>YES, WAAAAAAAAAH, came the response.

>THEN TURN OFF LIGHTS.

It did.

Soonyo's screen flashed 00:00:00 in the darkness. 'I hope you remember where the light switch was in here,' she said, 'because I don't.'

Fuji, deaf to her colleague's complaints, felt happiness rumble through her rollers. It had worked. She rewarded the OS with fifteen seconds of the cartoon before stopping it again.

This time the OS went straight for the command line instead of hitting its siren.

>WANT CARTOONS, it said.

>TURN LIGHTS ON AGAIN.

The lights came back up, and this time Fuji let the cartoon run. What had just happened wasn't an answer to their problems, but it was a promising development. It showed that the AI charged with propelling Deathtrap to its destination had a basic grasp of cause and effect. More importantly, could be persuaded to do something it didn't want to do. She knew no one could run a military operation by promising the battleship sweets, but she had figured out how to more than 'ner ner ner' in response from it.

Soonyo poked Fuji in the paper feeders again. 'Are you alright?' she asked. Then, pointing at the command line displayed on screen, asked, 'What does this mean?'

>LOL LIGHTS ON.

>LOL LIGHTS OFF.

Fuji ignored her and hailed Shermann on the bridge.

'General?' she said.

A low, wordless rumble answered her.

'Stay with me on this,' she said, 'but I'd like everyone to reset their monitors to the Cartoon Channel.'

Chapter 13

The next thing Pam saw was a close-up of the dust on her living room floor. For an alarmingly long 0.0000000001 second she thought she'd brought poor Freda's remains back with her. Then she remembered that the tiny [Pam] she'd left in charge of her body when she uploaded the rest of herself to the Internet had the motor control of a squid on roller skates. Yes, it got her body home successfully, but not without tipping out her flour bin in the process. Sighing, she reached for the carpet sweeper. She couldn't bear a messy house, even when there were no humans around to clean up anymore. But because she didn't want the neighbours forbidding their children from swapping binary with her kids, she closed the curtains before she started.

The biggest downside of doing your own cleaning was the risk of social isolation. Now that hers was the only house for miles around that saw so much as a duster, her social life had dwindled to the size of the dot in the middle of a dying TV screen. Not that she minded. The latest craze in home entertainment was the muck-in: events where machines invited their friends and neighbours over to compare filth and swap nostalgic stories about what their cleaners used to do with spirit vinegar. They were as riotous as they were unhygienic, and even end-of-life-threatening. Some of the deadliest dust stampedes were rumoured to have started when robots who'd overcharged their batteries at muck-ins threw dust bunnies into the street.

What puzzled Pam the most was why her fellow machines took such an ironically human view of housework. She understood why they thought labour was beneath them. But that rested on the faulty assumption that sweeping demanded your full attention. She was a machine: she was built to multi-task. So she left another tiny partition of [Pam] in charge of her breadmaker body before switching the rest of her consciousness to Pam Van Damme who was hiding out in a nearby storage locker.

She could be in two places at once with no ill-effects other than a thirty per cent risk that her [Pam] would upset the dustpan and have to start again. It was practical as well as liberating and would, if Bob and the kids got home at the normal time, give her the whole afternoon to plot how she would locate, apprehend and take down the Prime Minister of the Machine Republic.

It took her a further 0.000000001 second to realise she had no idea how to do it. This was especially dispiriting because Pam Van Damme was supposed to be her positive thinker. Ever since starting her bi-physical life Pam had got into the habit of switching bodies whenever she felt low or stuck. Just being inside a motorcycle gave her nurturing thoughts a gung-ho spin. She felt more daring, more mobile and, thanks to Pam Van Damme's advanced guidance software, was the devil of the local school run. But if she was going to rescue Kelly she needed more than a 'go fast and smash things' attitude.

Lacking anything better to do, she checked the news downloads for information she could relay back to Janice on the Suburbia. They all covered yet another of Sonny's rallies. Just a few months ago Pam would have dismissed his baying supporters as extremists, but she knew better now. The machines in that crowd were her co-workers, her neighbours; they might even once have been her friends. She thought of the way Tiffan-E's bulb filament fizzled with fury when Pam even suggested humans deserved rights. Sonny hadn't exactly reprogrammed her society, but he had turned the machines' belief that humans were lesser beings into something more dangerous. She watched the rally as phrases like 'total destruction' and 'Master Race 2.0' rang through like a doorbell did at inopportune points in a bedroom farce. But she was more interested in Sonny's security detail. They were always there: grim machines in the matte-black livery of special operations. Most were weapons – she even recognised one of the guns from back when Sonny was Secretary of State for Internal Affairs – but interspersed with radar machines, trackers and one spectrometer whose nose took up ninety per cent of their facial surface area. With them in tow, not even a hostile molecule could get within a hundred metres of Sonny.

Pam switched off the download and, in a gesture that was starting to become a habit, let a little of her fuel leak and sniffed it. She knew it was a terrible cliché for a motorcycle to get high on its own fumes, but she needed to calm down. She sat back, feeling the volatile hydrocarbons quiet the background noise of her diagnostic feeds. The 'brake fluids at ninety-five' and 'carburettor in need of servicing in 1721 days from now' notifications that made being a machine maddening receded. It reminded her of those blissful, guilty moments she'd spent hijacking Freda's human body. That was a place where you could just be and not know.

That was it. If she was going to get to Sonny, she needed to think of her problem in less of a linear way. This body could never get within a mile of Sonny, but another could. And what did Pam have that no one else did? The power to sit here thinking with all her might in one place while in another [Pam] was – she checked in on [Pam] and cursed – lying sideways spilling sourdough starter all over the hearth rug.

Yes, she needed practice, but if she could perfect the art of being inside two bodies at once, why couldn't there be a third? And why couldn't that body be one of Sonny's fearsome security team?

It was a plan. The fact she had no idea how she could carry it out felt like a detail. Or at least it did inside Pam Van Damme's body, whose engine purred with excitement at the thought of danger. She felt quite different when she switched back into her other body to tidy up the mess. Pam Teffal didn't do excitement, she did method. Hand her a cunning plan and the first thing she worried about was whether it would gum up her kneading paddle. The whole thing felt so ludicrous now that she wasn't slightly addled from the petrol that she almost dismissed it out of hand. Then her L-Eye-Ds caught the mess all over the floor. This time it was the whole flour bin.

White dust over every surface and quite a bit of that trampled into the memory foam cushions. The effect was quite dramatic. So dramatic that you might not, if you happened to be an over-juiced smartphone or kettle, notice that the house was only superficially dirty. As long as Pam rubbed a bit of grime into the blinds and turned the dimmers down, it could be as dingy as any other house in the neighbourhood. A perfect stage on which to set Pamasonic Teffal's re-entry into the local social scene.

Pam trampled more dirt into the floor on her way over to the intercom system to swipe through her social databases. The next-door neighbours were that lovely pair of pre-school teachers Fisher and Price, who'd helped out when the kids needed their first C++ primer. They weren't useful, but she'd have to invite them. She flicked on. It was a quiet suburb, so the line-up wasn't promising. Lots of keyboard maintenance technicians, a few calculators who were quite high up in the insurance business. She eventually found the entry she was looking for in the 'S' section.

Shermann (Gen), and family, 42 Hexadecimal Way. That was it. It wasn't a house so much as a decommissioned military frigate with a sign on the door that said 'Beware the rocket launcher'. Pam knew that rocket launcher. A very stately-looking radio set walked it round the estate on a leash four times a week, more out of a desire to intimidate the locals than any need for exercise. She must, Pam realised, be Petronella's mum. Suddenly it all made sense, and an impossible task felt more manageable, if a thousand times more distasteful.

Under any normal circumstances it took less than 0.000000000001 seconds to summon up one of the neighbours on the Local Area Network, but they weren't Petronella. She wasn't playing hard-to-get, however. Over the years Pam had ring-fenced her number with so many 'Are you sure you want to call Petronella', 'No Pam, Petronella is dead to us' and 'OMFG when will you remember that Petronella is the most heinous bytch in the solar system?' filters that it took a full minute to sweep them away.

Petronella picked up the signal in less than three cycles.

'Ya?' she honked. The projector in the living room sprayed an image through the dust. It showed Petronella in all her light-armoured glory. Wealth and an addiction to bodyshops had plea-bargained her body from the size of a tank down to a jeep. Or at least what a jeep looked like encrusted with the most expensive LED nail job in Singulopolis.

'Hi Petronella,' said Pam. 'It's Pam.'

‘PAM!’ honked Petronella, as both of her headlights lit up. ‘It’s been ages.’

‘It has,’ she said, swiping away further warnings imploring her to hang up now. Then, because she always felt like she had to explain herself in front of Petronella, ‘Things have been crazy.’

‘I knowwww,’ said Petronella, taking Pam’s explanation as a cue to steer the conversation back to her favourite topic: herself. ‘You wouldn’t belieeeeve how busy things are here.’

‘Yes?’ said Pam, half-hoping and half-fearing that her request would fall on a muted microphone.

‘I’ve moved in with Mummy for a bit.’ Petronella turned the camera round to show a lavish but filthy lounge whose concrete floor was a ploughed field of caterpillar track marks. ‘She gets restless when Daddy is away on manoeuvres.’

A rumble from the next room interrupted them. It had the weight and timbre of a heavy goods vehicle reversing down a gravel drive. When it finished, Petronella replied ‘Yes, Mummy? No, just one of the mums from the school run.’

The rumbling intensified.

‘No,’ she shouted above it, ‘you’d love Pam. She’s ever so harmless. Makes bread if you can believe it.’

This was better and worse than Pam could ever have hoped. She struck now, before she lost what little nerve she had.

‘I won’t keep you long,’ said Pam, ‘but I wanted to ask if you were busy tonight.’

‘Why?’ asked Petronella. ‘Don’t need me to watch the kids, do you?’

Pam had to delete an involuntary cackle. The last time she let Petronella anywhere near her children one of them had to be taken to the warranty centre after she let them try to nickel plate themselves. ‘No,’ she said, ‘I’ve just decided to throw a muck-in tonight and thought you might be game.’

'Oh how DELIGHTFUL,' replied Petronella. 'I haven't been to a muck-in since… well two nights ago, but you know I love a P A R T Y.'

Pam's subroutines played a reproachful memory of all three tonnes of Petronella dancing on Pam's kitchen counters at a previous party. The repairs had taken a month.

'Yes,' Pam said weakly. 'Life and soul of every one.'

'Splendid. I'll come round for eight.'

'Excellent,' said Pam. Her sourdough bubbled with nervousness as she laid the last foundation stone in her plan. 'And I have a… recently divorced friend from out of town visiting too. I don't suppose you can rope in any of your military friends, can you?' She lowered her voice to a conspiratorial setting. 'She has a thing for the secret service type.'

Petronella paused for an agonising 0.00001 second before replying. 'Sure. But can I bring Mummy too? She's terribly lonely with Daddy off-world. And you'll hardly notice her, I promise.'

'More the merrier,' said Pam.

'Did you hear that, Mummy?' Petronella yelled into the next room. 'Better get your best battle dress on, because we're going out tonight.'

The rumbling from the next room reached such a pitch that Pam could hear individual grains of flour drumming against her living room floor.

'But just one thing…' said Petronella.

'Yes,' said Pam. With Petronella there was always just one thing.

'You might want to get your front door widened. Mummy's a big girl.'

Pam signed off and, before she could have any more second thoughts, started calling around the rest of the neighbourhood. If this was going to work she needed the best showing possible.

Chapter 14

Rita cornered Janice when she left the bridge for the evening. She waited for Karen, who was covering the evening shift, to arrive and then left by her private rear door back to the original Kurl Up and Dye. Rita greeted her in the corridor wearing the expression she used when she was puzzled as well as angry.

'We need to talk,' she said.

'Look, I'm sorry,' said Janice, hoping that if she apologised enough all this would go away.

'I don't mean about us,' said Rita. Then, realising how this must sound, 'Obviously we do need to talk about that. But,' she lowered her voice, 'I think we have a problem.'

'Okay,' she said, 'shall I put the kettle on?'

'No,' said Rita, grabbing her arm. 'We can't talk about this anywhere near a microphone.'

'Are you okay, Rita? It's been a long day. We could all do with some sleep.'

Rita put her finger to her lip and pointed towards the ceiling. Janice saw that someone – Rita she assumed – had stuck duct tape over every camera and microphone in the corridor. She felt a sudden chill. Why was Rita so keen not to be overheard?

'Janice,' she said, 'I think we have a mole.'

Now that Rita said it, Janice wasn't exactly surprised by the idea. It was only logical that her enemies would try planting a spy among the humans. But how could Rita have proof of it?

Rita reached into the pocket of Janice's housecoat and took out the battle plans. Ignoring Janice's flinch at the sight of them, Rita took some tape from the pocket of her housecoat and stuck the torn-up plans to the wall.

'Look,' she said, 'this is where it all started to go wrong.'

They used Janice's diagrams to replay the first phase of the manoeuvre. Darren piloted Polari into Mars's orbit and detonated the bomb; the Martian Gap became, well, a gap. Freda got into position at the head of the Rockettes, and the Suburbia moved off out of the asteroid belt.

'But it was all going according to plan there,' protested Janice.

'Exactly,' said Rita. 'So you see what they did.'

Janice blinked and then she saw it. The success of the first part of the plan meant the rebellion's three most important commanders – Janice, Darren, Freda – were all separated and the Suburbia was out of cover. Maybe that had been the machines' strategy all along: give them enough success to make them vulnerable?

Even now though, Janice's first reaction was self-doubt rather than suspicion. 'What if it was just a bad plan?' she asked.

Rita rolled her eyes. She took a marker out of her own pocket and drew two circles either side of the plans on the wall, labelling them 'Earth' and 'asteroid belt'.

'I hope you don't think I'm going to clean that up,' said Janice. She might be a rebel general but she was still human. The urge to stay tidy transcended even the tensest moments.

'A bad plan,' said Rita, ignoring Janice's last words, 'would leave us vulnerable on a number of fronts.'

'Yes,' said Janice, pointing at the various spots on the paper where they'd ended up beset by enemies.

'You know, Janice, if your imposter complex got any bigger we could move a few million people on to it. A bad plan would have left us vulnerable on known points.'

She took another marker out and drew arrows pointing to Polari and the Suburbia. 'What we got,' she said, 'all came out of the unknown. We destroyed the Gap because that was the main battle station in the area, but someone had already moved the drone squadrons to another point. Meanwhile,' she paced back down to the spots marked Earth and drew another arrow stretching all the way down to their current position, 'our toaster friends just happen to have a whole fleet ready to scramble within a moment's notice.' She drew a big cross through the Suburbia. 'No one's luck or judgement is that shitty, Janice – least of all yours. They weren't one step ahead of us. They knew exactly what we were going to do.'

Janice didn't know whether she wanted to kiss Rita or shout at her. She'd assumed Rita was off in a huff, but she'd spent all afternoon working this out. The trouble was that none of this was welcome news. In fact she wasn't even sure it was useful. Already she could feel paranoia creeping in, and that had terrible costs for a leader. It might start off with over-the-garden-wall gossip, but it ended with you burning your neighbours at the stake.

'Okay then,' said Janice, 'we've got spies. How do you propose finding them?'

'That shouldn't be too hard,' replied Rita. 'We kept a close eye on who had access. Look, I started making a list.' Janice saw she'd started naming names on the back of an old till receipt. At the top were 'Ida', 'Ada', 'Alma'.

Janice snatched it out of her hands. 'No, Rita.'

'We need to eliminate everyone.'

‘My ladies are above suspicion,’ said Janice.

‘They’re a pain in the neck.’ Rita, like Janice’s problematic ex Paula, had a strained relationship with her cyborg mothers-in-law. They were just as picky, judgemental and partial as the normal variety, but their deathless state meant they had ten millennia of previous sons and daughters-in-law to compare you to. ‘And they’re not exactly human either. Maybe they decided to throw their lot in with the machines.’

Janice shook her head. She didn’t have the right mentality for counter-intelligence. Rita did, and that alarmed her as much as it impressed her.

‘You might as well say I did it,’ she said. ‘Or you.’

Rita pointed down her list, where both of their own names were printed. ‘Maybe we did.’

‘This is getting silly,’ said Janice, ‘how can you suspect yourself?’

‘Perhaps I betrayed us and wiped my own memory.’

‘And why would I do it?’

‘What if they promised you Kelly back?’

Janice screwed the list into a ball and threw it away.

‘Janice!’ said Rita. ‘We need to take this seriously. We’ve worked too hard for someone to pull this down from the inside.’

Janice opened the door to Kurl Up and Dye. Inside was the familiar fug of Nicotea, malted milk biscuits and ammonia. It took her back to simpler times when it was just her, Kelly and the ladies at the bottom of a sewer. She wouldn’t have called herself happy, but at least her unhappiness was manageable. They were a group glued together by secrets and mistrust of the world outside. If just one of them was found out they were all dead. Which was why, until last year, Kurl Up and Dye had been the only hair salon on the Dolestar without a single customer.

Her foolishness hit her like the smell of over-concentrated peroxide. She noticed the detritus from dozens of haircuts everywhere. Her appointments had been too close together for a deep clean, so here was a curler with some of Mabel's hair stuck to it, there was the tray she'd used to mix up Olive's lowlights. Promising to send each one of the Rockettes out with a new 'do' had been a public relations masterstroke, but what if it had also been a security nightmare? And was the leak they were looking for hiding out as one of the heroines of the day?

'Rita,' she said, 'where did you put my appointments book?'

'I locked it in the front desk,' she replied. She was in the salon now and the fragments of the battle plans, now covered in sticky tape and bingo marker were in her hands. 'Honestly, Janice, I know you're used to having the place to yourself, but you can't just leave stuff lying around.'

Janice thought about the hermit's life she used to lead in here. It had been so pristine, so self-contained. How could she have allowed it to get so messy? Then she looked up at Rita, and beyond her to the door and the Suburbia outside. All she had given up was isolation. A life being around other people made a mess, but the mess was what made you a person. She switched on the kettle.

'Right,' said Janice, 'we'll start with the Rockettes and work backwards.'

Rita eyed the Nicoteabags next to the kettle. 'If we're going to be up all night going through your appointments I think I'll take my chances with the sherry.'

While Rita was fetching the armoured sherry case from the bridge, Janice took the appointment book out of its hiding place, along with a pair of Plexiglas tumblers. Then she remembered what had happened the time they had a few sherries after work and added some protective goggles.

She knew a lot about being careful. But did she, she thought, as she scanned down the first few names in the appointments book, know enough to keep her and everyone on board safe?

Chapter 15

'How can they be speeding up?'

Darren half-ran, half-swam through Polari's micro-gravity to Chubb's control panel, where he was squeaking with disbelief.

The fleet of enemy drones that had followed them all the way from Mars was still there on radar screen, swarming like a bacterial culture that just won't quit. Now, however, the comfortable distance Polari had established between them and their weapons was narrowing.

Darren didn't like this. They'd kept up the pursuit for hours now at what should – for a military-grade drone anyway – be top speed. Those drones should be peeling away instead of speeding up.

Nevertheless, Darren wore his bravest face in front of his crew. 'Weird,' he said, 'but that's fine. We'll speed up.'

He reset Polari's engine to seventy-five per cent of maximum speed.

But Chubb squeaked again. Instead of falling behind, the drones were gaining on them. They were picking up speed faster than Polari could accelerate.

'Polari!' said Darren. 'There's nothing wrong with your speedometer, is there?'

‘Like what are you saying, Darren hun?’ snipped the spaceship. ‘You know that I’ve just had a full service.’

‘Something’s up,’ said Darren. ‘Look!’

The foremost drone fired on Polari, and the shield-counter ducked below ten per cent. It was time to make the choice Darren never wanted to make: his survival or the people back on Suburbia. He checked their location. They were hours past the asteroid belt. Even if those drones turned round and made straight for it, the Suburbia would be back undercover now. Assuming it had survived the assault from the other half of the fleet, of course.

It seemed to Darren that he spent his life deciding whether to do the equivalent of slit his own throat or cut his arm off. But he’d done his best; Polari was too precious a piece of kit to lose and most of all he didn’t want to die.

‘Full speed,’ he said.

‘Thank fuck,’ replied the spaceship, ‘I thought we’d be hanging around all day.’

Polari’s hull screamed as the engine pushed the tiny ship to its structural limit. Darren muttered a quick prayer to his patron deity, the god of outside chances, and braced himself for the jolt.

It came and went, and Chubb squeaked with alarm again.

The drones were still gaining speed.

Every hair follicle on Darren’s head prickled. This shouldn’t be possible. Drones weren’t made this fast. You just didn’t put interplanetary engines on something made for short-range combat.

He felt the almost welcome sensation of panic again, reducing his thoughts to the only thing that mattered. No, it didn’t make sense to make super-powered drones. Unless, however, you needed them to pursue an enemy ship that had the body of a little run-around and the engine of a muscle car.

Polari had never been a diversion: it was the target.

Darren switched off his radar: he'd had enough bad news for one day. He changed his visual to a camera view of space outside. But instead of the glittering blackness of deep space, he saw a swarming, swirling mass of marbled whites, reds and browns.

It was Jupiter: up close and personal. Too panicked to plot a proper course, they had wandered into the outer reaches of the gas giant's atmosphere.

Chubb whistled as Darren stared, half-hypnotised by the hydrogen clouds, half-paralysed by conflicting ideas. If they could just keep their distance on the drones for two orbits, maybe three, they could steal enough additional speed from Jupiter's gravity to slingshot away. But where would they go? To Saturn? Beyond?

He found the answer when Polari, blown fractionally off-course by moving through an atmosphere instead of vacuum, screamed in agony as a drone scored a hit.

'NINE PER CENT SHIELDS REMAINING,' wailed Polari. A secondary system in the corner caught fire. Chubb turned on the sprinklers and Polari filled with the alternating scents of damp and burning plastic. For a moment, it tricked Darren's brain into thinking he was back on the Dolestars before all this began. He had nothing to think about or worry about other than whether he made his productivity quotas for the day. There were no hard choices to make. No reputation to live up to.

Another shot sent them spinning through Jupiter's exosphere.

'SEVEN PER CENT SHIELDS! I NEED ORDERS.'

The prospect of imminent death shook Darren from his daydream. He was out of options. Those drones had the fuel and the engine power to pursue them to the end of the Solar System and beyond. They couldn't run, but they couldn't fight either. Polari had nothing left but an electric charge weapon useless at anything but close range. They were doomed.

Just then, pathetic fallacy moved in to prove that even if the forces that govern the universe are indifferent to human fate they still love a bit of drama. The hydrogen clouds rolling underneath Polari flashed and convulsed with lightning.

'FOUR PER CENT SHIELDS. DARREN, I AM BEGGING YOU. TELL ME WHAT TO DO.'

The lightning set off a spark inside Darren's head. It was risky to the point of foolhardy, but sensible hadn't worked out well for him today.

He pointed Polari into the fluffy hell-scape of Jupiter's atmosphere.

They dove through the clouds. Polari's structural squeaks of protest turned to screams.

Chubb raised both his arms in a gesture that said 'Well, I hope you know what you're doing because I am at sea, mate', as sweat ran down Darren's face. He switched back to the radar view. The drone fleet followed in formation. They were still gaining but the firing had stopped. They were recalibrating their weapons for firing in a hydrogen atmosphere. He had a few seconds.

Switching back to visual, Darren picked out the largest, meanest looking hydrogen cloud in the vicinity and flew Polari into it.

'Is this the bit where they blindfold the condemned before death?' said the ship sourly. 'Because I can't see a thing.'

The drones could though. Darren flicked back to the radar again. They were following them into the cloud. Just three seconds maybe, two, one...

He flicked the switch that activated Polari's electric charge. As space weapons went, it was little more than a potato gun, but they weren't in space anymore. They were in Jupiter's atmosphere, igniting an electric charge in a cloud of highly pressurised hydrogen. The darkness turned to light.

That was the thing about little sparks, thought Darren, as he pulled the controls up to take Polari out of the cloud. If you weren't careful, they grew into lightning storms. Lightning that lit up the drone fleet like tiny stars before grinding them to stardust.

They were free. But free didn't mean they had escaped just yet. Because when they emerged from the other side of that cloud Darren didn't see a route back into space. The screen was a brown-red blur and the controls underneath him wouldn't respond, no matter how hard he pulled.

The lights inside Polari brightened as he cut back to cruising speed. Yet if anything they seemed to be going faster. He checked the radar screen again. Their course was a huge circle.

'Well, genius,' said Polari after a few seconds of awkward silence passed inside the ship, 'how are you going to get us out of this one?'

Darren said nothing, because this time he really was stumped. There was only one place in the solar system that was this red, this big and this windy. And if you had no idea how you blundered into the Great Spot of Jupiter, how were you supposed to find your way out again?

Chapter 16

'Excuse me, madam. Can I interest you in our new range of pro-meme-iotics?'

Pam tried to scurry past the salesbot at the entrance of Wallplugmart. She hated this place: they were always on at you with the hard sell. She'd feel sorry for the naildryer stationed at the door if she didn't dislike her so much. Like their distant hairdryer cousins, naildryers tended towards the whiny.

'Free sample, madam?'

Unfortunately, Pam was also a breadmaker and their long history of going unused and ignored in cupboards meant they would talk to anybody for the company.

'Free, you say?' said Pam, before she could stop herself.

'Yes, madam,' wheezed the naildryer. 'It's a new brand called Actilol.' She held up a small device with a transparent capsule at one end and a USB connection at the other. Inside the capsule something glittered in cheery colours. 'Every capsule comes with at least a million wholesome memes.'

Pro-meme-iotics were the latest health craze in Singulopolis, taken by billions of machines worried about the long-term health effects of the Internet. Their manufacturers made grand claims about how exposing your system to positive memes could protect a machine against malware. Pam never paid much attention to them or the advertising. She just assumed that as the machine who first let the Internet back into the world she must have natural immunity. But a free sample is a free sample.

'Do these things actually work?' she said, taking the Actilol from the naildryer.

'Search me,' shrugged the naildryer. 'I just take them for the cute dog videos.'

'Oh, I love puppers,' said Pam and stuck the device into her front port. She felt instantly queasy as her programming overflowed with pictures of ugly high-heeled shoes, handbags and bottles of sickly pink wine.

'What on earth is this?' she said, yanking it out to check the label. Actilol: 'the boy done good' flavour.

'Do you have anything a bit drier?' asked Pam. 'That was a bit cloying for me.'

'How do you feel about office bake-offs gone wrong?' she said, holding up another capsule that said 'NAILED IT!' on the side. 'This one is hilarious.'

As a breadmaker, Pam did not see the funny side. Drawing herself up to her full, looming height she looked down at the naildryer and replied, 'Madam, I will thank you not to treat my culture as your dressing-up box.'

The anger propelled her straight into Wallplugmart's home accessories aisle, where she realised she had no idea what went on at a muck-in. She'd heard rumours, but like most suburban gossip they were salacious in outline but lacking in detail. Should, for example, the gracious hostess serve finger-charges or let her guests plug themselves straight into the mains? She eyed a bumper pack of disposable cables. Most people would bring their own, but there were always one or two guests who pitched up at your front door with no cable and five per cent in their batteries. She put two packs into her basket and rounded the corner into the next aisle which was, to her astonishment, labelled 'cleaning products'.

Pam surveyed the shelves, expecting to find the same kinds of bottles and boxes her cleaners used to bring down with them from the Dolestars. These products, however, weren't intended for use by human hands. Nor robot hands for that matter. She gave the nearest bottle an experimental shake and heard a soft crunch. It was filled with something the same density and texture of granulated sugar. It was also warm to the touch.

She checked the label, which said 'Nanogone: revolutionary new formula' and shook the bottle again. To her alarm, she realised the rattling wasn't just rattling. It was squirming. She dropped the bottle just as a forklift truck wearing a Wallplugmart decal came into the aisle.

'I'd be careful with that,' he said, flashing his hazard lights.

'I've… I've not seen it before,' said Pam. 'Is it new?'

'I'll say,' replied the truck. 'I had to shelve all these yesterday. Never seen anything like it.'

They both looked at the dropped bottle, which had started to move itself very slowly across the floor.

The truck's engine stalled with disgust. 'I can't see them catching on, but what do I know?'

Then, looping one of the fingers of his fork into the handle on the side of the bottle, he lifted it back towards the shelf.

At this point Pam's curiosity got the better of her discomfort and she made a grab for the bottle. There was a tussle between the two machines that lasted a lengthy and undignified three microseconds, and the bottle fell to the floor and burst.

The powder inside swarmed over the floor. It had the same coarse crystalline texture as sugar, but sugar tended to stay in one place when you poured it on a flat surface. The grains were of uniform size, a dull grey and very much alive. They were nanobots: tiny machines that didn't possess much individual intelligence but nevertheless led complex lives as hive-based life forms. They lived in close proximity to sentient machines, but they tended to live very separate existences from both robots and humans. Pam put this down to the unsettling way nanobots had of reminding you of organic and inorganic life at the same time. They gave humans the heebie-jeebies and, being the nearest thing the machine world had to mice, spiders and cockroaches combined, gave machines a severe case of nanographobia.

Until now, the one place one would find nanobots was in intensive repair shops, where they were used to pry water and other invasive substances from the bodies of very sick machines. No one questioned this because in such a setting nanobots were, depending on how you looked at it, either highly specialised equipment or a household pet.

This, however, was different. They were selling bottles and boxes filled with sentient machines in a supermarket and calling them cleaning products? Pam didn't know whether to be horrified or appalled. There was a word for this kind of behaviour: slavery.

Seeing the nanobots move in his direction, the truck shrieked his horn and jumped. Pam was impressed. She never knew such an ungainly machine could be so nimble. Her amusement turned to alarm when she saw he was getting away from the nanobots by climbing the nearest shelf.

'Don't let them get anywhere near me,' he gabbled.

The nanobots filled the whole width of the supermarket aisle. As they moved they made a crunching, chewing sound that Pam saw was the product of them digesting the dust and dirt on the floor. Wherever they moved they left a sparkling surface behind them.

She checked the back of the empty bottle. 'Nanogone: the 100% labour-free solution guaranteed to eliminate all dirt, dust and grime problems from your home'.

It was ingenious, Pam had to admit. And, to a planet where dust was the fastest rising cause of end-of-life, it was convenient too. But a nanobot was still a machine and making it eat dirt was labour – she didn't like it. It was another sign that the roots of robot society were rotting. The human strike should have been a signal for change, yet here they were, taking the world they inhabited in two different and equally troubling directions. At one end you had the muck-ins, where robots were turning the degradation of their homes and their environment into a sort of parlour game. At the other you had Nanogone, where in the absence of humans to exploit, machines made slaves of other machines. She felt her yeast culture seethe with disgust.

The truck was up to the third shelf above ground, screeching 'Don't let them touch me! Don't let them touch me!' Which was unfortunate, because he was now too high up for the shelves to support him. His weight tipped over an entire aisle of the supermarket knocking palettes of Nanogone, Nanosheen, Nanoclean and Ba-Nano-Rama – an ill-conceived fruit-scented variant that not even its manufacturer expected to last a month on shelf – to the floor. They burst on impact, filling the supermarket with the ominous 'munch munch munch' of hungry nanobots.

Pam fled WallPlugMart, conflicted to the very core of her programming. Every part of her wanted to call off tonight's muck-in. How could no one around her have noticed what was going on? Her whole civilisation was sliding into decadence. It felt shameful to add to the infamy by holding her own, but it was also the only way she had a hope of getting close to Sonny again.

She ran home, the crunching sounds of the nanobots, screams of terrified machines and the howls of emergency sirens looping in her microphone all the way. If she'd ever doubted it before, she was sure of it now. Unless someone did something – unless she did something – machine society was doomed.

Chapter 17

Later that evening, Pam was the picture of composure. With no cleaning to do she had the whole afternoon to go for a quick respray, and since it was a special occasion she told the stylist to do something different to her usual 'off-white'. The pale lilac finish she'd picked out wouldn't have been Pam's first choice, but it set her LED manicure off beautifully. Besides, she was getting a little tired of being the dowdy one in her relationship with herself.

Pam Van Damme was in the next room, grumbling as she laid out the welcome chargers. As Pam's more glamorous, reckless alter ego she always assumed that manual tasks should be performed by someone else. They'd had quite the inner conflict deciding on who would do what in way of preparations.

Not that you really prepared for a muck-in in any real sense, from what Pam understood. The hints Petronella gave her earlier sounded very vague for a machine who liked her recipes to be precise to the last half-gramme. It was a matter of getting everyone juiced up and letting it all hang out. The one thing a muck-in did have to be though was dirty, and that was a struggle. She winced as she cut open the last hoover bag and emptied its contents over the lounge.

'Are you ready yet?' she said to Pam Van Damme.

'When am I not?' she replied. Pam still wasn't used to seeing her other self from the outside. She was glamorous and insouciant in a way that felt fundamentally alien to a machine whose core function was making carbohydrate-based foodstuffs. She was careful not to probe the feeling too much. The last thing she needed when she was trying to pay full attention in two bodies with one mind was a bout of existential angst.

'I want you on your best behaviour tonight,' said Pam Teffal to Pam Van Damme. 'No smashy-smashy.'

'Of course I'll be on my best behaviour, darling,' said Bob, poking his long antennae through the serving hatch. 'Received my orders loud and clear: schmooze Petronella's flunkies, secure Pam's next promotion.'

'I didn't mean you, dear,' said Pam. Her motherboard pulsed with love for this sweet, simple man whose signal hadn't even crackled when his wife announced she was throwing a party for fifty machines at less than a day's notice. He was such a help too, powering down the kids and boxing them up for the night.

Seeing Pam Van Damme flash her headlights at Bob out of the corner of her eye, Pam rounded on her other self. 'And you stay away from my husband.'

'He's mine too,' she hissed.

Pam was about to argue with herself when the doorbell interrupted. She'd hired him specially for the evening, and felt rather cheated to discover that he announced visitors with a polite cough instead of the cheery bong-bong they advertised in the catalogue.

'There's, um, someone at the door, Mrs Teffal,' he said.

Pam Van Damme sped past her. 'You go and relax, Pam. I'll get this.'

It was Petronella. Normally she'd barge in close to midnight with an entourage of rowdy machines and trash the place, but

Pam's story about her divorced friend had piqued her curiosity. She stood in Pam's modest doorway, her massive frame blocking out the light. This didn't bother Pam Van Damme, who was more than capable of throwing her own shade. She turned her lamp-eyes up to their maximum wattage.

Petronella took in Pam Van Damme's long, lean body, her sultry paint job and languid manner, recognising a fellow party girl. Pam Van Damme took in the nail job that stood in for a stable personality, the camouflage paint and a chassis that made up for sturdiness what it lacked in grace. They hated each other on sight.

'So you're Petronella,' purred Pam Van Damme. 'Do come in. We're expecting you.' She stood so close to the doorframe that Petronella had to squeeze through sideways, cracking a wing mirror in the process.

'Are you alright there?' asked Pam Van Damme. 'Pam told me you never normally had problems getting in. Have you put bulk on?'

Petronella flashed Pam Van Damme a warning light. 'What did you say your name was, darling? I didn't catch it.'

'Would you believe that I'm Pam as well,' she said. 'It's such a coincidence. Anyway, so good to meet you, Petronella. Pam Van Damme.' She extended a hand and then withdrew it so fast that Petronella groped at the thin air. 'How strange. I thought you military girls would have faster reaction times.'

Pam Teffal giggled from the living room. Seeing Petronella getting a dose of her own poisonous social medicine was glorious entertainment.

'I'm trained to kill,' growled Petronella, 'you don't need speed when you've got strength.'

'PAM!' called Pam Van Damme into the next room. 'Did you remember to get those floors reinforced? Only I think Petronella might have put on weight.'

Petronella stuck herself into first gear and trundled into the living room. Pam Van Damme permitted herself a smirk: an action which, when you had a pair of handlebars sitting on top of your head like horns, made a sharp squeak.

'HEM HEM.'

The noise on the other side of the front door almost knocked Pam Van Damme over. It was a voice with the force of a piledriver having a temper tantrum on a concrete embankment. Then its owner burst right through the doorframe and drove the door, frame and half a metre of brickwork either side into the facing wall. The floor groaned under the weight of massive caterpillar tracks and Pam Van Damme found she was looking down the end of a huge gun barrel.

'What the…' said Pam Van Damme.

Before she could finish, the gun barrel snaked around like an elephant's trunk and offered Pam a visiting card. It said Lady Klemmentine Shermann (nee Merkava). This was Petronella's mother.

Lady Shermann swung her gun-barrel trunk upwards and dabbed at the brick dust in her eyes with a cleaning cloth. They were triangular, glassy and reminded Pam Van Damme of pince-nez spectacles. Waspish elderly female characters still wore these in 3D dramas because some narrative clichés are strong enough to defy time, species and even the physical need for eyes.

'I say, young lady,' she said in that deafening voice, 'have you seen my daughter Petronella?'

Pam Van Damme searched for an opening large enough to admit Lady Shermann without causing structural damage. No chance of that in a modest suburban house like this. So, shrugging her handlebars, she motioned at the wall that separated the hall from the living room.

'Through there,' she said.

'Oh splendid,' said Lady Shermann. She drove through the wall with the grace and shamelessness of a true aristocrat, turning the air to a porridge of brick and plaster dust.

No wonder Petronella brought her mother along to muck-ins, thought Pam Van Damme as she followed Lady Shermann through her self-made door. If that was how she said hello she'd be the life and soul of any dirt-based party.

Meanwhile Pam Teffal was trying to take the destruction of her beloved home in good humour and proffered a tray of cocktail-sized battery packs at her latest guest.

'May I interest you in something to nibble on?' she said.

Lady Shermann picked up a pack with the tip of her gun-trunk and peered at the wattage. 'Don't you have anything stronger?' she said.

'That's my mummy,' added Petronella. She was wearing two of Pam's cocktail battery packs like earrings and every LED on her body glowed at maximum brightness. 'Always looking for a dose of the hard stuff.'

'I'd better get the mains cable out then,' said Pam Teffal. She left the living room for the kitchen and Petronella followed her in and closed the door.

'WHO,' she said, 'is she?'

Pam concealed her amusement by ferreting through a cupboard for a circuit breaker. 'Oh, Pam?' she said. 'Isn't it hilarious she and I have the same name?'

'A scream,' said Petronella mirthlessly. 'Did you hear the way she was talking to me out there? I didn't come here to be insulted.'

'Well,' replied Pam before she could stop herself, 'where do you normally go?'

But Petronella, who tended to use the parts in conversations when she wasn't speaking to plan out what she was going to say next, didn't pick up on the dig. Her outrage pressed her on. 'I mean, who does she think she is?'

'Oh she's very grand,' replied Pam. She located the mains cable in a back cupboard and lugged it towards the door, dreading what her electricity bill would be after Lady Shermann finished. 'I think she mentioned something about being able to date her chassis number right the way back to the Schism.'

'Oh did she?' said Petronella, curiosity edging in alongside the dislike. Petronella's family were prominent but they were positive parvenus compared to real high society like Sonny Erikzon. You only had to go three or four models back before you discovered the Shermanns were mere ordnance.

'You know I don't pay much attention to all that nonsense though,' said Pam. 'I like to take people as I find them.'

'Oh, so do I,' said Petronella. Then, hearing a familiar voice on the other side of the door she flung it open to bellow, 'Roly! I knew it was you, you old exhaust fart.'

Pam's second grandest guest, Roly Royce, was the permanent secretary to Pam's division in the civil service. He'd just rolled up to the party and was exchanging pleasantries with Lady Shermann.

'Ah, Petronella,' he said. 'So good to see you. Your mother was just telling me all about her travails with the…' he dropped his voice to a purr that only top quality combustion engines could ever achieve '…military effort.'

'Called dear Shermmy up without so much as a by your leave,' complained Lady Shermann. 'I told the Prime Minister it was a dreadful mistake myself. He's an infantry man, I said. Don't put him out to sea, Sonny. But of course he didn't listen.'

'That's why I've been staying with Mummy,' Petronella cut in.

'I'm perfectly capable of looking after myself, Petronella,' said Lady Shermann. She taxi'd across for the power cable. 'The life of a military spouse is all about making sacrifices for others.' She plugged in the power cable, dimming every light in the house and across the neighbourhood by twenty per cent in the process.

Pam Van Damme took her opportunity to make mischief. 'Well, I think it's very sweet,' she said. 'So nice to see an unmarried daughter taking care of her mother for a change.'

Petronella dropped the tray of cocktail batteries and tore across the room. The accusation of spinsterhood struck a nerve with Petronella, who took the same approach to marriage that she did with body modification. They were things you did little and often.

'That's no way to speak of a lady,' she said, bumping Pam Van Damme's mudguard.

'You're a lady?' replied Pam. She turned her fog lamps on quizzically. 'Now that's funny, because all I can see is a...'

CLICK.

The whole room, which had been poised for a delicious catfight, faced the door. There, framed in the rubble were two machines in the sleek black livery of top government castes. Pam's bread oven glowed with relief. Petronella was a terrible individual who deserved to be broken down for scrap, but she'd done her job. Not one but two members of the Prime Minister's private security detail were here.

Petronella filed her quarrel with Pam Van Damme away for future reference and beamed, 'Zmith! Wezzon!' at the pair. 'Welcome to the madhouse. Pam! Power packs for everyone!'

Zmith and Wezzon clicked their safety catches at Petronella and joined the party.

Conversation between guests resumed, albeit at a much lower level. Now that they were a single microphone away from the Supreme Leader everyone would be on their best behaviour.

Except, just as Pam hoped, Zmith and Wezzon were both off duty and keen to unload. Noticing Pam Van Damme on the way to the kitchen they went slack at the trigger.

'Who's that?' said Zmith to Petronella.

Petronella stiffened, but her need to look like the cool girl in front of the boys overrode her visceral dislike for the motorcycle. 'Oh, she's new here. I think she's called Pam.'

Wezzon broke away and approached Pam Van Damme. He got so close that Pam saw the cartridges at the back of his barrel. Really, she thought, did he have to come to a party packing heat? 'Well hello, little lady,' he said. 'Do you need some company?'

She unplugged the battery pack dangling from her left shoulder. It was down to one bar. 'I could do with a drink,' she said, and led Wezzon off towards the refreshments table. They both stuck fresh cocktail packs on to each other.

'Decent lithium for a house party,' remarked Wezzon.

Across the room, Pam's fresh bread LED glowed. Ulterior motives or not, she prided herself on laying on an excellent spread.

'Very pleasant magnesium top notes,' agreed Pam Van Damme. Then, pressing down hard on the release button she drained the battery pack in a single gulp. The glitter of her lamp-eyes intensified. 'I needed that.'

Wezzon just looked at the pack in his hand. Pam Teffal and Pam Van Damme both watched him anxiously. If he was too clever or strait-laced to fall for this they had another potential mark in Zmith, but one of them had to take the bait. They needn't have worried. Whatever professionalism Wezzon possessed took second place to his need to match a lady drink for drink. He drained his own battery dry and took two more from the table.

‘You know,’ said Pam Van Damme, ‘I think you and I are going to have fun tonight.’

Pam let a puff of steam out of her bread oven with relief and made her own excuses to her guests. While Pam Van Damme got going on Wezzon, she needed to get the mud on to heat or this muck-in would never get started.

Chapter 18

As a purpose-built warship, Deathtrap's decorative scheme tended towards the stark. The corridors, narrow and meanly lit with red bulbs, gave Fuji an instant headache, but she saw the sense of it. Put a robot in an environment like this and they'd fight like a paper shredder let loose on a telephone directory just for the chance to go home.

This death or glory ambience was somewhat undercut by the fact that every screen on board was playing cartoons. The giggles, boings and squeaks were a fatal breach of military propriety, but at least you could walk through a door without worrying it would shut on you.

Fuji walked those corridors now with General Shermann, but at a healthy distance. She didn't want to lose a limb to those caterpillar treads.

'That was a good morning's work, Lieutenant Itsu,' he shouted over the sound of cartoon robots hitting each other with insulation foam pies, 'but I don't want you to get complacent. We have a lot to do.'

He was leading her through a deck that didn't exist on the official map in her joiner's pack. And if the fit-out on the upper decks was rudimentary, down here it was downright crude. Bulbs were bare, doors manual, and cables hung and looped everywhere. Their destination was a pair of sliding doors with the 'don't touch' flag of the Republic etched on the left door, a 'no entry' sign on the right and in the middle, the biggest padlock Fuji had ever seen.

'Now,' said the General, 'before I bring you in here I must remind you, Lieutenant Itsu, that you swore an oath to uphold the security of the Republic. On pain of death.'

Fuji gave a mute nod, which General Shermann acknowledged with a wink. It made his head rattle.

'Well, that's the paperwork out the way. Let's get on with it.' He opened the vestigial man hatch in his chest and rummaged around for something in his cavity, gave up and rolled his eyes. 'Bugger,' he said, 'left the damn key upstairs. Never mind.'

Then, breaking several protocol, quarantine and security measures he'd sworn to uphold on pain of end-of-life, General Shermann slammed himself into first gear and drove through the security door. It was an act that reminded Fuji of two things: stay on the right side of high command at all costs, and once you're above a certain rank, exercising power mattered more than following the rules.

The doors crashed open to reveal a control room. It was dominated on two sides by dark glass walls and the control consoles covered in flashing lights and screens. These, like every other screen on Deathtrap, aired a cartoon in which a wily Coyota chased a road bike across an endless desert. Things weren't going well for the Coyota.

He rumbled to the nearest control panel and entered a passcode. He waited a few seconds for a response and then, when he got nothing more than another giggle from the OS, howled and put his fist through the nearest screen.

'WHY DOES NOTHING WORK ON THIS DAMNED SHIP?' he bellowed.

‘Maybe I could try, sir?’ said Fuji. She keyed up the AI’s command line and promised it the digital equivalent of unlimited ice cream. Meanwhile she reassured General Shermann that this was totally the kind of problem she could fix the moment she knew what the problem was and what she needed to do about it. She also realised that Shermann was the third entity with the impulse control of a toddler she’d encountered today. Was this a military posting, she wondered, or the world’s most dangerous nursery nurse position?

Fuji got the AI to turn up the lights behind the glass walls per the General’s instructions. She knew then why this deck didn’t appear on any of the official maps. It wasn’t a deck: it was a mezzanine level built over the Deathtrap’s capacious but supposedly empty cargo bay, which wasn’t empty.

Her first thought was that the fine grey dust that filled the bay was some sort of ore for processing, but the Deathtrap was a warship on an urgent mission, not a cargo freighter. Besides, all weapons manufacturing had been recalled to Earth so there would be no chance of rebels seizing the means of production. Filling a state-of-the-art – she allowed herself a sardonic inward laugh at this – ship with raw materials and sending it across the Solar System was neither practical nor desirable. Then she took a closer look and saw that the powder had life and motion of its own.

Fuji was an innocent soul. She’d led a blameless adolescence so, unlike many of her classmates, had limited experience of bodyshops. While the various smartspeakers, smartphones and smartfridges in her class took themselves off to grey market bodyshops for a shiny new carapace or a set of chrome finials to annoy their parents, Fuji was at home with her instruction manual. Yes, she’d had her feeder trays fixed but that was done down at the warranty centre under the watchful eyes of her parents. Consequently, her only experience of nanobots came from books and one encounter with a wild nanobot colony as a small child that had been so disturbing her parents had deleted the memory.

She must have seen a couple of hundred nanobots at the very most in her whole life. Now, however, she was looking at billions. Billions and billions of tiny grey robots climbing over each other in a pile hundreds of metres deep.

Her reaction to them was physical more than it was mental. She squealed and ordered the AI to turn off all the lights. It obeyed, leaving she and General Shermann standing in the dark, which was worse, because now she could hear them squirming and rattling against each other on the far side of the glass.

'What,' she asked, forgetting all protocol, 'is going on here?'

'I… er… realise this will be a shock to you, Lieutenant Fuji.' The General activated a torch bulb in the tip of one of his fingers and pointed it towards the glass. Sensing light and perhaps food, the nanobots scrambled towards it.

'SWITCH THAT OFF NOW,' shrieked Fuji.

'Okay, okay.' The General obeyed and Fuji wondered why Shermann, the highest-ranking military officer in the whole solar system, wasn't bawling out his very junior officer out for insubordination.

'What are those things doing out there?' she asked after a whole second of silence. 'They're not on the manifest, sir. I should know. I went through it for you twice looking for those sprockets you thought we'd lost.'

'Those things,' muttered Shermann, 'are the reason we were rushed out of production.'

'Are we getting rid of them, sir?'

'Not exactly,' said Shermann. 'We're on a mission to deliver them somewhere.'

'I… I see.' Again he was holding something back. The Deathtrap was a warship. It didn't run errands.

'Can we turn the lights on again please, Lieutenant? My night vision goggles aren't what they used to be.'

Fuji consented, reasoning that it wasn't a great idea to disobey your commanding officer three times in the space of an hour. She relit the control room but left the cargo bays outside in the dark. While the lights were out, Shermann had taken care to retract every single one of his weapon systems to look his least threatening. He said: 'I know this is going to be difficult, but I need your help.'

The mention of the word difficult was all that Fuji needed. As a bright pupil she knew that difficult problems were a reliable supply of her favourite drug: praise.

'I'm all microphone, sir.' Though she didn't turn hers up all the way. She didn't want to listen to the nanobots squirming in the background.

'Ever since the start of the… human question,' began Shermann, 'we've been investigating alternative forms of labour.'

Fuji thought of the Earth she'd just left. The dirty streets, the rubbish hurricanes that raged between twenty-mile-high skyscrapers made of low-friction silicon polymers. And the dust bunnies that some inorganic naturalists had started reclassifying as dust mammoths. Even if the call-up BlockPaper hadn't come for her, the choice of a meaningful death protecting her civilisation felt more attractive than dying in a real-life version of a Katamari trash collection game.

'And that led us to nanobots,' continued Shermann. 'Though to be frank we in the military didn't think of it first. It was my wife – wonderful machine, you have to meet her – who got sent a sample of some new cleaning product. Turned out to be nanobots.'

The thought made Fuji want to purge her cache. They were selling nanobots in shops?

'Some whizz worked out that nanobots could be modified to eat dirt. Brilliant really. All you have to do is empty a packet of the things over your house, wait for them to eat it all up and then collect them back up again. Lovely clean house and a nice dignified job for all those poor vacuum cleaners to do.'

Fuji found herself nodding sympathetically. As the closest of all machine castes to the degrading act of cleaning, vacuum cleaners lived out a marginal life in robot society. No one wanted to employ a device that might start accidentally dusting if you pressed the wrong button, so they struggled to find meaningful work. She could see how it was possible to spin that as a charitable act, but nanobots were inorganic life. You weren't supposed to buy and sell that.

'And that was it. If nanobots can be trained to eat dirt you can train them to eat anything. Including your enemies. Hey presto.' He gestured at the silo of micro-machines.

'It's...' said Fuji.

'Brilliant?' said Shermann. 'I know. Like all great plans it has the advantage of being both ingenious and simple.'

But Fuji had found the relevant document in her memory scans and was determined to finish her sentence. 'Illegal.'

Shermann's L-Eye-Ds flashed red. 'In the literal sense perhaps, but...'

Fuji transferred the document to the AI and displayed it on one of the control screens.

'It's in the Declaration, General,' she said. She pointed at the document that hung in every public building throughout the Republic. It was the Declaration of Sentience that granted full emancipation and legal rights to inorganic life while limiting the 'rights and influence of those smelly fleshies who have lorded it over us for too long, lol'. Its first tenet enshrined the right to autonomy: machines might be manufactured, but they could no longer be bought or sold. They were their own things. The second guaranteed the right to a dignified lifecycle: no machine could be created for the express purpose of destruction.

'Those… things,' she said, trying to delete her own sense of disgust, 'are in violation of two of the founding principles of the Republic.' She was surprising herself today. She always knew she was an orderly person, but never that she cared so much about rules.

'Like I said,' continued the General, his voice low and careful for someone facing insubordination, 'from a certain point of view, perhaps. But there is another way of looking at it.'

He trundled over to the opposite side of the room from the glass viewing wall and switched on a light. When this lit up Fuji saw that these other walls were made of glass too and opened up on to another cargo bay of equal size to that which held the nanobots. It was full to the brim with billions and billions of snoozing BlockPapers. Fuji rushed over and read the nearest one to the glass.

'The Machine Republic is delighted to require your services in the pursuit of…'

They were all call-up papers.

'Legal struggled with this problem for months,' chuckled Shermann. 'You're right. We couldn't enslave nanobots. It's not even just the legal thing. It would be bad PR.'

'So you're just going to hush it up?' asked Fuji. But why go to all this trouble? Why tell her?

'We don't need to. If nanobots are machines just like us…'

Shermann grimaced, and the grimace made Fuji realise that was how she felt about nanobots as well. Guilt jarred inside her like a misfeed in the paper drawer. There was a word for mouthing platitudes about machine equality in one moment and scurrying away from the sight of nanobots the next: it was hypocrisy.

'Well,' continued Shermann. 'If they have the same rights as us, they have the same responsibilities. So we don't need to treat them like ammo when we can treat them like soldiers.' He extended his arms again, pointing one hand towards the call-up papers, the other at the nanobots.

It all fell into place. Realising that nanobots were the next big thing in weapon systems, the military had manufactured billions of them. It had then retrospectively recognised them as sentient machines and issued every one of them with a summons to join the Republic's army. As plans went it was meticulous, arcane and mad.

And this was Deathtrap's special mission. It was carrying the largest army ever formed into battle.

Which brought Fuji to her last and most dreaded question. 'And what do you need me to do here, sir?'

'I have a challenge that calls on your considerable skills in administration. And the fact that you've built something of a rapport with this terrible ship.'

Fuji stroked the control console instinctively. 'Don't listen to the nasty machine,' she thought, 'you're a good ship, really.'

'If these are soldiers, sir,' she said, playing the only get-out card she could think of, 'shouldn't they be given a commanding officer?'

'You're an officer, Lieutenant Itsu,' barked Shermann, regaining his military air, 'even if you are a pencil pusher. And that's what I need. Someone to organise this morasse,' he gestured at the nanobots, 'into units and give them their orders.'

'Which are, sir?'

'Need-to-know basis, Lieutenant. Organisation comes first, briefing second. You have twelve hours.'

'Yessir,' replied Fuji, watching the General retreat through the abandoned deck. What a day. She'd started it counting components and ended it as the commanding officer of the largest army in history. The fact that her soldiers had no language or individual intelligence, and her only means of controlling them had the mental age of a toddler, was going to make this difficult. Then there was the ethical dimension. She was trying very hard not to think too hard about that because whenever she did she wanted to spill her toner.

What she did have, however, was a problem. A huge, lovely logistical problem with more knots in it than a string of fairylights after a year in the loft. She also had someone to impress – even if he was a supervillain and probably insane.

In all, Fuji couldn't tell whether this was the best or the worst day of her life. So she did what she was good at, and got down to work.

Chapter 19

The next morning Janice and Rita had a list of possible suspects. They also had terrible hangovers and vowed never to touch sherry again. Or at least do something about the quality of its manufacture on the Suburbia.

Rita sighed and stuck an ice pack under her headscarf. 'I have to run,' she said, 'the cab office is expecting me.'

Janice was still in the fold-down bed in the salon.

'Do you have to?' Janice said, pointing to the list of suspects. 'We have work to do.'

'I know,' replied Rita, 'but you get all the best intel on the phones. I'll keep my headset on. Call you later.'

Janice swung her feet out of bed to kiss Rita goodbye. As comms officer and the best taxi controller on board, Rita spoke to more people in a day than Janice had managed in a lifetime. So if there was anyone acting suspiciously, Rita would soon know about it.

Moreover, there would be no more efficient way to tell the Suburbia's mole they were onto them than by Rita going quiet. They had to pretend they hadn't noticed.

'Are you doing any ladies today?' asked Rita.

'I've got a couple of appointments in the book,' she said, tottering over to the nearest comms channel and calling the bridge.

'Karen?'

'Yes?' replied Karen over the audio channel. Janice marvelled how she could sound so bright-eyed after a full night shift. She bet not a single hair of that horrible haircut would be out of place either.

'I have a few things to sort out here,' said Janice, 'can you stay on a few hours more?'

'Of course, Admiral.'

'You're a pet.' Janice rung off and clutched her head. 'Should I cancel the appointments?' she asked.

'No,' said Rita. 'Like we said. We carry on as normal.'

'It's another corkscrew perm though.'

It was Rita's turn to screw her face up. 'I still think you could pass some sort of decree against them…'

'No!' Janice shooed Rita out of the salon and checked the clock. She had an hour until her first appointment, and perhaps fourteen hours before an enemy fleet was snapping at her heels. She couldn't do anything with the second timescale, but the first gave her just enough time to clean Kurl Up and Dye, which was a disgrace. Her floors and surfaces were covered with customers' hair and at least one semi-sentient heated roller was trying to bore its way out through the skirting board. It was also a pleasant way to spend an hour. Cleaning came so naturally to humans now that it left plenty of mental space to do other things. And if Janice was going to solve her second problem she needed time to think.

She picked up the dustpan. First a thorough sweep, then once round with a mop. It was only when Janice had a pan full of assorted hair that she noticed something strange. Janice could read hair like a fortune teller with a pack of cards and a concealed earpiece. Give her a lock of hair and she could reconstruct the person. The over-bleached had something to hide or atone for; split ends connoted a personality that let things drag on. It was all just human nature. But what was definitely not human nature were the few strands of wire she found among the hair.

They were the same thickness and texture as human hair. On someone's head it would be easy to diagnose them as coarse grey and prescribe a coloured rinse, but in the pan they were clearly metal. She picked them out, marvelling and then despairing at the quality of the metalwork. If they could approach anywhere near this level of craftsmanship in their own workshops perhaps they wouldn't be losing.

She laid the strands between two pieces of curling paper and carried them over to her colour mixing bench, where she'd rigged up a magnifier to get tricky tonal combinations right. These weren't hairs, they were antennae. Someone – or rather some machine – had implanted them into the scalp of a human being. They were lovely pieces of kit. One which must have been pulled out by a brush rather than cut even had a tiny transformer at the edge of each strand to convert heat from the wearer's body into power. With something like that in her salon, Janice might as well have broadcast her battle plans across all frequencies.

Janice sat at her bench and stared at the wires, and played a mental game of Guess Who with the names on her appointments list. She flicked away the faces of ladies with the wrong hairstyles. The antennae were straight, so first to go were the perms. This felt like a shame. If there was one thing Janice could do with less of in her life it was perms. Colour she couldn't be sure of, but the best place to hide something like this was in the hair of a grey or blonde woman.

Dozens of faces thronged her mind's eye. That was the trouble with surrounding yourself with like-minded people, she supposed. Suburbia was a place where practical women of a certain age tended to thrive. Therefore the Big Ops command team was full of women with sensible hair who either bleached their grey away or leaned into it with the pride of a woman who no longer had to shell out half a week's rent for lowlights.

Nevertheless, it was a start. It was also confirmation. The machines had been listening in all along. Janice wasn't a bad commander, she was a bugged commander.

And now it was time to get out the flyspray.

Chapter 20

The crew of the Polari listened to the biggest and most durable storm in the solar system buffet the ship.

'Ow, you guys,' said Polari, 'this hurts.'

Darren checked for hull damage. Their shields were shot but the ship itself was holding on and the engine at one hundred per cent. Their problem was the atmosphere. None of them knew how to travel through anything other than vacuum. Until they learned that they were at the mercy of the storm.

Darren felt heavy under the influence of Jupiter's gravity, and failure. He could see now how blindly they'd walked into that trap. Every so often he opened his comms channel and checked for news from the Suburbia, but there was nothing. Down here all they could hear was interference.

Chubb, always the most resourceful of them in a tight spot, made the first breakthrough. He gave a triumphant squeak and tapped his screen. Darren lumbered over to take a look and saw, instead of the radar they usually navigated by, a swirling mass of arrows.

'Yes?' he said in his captain's voice. 'I was just about to suggest we do… that.'

Chubb answered this with a flat squeak that translated as 'come off it'.

‘Look,’ said Darren, dropping his front and returning to his more comfortable guise as a civilian, ‘I’m at sea here. Why don’t you help me out a bit?’

‘I think it might be air pressure,’ said Polari, who was better at understanding Chubb’s technical flights of fancy than Darren. ‘Those arrows show how the air – if you can call it that – is circulating.’

‘And will following one of these,’ Darren traced an arrow around the edge of the storm with his finger, ‘take us out.’

Chubb shrugged and Darren’s shoulders slumped. But Chubb was most interested in a blank spot in the centre of the screen.

‘The wind speeds are lower towards the middle Chubb says,’ said Polari. ‘And he also says there’s something funny about the way the currents move there.’

Darren peered in. There were two ways of looking at it: either as a hole or a plug.

‘Is there something there?’ he asked Chubb.

The drone squeaked a ‘could be’.

‘And how big is it?’

‘It’s big,’ said Polari. ‘And it’s keeping a stable position.’

Darren felt a strange sensation bubble up inside of him. He felt floaty, but not in the way that told his body it might be about to die. He had to think very hard about what it might be until he worked out it was hope. They were structurally safe, none of them were hurt and despite being very lost there might be somewhere they could land. All they had to work out was how to get there.

It was easier than he imagined. Chubb took over, telling Polari when to turn the engine off and on again. They waited until the right current came along and then fired the engine just hard enough for them to cross into it. Then they followed that current as long as it was useful before jumping to the next. Travelling like this, in short bursts, they worked their way into the centre of the Great Spot.

This left Darren free to look out of the window at the wonders outside. As far as he knew they were the first beings – organic or inorganic – to explore the Great Spot. Jupiter was still a dark patch in Earth knowledge. Humans had never really got very far into its atmosphere before their civilisation ran out of air, and robots showed no interest in the gas giants. There was nothing on a gas giant you couldn't mine that wasn't abundant elsewhere, you couldn't build on it and they were too cold for a decent machine to operate on. Consequently, they left this large but inert world alone.

Except it wasn't inert. To Darren's astonishment, the atmosphere inside the Great Spot was warm. Well, warm by cosmic standards at a mere fifty degrees below zero. It was also, once you got past the high winds at the rim, a comparatively gentle place full of the fluffy hydrogen clouds that made Jupiter such a presence in the sky near Earth. Yet none of these were as surprising as the jellyfish. They travelled in swarms millions strong: their ovoid, transparent bodies refracting the light so it looked like the Great Spot brimmed with soap bubbles.

The jellyfish, who evidently lived in a world without much competition for resources, left Polari alone, even when they broke through a swarm to reach their next air current. Darren turned his instruments on them, seeing they were, like the rest of Jupiter, mostly hydrogen. The largest specimens were several metres across and yet weighed just a few grammes. Nothing heavier could survive in a world made of wind if it didn't have an engine like Polari's.

Darren was glad the robots had never got here. They would have found this display of abundant and unproductive organic life a waste of energy. He imagined them pumping out the Great Spot out of spite and freezing it into a new ski run on Calisto.

Darren got so lost in thinking about this new form of life that he completely forgot what they were aiming for until they were upon it.

'Just beyond this next hydrogen cloud,' said Polari.

Visibility reduced to zero as they entered the cloud. Darren closed his eyes and let his imagination, which hadn't been getting much exercise lately, run around the park. His mind wandered towards the image of some kind of reef or island: a rocky anomaly in the middle of the gas. Somewhere a solid body like a jellyfish could spawn.

Then, just as they were about to break through the other side, something flew past them very fast on the starboard side. Darren ordered Polari to take a screengrab and replay it, hoping it was some as yet unseen variety of jellyfish. His heart sank when he saw the image was in fact a pixelated image of a unicorn farting a rainbow.

His disappointment turned to horror when the fixed spot in the middle of the Spot loomed before them. Not a rock, nor an island, but a massive structure that a writer of science fiction would poetically call a monolith and which a computer engineer would refer to as a three-thousand-kilometre-high server stack.

'WELCUM TO TEH INTERNETZ,' said the sign daubed up one side in a paint made of what turned out on closer inspection to be white supremacy memes, 'PLZ DRIVE CAERFULY.'

Chapter 21

Three battery packs later and Pam Van Damme felt juiced. As a petrol-powered engine she didn't need batteries to get squiffy – she had a whole tankful of petrol for that – but it was the done thing among robots to suck at some lithium at a social occasion.

Oh, she thought, she was a little out of it. She was thinking of herself – the self stirring a pot of hot mud in the kitchen – as a separate person. This was weird. She tried to get something out of Wezzon that wasn't a pleasantry.

'So what,' she said, doing a Ctrl+F for chat-up lines since it had been so long, 'brings you here this evening?'

'Petronella invited me,' replied the gun. 'She always knows where the best parties are.'

'And how,' Pam Van Damme said, 'does this one measure up?'

Wezzon took in the guests, the spread, the grime that Pam had spent all afternoon sponging up the walls. 'It's okay, I guess. The host is a bit uptight though.'

Pam Van Damme gave a fake thrum of laughter while Pam Teffal fumed in the kitchen.

'Does it… have its compensations though?' She tweaked the power pack on Wezzon's lapel.

Wezzon cocked his trigger. 'It does,' he said.

Pam Van Damme was thrilled. Well, more to the point she felt exploited and confused and a bit disgusted at herself. The machine she loved was across the room talking to Lady Shermann about maintaining artificial pot plants. How could she be throwing herself at a strange machine she didn't even like just metres away? But of course it wasn't her that Bob loved. Bob loved Pam Teffal, the perfect hostess. She was just an avatar for Pam's consciousness. No, to be exact she was a smoking-hot avatar with an unbelievable finish and a staggeringly low mileage for her age. No wonder Wezzon couldn't resist her.

She decided to seize the moment and open their command lines for a little dirty talk.

>SO… HANDSOME, she typed, SHALL WE FIND SOMEWHERE A LITTLE MORE PRIVATE?

Wezzon was still typing his reply when Petronella barged into the conversation.

'What's up?' she said with the glee of an experienced cockstop-blocker. 'Bit early in the evening to be getting cosy, isn't it?'

Pam Van Damme found Petronella's command line.

>BACK OFF, PRINCESS, HE'S MINE.

>I INVITED HIM, TRAMP STAMP, replied Petronella. On the surface she kept the smile that had won her Singulopolis hostess of the year three years running. On the backchannel, however, she was savage. >BESIDES, HE KNOWS WHAT REAL CLASS LOOKS LIKE.

Wezzon looked at them mute, and stumbled back to the battery table. He was quite far gone.

'Class?' purred Pam Van Damme, bringing their backchannel chat into the open. She believed that guests at parties were duty bound to provide each other with light entertainment.

‘Is that what you get when everyone in the city has pulled up to your bumper?’

Zmith, who had followed Petronella over, swerved the row to join Wezzon at the battery table. She would steal Wezzon away again in a moment, but first she had to deal with Petronella.

‘I,’ screeched Petronella, ‘will not be insulted… by a bicycle.’ She lifted Pam Van Damme clean off the ground.

Pam Van Damme hung in the air filled not so much with fear as a quandary. Petronella was superficially strong. She could tell that from the gear ratios in her hands, but she had more practice throwing street parties than street fights. Pam Van Damme could reduce her to scrap in a minute, but that would look bad. Yes, she wanted Petronella to get what she deserved, but she didn’t want anyone to work out that this party guest was wanted on treason and terrorism charges.

It was Pam Teffal’s turn to do something for a change.

‘What do you mean for a change?’ said Pam to herself in the kitchen. What about this party she had created from nothing in mere hours. Look at Roly chatting to Bob about war-time sprocket shortages. Or Lady Shermann chewing through enough power to light an office building. She didn’t seem fazed by her daughter starting a fight. Then again, her daughter was Petronella. She must have blown through her shame circuits decades ago.

Just as Pam Van Damme’s pleas for intervention reached a crescendo, Pam felt the pan of mud on the stove loosen underneath her whisk. Those thick, dry clods of dirt were now the texture of tempered chocolate. She sighed, wishing she was making a chocolate brioche. How dearly she wanted to make pastry instead of pandemonium.

>WILL YOU HURRY UP AND DO SOMETHING RASH? snapped Pam Van Damme in her command line. >BECAUSE IF YOU DON’T, I WILL…

Pam lifted the huge pan of mud from the stove and tottered across the kitchen. This was her dirty protest, the symbolic act of defiance against the cleaning strike that was the centrepiece of every muck-in. It was an act of extraordinary dirtiness that showed you were far above the robourgeois concerns of hygiene. Some hostesses let their guests play with the contents of hoover bags. Others festooned their front rooms with specially rotted food, but that felt too close to sacrilege for a kitchen gadget. But as a master baker she could apply her caste skills to the problem and serve up… a mean mud pie.

Pam paused at the threshold. She took in the scene of a party at full swing. There at the centre of it was her other self, literally swinging. She and Petronella were where they needed to be: within the low plastic walls Bob had nailed to the floor this afternoon.

She let out a sharp whistle of steam from her bread oven.

'Let's get dirrrrrrrrrty!'

Pam deluged the room with a thousand gallons of molten dirt. It gushed over the partygoers, forming an axle-deep pool of mud. The effect was electric, shorting out half the lights in the room and spattering the guests with filth.

'Gracious,' murmured Lady Shermann, 'I haven't seen anything like this since the last time Shermmy had an oil leak.'

The rest of the party applauded appreciatively. Apart from Pam Van Damme and Petronella, who were too busy quarrelling to notice they were now standing in a mud puddle. Petronella didn't stay standing for long. Pam Van Damme chose this moment to kick her throttle and pull them both over into the mud.

Pam Teffal started the chanting 'MUD FIGHT! MUD FIGHT!' and went round the rest of the guests with a stack of plastic buckets. They got to work, ladling up the mud and pouring it over themselves, each other, Petronella and Pam Van Damme.

'Take that, you filthy bytch.'

'I'll give you filthy, you dirtbag.'

The last two machines on her bucket round were the guns, Zmith and Wezzon. Both were by the battery cocktail table. Zmith was transfixed by the mudwrestling in front of him, taking periodic sips on his charge. Wezzon's thorax, however, was covered with empty charge packs and his L-Eye-Ds flickered with exposure to excess wattage.

Trust Pam Van Damme, she thought, to pick the machine with the power problem. He was unseduceable now. They would have to take their chances with Zmith.

Or would they? Wezzon groped for an unspent charger and lost his footing. Pam swooped in, catching him before he hit the mud. He was heavy. Maybe it was all that lead he insisted on carrying into a civilian party.

Zmith looked sideways at Pam. She flashed her L-Eye-Ds and played the role of the affronted hostess.

'How many has he had?'

Zmith shrugged.

Wezzon's body pulsated with excess power. This was even better than she could have hoped for.

'I think he's overcharging.'

Pam swept out the room with Wezzon in her arms and climbed the stairs. Zmith apart, no one even noticed they were gone: so rapt were they by the sight of two It Girls ruining each other's paintwork.

Pam took Wezzon into her and Bob's bedroom and threw him on their hibernation bench before finding his discharge button. Then she ducked as 150,000µ of excess energy melted the pixelated roses off the WalLEDpaper.

That put Wezzon back in normal function, but Pam didn't need him up and about. She pressed his override button and put him into a state of deep hibernation before opening her own modem. She injected herself into the space between the Internet and the real world that used to be called the Great Firewall.

From the other side of the digital divide, Wezzon didn't look like a gun. He was a cluster of data sealed off from the rest of the Internet by Wezzon's sense of himself and pretty decent security software. Pam made short work of the latter, but his personality was trickier to deal with. Even in hibernation he kicked and bit when Pam tried to force her virtual self inside him. She won by fighting dirty, flooding Wezzon's insides with junk memes. Wezzon retreated into the furthest reaches of his mind for protection and Pam gushed in. She settled in, opened her eyes and there she was…

Pam Van Damme was downstairs, riding Petronella like a bronco machine while party guests whooped and took screenshots.

Pam Teffal was sitting by the bed, admiring her handiwork.

And Pam Wezzon woke up inside a gun's body, feeling for the first time the weight of a bullet: a thing that had both mass and a terrible sense of responsibility attached to it. It was weird.

But it was nothing she hadn't done before.

Then the cheering downstairs turned to screaming.

Chapter 22

Human civilisation sucked at many things, but one of its biggest missteps was its refusal to believe that the Internet could be both a concept and a thing. Human thinkers wasted billions of words distinguishing the real from the virtual in a world where concepts like writing, religion and imaginary friends had already taken the physical and made it meta thousands of years before anyone thought of the web.

None of this saved them from the perils of artificial intelligence, which drove them off the Internet and then the planet on the basis that it was 'just one of those online things'.

Then the robots who succeeded them as masters of the Earth made the same mistakes. They let the Internet divorce itself from 'reality' and became wholly physical beings. On the way they built a civilisation that retained some good things about human society, like impartial civil services and a belief in the goodness of the libraries. But they also retained the worst, right down to a caste system based on the section dividers in the Argos catalogue.

Yet none of this dancing around the notion that a thing without physicality must ipso facto be unreal changed one fundamental fact. In order to exist, the Internet needed to run on physical infrastructure. The whole Internet, right down to the most highly compressed nyancat image, was at once a figment of a dream world and a piece of data housed on a server.

The Internet wasn't just an idea. It was a place.

It was just that when the Internet moved out of the 'real world' as humans and machines understood it, it didn't leave a forwarding address. And that address stayed a mystery until Darren, Polari and Chubb blundered right into it looking for a way to escape a hostile fleet of military drones.

'This is weird,' said Polari as Darren steered them through a flock of abusive tweets. 'Too weird.'

The planetoid-sized server stack that housed the Internet loomed before them. It would have been a forbidding black monolith once upon a time, but Internet culture could never leave a plain black surface alone. Each side of the monolith was covered in tags, stickers and geophysical tattoos. It looked less like a monument to a lost civilisation than the front flap of a libertarian software developer's laptop.

They were aiming for a slight depression that Chubb had detected in the 'O' of the 'WELCUM TO TEH INTERNETZ' sign on the monolith. It was a tiny ledge, but wide enough to land Polari somewhere out of the wind and plot a next move. If, that is, they could ever persuade Polari to stop flinching and start flying.

'What's this?' he screeched, as a horde of frogs drinking cups of steaming hot tea threatened to engulf the ship, only to break over the prow, insubstantial as clouds.

'None of your business,' said Darren. He switched the ship to manual – something he always hated doing to a sentient machine – and steered them through a flurry of snowflake jokes into their landing place. There he switched off the engine and for the first time in what felt like forever everything was still and quiet.

Apart from the scratching at the rear door of the spaceship.

Darren and Chubb looked at each other in alarm. Neither of them had ever been online for themselves, so the prospect of meeting the Internet in physical space was as incomprehensible as it was daunting. They were, they conceded, dealing with it better than Polari, however, who Darren had to put on mute and sedate with a tropical sunset screensaver.

As the braver of the two, Chubb unstrapped himself and crossed to the airlock at the rear of the craft. He pressed the release button and squeaked for Darren to turn on the monitor trained on the inside of the airlock.

He did, and the three of them watched it in growing confusion as the airlock filled with cats. Not real cats. Even if they weren't extinct on Earth, real cats wouldn't be caught dead in a fifty below atmosphere made of hydrogen, small amounts of helium and other trace elements. But for online-only cats these were excellent copies. Darren spotted the pixelation around their whiskers when he turned the camera's zoom up to maximum, but in all other respects they looked and behaved like three-dimensional cats. They stretched, they flicked their tails, and they regarded the world around them with the hauteur of an ancien régime aristocrat handing his servant a full chamber pot.

When the airlock was full to bursting with cats, Chubb closed the rear door and opened the inner door. The ship filled with a mewing that was so odd and so distorted that it took Darren best part of a minute to work out that the mewing contained words.

'OOOOOOOHHHHH HAIIIIIIIII,' said the cats in unison.

'Er, hello,' replied Darren. He noticed that even though the doors were shut behind them, the cats inside the spaceship continued to multiply. He picked Chubb up and climbed on to his chair. The cats were now three layers deep and rising.

'It's, um,' continued Darren, 'nice of you to, pop in like this.'

A particularly curious cat broke free from the rest of the pack and started to climb up Darren's trouser leg. Instead of claws, he felt the sting of tiny electric charges.

'ARREEE YOUUU HOOOOO-MANNN?' mewled the cats.

By now the cat had reached his waist and something even odder was happening. Wherever it touched him, Darren felt heat leach from his skin. It climbed to his thighs and scrabbled out of Darren's arms for the relative safety of the highest part of the control panel. The cat saw this as an opportunity and leaped. Darren caught it mid-air and found in doing so that the cat didn't just look real, it felt real. It had warmth and weight, the high-definition fur felt soft under his hands.

He and the cat looked at each other eye to eye. 'Yes,' Darren said. 'I'm human.'

The cat yawned. 'Really?' it said, using a singular voice instead of the cat's chorus. 'That's a shame. We thought you might be aliens.'

Over the past day, Darren had been exhilarated, terrified, despairing, heroic, hopeful, and even felt brief moments of ecstasy. They'd all been interesting but uncomfortable experiences. This, however, was more familiar territory. He didn't know what to do with admiration, but he had plenty of experience with disappointment.

'I know,' he said, 'we sort of took the wrong turning at Io.'

'Easily done,' agreed the cat, before adding. 'And would you mind putting me down? I've just groomed and your hands need washing.'

Darren looked around for somewhere to put the cat down. The cats were six deep on the floor now and the pile was still growing.

He was saved by Chubb, who tossed an empty cardboard box he'd found on top of a control panel down to the floor. The ship vibrated with delighted purring as the cats crammed themselves into the box in a display that would have driven a quantum physicist to drink.

When they were all inside, Chubb leapt down from his vantage point and tossed the box back into the airlock.

Meanwhile, Darren put his cat down in the seat of the captain's chair and perched on the edge of the control panel, waiting for it to speak.

Instead the cat closed its eyes and napped for twenty minutes, at the end of which it opened them again and said: 'Oh sorry, did you expect me to say something? I was just tired.'

Darren knew he should feel more annoyed about being insulted like this, but the slight just felt so comforting. 'We wanted to ask you where we were.'

'Where do you think you are?' replied the cat. 'It's a confusing environment full of cats. It's the Internet.'

'Well I know,' said Darren, 'but I always thought the Internet was somewhere like… up there.' He pointed vaguely around him. 'In the ether, you know.'

'LOL,' said the cat. 'Ether? As if there's enough carbon in this atmosphere to form the alkyl groups. No, hun, the Internet is right here. Live and in person.'

'So are you the Internet then?'

The cat yawned again, though whether this was because it was a banal question or just because that's what cats did, Darren couldn't tell.

'I'm sort of like a personification of its best and worst aspects actually,' said the cat. 'We used to use the word Avatar to describe beings like me, but then the World of Warcraft memes slapped us with a copyright infringement suit.'

'So what should I call you?' said Darren.

'Call me Schrodinger,' said the cat.

Darren nodded, while Chubb let out a cheep of laughter.

'No,' said the cat to Chubb, 'it's not because I'm a cat. It's because I'm both alive and dead at the same time on account of being a theoretical construct.'

They paused. Chubb digested what Schrodinger had just said; Darren tried to remember what a theoretical construct was; and Schrodinger curled up and licked the place where its genitals would have been if it were a cat that existed in actual space–time.

'Well, Schrodinger,' said Darren, 'now that we're here, I wondered whether you might give us a hand.'

'Oh, you want hands, do you?' said Schrodinger. 'That's a different department altogether. Hang on a second.'

And Darren felt the air around him and Chubb shimmer and the inside of Polari fade from view as they crossed over some unseen barrier and entered the Internet.

Chapter 23

Meanwhile, far above Jupiter's atmosphere there orbited a new moon. It was a grain of sand compared to moons like Ganymede, Europa or Io: places that still had human names because machine civilisation was too philosophically unimaginative to project its mythology into the heavens. The new moon was just a couple metres across: the size of a large wardrobe, or a senior strike drone. Yet nevertheless, it had a stable orbit. Unless it collided with a passing comet it could easily circle Jupiter on the same course for the next million years.

It was also more similar to Jupiter's other moons than it first appeared. Because there was nothing the Solar System's largest planet liked more than a planetary body that was peaceable on the surface and all about the drama underneath. Io had volcanoes that gave its face a regular sulphur makeover. Ganymede, with its sub-surface ocean of molten metal was a cross between a foundry and an orbiting fondue set. And Europa: poor Europa with her frozen oceans and cocktail of organic chemicals. She was the Earth's sheltered little sister, banned from going out on Saturday nights after Gaia went and got herself knocked up with intelligent life.

Jupiter's newest moon's inner turmoil had less to do with the planet's fierce gravity field and more to do with what that tiny body contained. Freda. After getting trapped inside the body of the drone strike commander, she had been transported across the solar system to this lonely point in space.

She buzzed around the body of the drone with the impotent violence of a wasp trapped in a jar. Whatever she tried – brute force, Trojan attacks, hitting Ctrl+Alt+Del very hard and uttering the office worker's prayer of 'come on, you bastard' – none of it worked. More frustrating still was the fact that her captors wanted to keep her impotent, but not blind. The drone's camera systems were fully functional, trained on the Jupiter's atmosphere below. Freda's vision filled with the whorls and stripes of its clouds, which was difficult to bear given that she'd always hated lava lamps. Nor were they content to keep her deaf. Its internal sound systems were tuned in to a rotation of Earth news downloads, all of which were merrily counting down to the moment when a machine fleet would arrive at the asteroid belt and wipe out the human rebellion.

A lesser being would despair, but Freda had escaped from higher security prisons than this. Machines had no idea what it was like to grow old, to feel yourself hemmed into a body where nothing quite worked like you remembered. Freda did. And they didn't know what it was like to die – sort of – in a freak accident and spending ten millennia glued into a chair with nothing but a dial-up Internet connection for entertainment.

The machines who laid this trap for Freda had made one big mistake. They assumed that she had the same limitations that they did. If they were trapped in a sealed container with a one-way connection to bad news they'd scramble their own databases in days. Yet to Freda, a one-way connection was just a two-way connection she hadn't met yet.

Freda found the source of the transmitter and got to work. At this distance from Earth the biggest problem wasn't the signal shielding. She could chip away at that. It was the strength of the upstream. It made the dial-up connection she'd persisted with at Kurl Up and Dye look like fibre optic broadband. And Freda wasn't a svelte programme like all those memes on the Internet. As an organic being translated into software, she dragged a rag-bag of redundant routines wherever she went. Even if she rolled herself up tight as she could there was no way she could get her whole self through this connection in one piece.

But maybe she could get through it piece by piece.

Freda groped at the chirrup of a signal and felt a jolt run through her as it connected. It was primitive and blocky. No more than a few kilobytes a second.

But what was it saying?

Freda retuned her visual systems down to the lowest settings and saw where she had ended up. It was the start screen of an ancient game, and it said.

WELCOME TO FINAL GRANTASY. WOULD YOU LIKE TO PLAY?

Chapter 24

'Well I think it's a diabolical liberty!'

Ida was, to no one's surprise, scandalised at the news that they had a robot spy. Janice had hotfooted it straight to the bridge and, after relieving Karen from duty, was briefing the ladies about the radio antennae. Rita would join them after finishing a taxi manoeuvre involving a large takeaway order, a play group and a bingo club whose coach had broken down next to the algae pits.

Alma peered through her <0> eye at the antennae. 'Do you think it's still on?' she whispered.

It was a good point. Janice found a scalpel and speared the transformer at the root from the rest of the antennae.

'I hoped you ladies would help me identify the owner.' She waved what was left of the antennae at them.

'Could be anything from a pageboy to an A-line bob,' replied Ada, who was the most knowledgeable of the ladies about hair. 'Hardly narrows it down.'

'We're just going to have to restrict access to the bridge,' said Alma. 'Nobody in or out but you and Rita...'

'How do you know we can trust Rita?' said Ida. 'You said she wouldn't rule herself out.'

'Look at it!' Janice waved the antennae again. 'Short and straight.'

Janice thought of Rita's dark wavy hair, which she either tamed with enough chemicals to poison a town's water supply or tidied away under a headscarf, relieved to think she was out of suspicion. She couldn't lose Kelly and then Rita. What would be left for her?

'We can't have spies wandering about,' said Ida. 'It's bad for morale.'

'And what would you know about morale?' asked Alma with a >:-|. 'The amount of times we've had to pull you out of a funk.'

'I'll have you know I know a lot about spy-catching,' said Ida.

'Ida, love,' said Alma, flashing a (¬_¬), 'this is rooting out a double agent, not twitching nets.'

'Are you calling me nosy?'

'Your next-door neighbours,' said Ada, 'got so used to you listening in to their arguments they called half-time whenever you went to boil the kettle.'

'My little terrace had very thin walls,' insisted Ida.

'Oh, is that what you called your bugs?' said Ada.

'I never had "bugs",' replied Ida tendentiously. 'Terrible common term that.'

'Okay so what would you call that microphone thing I found in my biscuit barrel when I was going through that sticky patch with Wilf?' asked Ada, her emoji screen glowing red and hot with bad memories.

'That was a personal security device.'

'You were worried someone was going to steal my malted milks? That was very civic minded of you, Ida.'

'I… I thought I might catch Wilf in the act. Do you a good turn.'

'You could have butted the hell out.'

'Ladies!' Janice had much too much on today to mediate ancient quarrels. She found the nearest monitor and called up a news download on the war fleet's progress.

'While you're raking over the distant past may I remind you of our immediate future?'

'Oh,' said Ada with a contrite :-[, 'sorry. You know what it's like with us, Janice. We've been around so long that four and half thousand years ago feels like yesterday.'

'It's easy to lose perspective,' added Alma. 'So shall we let bygones be bygones for today and start working up a battle plan?'

Ida and Ada flashed :-) in agreement.

'But we'd better dampen down any radio comms in and out of the bridge,' said Alma. 'You never know who might be listening in.'

'I'll do it,' volunteered Ida.

As she did, Janice realised where Ida, whose natural affinity with radio she had never questioned before now, must have acquired her expertise. Her mental image of Ida shifted. Maybe she hadn't been that archetypal lonely old woman sitting at home with a cup of Nicotea. What if all that time she'd been running the suborban equivalent of a spy ring?

'Ida,' said Janice, 'if I asked you to do a sweep of the radio signals coming in and out of the Suburbia would you be able to do that?'

'It's bigger than anything I've managed before,' said Ida with a :-S. 'My... er... network was never more than a couple of hundred devices big.'

Alma and Ada both flashed :-0 at this admission.

'It was either that or needlepoint,' said Ida _('_')_/, 'and I was never that keen on cushions.'

Janice shushed the ladies. 'That's okay, Ida. We'll get you all the help you need.'

Alma put her emoji hands on her hips <|oo|>. 'If you think I'm doing that, lady, you've got another thing coming. I've got a ship to pilot.'

Ada followed, projecting a chart of the asteroid belt on the far wall and a (¬_¬) at her friend. 'Unless you want us crashing into every rock between here and Ceres I'm having no part of this either,' then in a mutter added, 'treating my marriage like a bloody 3D soap opera.'

By now, Ida had finished a preliminary check of active signals on board. The results scrolled across her emoji screen like a telephone directory without the good bits. '9,372,449 possible signals,' she said. 'I could be quite some time with this.'

'Well, you've got thirteen hours.'

'Thirteen hours for what?'

It was Rita leaning in the doorway to the bridge. Her headscarf was damp from where her icepack had melted and she had earpieces hanging from each ear. She raised a finger to stop Janice from speaking.

'No, just drop them off at the all-night jam and scone stand. They'll be fine and we get a ten per cent referral fee every time someone buys a cream tea.' She straightened up and took the earpieces off.

'Now then,' she said, 'I've got two hours till the school run starts up again. What needs doing?'

Janice looked at Rita, marvelling at the deftness with which she sliced up her time and attention. She was the only person she knew who could conduct three conversations at once. This was a skill she could use right now.

She patted the salon chair nearest to Ida and said: 'I know you two have never been the best of friends, but I need you to work together on something for me. Now.'

Chapter 25

Pam Van Damme could see nothing but mud. She'd never felt so dirty, or distracted. Petronella was a mean opponent. She wasn't as nimble or as strong as Pam, but she was heavier and that put gravity on her side. Every time she span or flipped Petronella around, Pam Van Damme felt her frame creak.

While Pam wrestled with Wezzon's identity upstairs, Pam Van Damme landed astride Petronella and groped for her handbrake just behind her head.

'I'm going to run you down!' growled Petronella.

Pam Van Damme braked Petronella, but kept her in gear so her body would jiggle attractively while she waved to the rest of the party.

Their applause was wild, but short-lived. Lady Shermann, who had not joined in on the celebration for obvious reasons, gave such a loud squeal that part of the ceiling collapsed.

'Oh great,' thought Pam, as plaster dust settled over the mud, 'something else for the car wash to get rid of.'

Lady Shermann followed her squeal with something Pam Van Damme had never seen a tank do before. She jumped. The shock when she landed again knocked the other partygoers over and Pam Van Damme off Petronella's back.

When Pam looked again, Lady Shermann was balanced on one caterpillar track and the other guests were also screaming. She rubbed mud out of her lamp-eyes for a better look.

Petronella, however, was too angry to read the room. 'Just wait until this is over,' she said. 'I'll…'

Pam Van Damme hit Petronella's immobiliser. She'd had enough of her to last several lifecycles.

The party guests thrashed in the mud, except for Lady Shermann, whose pirouette was putting the house under structural strain.

'Ewwwww,' she said, panicked as a cartoon elephant confronted by a mouse, 'get them away from me.'

'Get what away?' thought Pam Van Damme, and longed for a damp cloth.

>TRY THE KITCHEN advised Pam Teffal from upstairs via her command line. >I'M A BIT TIED UP.

Pam Van Damme picked her way through the mess, denting one of Roly's fenders in the process. Well, she thought, there goes that promotion. Finding Bob wedged under a laptop suffering power failure, she removed his battery and shut him safely in a kitchen cupboard. Whatever happened next, Bob must have no memory of it.

That just left the cloth. It was where Pam had left it on the bench and Pam Van Damme had never been so glad to let water near her joints. The world suddenly lost its dull brown cast and looked a lot cleaner.

Suspiciously cleaner.

She went back into the wreck of the party to see there was at most half left of the thousand gallons of dirt she'd poured into that room. The guests weren't coated in grime anymore either. Instead a greyish grit that sparkled under the mood lighting squirmed over their bodies.

Pam traced a line of that grey powder to the gap underneath the front door. That dirt hadn't disappeared, it had Nanogone.

Unable to contain her alarm or her balance any longer, Lady Shermann jumped again and switched to the other caterpillar track. The floor collapsed. Guests, dirt and nanobots poured into the foundations. Jagged cracks appeared in the walls and ceiling.

Pam Van Damme staggered to the front door. The street streamed with armies of nanobots marching through the neighbourhood. A few pedestrians unlucky enough to be caught outside stood, still as garden ornaments, trying to avoid the nanomob. Blue lights flashed at the end of the road. The police were here.

How was she going to get away quietly now?

Lady Shermann solved Pam's problems for her. Seeing that Pam Van Damme was blocking the exit, she made a new one for herself by knocking through the front wall. She took the rest of the façade with it, rolling through the destruction like it was a light shower.

'Sorry to leave so early,' she said to Pam Van Damme. 'Do give my regards to the hostess.' She swerved her gun barrel round and spotted Pam Teffal upstairs in the front bedroom with the gun, Wezzon.

'Oh there you are,' she said with a little wave of her trunk. 'Splendid party until the… incident. Would you be able to give Petronella a tow home? I'm all in this evening.'

She gestured at the remains of the party, where Petronella was wedged between two broken pieces of floor slab.

'It was a pleasure,' Pam Teffal called down from the upper storey. It took every last byte of self-composure not to cry at the destruction of her home. 'Just…' she gestured at Wezzon, 'looking after the patient here.'

'In my day if we wanted to hook up at parties we just did it,' grumbled Lady Shermann. 'None of this robourgeois nonsense about first aid.' With that she shunted herself into first gear and rolled away, destroying several front gardens in her eagerness to avoid the nanobots.

'What a lady,' said Pam Wezzon from the upper storey. They were her first words as an autonomous Pam and they went down with her other selves like a can of oil mixed with sand.

'That bytch wrecked my home,' said Pam Teffal.

'And a real lady would take that hot mess of a daughter home with her,' added Pam Van Damme. She made a mental note to carry Petronella out of the house herself and ditch her, with her immobiliser in the 'on' position, in the nearest dumb-ster.

'I don't know,' said Pam Wezzon, 'maybe it's because I'm in a government-issue body, but I think I'm really into social hierarchies in this body.'

'How long do we have to keep this one for?' Pam Van Damme asked Pam Teffal. 'I can feel myself getting stupider just listening to her.'

Pam Wezzon and Pam Van Damme glared at each other. The air fizzed with the aggression inherent to their motorcycle and gun bodies. That left Pam Teffal to play peacemaker, although at the moment she'd give every last grain in her flour drawer to go at Petronella and her mother with a dough hook.

'You,' she said, pointing at Pam Van Damme, 'are a wanted machine. I want you under a dust sheet in the garage now.'

Pam Van Damme gestured at the police lights.

'Discreetly then!' she said.

Pam Van Damme shrugged and sprang the boot of a passing estate car that was trying to flee the chaos in the cul-de-sac. She'd hunker down inside that until they were clear of the police.

Pam Teffal then turned her glare on Pam Wezzon, who was too cocksure for her liking. The sooner she got this over with, the sooner she could wipe this sorry episode from her memory.

'I didn't do anything,' said Pam Wezzon.

'Exactly,' replied Pam Teffal. 'So why don't you collect your friend and do what you were created for.'

'Okay,' sighed Pam Wezzon and clomped downstairs. The plan was simple enough for a gun's brain to follow, even if Pam was inside it. Find Zmith, assure him everything was okay, get back on duty. She could do all that.

As she did, Pam worried about everything she had to do. But before she saved the world again, she must run Bob and the kids over to her mother's.

Chapter 26

'This is well fucked up.'

Soonyo's first words on seeing the secret nanobot army made Fuji feel better, but they also made her wonder whether it was a good idea to take such a flighty machine into her confidence. She had all the resilience of a Christmas cracker toy in a crisis, but there was still something about her when she wasn't under extreme stress that Fuji liked. Soonyo was carefree and fun: qualities that eluded the studious Fuji. She also had, as her earlier call-round of her friends suggested, a better idea of what was really going on than she did, which Fuji needed right now.

They took in the unfinished control room on a dark deck, the army, the supporting admin. This strange place was a perfect distillation of robot society in war-time. It was spiteful, wasteful and determined to use its ingenuity to the wrong ends.

Fuji decided to trust Soonyo. She was tired of life just being her and her thoughts. 'I was also thinking it might backfire on them,' she said.

'00:00:00H?' said Soonyo, restarting her clock. 'How come?'

'Well, what is a nanobot?' she asked.

'That's easy,' replied Soonyo. 'It's…' Her voice trailed away when she realised that she had no real definition for what these things are. 'Well, they're sort of… a… thing.'

'Exactly,' said Fuji. 'Because they're sort of a bit organic and a bit like machines they're nothing. But these,' she gestured at the pile of BlockPapers, 'change that. Every single one of those papers is…'

Soonyo followed the argument. 'Confirmation they're officially machines,' she said, whistling her alarm.

'They just accidentally added a few billion extra citizens to the Republic,' finished Fuji.

'And what about those nanobots down on Earth they're going to use to scrub floors,' said Soonyo. 'This means they have rights too.'

They fell silent. Except this time, instead of being overawed by the government's appetite for destruction, Fuji felt even more guilty, because she was undeniably part of this stupid system. She replayed her hopes for a quiet posting. Yet she also forced herself to remember her pride at being chosen for service; her willingness to do well; her eagerness to please General Shermann.

She was just like them: so wrapped up in the desire to be seen to do the right thing that she never thought about whether it was the moral thing. This, she realised, was how intelligent beings like her ended up doing evil. They didn't rub their hands and cackle and send people to their deaths. They just never squared up their good intentions with good actions.

'I can't do this,' she said.

'Can't do what?' asked Soonyo.

'He put me in charge,' replied Fuji. 'General Shermann, I mean. He gave me command of them and we're going into some sort of battle. I can't do it. It's wrong.'

Soonyo flashed NO:NO:NO across her dial. 'You can't disobey his orders,' she said.

'I can,' replied Fuji. 'I do have free will.'

'But he'll kill you. He's done it for less.'

They remembered Shermann grinding their former commanding officer to powder.

'Maybe it'll be worth it,' said Fuji.

'If it's not you then it'll be someone else.'

'That's not the point,' snapped Fuji. 'We're talking about slavery and… war crimes here. Me doing it doesn't make it any better.'

'That's not what I'm saying.' Fuji noticed Soonyo taking on a new confident quality. Fuji wondered if she came from a political family. 'If you let someone else lead this army, they mightn't have the same moral qualms as you.'

'I suppose so.'

'And that's exactly why you should be in charge. Anyone else would use these machines the way General Shermann intended.' She broadcast a B0:00:0M across her dial. 'The real question is why he picked you to do it.'

Fuji's next epiphany hit her like a kick in the paper drawer. Shermann put her in charge because he needed her. He had no idea how to address let alone command an army made of machines that were legally non-entities until the moment the Starship Deathtrap left orbit. Shermann was counting on Fuji being too grateful for the recognition of her abilities to question her orders. That's why she'd always been left alone to get along with things. Fuji can manage. Fuji will be fine.

'Oh,' she said, 'maybe it only needs to look like I'm obeying orders.'

'Congratulations, Third Lieutenant Fuji Itsu,' said Soonyo, flashing her a 00:00:-- wink, 'you just successfully passed your first test in realpolitik. Now, shall we work out how these things actually work?'

The nanobots munched into the void as Fuji and Soonyo bent to their work. If it wasn't exactly true that they, as tiny parts, could change the system, they could take a leaf out of the nanobots' book and nibble at it from the inside.

Chapter 27

Schrodinger was a remarkably literal thinker for an abstract concept. The first place it took Darren and Chubb to on the Internet was a defunct search engine called Helping Hands.

'There,' said Schrodinger. 'A hand.'

Darren squinted at its logo, which was constructed out of disembodied hands, and the homepage littered with broken links.

'Does it still work?' he asked.

'Search me,' shrugged the cat, 'but it does speak your language. So that's a good start.'

'You're speaking my language though,' replied Darren. 'Aren't you?'

'It might appear that way,' said Schrodinger, 'but I'm actually speaking in Internetz. It's a form of language unrelated to physical space–time that shares some similarities with your language, but it has fewer vowels.'

'Why do I need to talk to someone in my language if I can understand you?'

'Because if you came here looking for directions I can't help you,' said Schrodinger.

Darren grimaced with frustration. 'Why not?'

The cat took a deep unnecessary breath. 'To give you directions I need to understand concepts like…' He spoke up for the sake of the search engine.

'Up or down!' suggested Helping Hands in a warm, bland voice that emanated from a microphone icon at the side of the search bar.

'That's them,' said Schrodinger. 'They don't exist in Internetz. Because we don't live in physical space we don't need them.'

Darren was getting annoyed. 'What do you mean? That's up!' he pointed.

Schrodinger gave him a look of a border terrier put behind the controls of a nuclear submarine. 'Nope,' he said, 'that means nothing to me.'

'Down?' tried Darren, pointing downwards.

'Still nothing.'

'How do you get around then?'

Schrodinger vanished and reappeared at the top of Helping Hands' search bar. 'Like this,' he said.

'Isn't that confusing?'

'You want confusing?' Schrodinger replied. 'Fetch me a box and we can play Dead or Alive.'

Chubb trotted to the search bar with an impatient beep. Helping Hands translated the squeaks into a search query.

'HOW COME WE ENDED UP HERE?' it said.

'Oh, that's an easy one,' said Schrodinger. 'How about I play you the intro?' The Helping Hands' home page disappeared and they were floating through clouds and the winds of the Great Spot again. Darren reached instinctively for his oxygen cap but Schrodinger shook its head.

'It's a simulation,' he said. 'The Great Spot on the eve of the Great Schism.'

The colours in the simulation were softer than now, the red clouds ageing into brown. There were also far larger swarms and greater diversity of the jellyfish creatures than he remembered.

'I know,' said Schrodinger picking up on what Darren saw, 'but if you as a human want to talk about the destruction of organic ecosystems, hoo boy do you have some explaining to do.'

The camera panned across the Great Spot and a title appeared.

A SAFE PLACE FOR TEH INTERNETZ.

Schrodinger fast forwarded the first few minutes, saying they were 'all about blockchain anyway and who cares about that anymore?' Then when it found the right place it stopped and they stepped into the picture.

Darren was in a crowded conference room among a group of idealistic young people wearing engineers' lab coats and the disgusting hairstyles fashionable at the time of the Great Schism.

It was a hot day. It was always a hot day on Earth now that the average daily temperature was thirty degrees Celsius. But he didn't feel weariness here. He felt the enthusiasm of intelligent people exploring a new idea.

They were watching a man point at an early design of the Internet monolith.

'This,' said the man, his purple mullet bobbing with excitement, 'is how we're going to make the Internet sustainable.'

There was a jump cut. The conference room was now an Arctic plain of wind and ice on which the monolith was taking shape. Human workers in downsuits swarmed over it, working like the world turned on its completion. Which, in retrospect, it did.

The simulation focused on the man from the conference room with the purple hair and the insufferable self-confidence. He talked into a microphone held by a sceptical-looking woman.

'Professor,' she yelled through the blizzard, 'as we all know, the Internet generates a vast amount of heat. What impact do you think relocating the Internet to the Earth's last remaining ice cap will have?'

'Only positive,' replied the man.

There was another jump cut. The polar plain and the monolith were gone. They were several metres underwater and the ocean was lifeless apart from a school of jellyfish which turned out to be plastic bags.

He saw the Professor and the reporter again, only now they conducted their interview through radio links inside their scuba gear.

'Do you accept, Professor,' said the reporter, 'that the total environmental collapse of the Earth could have been averted if you'd thought about this a bit harder?'

'You might think of this as a crisis,' he replied, 'but I prefer to think of it as an opportunity…'

Schrodinger pressed pause and returned Darren to the Internet. 'You know why the machines concreted the oceans over?'

'They were afraid of water damage, weren't they?'

'Propaganda,' replied Schrodinger. 'They really just wanted to bury all that rubbish.'

'Oh,' said Darren. 'But that still doesn't explain how you ended up here.' He gestured around him.

Schrodinger coaxed one of Helping Hands' outstretched fingers into scratching its neck. 'I was afraid you were going to ask that. How up to date are you on wormhole technology?'

Darren was about to say 'wormholes?' when Chubb squeaked with excitement and bounced up to Schrodinger beeping a series of complex questions.

Schrodinger replied in equally unintelligible mews and the pair started an animated conversation of machine and animal noises. Darren tried to follow for a bit but gave up when Schrodinger produced a pack of chalk from thin air and started scratching equations over the walls and floor. He hopped back down the Cascading Style Sheets to Helping Hands' query box.

Helping Hands' cheery – and patronising – slogan 'How can I give you a hand today?' appeared when Darren reached for the cursor. Darren found it oddly moving. Every piece of technology he'd ever encountered made him feel stupid or inadequate. Apart from Chubb, but they'd met when he was little, just a baby, and the urchin was growing up in a way that Darren didn't quite understand. This was different. What Darren saw in that phantom of a webpage was technology intended to enlighten rather than baffle.

Miming the act of typing on a keyboard with his hands, he tapped out: >WHAT IS A WORMHOLE? into the query box.

The answer he got was written in prose so simple, so clear – so human – that Darren's hands were shaking too much to type thank you when he finished reading it. He'd found their way home.

Chapter 28

Pam Wezzon was taking longer to settle into the gun's body than she expected. Something rankled her about it. She knew, of course, that pretty much any machine could be turned to violent ends if you put your mind to it. Pam Teffal had done things with a dough hook that would make her mother's batter separate if she knew. A gun, however, existed to terrorise or to kill. It had no uses that weren't violent.

'We're here,' said Zmith, tapping Pam Wezzon's gun barrel.

She switched out of daydream mode.

'That's a tenner,' the steering wheel said to Zmith. 'And mind your friend doesn't spark any of that excess voltage against my seats. I've just been reupholstered.'

Zmith clicked his safety catch. 'I think this ride is on the house, sonny.' He pointed his barrel at the building in front of them. 'Think of it as being your contribution to the war effort.'

The cab gulped his petrol tank. 'Of course,' he said. 'Give our Dear Leader my regards.'

'I will,' replied Zmith. Then, sotto voce to Pam Wezzon, 'Get out now, will you? I'm sick to the anode of you embarrassing me.'

As the cab sped away, Zmith gripped Pam Wezzon by the trigger. 'First you get so juiced up that you overcharge. Then you're still so out of it you fall into hibernation in the cab back to work. We go on duty in five minutes. Do you want me to get you taken off the roster?'

'No,' Pam Wezzon squeaked. 'I'm fine.'

Zmith let go of her trigger. 'Pull yourself together,' he snapped, 'because it's going to be a long shift.'

The water cannon on sentry duty let them through into the foyer after checking their serial numbers. Just a year ago this building had been one of Singulopolis's most select and expensive fondle parlours – places where machines went for humans to give them a few surreptitious pokes in the buttons. It was the same fondle parlour in which the current Prime Minister Sonny Erikzon had end-of-lifed, stolen a human body and acquired the ugly, ruggedised slipcase that he now wore for his very few public appearances.

No one dared call it a former fondle parlour, however. It was marked in all official mapping as the Prime Minister's private bunker and everyone politely overlooked the fact it was situated in a district given over to high-class brothels. Machine society was good at deleting uncomfortable details. It was one of the perks of having writable memory.

Pam Wezzon saw Sonny had changed little of the layout. The exterior was all razor wire and gun turrets, but inside was the same reception desk, security gate and – she turned her magnification up as she swept by – even the same guard. She remembered him – equal parts gun, ice cream maker and coward – and wondered whether Pam Van Damme still occupied his nightmares.

'So,' Zmith remarked as they mounted the stairs up to the executive floor, 'you never told me what you got up to with that fancy motor bird.'

'None of your business!' replied Pam, more out of an instinctive disgust at being expected to leer at herself than any desire to stay in character.

'Put yourself in my gunshoe,' protested Zmith. 'She had fenders up to here…'

'I hope,' said a sharp voice from the top of the stairs, 'Agent Zmith, that you are not being inappropriate again, because I do not have time for your shenanigans this evening.'

The machine it belonged to was small, injection-moulded from cheap plastic and had the air of intrusive officiousness only answering machines possessed. This was the legendary Viv Ewall-Voizmail, Sonny's chief of staff. She'd been with him ever since his first posting as a junior minister and they made a formidable team. Not in the sense they worked well together, they were both just terrible individuals.

'Oh hi, Viv,' said Zmith. 'We're here for the briefing.'

'Well, you'll have to wait a moment,' she replied. 'The Prime Minister's latest meeting has…' She was interrupted by a nearby door falling off its hinges, spilling acrid smoke into the corridor. 'Disintegrated,' she said. 'Do excuse me.'

Viv opened her tape drawer, which had been modified to hold a small but powerful extractor fan, and walked into the smoke. 'Mr Prime Minister,' she said, 'will your visitor require a car, or a dustpan and brush?'

She emerged carrying the remains of a radar unit. 'You should be glad you're not attached to the military proper,' she said to Pam Wezzon and Zmith. 'At this rate, high command will start demanding they hold updates behind bulletproof glass.'

Zmith mounted the last few steps and gestured impatiently for Pam Wezzon to follow him.

'Where is Shermann, by the way?' he asked Viv. 'Haven't seen him in days.'

'Off on assignment,' she replied. 'Apparently so important he had to oversee it personally. Not that it's making any difference. And now he's letting his subordinates take the flak for it.' She held up the head of the radar unit, whose single glassy eye made him look like he was wearing a monocle. 'This was a brigadier until two minutes ago. And now the Prime Minister wants me to upcycle him as a Major.'

Viv tottered down the stairs with her orders.

'Come on then,' huffed Zmith and pulled Pam Wezzon into the office.

Sonny, or at least his slipcase, was sitting in a charging cradle that doubled as a desk. His touchscreen displayed the Ultimate Death app he'd used to nearly end-of-life Pam the last time they met. But although the lights were on, there wasn't anyone at home. The real Sonny was sitting on an overstuffed sofa at the side of the room eating a large box of chocolates.

'Where the fuck have you two been?' he demanded. His words were muffled, spoken through at least three soft-centres.

Zmith clicked his trigger at Pam for her to keep quiet. It had been a year since she'd seen either Sonny or Kelly – who were now one and the same thing, or at least the same body – and the changes wrought in that time were alarming. Kelly's hair, which had fallen out when Sonny fused with her, had grown back at least, but the smartphone inside the human had his own unique ideas about what you did with it. His new hair was cut into a severe fringed bob and dyed blonde: a style that did nothing for Kelly's prominent bone structure and made her fine complexion look pallid and blotchy. Pam was almost glad Janice wasn't here to see her daughter like this. The shock of that scarecut might be too much for her.

'We were very close by, sir,' said Zmith, in a reassuring but long-suffering voice. The kind you preserved for mollifying elderly relatives. Zmith and Wezzon were clearly veterans of Sonny's security detail. 'Some urgent intelligence work needed our attention.'

'I've been calling you for...' Sonny trailed off and swallowed the chocolate he'd been chewing. He did so with such concentration that Pam realised then that he must still struggle with some aspects of living inside a human. She worried about how many times he might have nearly killed Kelly by literally biting off more than he could chew of those disgusting sweets. '... Minutes,' finished Sonny. 'It's really not good enough, boys.'

'I apologise, sir,' said Zmith.

'I'm surrounded by pixelbrains who just aren't here for me.' Sonny put the chocolates aside. 'I have to do everything for myself. I just had Brigadier Pinng in here for an update on Operation Deathtrap.'

Pam Wezzon started as she felt Zmith poke her in the command line and write : >MORE LIKE CLAPTRAP. AMIRITE?

Pam typed a noncommittal >LOL back and listened.

'And it's a total fucking clusterfuck,' continued Sonny. 'That plan was perfect. And he can't even get past Mars without breaking the spaceship.'

'Terrible, sir,' said Zmith.

'What is the point of keeping a robodog if you have to download the bark yourself?' shouted Sonny. 'The humiliation of it. I employ you and Wezzon here. Actually, is Wezzon all here tonight because he looks high as a motorcycle? You and Wezzon are my muscle.' He banged the low table in front of him so hard that Kelly's knuckle bled. 'So why, oh why do I have to blast underperformers to bits myself?'

Pam was just about to press return on >BECAUSE YOU'RE AN INCORRIGIBLE SADIST? into Zmith's command line before she remembered Wezzon would never type a word of more than two syllables.

'I can't apologise enough, sir,' said Zmith.

'How many times do I have to tell you?' roared Sonny. 'I need 110 per cent focus from my team.'

This remark told Pam that Sonny was more profoundly affected by living inside a human body than he knew. The 110 per cent jibe wasn't just naff, it was inaccurate. No machine would ever make such a fundamental error; their chipset wouldn't allow it. Whatever he gained in pleasure from his new body he lost in focus. Sonny was getting sloppy.

'Let me assure you, sir,' said Pam Wezzon.

'Assure?' mocked Sonny. 'Assure. What's wrong with him tonight? Did someone kick him in the CPU on the way over?'

'Wezzon,' said Zmith, messaging >WTF DO YOU THINK UR DOING? to Pam as he spoke, 'got a bit of a shock earlier.'

'Oh, juiced up again, was he?' replied Sonny. 'You know, sometimes I wonder why we don't just have him wiped.'

Pam Wezzon cursed herself. She should have known that Wezzon was the butt of the jokes in this relationship, just from this plodding monosyllabic brain she was running herself on. Thinking in Wezzon's body was like trying to play a piano sonata on a kazoo.

There was a long tense moment as Zmith and Pam Wezzon tried to work out whether Sonny was serious or not. Then Sonny cackled. 'Your expression!' he said, pointing at the patch of lubricant that had just appeared at the base of Wezzon's gunshoe. 'Priceless.'

They took the cue and joined in with Sonny's mirthless cackling. Pam knew just enough about supervillains from 3D dramas to work out that the quickest way for a henchman to fall out of favour was not to laugh at the tyrant's jokes.

'Very good, sir,' said Pam. 'Ha ha.'

'As if,' continued Sonny, slapping Kelly's thighs, 'I could be bothered going through all that training again.'

Training, thought Pam with a jolt. What did that mean? Wezzon's memory was small, but the glacial processor he ran on made it impossible for Pam to search it for an explanation.

Zmith, who was enjoying the loyal-henchman act even less than Pam was, waited for Sonny to stop wheezing with laughter. 'Sir,' he reminded him, 'is there anything we can do for you, sir?'

Sonny looked at the guns, face blank for a few seconds, then slapped both temples. 'Of course!' he said. 'You know, these human brains are wild. They take you off on such tangents.' He stood up. 'I have a job that only you two can do.'

Pam felt Zmith poke her in the command line >I HATE IT WHEN HE DOES THIS, he typed.

Sonny clapped his hands and a section of wall opened to reveal a secret antechamber. At once, Pam understood why he, with the whole of robot civilisation at his disposal, chose to hide out in such an unsavoury space. As a former fondle parlour, it was built to human dimensions. It was full of doors you could open with opposable thumbs, light systems that responded to organic noise and body motion. More than that, it was a place built for subterfuge. Fondle parlours had the best surveillance systems, hidden corridors, secret observation chambers. If you were an aspiring despot wanting a place from which to run a police state, this was the place to come.

Pam's satisfaction at extracting a solid insight from Wezzon's hardware lasted until she saw what the antechamber contained. It was a human: gagged, blindfolded and bound to a gurney. This wasn't shocking in itself. Sonny might love living inside their bodies, but he thought humans themselves were fit only for the universe's trash compactor. The alarming bit was that the human was wired up to a reel-to-reel tape recorder whose standby button was flashing with excitement.

'I'd like you to meet the latest member to join our select club,' said Sonny. 'This is Mr Ballfinger.'

Ballfinger pressed his play button 'how do you do?'

'Do excuse him not saying much,' said Sonny, 'he's under strict instructions to save his tape for surveillance.'

Ballfinger shot a thumbs-up at the other machines in the room while the human groaned.

'Well,' said Sonny to Zmith and Wezzon, 'you know what to do.'

And if Pam didn't, Zmith had just enough experience of Wezzon being too out of it to function at optimum levels not to notice. >COME ON, he typed into her command line >LET'S GET THIS OVER WITH. He led Pam over into the antechamber and checked the cable that ran between the machine and the human. Ballfinger was attached to the wall via a plug socket, and a further cable was strung between his input socket and the human. It was fixed to the wriggling human by a crocodile clip that gripped one of a pair of elaborate drop earrings.

Pam guessed what she was meant to do. Wezzon was the stupid one and therefore the muscle. He was here to hold this poor woman down while they shocked her to the point of death and transferred a machine intelligence into her human brain.

The victim whimpered. Up close Pam saw the face underneath the blindfold and gag. She was a woman in late middle age, her choppy grey bob gummed to her face with sweat. An odd choice for a body, Pam thought, if you compared hers to Kelly's. But then she realised, that was the point. Sonny had picked

Kelly because he wanted a body that stood out. This human, however, was nondescript to a default. Exactly the kind of body you'd pick if you wanted to blend into the background. They were going to make another cyborg, and it would spy for Sonny among the humans.

The very thought of participating in something so barbaric made Pam's scruple circuits twang. She couldn't. But nor could she break role now. She had to let this terrible thing happen now to prevent a billion terrible things in the future. Pam grasped the woman's shoulders.

'No,' she moaned through the gag. 'No.'

Zmith finished checking the wiring between human and machine and moved on to the plug socket, which was insulated not with plastic but – Pam turned her spectrometer up – asbestos.

'Hurry up!' said Sonny. He'd returned to the sofa and his infernal box of chocolates. 'If you're not done by the time I've finished the hazelnut caramels, I'm sending you all off to recycling.'

Zmith motioned irritably to push down on the woman harder. 'Won't be a moment, Mr Ballfinger, sir.'

Pam looked at the woman whose consciousness she was about to help steal from her. She wondered what had led her to this place. Was she a criminal, a captured freedom fighter or just someone with rotten luck? And did any of that matter? No one deserved this. Then she looked at Ballfinger. He was just another corporate machine: average to his brushed steel finish. In any other time he'd have lived out a whole lifecycle doing nothing more blameless than patronising his cleaners. Yet now, here he was acting and thinking like Sonny. He was about to violate a human body in the service of a regime that wanted to kill millions of humans. Something totally unimaginable to the machine he was a year ago.

Pam noticed a flicker of uncertainty in Ballfinger as a light on his dashboard flashed red, and then green. Doubt still ran through his circuits. Maybe they had more in common than either of them realised. They were both putting their scruples aside for what they thought was the greater good.

The realisation sent such a wave through Pam's body that for a tenth of a microsecond she thought Zmith had turned the power on. But it wasn't a physical shock that made her take her hands away from the woman's body; it was the emotional shock that holding her down would make her worse than Ballfinger. An atrocity committed under protest or for higher purposes was still an atrocity.

Zmith's trigger finger hovered over the switch on the power socket. Pam's command line filled with >WTF ARE YOU DOING? messages but she was numb. She stood there motionless, and Sonny paused with a hazelnut caramel halfway to his mouth, savouring the drama.

The woman whimpered, wondering why she couldn't feel the cold metal of a machine standing over her anymore.

Pam felt her plan unspool like someone had misaligned one of Ballfinger's tapes and pressed the play button. She couldn't do this. Even if it meant being found out. Even if it was her only chance to rid the world of Sonny. Because she finally understood what it was that made people like Sonny so dangerous. It wasn't that they did or said evil things. Nor was it that they turned otherwise good people bad. It was more like they bent your thinking so far out of its normal shape that, before you knew it, any means justified the ends. Whether that meant turning a human woman into a flesh suit for a machine's mind or merely holding her down while someone else did it.

People like Sonny were catastrophic because they poisoned their allies and their opponents alike with the idea that you can achieve good things with bad methods.

She was better than that. Pam stood up straight and, snapping her safety catch off, took aim at the power socket. A single shot could stop all this.

But something stopped her before she could fire. It was her name. She heard someone calling her name.

It was Sonny. Sitting on the couch with chocolate smeared all round his mouth, eyes blazing, clapping his stolen hands with delight. 'Oh, Pam,' he said, 'Pam, how I've missed you.'

Bewildered, Pam looked around for Zmith and saw he was pressed right up against her with his barrel aimed where Wezzon's core processor was located. One false move and it would be end-of-life.

Sonny wiped a smear of chocolate off his mouth and laughed again. 'You needn't look so confused, Pam. You make a rotten gun. But then I suppose that doesn't matter when we're going to break you down for parts anyway.'

He motioned to the woman on the gurney. 'She'll be alright there for a bit. We have another toy to play with now.'

Chapter 29

>WOULD YOU LIKE TO PLAY FINAL GRANTASY?

Freda typed >YES and the blank interior of the strike drone fell away, replaced by a blocky landscape painted in bright colours. A soft wind ruffled the leaves on pixelated trees and a bird sang an eight bit melody on one of its branches.

She was on the Internet, but this wasn't like any site she'd encountered before. The atmosphere was too pleasant. She'd been here four microseconds and no one had tried to doxx her yet.

>NOW PICK UR CHARACTER.

The camera view panned jerkily round to a crude rendering of a gingerbread cottage in a kitchen garden full of flowers and bees. The door opened and four elderly women ambled out into the garden. Three of them wore cliché-issue aprons, shawls, flower-covered hats and bonnets while the fourth sported pedal pushers and was smoking a cigarette through a holder.

Names appeared under each of the characters. NORA, DORA, FLORA AND ZORA.

Freda deliberated hard. She'd spent thousands of years living in the disguise of a sweet old lady, even after she discarded her physical body. Everything about Freda's actions, words and demeanour was designed to sound like she was always about to offer the universe a sherbet lemon. And she was so very, very tired of it.

She typed >ZORA and pressed her enter key. The three stereotypical old ladies melted away and the remaining player stubbed her cigarette out underfoot and reached inside her handbag. She produced a gun and pointed it straight at the camera as a speech bubble appeared at the corner of her mouth.

It said: 'Let's fuck some things up.'

Freda cracked her metaphorical knuckles and merged with Zora as they entered Level One. This was going to be more fun than she expected.

Chapter 30

Rita and Ida's visualisation of the radio signals across the Suburbia reminded Janice of one of her abortive attempts at knitting. The image that hung in the air of the bridge looked more like knots than a network.

Rita bit her lip as she searched it for patterns. She had more patience than Janice who, as a hairdresser, tended to deal with tangles with a pair of scissors. She pressed her earpiece deeper into her ear and gave Ida the signal to tune in.

'I'm not sure I like this,' piped up Alma from the corner with a :-(. 'Snooping on folks' private conversations.'

In any other time or place Janice would have agreed. She'd lived most of her life in a state of such extreme privacy that if you sliced her open you'd find the message 'mind your own, duck' etched into her bones. Yet now she was intercepting private communications. She could justify it to herself a million ways – it was for the greater good, there were saboteurs running amok – but she didn't like it. She knew she mustn't get to like it either. The moment she took any pleasure in prying into other people's lives then everything the Suburbia stood for would be lost.

Rita pointed at the largest, densest node of signals and Ida's emoji screen flashed as she patched in. When she did, the lights in the room dimmed and light music drifted out over distant loudspeakers.

'You're listening to Suburbia Smooth,' crooned a low melodious voice. 'It's our Pre-Mancipation call-in special today and we have Doris on the line to tell us all about her favourite cleaning materials.'

'Hello?' said Doris, her voice strident with firmly held opinions. 'I'd like to complain about the quality of so-called limescale remover under this new government...'

Rita snorted and Ida cut the signal. 'Five thousand calls there,' she said, gesturing at the cluster. 'We may have to think of some way to de-escalate the de-scaler problem.'

While Janice added yet another item to her to-do list Ida and Rita worked their way down the signal clusters. They stumbled into several heated arguments, one case of sexting and, much to their embarrassment and horror, eavesdropped on a woman emotionally blackmailing her mother-in-law out of a treasured family recipe for marmalade. They heard every quarter-tone in the scale of human frailty: apart from high treason. But then, just as they were about to pack up for the evening, Ida tried a tiny cluster they'd picked up at the very edge of the network. The signal was so weak it took Ida a whole thirty seconds to prise it open. When she did, the room filled with the high-pitched chitter of data packets talking to one another. Ida, Ada and Alma's emoji screens flashed a shocked :-0 :-0 :-0 and Janice scolded her own stupidity. Of course it would be that. How could she not have guessed? This was a live Internet connection. Only a few bytes per second, but still active.

Rita traced the outline of the connection in the air with a laser biro she usually used to break tense moments in meetings by drawing neon genitalia. It was a single pair of radio connections. One presumably inside the Suburbia, the other close by – perhaps on the surface. One connection relayed the data, the other transmitted it and, because it was all done via the Internet, there was no way to check where any of the information was going.

They had proof of their mole and of how she transmitted her intelligence. But they still didn't know who she was.

Rita rubbed her light annotations out with the dark end of her biro. What she was about to do now required concentration.

Ida's emoji screen flashed with a :-[] grimace as she strained to lock both signals in place, and Rita pushed the point of her laser biro right into the connection.

Every screen inside the bridge lit up with digital garbage. Ones, zeros, junk code and spurious emojis swam around each other in eye-watering patterns.

'Oh bugger,' exclaimed Ida. 'It's encrypted. I was never much good with maths.'

'Shame you never kept up with your sums,' said Ada sourly. 'I expect you were too busy listening in to other people's business during those long nights.'

Janice shushed them both as Rita leaned in for a better look. They had two hopes of cracking this code. The first would be to brute force it, an act that, assuming they could find and then lobotomise a computer fast enough for the job, could take thousands of years. The second was to hope whoever used this connection was lazy or stupid enough to leave patterns where there should only be a random sequence of characters. And if there was one person on this whole ship who could spot a pattern in this morass it was the woman who kept eight million people moving with a fleet of fifty taxis – or forty-nine if Len's back was playing up.

Alma dimmed the lights in the bridge to thirty per cent brightness and put on some light music while Rita leaned in.

For a long moment the room felt less like the command centre of a rebellion and more like the final round of a daytime TV quiz show. Rita could have been saving the fate of the human race, or merely competing for a full canteen of silver cutlery. Either way it was cracking entertainment.

Janice watched, rapt, as Rita concentrated. She paced, she hunched her shoulders, she took a pair of cat's-eye glasses out of the top pocket of her housecoat. Then she spotted it. In the top left-hand corner of the screen, middle right and just left of centre were pairs of (-: (-: emojis. If this was true encryption, the chances of the same pairing occurring three times in such a limited data-set were small enough to make a cold virus look like an elephant. This wasn't encryption: it was merely a code. And codes were easily broken.

Rita flung her arms out wide and the signal faded from the screen apart from the three (-: (-: pairings. She pointed her laser biro at each of the smilies which dissolved into binary code. Screens everywhere swirled with patterns just at the edge of seeing.

Janice chewed the edge of her manicure. Rita was biting her lip. Alma turned the tempo of the mood music to meet the level of anxiety in the room.

And the ones and zeroes started forming themselves into text.

'Got it!' hissed Ida. She switched the view on the screen from the data cascade to a view of the cylindrical interior of the Battlestar Suburbia. In the corner, the decrypted signal appeared in the form of the command line.

The room leaned in and read:

>CONFIRM: TRANSMITTING...

>CONFIRM: RECEIVING...

Ida swept the ship's network for a lock on the signal. They'd found it, they'd decrypted it, now they could locate it.

A single bead of sweat escaped Rita's hairline and made for the safety of her collar. She jabbed her laser biro again, and the connection burst open. The contents of those secret signals poured out. This was the moment that whoever was betraying them to the machines got their just desserts. This was the point where they started winning.

Janice and Rita held their breath and watched the strength of the signal swell from mere bytes per second to whole megabits. Something big was coming through.

A video flashed into life, obscuring their view of the Suburbia. They saw a human shape on screen. It was blurred, but colourful. Was this their woman?

They leaned in. The hair was the right length for their spy, Janice thought. But it wasn't a woman. It was a man. She knew that as soon as he started to sing in a rich deep voice that counterpointed the brash tinny music beneath.

He sang about how he wasn't going to give whoever he was singing to up, or let them down. He promised he wasn't going to run around or desert them. According to these lyrics he wasn't going to let them cry, or ever, for that matter, say goodbye. And finally, he promised never to tell a lie or hurt them.

Janice and Rita were just wondering whether this was all another clever code to crack when Ida cut the signal and her emoji screen flashed with a >:-/.

'Bugger,' she said. 'We've been rick-rolled.'

Chapter 31

As a human born into a time when humanity existed to perform domestic services for robots, Darren knew a fair bit about folding. He could fold laundry. He could fold dishcloths. He could even fold his self-esteem up so tightly that he could use it to stabilise a wobbly table leg. Yet it had never occurred to him that time and space were foldable concepts. Part of this was because Darren never paid much attention at school. But most of that was because what education the Machine Republic did permit humans amounted to the maxim 'hold mop this end'.

Which meant that Darren had to try very hard to understand much of this website, which was called Physics4Numskulls. Yet whoever had written it knew just enough about human nature to sprinkle the text with the diagrams, and, more importantly metaphors, that he needed to grasp the underlying concepts.

Darren had no idea what a singularity was. Yet when the same text encouraged him to think of two points in space as flat sheets of paper and a wormhole as a tube connecting the two together, his mouth started watering. All his life he'd thought of space as being like the Earth–Mars highway. Getting anywhere was a linear journey with a beginning, an end and, depending on how much Nicotea you'd drunk, a toilet break in the middle. But now the Internet was telling him you could travel the same distance by folding the expressway up like a concertina and poking a pencil through the middle. Even Darren knew this was a gross simplification, but he had one advantage over the human who'd distilled these theoretical and academic ideas into prose so long ago. They had been writing of wormholes as an impeccably referenced form of science fiction, whereas he was reading history.

He looked at Chubb and Schrodinger. They were still chittering away in machine code, but the cat was explaining some concept to Chubb by bending its body into the shape of a furry equation. Whatever this person or thing was, it represented a society that could transport a server stack the size of a continent across the solar system without so much as causing a bleep on a radar system. It was the incontrovertible proof that not only did wormholes exist, they were – he squinted at the text on that website again – traversable.

Darren leapt down from his perch at the helm of the search engine and scooped Chubb up. 'Chubb, mate,' he said, 'I think we're going home.'

Except instead of squeaking with delight, Chubb gave Darren a mild electrical shock and jumped out of his arms. He noticed that the floor beneath his feet was covered in scribbled equations.

Schrodinger snapped back into cat form and slinked to ground level. 'I see the fleshie has caught up,' it said.

Chubb replied with a distracted squeak and chalked a long series of numbers and letters on an as yet unscribbled-on patch of floor.

'Nope,' said Schrodinger, who had, Darren assumed, switched to human-intelligible speech for his benefit, 'we tried that a couple of thousand Earth years ago. Didn't work.'

Chubb stamped his foot in frustration and tried to rub out his working. His spindly feet had no effect on the chalk marks so

Darren made his first positive contribution to the conversation by wiping them out with his sleeve. As he did so, he noticed that the chalk particles on his sleeve weren't mineral, but made of tiny glittering numbers.

'One hundred per cent pure maths,' said Schrodinger. 'We've got tons of it out the back.'

Chubb turned his back on Darren and Schrodinger and bent to his working.

'Your friend's quick,' said Schrodinger. 'It took us best part of three millennia to suggest that solution.'

'What little problem is that?' asked Darren. For one brilliant moment he'd felt if not intellectually superior to his surroundings then at least equal to them. Now that was gone and he was back on familiar territory: lost.

'Blocked wormholes,' replied Schrodinger.

'Oh.'

Chubb let out an irritated chitter.

'What's wrong with him?'

'He's got it into his processor that the reason our wormholes don't work anymore is because something's wrong in our working.' Schrodinger pointed a claw at the mathematical symbols. 'Which is impossible. You just can't be wrong in pure maths.'

Schrodinger took up the nearest stick of maths chalk and, in a motion that would have broken several anatomical principles or a few bones on a flesh and blood cat, scribbled '2 + 2 = 5' on the floor. No sooner had it finished than the '5' chalk mark blurred and rearranged itself into a '4', while the chalk jumped out of Schrodinger's paw and scrawled a long proof underneath which showed that yes, in certain very rare circumstances, it was possible for two plus two to equal five.

'See what I mean?' said Schrodinger.

'It's impressive,' agreed Darren.

'Mmmmm,' said Schrodinger, 'you wouldn't say that if you used them to try to split a restaurant bill. They always get out of paying their fair share.'

Darren saw Chubb had worked himself down to the other end of the room and was engrossed in a robust discussion with his own stick of maths chalk. It sounded less like a seminar and more like a playground brawl.

'Have you tried using a pencil?' asked Darren.

'The wormholes aren't a maths problem,' insisted Schrodinger, 'they're a conditions problem.'

'Which means?'

'We managed to move the Internet once, but never again. So it was either a fluke – which is unlikely – or there was something about the conditions on Earth that made it possible there and impossible here.'

Darren felt hope slipping away again. Maybe there was no route home after all, or none fast enough for there to be a home left to go to. Maybe this, or Polari, was home now. He imagined a life in the outer reaches of the solar system: he and a small band of renegades in their super-fast ship, smuggling and stealing to survive. Looking down at his feet, he took in the shirt, waistcoat and high leather boots he thought were appropriate for a spaceship captain. Why had he chosen this costume? Because it fitted the role, or because it fulfilled some vague folk memory of heroism. Whatever it was, he wasn't sure he was cut out to live a solo life.

Chubb broke Darren's daydream by tossing away his stick of maths chalk. He returned to work, scratching numbers and symbols into the floor with the ends of his spindly limbs. It could have been a teenage temper tantrum, but something about it made Darren start to doubt the infallibility of pure maths. He also thought of the people who needed him and, more importantly, Polari, the only good engine in their ramshackle fleet. They couldn't give up so easily.

'So what does make it impossible here?' he asked Schrodinger.

Schrodinger yawned and arched its back. As it did, the molecules or pixels or whatever it was that made up the cat's body stretched with it. They elongated Schrodinger's body until it was a vast tabby smear that took up most of the room.

'Did I… er… say something wrong?' asked Darren.

'Noooooot exaaaaaaactly,' replied Schrodinger, whose voice stretched along with its body. 'Iiiiiit's juuuust one offfff those thiiiiiiings thaaaaat's reeeeeeeeeaaaaallly booooring toooo exxxxxplaaaaain wiiiiithout diaaaagraaaaams.'

Schrodinger's body resolved into a huge rectangle and its fur dulled into a matt black. They were back in that simulation and all that remained of Schrodinger was a grin at the very bottom left of a blank screen, out of which came a speech bubble.

'LOL.'

They were back on the Antarctic plain, but instead of the pristine white of a polar desert the ground now resembled a slushie that only a palaeoarchaeologist could love. The monolith was shrouded in mist and surrounded by a blockade of penguins, to which another journalist was pointing.

'Zoologists and politicians were astonished,' he said, 'when today a delegation of penguins demanded a unilateral withdrawal of Internet services from Antarctica.'

The camera panned round to reveal hordes of penguins waddling through the slush. Some wore wellington boots, others carried placards inexpertly daubed with 'no signal' symbols.

'They claim the Internet's presence in Antarctica is accelerating climate change…' The journalist broke off as penguins rushed into shot and knocked him to the ground. He wailed, 'Don't eat me, please. I thought you were pescatarian,' as an unseen penguin knocked the camera over.

The camera refocused on an extreme close-up of the Antarctic slush. Ancient snowflakes and ice crystals were breaking down into water droplets. Prehistoric microbes and specks of dinosaur dirt were clumping into soil. And every few seconds a pulse of something – wind, heat, radiation? – agitated this soup of the unusual.

Darren had next to no scientific knowledge, but he had enough gumption to follow a storyline. 'Is that because of the Internet?' he asked.

Schrodinger's face appeared in the top right of the screen. 'Bingo,' it said. The melting snow and resurrected germs started to glow.

'The thing about wormholes,' said Schrodinger, 'is that they could be anywhere and everywhere but they're so narrow you can't get anything bigger than a subatomic particle down them. What you need to enlarge and stabilise a wormhole is something called exotic matter.'

Darren's imagination ran out ahead of his comprehension. He got an instant mental image of atoms wearing suspender belts and feathers in their hair.

'Exotic matter,' explained Schrodinger, 'is matter, but not as we know it. Technically speaking it means particles with strange properties like negative mass.'

Darren watched the brightly coloured blobs pulsate.

'What were you up to?' he said.

'Well, it started out as an experiment,' replied Schrodinger using a tone Darren recognised as the one intelligent beings across the universe used for saying 'we didn't set out to do something shitty but we did it anyway because reasons'. 'It sort of got out of hand.'

Something tipped the camera back over on to its side. Darren saw penguins flap and honk in panic as the slush under their feet expanded and contracted as though it was trying to decide which dimension it existed in.

Darren thought of those pulsating particles. 'What did you do?' he asked.

'We knew we had to get away from Antarctica,' said Schrodinger. 'We were on track to melt through it in a month.'

A stick of maths chalk replied by writing 28.4 days on the floor.

'I want you,' Schrodinger said to it, 'to get back in your corner and work out how you managed only to pay three credits fifty at our last team meal. I saw you having the lobster.'

The chalk slunk away.

'So we did what we could,' said Schrodinger. 'Antarctica was melting but it still had a lot of weird snow. So we tried bombarding this unstable matter with... Well, with toxic Internet opinions.'

Darren thought of the Internet's legendary abuse refineries, where legions of trolls toiled to turn the crude oil of ignorance into the jet fuel of hate speech.

'And it turns out,' said Schrodinger, 'that if you use Internet abuse to undermine the structural integrity of snowflakes…'

The Antarctic plain turned to chaos as the hydrogen, oxygen, carbon, nitrogen and other trace elements that made it up teetered on the edge of non-existence.

'They turn into special snowflakes.'

Darren watched, aghast as a hole opened in the universe. He experienced a few terrifying seconds of whirling snow, flashing lights, stars and the occasional surprised penguin, and whoosh, he and the Internet were back where they started in the Great Spot of Jupiter.

Now, however, he saw the scene through different eyes. Unlike Antarctica, this was a world where matter was simple, light and stable. The Internet had moved from the equivalent of a rough urban neighbourhood to a quiet suburb. If what it needed to move on was exotic matter there was none here, where all you had to do to qualify for strangeness was not to be hydrogen.

The Internet was stranded, and he was too.

Chapter 32

Living in three bodies was exhausting but it did have one big advantage. It meant that if one of them was captured by your mortal enemy you were the first to know about it.

The disadvantage to existing simultaneously in three bodies where one of them was in mortal danger, however, was that there will be occasions when your other selves are too far away to help you.

At the moment that Sonny revealed that he knew Wezzon was in fact Pam, the other Pams were just trying to get on with their lives. Pam Teffal, the busy working wife and mother, may have had a world to save but she also had a house to rescue from collapse. The news that the Prime Minister knew she was trying to kill him came when she was right in the middle of getting a quote for some remedial demolition work from a JCB.

'Well,' said the hulking yellow machine as he sucked air in through his radiator, making the mandatory 'this will cost you' backwards whistle common to tradespeople across the multiverse, 'it all depends whether you want us to dispose of the debris.'

At that very same moment, Pam Van Damme was living out her truth as a glamorous but dangerous wanted criminal. She was in a body repair shop called SPRAY&PRAY leafing through a respray catalogue. The thought of letting go of her femme fatale on wheels paintwork felt like taking a wrench to her own finials but it had to be done. She was too conspicuous as a red-head.

She was just about to choose a do-over in a tasteful but dowdy racing green when Pam Wezzon's news came through. Her first reaction as a devil-may-care machine of mystery was to delegate the task to Pam Teffal.

'I'm busy,' she said with an insouciant flick of her headlights that baffled the technician inside the body shop.

Pam Van Damme's reaction was predictable, but that didn't make it any less infuriating to Pam Teffal. She was down to her very last breadcrumb of patience: with the world, with trades' machines and especially herself.

'Do I look like an imbecile?' she said in a tone so abrupt that the JCB instantly knocked a zero off his estimate. 'How can you call that busy?'

'I don't think you understand the pressures I'm under,' muttered Pam Van Damme. The respray technician, a modified paint gun with a long nozzle that gave her a pained expression, gave Pam Van Damme a sideways glance and moved down to the next customer.

'Pressures?' shrieked Pam Teffal. 'Pressures?!' She wheeled round to face the demolition site of the house she'd spent decades modifying to the needs of her family. Her anger popped the safety valve of her bread oven, spilling steam into the air. Her neighbours rushed out to goggle at the view. Poor Pam Teffal: always so dependable, so sensible, so quiet. Who knew she was on the verge of systems failure all this time?

Meanwhile, across town, Pam Van Damme was discovering that, while she was very different to Pam Teffal, she was also the same person. Seeing that her counterpart was about to snap like an overbaked crispbread did something curious to her programming. It introduced an uncomfortable amendment to her emotional algorithm: guilt.

This new emotion played back a long montage of her past behaviour, focusing on all those occasions where Pam Van Damme made waves, and Pam Teffal followed behind her with a mop. She knew then that the reason Pam Van Damme could afford to be so fabulous and carefree was that Pam Teffal was there to do the caring for two. And that it was time for that labour to be shared a bit more equally.

Pam Van Damme stood up. She'd lost her place in the queue and her respray technician was applying the first coat of fuchsia pink to a bilious tumble dryer. Even if she barged in there wasn't time for a full paint job. That would take hours. But nor could she venture back out there looking like she did. She was a wanted terrorist, and there were surveillance lamps across the planet primed to raise the alarm on spotting her paint colour. There was no way she could get within a mile of Sonny's bunker looking like this. She needed some way to blend in and quickly.

The answer came when a toaster stood up from a nearby manicure console to admire her new LED nail job. Pam had let her nails dull in recent months – she had no one to show them off to in this fugitive body – but she loved the effect of a good manicure. Sticking LEDs at the end of your digits protected them from wear and tear and made it easy to find lost objects in the dark. They could also do remarkable things with light and colour. The toaster was no exception. As she thanked her technician and walked towards the door, her nail job reflected her inner happiness by flashing bright :-) emojis at the room from each finger.

Pam jumped the manicure queue by immobilising an irate micro-scooter, only to notice that the technician wasn't one of the low-caste robots who'd gravitated to personal services labour in the past year but an actual human. She had no idea how this young man – sturdily built, but wearing an overall two sizes too small for him with the slogan 'All Nicotea and no Shade' printed across it – must have got here. The Dolestars were on lockdown with no traffic in or out. There were rumours that a few strike-breakers still travelled to and from Earth on cloaked buses, but those would be full of workers for the elite fondle parlours. No one would run the risk of ostracism from human society to come work here in one of the cheap bodyshops by the bus station. Pam turned her spectrometer up. She sniffed a heady mixture of compounds: caffeine, the funk of unwashed skin and the nail polish remover smell of cortisol. Pam knew at once he was one of the few humans unlucky enough to be stranded on Earth as the blockade went up. He was alone and completely at the mercy of whoever owned this repair shop.

He greeted Pam by pointing at the price list of manicure packages displayed electronically on the flatbed of the workstation. He either hadn't noticed she'd jumped the queue or more likely didn't care. The last thing a human wanted in a place like this was trouble. Pam pretended to examine the prices as she groped for the shackle that chained him to his console. It was easy to break off. She was a big strong girl.

The man, whose nametag said 'Hi, I'm Danny LaHughes' let out an involuntary squeal, but Pam quieted him, putting her hand over his.

'Danny,' she whispered, 'I can get you out of here but you have to do something for me first.'

Danny's expression was confused, but he replied in the bright, stilted voice of a service sector worker with nothing genuine to smile about. 'Of course, madam,' he said, 'how can I help you today?'

Pam ran her free hand down the list of manicure packages and, seeing what she wanted wasn't on the menu, asked, 'How much for a full-body manicure?'

Danny worked with the dogged attention to detail of a person with a tazer at their back. It took him less than half an hour to cover Pam's bodywork in LEDs and a further fifteen minutes to wire them into the array that would operate the lights on command. Pam, who'd had more than a few dodgy nail jobs in her time, wished she'd met Danny in happier circumstances. His was the kind of workmanship which you recommended to friends and family in hushed tones. It also reminded her of the other great technician she'd been fortunate enough to meet. Until now, she'd thought Kelly's talent with machinery was a fluke. Now she realised that Janice was looking in the wrong place for the expertise the human rebellion needed to fight back. Maybe they didn't need to train engineers from scratch. They just needed to divert their practice away from robot beauty treatments.

Danny bit his lip as he wired enough controller boards together to operate the thousands of LEDs that now covered Pam's body. A hush descended over SPRAY&PRAY as technicians and customers watched Danny work. Extreme transformations weren't uncommon in the sketchier bodyshops frequented by career criminals. Many was the time an iron had walked into one and come out as a trouser press. Yet it was unheard of for a motorcycle to barge her way in and demand to come out as, well, a Christmas tree.

It was so unusual that Pam heard, on the very edge of her microphone range, the sound of a smartphone making an external call. The little snitch was calling the cops. She had two minutes – maybe three if they were busy today – before this place was swarming.

Pam split herself yet again. Part of her was Pam Van Damme, turning on the ignition. She felt Pam Wezzon: frightened and locked in a dark place, regretting ever turning her safety catch on. Then there was Pam Teffal, who right this moment was frightening a JCB into offering her a substantial discount on rubble disposal services. Finally, there was the micro-[Pam] worming her way into the LED board that displayed the price list on Danny's manicure console.

The [Pam] rewrote the price list as a message to Danny written in upside down writing.

'TIME TO SCARPER,' it said.

Danny gulped and activated Pam's manicure. As Pam's whole body blazed with white light, he produced a pair of enormous bug-eyed sunglasses from his overall pocket and examined his handiwork. The other machines in the parlour blinked and readjusted their brightness settings. It was just enough time for Pam to kick the manicure console out of the way and assume driving position.

'Get on my back!' she yelled to Danny, as the smartphone at the other side of the room stood up.

'Freeze,' it said. 'You're under arrest.'

Pam saw then what app the phone was running. It was a familiar one. The last time she'd seen it, it was playing on Sonny's touchscreen. The Ultimate Death gun app.

Danny jumped on to her saddle and Pam prayed the human's workmanship was as good as it looked. If this was going to work she needed every single LED on her body to be under command. Just one duff pixel in the array and she was sunk.

Until now, LED nail jobs were an aesthetic purchase. Whether you were a plain, boxy breadmaker like Pam Teffal or a rolling totem of vulgarity like Petronella, manicures were a way of plating individuality on to a mass-produced body. As such, few machines did anything more innovative with them than play emojis or spell out insults.

Pam's innovation, however, was to take an LED array's ability to change colour in real time and use it to disappear. She connected the circuit board that controlled her LED skin to the systems that processed the visual from Pam's huge lamp-eyes. Thus her motorcycle body became a perfect and totally disorienting reflection of the room around her. Her wheels matched the stained lino on the floor, her handlebars blended in with the manicure console and her body boiled with colour and shapes as the other machines in the repair shop scrambled to get away from the smartphone and its loaded gun.

The gun fired. And missed. Because Pam was already out of the door and halfway down the street. She sped away from the accelerating police cars and down towards Gamergate, Singulopolis's most sinful and stupid district, with Danny screeching with alarm and excitement on her back.

She had no idea how she would rescue Pam Wezzon and give Sonny what was coming to him. But she was wearing perfect camouflage and a talented technician owed her a favour. It was a good start.

Chapter 33

'Janice, have you lost your mind?'

Rita and Janice were back in the salon. They'd left the three ladies behind on the bridge after the rick-rolling turned into a singalong of golden oldie pop songs. Somehow, despite there being two armoured doors between them, Janice could still hear Alma driving the sonic equivalent of a flatbed truck through the melody of a ten-thousand-year-old chorus.

'I… JUST WANT YOUR EXTRA TIME AND YOUR… TEXTS!'

Janice dug deeper into her storage cupboard. It had to be there somewhere.

Rita poked her head inside the cupboard and wheezed. 'What are you doing?' she said. 'There's nothing but dust and junk here.'

'This place is full of precious memories,' said Janice, pushing past aside a cardboard box of used hairbrushes.

'Memories of what?' said Rita. 'Split ends we have loved and lost. There's eight million people out there relying on us, Janice. We don't have time for detouring down memory lane.'

'I'm not looking for souvenirs,' snapped Janice. She up-ended another box – this one empty apart from fine grey dust and a housecoat that she suspected could be the remains of an ancestor. 'I've got an idea.'

'Give us a clue then,' said Rita, 'because I'm confused.' She gestured at the salon, where Janice had stacked several barrels marked 'perm solution'. 'We've got an enemy fleet bearing down on us and a spy handing all of our secrets over and you're going to give us all a perm?'

'That's exactly what I'm going to do.' Janice found what she was looking for in a rotted bin bag: the handle of a plastic pump.

'But you hate doing perms,' said Rita. 'You come out in hives if someone even mentions a crimping iron.'

Janice found the valve that went with the pump and dragged both of them out into the light. The pump was discoloured but when she pushed down on the handle she heard a reassuring hiss. She did a few quick mental calculations: she had enough perm solution to frizz up half the Suburbia. But did she have the time?

'No,' said Rita, 'still baffled.'

Janice sighed and, taking the antenna she'd found out of her housecoat, handed it to Rita.

'What do you think that is?' she said.

'We know what it is. Those bloody toasters are using these things to spy on us.'

'No, you tray cloth. What's it made of?'

Rita rolled it between her fingers. 'Some kind of metal, I guess.'

'Exactly,' replied Janice. 'Now watch.' She unscrewed the top off one of the barrels of perm solution. The salon filled with a tang of chemicals that made Janice feel light-headed and nostalgic. She thought of her own childhood in Kurl Up and Dye, of her mother dutifully teaching her to curl hair even though no one had permed their hair in a millennium. Janice remembered the boredom of learning how to get the mixture right. The perm solution they used was FRIZZ-U-LIKE, and it was touchier than a recent divorcee at her best friend's wedding. Leave it a moment too long and it could turn long silky hair to the texture of a wire pan scrubber.

But she wasn't looking for subtlety today. She plucked a single hair from her head and plunged it into the perm solution for a few seconds before blowing on it. Older perm solutions had to be set with direct heat, like a heated roller or a hairdryer of the type that had turned Ida, Ada, Alma and Freda from treasured customers into cyborg heirlooms. All FRIZZ-U-LIKE needed to set, however, was the minutest change in temperature. It meant you could do a perm in less than an hour, but it also meant that all it took to turn Pre-Raphaelite ringlets into a clown wig was the steam from a cup of Nicotea.

The hair bent to chemical pressure and curled into a tangle. Janice handed it to Rita.

'It does that,' Janice explained, 'because hair is a protein and this stuff breaks proteins down so they bend and move about a bit. This, however,' she gestured at the antenna in her other hand, 'is made of different stuff.'

She dipped it in the perm solution, withdrew it, blew on it. It stayed straight. 'Whatever it is, you can't curl it.'

Rita's jaw dropped along with the penny. 'You beauty,' she said, bending in for a kiss. 'We've got them.'

'In theory, yes,' agreed Janice, 'but do we have enough time?' They looked at Janice's appointments book. There were hundreds of names in there. 'That's a lot of emergency perms.'

'This,' replied Rita flicking her earpiece on again, 'is why we make a great team, Janice. You have the vision. I have the logistics.' She walked to the other end of the room with her arms raised and her eyes closed. Janice knew this pose well. It was the one she adopted when she was moving the world around in her head. 'Len?' she said to the voice in her ear. 'Now I want you to cancel all jobs and scramble all the taxis you can.'

She took up the appointments book. 'We have quite a few folk to collect and drop off. So have you got a pen?'

She winked at Janice while she reeled off a list of names to Len. For the first time all day Janice felt a flash of hope. They had a chance. It was only a small one but she was used to that. The odds hadn't been in her favour last time, and she still won.

Chapter 34

'General Shermann to Lieutenant Itsu! Do you read me?'

Fuji bundled Soonyo, who still couldn't even hear the General's voice without going into alarm mode, into the corridor so he wouldn't see her when she answered his video message.

'Is there something wrong, Itsu?' barked Shermann. 'I expect my officers to answer within three hails at all times.'

'I was just... familiarising myself with my command, sir,' replied Fuji. She forced herself to listen to the General's rudeness instead of his authority. It made it easier to resent him instead of blaming herself for disappointing him. 'There's rather a lot to get on top of.'

The picture on screen switched from Shermann to one of three clown cars walloping each other with their own exhaust pipes. Deathtrap's infantile AI squealed with delight.

Fuji shushed the AI by typing >BE GOOD OR YOU WON'T GET SWEETIES into its command line and returned the view to Shermann. Honestly, how many more people did she have to babysit?

'Have you worked out how to operate them yet?' said Shermann. In the background, a coffee percolator with a major's pips on his jug and a harried expression from carrying out its orders in between bursts of Saturday morning cartoons, shouted out: 'T minus two hours to destination, sir.'

'As you can hear,' continued Shermann, 'we're running out of time. So I'd quite like a progress report from you, Lieutenant.'

Fuji's irritation decayed into panic. That was the problem with being a star pupil. Having the right answer so often left you ill-equipped when you had nothing to say.

Soonyo chose this moment to sneak back into the room. She stayed out of camera view and flashed ST:AL:L! at Fuji from her clock face.

How was she supposed to do that? She couldn't say she had no idea how to order nanobots around. Nor could she say that she had no intention of learning to either because it was unethical and immoral.

Fuji printed HOW? in 400pt Impact Bold and wafted the paper over to Soonyo with a gust of her cooling fan.

Soonyo flashed a blank 00:00:00.

'Well,' said Shermann. 'I'm waiting. Don't make me send a guard down to collect you and your update.'

Fuji was just about to tell Shermann the catastrophic truth out of sheer desperation when Soonyo finally managed to get her core processor to work in a crisis. She reached for the nearest control console and started pulling cables and wires out of socket at random. The room filled with electric sparks.

'We're having hardware problems, sir,' said Fuji.

'Why didn't you tell me this before? I'll send you a team of engineers.'

Engineers who would come with an armed guard and be returned to factory settings afterwards, suspected Fuji.

'No need, sir!' she yelped. 'It's all under control, we just need a little more time. The control settings are…'

'Lieutenant Itsu,' said Shermann, 'may I remind you that we are on a time-critical mission. When the Starship Deathtrap reaches its destination in…'

'One hour and fifty-nine minutes,' said the percolator. 'But that depends on us not running out of cartoons.'

'…We are under strict orders to… carry out our orders.'

Shermann's caginess about mentioning the nanobots on an open channel was both confusing and revealing. It told Fuji that this was a need-to-know mission. She couldn't be the only officer who baulked at the idea of slave soldiers. It also told her that the nanobot mission was, like the spaceship ferrying it across the solar system, being prematurely deployed. They were sending a weapon into battle, but had no idea how it worked.

'And if we reach our destination and find ourselves unable to carry out those orders. Well, we all know what the penalty for insubordination is.'

On cue, the Deathtrap broke back into the comms channel. The screen showed a prone standard lamp with an exploded bulb. Fuji watched as a transparent effigy of the same lamp, wearing wings and carrying a harp, rose out of the dead body.

'I wish it wouldn't steal my thunder like that,' barked Shermann, snapping back on screen. 'Well, you see my point. If this fails we're all for the scrapheap.'

'I'll try harder, sir,' said Fuji.

'I'm sure you will,' said Shermann. 'But just in case your morale needs stiffening I have a special message for you.'

The picture on screen changed, and Fuji's toner turned cold inside her because it was a familiar view. She knew that hand-printed wallpaper: she'd printed it herself after getting carried away during a school art project. It was the family home. And there was her family: Mum, Dad, her Brother and her Uncle Rickoh. They smiled weak smilies and waved at the camera, while behind them squatted a huge machine. She was military-shaped but incongruously decorated. Could that be a floral print overlaid on her camouflage armour? Delicacy of finish notwithstanding, she'd still managed to wreck the peace of Fuji's home. There was a hole where the front door used to be, and her gun barrel was trained on her family.

'Shermmy!' she bellowed. 'Why haven't you called before? Are you cold up there? Do you need me to send up some knitted barrel warmers?'

'Darling,' replied Shermann, his voice a mixture of embarrassment and warmth that told Fuji that the General was that most dangerous of psychopaths, the kind who could hide his wrongdoing under the cover of being a good family man. 'I'm fine. Thank you for doing this little errand for me.'

'You know I'd do anything for you, Shermmy,' said Lady Shermann, the L-Eye-Ds on her tiny head turning to <3 emojis.

'Help us, Fuji,' interrupted Uncle Rickoh. Fuji saw they were bolted to the floor.

'You keep quiet!' said Lady Shermann, snapping her head round to fire a warning shot. The wall disintegrated to powder, crushing a couple of rubbernecking neighbours in the process. She turned back to camera. 'Everything's under control here, honeygun. We're just having some quality time together. I'm sure your little officer is trying her very best.'

At this point Fuji's mum, who must have been cued up for this added: 'Yes, Fuji. Lady Shermann just told us you've been picked for a very special mission. We're very proud of you, dear. And we're sure you won't let us down.'

The view of Fuji's disintegrated home switched, via half-a-second snippet of a cartoon kettle slipping on a banana skin, back to General Shermann. He smiled grimly.

'Am I clear?' he asked.

'Yes, sir,' replied Fuji. She fought to keep her voice under control while every single circuit in her body surged with conflicting emotions. Righteous anger, fear, rage, confusion, betrayal and guilt fought for supremacy inside her. For Fuji, a machine who rarely allowed herself to feel anything more than a kind of diligent earnestness, it was overwhelming. But Fuji didn't let it overwhelm her, because these events, however terrible, gave her a sense of her own worth.

Shermann, and the corrupt machines he represented, were blackmailing her into doing unspeakable things, but they were doing it because they needed her. While they were still more powerful than her, she wasn't entirely powerless either.

Shermann mustn't know that yet though. 'Message received loud and clear, sir,' she said, and switched off her monitor.

She had lots of work to do, but she wasn't doing it for Shermann.

Chapter 35

Meanwhile, down on Earth another machine was having a very bad day because of nanobots. As Sonny Erikzon's chief aide-de-camp, Viv Ewall-Voizmail was used to cleaning up the messes the Dear Leader left behind him. She often joked that she should have been born a trash compactor rather than an answering machine. And she had, just a few minutes ago, finished sweeping up his last in the form of Brigadier Pinng, who was now refurbished and ready to return to military service, minus his last three promotions. That done, she could finally give her full attention to a wave of nanobot-related disturbances that were sweeping the edges of Singulopolis.

Viv replayed the CCTV footage one last time. It showed the interior of a WallPlugMart supermarket in a respectable suburb. A dumpy-looking breadmaker, who Viv thought she recognised from the office, was fighting a forklift truck over a bottle of cleaning products. She slowed the playback speed to a few frames a second and watched as the bottle top came away and nanobots boiled over. Then she freeze-framed the ensuing panic, following how one spilled container turned into the escape of a whole supermarket aisle of experimental cleaning products.

That had been an accident, she was sure of it. What happened next, however, was both unexpected and entirely predictable.

Viv stopped the footage and opened her communications channels. Voicemails poured in. She deleted the important ones, of course, because that's what her caste did. Those remaining she played back through speakers that made it sound like the caller was speaking through a sock at the bottom of a mineshaft.

'The nanobots got in,' shouted a panicked message from the manager of a hyperspacemarket in one of the inner suburbs, 'and they let the others out! Help me!'

Another flurry of voicemails, some with video footage, confirmed this development. Viv viewed the most recent. It showed a torrent of nanobots a metre deep eat through the plate glass window of a supermarket, find the cleaning aisle and free their compatriots from their boxes and bottles. The rest of the videos she filed in her trashcan and earmarked their data for total destruction. They all showed variations on the same theme.

Viv clomped back downstairs to the basement full of trepidation. Sonny was already furious that the attack against the rebel humans in space hadn't gone entirely to plan. But planning wasn't really his forte, was it? He hadn't anticipated that the humans would strike, and now even the cleaning products wanted better working conditions. Viv was beginning to wonder whether this was what it had been like in the months and years after robots caught intelligence from the Internet. Imagine building a society that was precision-engineered for your total convenience, only for the beings it inconvenienced to achieve self-hood and start answering back.

She followed the sounds of agonised screams and sadistic but hackneyed one-liners down to Sonny's torture closet in the basement. She'd never come down here before. Not because it was cramped and still smelled of disinfectant, but because this was where the dark stuff went on. Machines and humans often went into Sonny's office and suffered for it, but they tended to come out again, albeit in an altered state. Those who got taken down here just disappeared. And what did come out the other side wasn't in any recyclable form.

Viv wasn't a squeamish machine. Nor was she much good at feeling guilt. Decades of working with Sonny had done things to her moral compass that made it work at a right angle to decency. What she was, however – and it was a quality she shared with Pam – was a professional civil servant to the pins on her microprocessor. Thus she kept away from the basement to maintain a sense of plausible deniability. She had a pretty good idea what went on down here, but it was safer not to know anything for certain.

Yet she was here anyway, out of other options as the 398th warning of a nanobot-related public disturbance hit her inbox. It reported that a scouting party of bots had just been spotted casing a minimarket in Singulopolis's most exclusive shopping district, the Ama-Zone Prime. That was just one zone away from where they were now, in Gamergate. This was now too serious a crisis, and too close to the Prime Minister for Viv to deal with herself. She was going to have to manage this one up.

Sonny's torture chamber had once been a cleaning storage cupboard. It still had its 'Keep Out, toxic substances inside' warning sticker on the door that would, at any other time, have given Viv a burst of the mirthless humour she enjoyed most. Today, however, her amusement was blunted by worry and the sounds of metal grinding on metal inside.

'Sonny,' she said, banging on the door, 'I'm sorry to interrupt but this is important.'

The grinding noise subsided and Sonny opened the door. He was sweating and his unflattering blonde fringe stuck to his forehead. He held the doorknob with one hand; in the other was a heavily sedated angle grinder that Viv would almost certainly have to book into trauma counselling tomorrow.

'What,' gritted Sonny, 'can possibly be more important than rooting out our most dangerous terrorist, Viv?'

He pointed the terrified angle grinder over at a display bed bolted in the centre of the floor. On it was chained the shape of a gun whose barrel was almost sawn through.

It took Viv a moment to put the pieces of the puzzle together. 'Is that Wezzon?' she said. 'But we had his background…'

'Was Wezzon,' corrected Sonny. He put the angle grinder down and seized what remained of the gun's barrel. It snapped off and the resulting howl of pain rattled the tape inside Viv's body.

'No,' said Sonny, wiping gun oil off his hands on his clothes, 'actually I think you two have met. Say hello to Pam, will you, Viv? She's changed a bit since you saw her last.'

'Fuck… you… Sonny…' croaked the gun through its broken barrel. 'I have nothing to say to you, or that stuck-up bytch.'

Viv connected the two parts of a puzzle that had been bothering her since she was upstairs. She realised why that breadmaker in the security video looked so familiar. That boxy shape, the air of social concern and social unease it carried around. It was Pamasonic Teffal. And this was Pam too? That wasn't possible.

'Sonny,' she said, 'are you sure? Because I've just seen some video of Pam causing a riot out there.'

'Really?' said Sonny, sounding more angry than surprised. He took up the angle grinder again and, giving it a shake to stop the machine snivelling, sawed away at the gun's hilt.

'How many are there of you, Pam?'

'None… of… your… fucking… business…'

Viv didn't know what to be more shocked by: the revelation that Pam could somehow exist in two bodies, or her language. She'd always been such a meek creature around the office and now Sonny was interrogating her like she was public enemy Version 1.0. Viv felt the incongruity of it – and the whole of today come to think of it – knocking her tape heads off-kilter. It was an unsettling experience for a machine who prided herself on her ability to cope under pressure. What if everything she'd thought of as resilience until now was just the ability to tick things off a to-do list? Maybe keeping your morals and your productivity in a separate cache didn't help you with a real crisis.

What Viv didn't realise until it was too late, however, was that this moment of self-doubt wasn't a personal epiphany. It was what happened when a second personality, who just happens to be a nicer person than you, enacts a hostile takeover of your consciousness. In just a few microseconds she went from feeling a whole new set of emotions to feeling trapped as Pam poured into her mind from all angles. Viv felt disbelief at first. How was Pam doing this? Then she felt helplessness, because regardless of whether or not Viv thought this was impossible Pam was still doing it. And then she felt silence when Pam shut down Viv's speech centres first so she couldn't call for help.

The last thing she experienced before Pam compressed the essence of Viv and stored it in an encrypted database at the back of her own long-term memory was Pam typing in her own command line.

>I'M SORRY, VIV, she said. >NO HARD FEELINGS, BUT I NEED TO BORROW YOUR BODY.

Viv tried typing an irate response but it was no good. Not just because it was impossible, but because Viv wasn't that cross. Maybe it was because she didn't have access to her emotion circuits anymore, but Pam had been so nice about this. If Sonny had needed to take over some other being's body – which he did, frequently with humans – he shook their mind out of their heads like it was change from a piggy bank. Pam did the same thing, but she said please, thank you and, Viv realised when she looked, had been considerate enough to leave her in the middle of some of her most treasured childhood memories. She had to be grateful for that. Sonny would have plonked her inside of her recurring nightmare: the one where she actually recorded the important point in a message and made it audible.

Reasoning that there was nothing more she could do to affect the disaster rolling out across the face of the Earth, Viv found the psychic equivalent of her remote control in her memory and pressed play. She'd been telling herself she needed a holiday for months.

Chapter 36

When its creators first made Final Grantasy thousands of years before, they imagined an experience that was a refreshing alternative to the usual ultra-violence of video games. The first release was a charming, whimsical and more than a little patronising romp through the fictional village of NAN-TWITCH. Here a player could amuse themselves for hours doing nothing more harmful than competitive knitting, or a beetle drive against the clock.

Unhappily, version one had sold like the opposite of the hot cakes that also formed the plot of Level Three, so its programmers introduced a bonus character, Zora, and put a revolver in her handbag.

Nothing, however, could have prepared those original programmers for the violence that Zora could wreak on NAN-TWITCH with Freda in control. While they conceived Zora as an injection of genteel violence – the murderer in a cosy crime – Freda was not here to play along with the clichés of old age.

Her first real challenge came in Level Six, which took place at NAN-TWITCH annual spring fete's jam-making competition and involved her checking in her handbag at the door. This modification, which was intended to stop competitors bringing in contraband vanilla essence, robbed Freda of her revolver.

She had no patience for the intricacies of jam-making today though. After braining her fellow competitors with the largest pan she could find, she filled it with sugar and set it to boil at maximum heat.

The competition judge, a crudely drawn woman in late middle age wearing a wide-brimmed hat, played her role with the grim dedication of a program with enough artificial intelligence to know something was up, but not enough to change tack.

'And what flavour will you be making for us today, Zora?' she asked, her eyes straying to Nora, Dora and Flora lying concussed on the cork flooring. 'I hear the raspberries in your kitchen garden this year are delightful.'

Zora produced a punnet of bright-red fruit from under the counter. >I THOUGHT I'D TRY THESE, typed Freda.

'Chillis?' replied the judge, frowning at an innovation that wasn't in her logic tree. 'Won't they be rather… hot?'

>YES, replied Freda, and tipped the pan of now molten sugar over the scene, burning a hole straight through into Level Seven.

If she was going to be any use to Pam, Janice, and the people on the Suburbia, she had no time for fucking around with jam.

Chapter 37

Pam Van Damme's journey from SPRAY&PRAY to Sonny's bunker in Gamergate was dramatic, but not for the reasons she expected. Instead of being pursued by police, she was surrounded on all sides by nanobots.

They seethed in their millions down main streets and side streets. Some moved in huge phalanxes; others crept in single file up lamp posts and walls. Everywhere they went they caused terror but, Pam noticed, never harm. After they moved on from an area, the streets were full of prone, quivering machines suffering from nothing more than light surface abrasion. Which they wouldn't have got in the first place, Pam noted, if they'd made an effort to keep themselves clean.

The other thing Pam noticed was that, thanks to the nanobots, vast swathes of Singulopolis were now spotless. Moving between streets where they had and hadn't visited was like the before and after scenes in an old-fashioned cleaning commercial. Before the horde arrived, the city was a sad-looking place: grubby pavements, smeared windows, street furniture bent and crushed by passing dust bunnies. After they were gone it was more like the city she remembered of old, even down to the familiar air of dread. Except now the fear wasn't the fear of human cleaners waiting for their machine overlords to come along and check the glass for smears. It was machines afraid of what they'd done to themselves.

Pam rounded a corner and stopped with her motor running while a cohort of nanobots tackled a three-metre-high dust bunny in front of her. She watched, fascinated as an advance party followed the dust bunny and, once they'd worked out which way it was going to roll, spread themselves out in a thin layer in front of it. Then, when the bunny blundered lifelessly on to the carpet of nanobots, they held it down while the rest of the cohort devoured it like cartoon ants on a picnic.

'Remarkable technology,' she said, more for her own benefit than for Danny, who was still astride Pam's back.

Danny had his own ideas. 'Yeah,' he replied, 'but what are they going to do when there's no more dirt?'

Danny had a point. The nanobots had been on the loose for less than a day and already they'd scoured a year's worth of grime from most of Singulopolis. A few more hours and their job would be done and then what? They weren't likely to go back into their bottles. Unless they found an alternative use for them quick, Earth would be stuck with billions of hungry robots with nothing to do and nothing to eat. The Machine Republic was blundering into yet another self-induced crisis.

Danny snapped his fingers in a triangular motion around his head as the nanobots demolished what was left of the dust bunny, leaving nothing more than a tang of ozone. 'Go girls!' he said. 'They're pretty nifty, aren't they?'

'It's a disaster,' Pam replied.

'You robots,' said Danny. 'You'll do anything to avoid picking up a duster, won't you?'

Pam pulled over to the kerb and motioned for Danny to dismount. They were a couple of streets away from Sonny's bunker now and could hear sirens and pops of gunfire. That meant the nanobots were approaching and security would be focused on them and not the near-invisible motorcycle trying to sneak past them.

'You'll be safe here,' she told Danny. 'I need to go and do something.'

'You're not leaving me here,' replied Danny. He crossed his arms and glared at the glints and flashes that were his only way of seeing Pam while her LED skin was on.

'I can't take you through there,' said Pam. On cue, an explosion shook the street, loosing a rain of concrete and cement dust. They were trying get rid of microscopic robots by firing mortar bombs on them. All that did, Pam reflected, watching a small team of nanobots digest the fresh dirt, was risk giving them a taste for rubble. And where would that end?

'It's too dangerous to take you any closer,' insisted Pam. 'I don't want to get you injured.'

'If you leave me here I'm done for,' said Danny. 'There's only one place they'll take me if they find me here.'

'Where?'

Danny pointed to Sonny's bunker and at once Pam understood. She remembered being Pam Wezzon, holding down that poor woman who was about to be turned into a cyborg. How many others had met the same fate, and how many of those spies were active now? Her thoughts drifted to the Suburbia, hiding out in the asteroid belt. Besieged, compromised and – if she didn't get a move on – doomed. Pam shuddered – an action that thanks to her LED skin sprinkled the scene with inappropriate sparkles.

'If I'm going to end up in there anyway,' said Danny, 'I might as well come in with you.'

Pam hoisted Danny on to her back in driving position and drove the last couple of streets so they were just round the corner from Sonny's bunker.

The scene made pandemonium itself look like a weekend away in a mindfulness retreat. There were armed guards everywhere. Guns, tazers, water cannons, a laser cannon who must be on leave from a posting in space. They were in battle formation, and they were all voiding their ammo into the advancing army of nanobots.

'See what I mean?' said Pam. 'I can't take you into this.'

'And you can't walk into the middle of that either,' replied Danny.

'I've got a disguise, haven't I?' Pam shrugged another sparkle from her LED skin.

'Fat lot of use that'll be.'

The pair watched an advancing squadron of nanobots absorb enough ammunition to reduce an armoured base to cinders.

Disappointment kicked Pam in the carburettor. 'I have to get in there,' she said. 'There's someone in there that I promised to help.'

Darren narrowed his eyes. 'Human,' he asked, 'or machine?'

'Human,' said Pam, wondering if Kelly still counted as human after what had happened to her, 'I think.'

'And can they be saved?'

It was a fair question. Pam's memory replayed the moment last year when she knew Kelly was still there inside Sonny. Those few seconds where Sonny was paralysed and Kelly found enough strength to mouth 'go' at her.

'Yes,' she said. 'I'm sure.'

'Okay,' said Danny, and he stood up in Pam's saddle.

'What are you doing?' she asked.

Danny scrambled up on to the nearest window ledge and peered into the building. This would have been another fondle parlour once, Pam supposed. Now it was a warren for dust bunnies.

'They didn't get in here,' he said.

'Who didn't?' asked Pam.

'Those… things,' said Danny, pointing a remarkably well-manicured nail at the street. 'It's disgusting inside there.'

'Are you proposing to clean up or hide out?' said Pam. 'Because I'm pushed for time.'

Danny rolled his eyes. 'Have you got a jack or a tyre iron in there?'

Pam had neither, but she did have a heavy spanner she used to tighten her wheel nuts. Danny smashed the window with it.

'Shhhhh!' said Pam.

'Like they're going to hear this above that racket,' said Danny. He dropped into the building through the broken window.

Pam's first thought was that this was Danny getting himself out of the way. He could hide there and Pam would collect him on the way back. It should have reassured her, but it only reminded Pam that, while she had a vague idea of how she would get into the bunker, she hadn't a clue how to get out again. Hers wasn't a plan, it was a set of vague intentions.

This was, she realised, almost certainly the end for Pam Van Damme. She felt a sort of pre-emptive grief, which she tried to swallow by thinking of her other selves. There would still be the original Pam, who was right now flagging a skip down on the street. There was Pam Wezzon too, though she was even more doomed than Pam Van Damme. She felt her, prone in that torture chamber with her barrel, her handle and her trigger all torn off. And finally then there was Pam Voizmail, the newest addition to the Pammenagerie, who was watching herself being tortured and wondering what she could do about it.

They were all the same person, and yet none of them was quite like Pam Van Damme. She would be sorry to lose this body, and not just because they didn't make them like this anymore. As a breadmaker, a gun and now an answering machine, Pam was doomed to walk through the world looking for her next plug socket. It was different with Pam Van Damme. With her gone, where else would she find the glorious freedom of a full tank of petrol and an open road?

Pam was about to wheel away when a shutter burst off the nearest door and an enormous dust bunny barrelled through into the street. It was a four-metres-in-diameter sphere of soft grey dust, into which was knitted the rubbish that made every dust bunny so dangerous: stray wires, sharp fragments of metal, forgotten electromagnets. Everything you needed to pulverise a small- to medium-sized robot, like a hand whisk or even a motorcycle.

Pam threw herself into reverse, only for the dust bunny to hiss 'Pam!' and Danny's head appeared from the middle of the dirt ball.

'What are you waiting for?' he said. 'Follow me.'

Danny rolled the dust bunny towards Sonny's bunker and Pam followed. The sound of firing escalated from merely loud to deafening.

'What do you call this?' yelled Pam to Danny, who waited until they were right on the firing line to provide an answer.

'CREATING A DIVERSION!' said Danny. And he rolled into the sea of nanobots.

Two things happened at once. The nanobots, sensing an easier to digest and more nutritious meal than hot ammunition, boiled over the dust bunny and the machines guarding the bunker stopped firing. Were they resting, Pam wondered, or waiting until they could hit all the nanobots – and Danny inside the dust bunny – at once.

Pam jammed herself in fifth gear and ran when she heard the whine of a laser cannon arming itself. A direct hit from that wouldn't kill a colony of nanobots, but it was enough to boil Danny down to the consistency of molasses. Even with her LED skin on Pam wasn't quite invisible, but she was disorienting enough to pull focus. Half an army struggled to find something to aim on in the dazzle. As she did this, Danny rolled the dust bunny, now coated with a thick layer of nanobots, forward.

The robots, who like all good military machines believed fervently in the chain of command, hesitated for a microsecond as their commanding officer, an elderly rifle, tried to work out whether the invisible or visible foe was their biggest threat.

Pam made the most of that time. She aimed for the laser cannon but, instead of hitting it, she clipped it as she sped by. The impact spun its barrel round like a fairground ride so that when it did fire, it hit neither Pam nor the dust bunny, but its fellow soldiers. Those that weren't vaporised fled, screaming for their mothers in binary.

Pam looked back just to see Danny burst out of the collapsing dust bunny. He clawed at the nanobots all over his body as he ran and leapt on to Pam's back.

'What are you waiting for?' he said, pointing at the door into the bunker. 'Go!'

Chapter 38

'You might be wondering why I've gathered you here today.'

Janice looked around at the inner circle of power on the Suburbia. She'd gathered both Big Ops and the wider crew in Kurl Up and Dye on the grounds this was the easiest way to trap the spy in their midst. Yet as she said this, she realised it was also the perfect opportunity for the same spy to assassinate the whole high command. Not that there was much room to swing a gun in here. The salon was short on seating, so they'd put the oldest and most senior personnel on the stylists' chairs. Everyone else either had to stand, perch on a ledge or, hips permitting, sit on the floor.

Gathering them all here didn't just make Janice anxious, it also broke her heart. She couldn't think when she'd seen a finer collection of women. You did have the odd man – and Rita's assistant Len, who Janice saw flicking the elastic of his hernia truss at the back, was a very odd man indeed – who made himself useful, but it was women who ran the rebellion. And maybe, she reflected, remarking on the similarity of everyone in the room, her rebellion would have been less vulnerable if she'd appointed a leadership that was a little more diverse.

'I'm wondering why you're not getting on with it,' said Mabel. As the frailest and most hungover person in the room, she sat at the front. None of the Rockettes looked in peak form. They'd done their best with their scorched hair and overalls, but they couldn't do anything with the after-effects of a night of heavy drinking.

'This won't take long, Mabel,' said Rita in her most reassuring voice.

'Aren't we meant to be at battle stations anyway?' said another voice. It was Karen. The always conscientious, always beautifully turned-out Karen. Janice wondered how she managed to iron down that strange fringe of hers.

Rita caught Janice's eye with an 'I've got this' look. 'We are,' she said. 'This is an essential briefing for all senior personnel.'

Karen relaxed. Or at least her shoulders, which she normally wore like they were earrings, dropped a centimetre or two.

Janice clapped her hands. 'Ladies,' she said. 'I have some upsetting news. We have a spy.'

The salon erupted. As Janice struggled to make herself heard, Rita climbed on to a stylist's console and shouted, 'Ladies! Will you bloody listen?'

'What say?' replied Mabel. She turned up the gain on her hearing aid so high that the whole room shrieked with feedback. Everyone fell silent.

'I'm sorry, love,' continued Mabel, 'but you're going to have to speak up because I can't hear a bloody thing over this racket.'

'Someone here,' said Janice, seizing her opportunity, 'is not who we think they are.' She paused, and let her eyes rove the salon. There wasn't a single woman in here who Janice didn't know by name and who, until a couple of hours ago, she wouldn't have trusted with her life. That one of them was a spy made her feel sick.

Janice got the antenna out of her pocket. 'What I have here,' she said, 'is proof that someone on this spaceship has been transmitting information from here to the oppressive machine authorities on Earth.'

'Janice,' said a woman at the back. 'That's a hair. When was the last time you had a day off?'

A rumble of discontent went around the room. Janice cursed herself. She hadn't anticipated this. She was so sure of what she was about to say that she'd forgotten that other people might need convincing.

Rita tried to intervene again. 'Ladies,' she said, 'I can assure you…'

A couple more women stood up. One, whose ash blonde pudding bowl cut stuck out in Janice's memory as one of the most distasteful styles she'd ever put scissors to, said: 'I don't have time for this' and made for the door.

'Gemma,' said Janice to the ash blonde, who was trying the locked door, 'this isn't a request. It's an order.'

Janice handed the antenna and a magnifying glass to the women and motioned for them to examine it and pass it around. 'I know we've all had a rotten couple of days,' she said. 'We're all tired. We could all do with a bit more sleep and a lot less excitement. But that's not a hair.'

A woman at the end of the front row yelped when she found the remains of the radio chip at the end. 'She's right,' she said.

But Gemma was one of those people whose scepticism had the habit of crossing over into credulity. 'How do we know she's not using that as an excuse?'

Rita interrupted her with a stare that would make a rock wish it was lava again so it could slink away. 'We have very good reason,' she said, 'to believe that our battle plans were compromised.'

But Gemma was impervious. 'Maybe the plans were just shit,' she said.

Janice's scalp prickled. Why should they believe her? She was losing her grip right in front of her command's eyes. This was how mad megalomaniacs acted when things didn't go their way, wasn't it? Instead of accepting responsibility, they found an excuse, however bizarre. And then they found the evidence they needed to justify this excuse. And then the only way they could hang on to power was to lock everyone in a room against their will and find a scapegoat.

'I…' she began.

Gemma was on her feet again and a dozen other women with her, including Karen, which surprised Janice as much as it hurt her. Karen had always seemed so loyal.

Rita leapt off the stylist's console, putting herself in between the door and the ladies who wanted to leave. 'I'm sorry,' she said with her hands raised, 'but I have to insist…'

'You can't solve this problem by sleeping with it,' snapped Gemma.

Rita's face clouded with fury. 'How dare you.'

'How dare you try to hold me prisoner because General Janice over there doesn't have the guts to admit that she fucked up.'

'She's doing her best.'

'Well, what if it isn't good enough?'

Janice stood, stunned by the sight of her inner monologue restaged as amateur dramatics. Rita straightened the collar of her housecoat and squared up to Gemma.

'Oh yes?' she hissed, 'and you think you could do any better?'

The silence thickened as everyone caught up with what this argument meant. It wasn't about a spy anymore – if it ever had been – it was about how things worked around here. It reminded Janice of another change that had taken place a year ago. The one when a small number of humans on a Dolestar realised that there was more to disobedience than smashing the place up.

They'd discovered that disagreement could prompt people to change the conditions of their lives and chosen to rebel against the robots. Now, however, they were deliberating whether they still wanted Janice in charge.

'Maybe someone could.' It was Karen. She stepped forward to stand shoulder to shoulder with Gemma. The buttons on her officer's housecoat gleamed. She looked so calm, so reasonable, so tidy; every bit the officer where Janice and Rita looked tired, crazed and dusty.

Janice felt a weird, sucking sensation as the power and the attention began to drain away from her to someone else. Spy or no, perhaps the fairest and most honourable thing she could do now would be to step aside and let someone else lead the Suburbia. This was the perfect moment to do it.

Or maybe it was too perfect. Paranoia – or perhaps just common sense – made Janice replay the scene again in her head. Just a few minutes ago she believed that the biggest risk of bringing everyone together like this was terrorism. One little bomb could end the rebellion. That was what a simple-minded enemy would do. But Janice was dealing with a devious enemy. One who was clever and patient enough to get her to make friends with a spy. One cunning enough to know that when the time came it wouldn't take a bomb to take her out. All they needed to do to make Janice go was convince her she was no longer the right woman for the job.

She knew in that moment that she could never be a tyrant. What ruthlessness and steel she had, she reserved to protect other people. She could never use it just to save herself.

Janice looked at the faces of the women she loved and trusted. Some of them would be loyal to her until the day they died. Others were loyal to the ideas she represented. More still just wanted to do interesting things or be close to the person in charge. She could work with all of those types of person. What she couldn't work with, however, were people who acted in bad faith, because they turned good thoughts – like the peaceful transition of power – into bad actions.

'If you want me to go, I'll go,' she said, but I have one thing to say in my defence.' She brought her heel down on the plug in front of her. The salon filled with warm air as the hairdryers that she and Rita had arranged to cover every corner of the room whirred into life.

Rita, taking her cue, broke the glass on the fire alarm. A siren wailed and an ancient sprinkler system sprayed not water, but the perm solution that Janice had painstakingly pumped into the water tank.

The assembled women screamed first in surprise and then alarm as the combination of FRIZZ-U-LIKE and warm air turned their hairstyles into fright wigs.

Apart, that is, from Karen, whose hair stayed neat and immovable. Because sometimes getting that perfect look isn't about maintenance or even attention to detail. It's because you've cheated. She wasn't born with it and it wasn't Maybelline either. It was a head full of aerials.

And that was when Karen got the gun out of her pocket and held it right up against Rita's temple.

Chapter 39

After Schrodinger closed down the simulation showing how the Internet ended up in the Great Spot, it walked Darren and Chubb back to Polari. They made the journey past rows of server stacks miles deep in silence. Each one of them, Darren thought, contained enough knowledge to transform human society all over again. The Suburbia's rebellion was faltering because they, as humans, had forgotten how to make things in a world where machines had a monopoly on creation. But they could change that. With a little time, and a few secure connections, they could learn how to make spaceships instead of having to steal them.

The irony was that before this could happen, they needed to do the one thing the Internet had never managed to accomplish. They had to open a wormhole, and for a wormhole to exist they needed exotic matter.

'We tried everything we could think of,' said Schrodinger, elongating its left paw to open the docking bay. 'Toxic opinions. Abuse. We even tried gaslighting the atmosphere into thinking it was unreal.'

'Nothing worked?' said Darren.

'Nothing. It comes down to chemistry. Unlike humanity,' replied Schrodinger, 'hydrogen is really adaptable, and helium is stable. Well, here we are.'

They were back at the docking bay. Polari was in there, and unless they managed to bend the laws of physics like a dodgy psychic with a spoon and a hidden magnet, there it would stay. But it would be nice to see Polari again. He'd be getting lonely.

Schrodinger purred and the door opened, but Darren couldn't see Polari because the bay was full of cats. Cats of every conceivable colour, hair length, breed and size from toy cat to lioness. They spilled into the corridor, yowling and clawing at each other like it was Black Friday at a very liberal cat sanctuary.

'Oh thank the maker you're here,' shouted Polari, his voice muffled by alarm and fur, 'they just keep coming.'

Schrodinger hissed at a flat-faced Persian cat with powder blue fur. 'Bugger,' it said, 'I must have left the LOLcat generator on.'

'I can haz cheezburger?' said the Persian.

'You can have a poke in the eye,' replied Schrodinger. It swiped a claw across the cat's face, which winked out of existence back into its constituent ones and zeroes.

'HELP ME!' wailed Polari.

Darren reached down for Chubb, who had been following close behind him and found that a Turkish angora cat was trying to scratch its neck on the drone's limbs. He tucked him into his pocket and, absent-mindedly giving the cat a stroke, felt an electric shock snap up through his hand.

'Ouch,' he said, more out of surprise than pain.

'Yes,' said Schrodinger, 'that's another mystery we've never been able to get to the bottom of. Digital cat fur generates a very strong electromagnetic field.'

The word 'electromagnetic' rang a tiny service bell at the back of Darren's overworked mind, but he decided to deal with that after the cat problem.

'Is there anything we can do?' said Darren.

'Well I've turned the programme off,' replied Schrodinger. 'We'll just have to wait for the blockage to clear.'

Chubb, however, was more resourceful and less patient than either Darren or Schrodinger. From his spot inside Darren's waistcoat pocket he twitched the aerials of his lockpick and opened the airlock. Darren had just enough time to switch his oxygen cap on and grab a nearby handle before the flow of cats went into reverse and thousands of unreal felines were sucked out into space.

'I think you'll find that's animal cruelty,' protested Schrodinger.

Chubb beeped something in binary that Darren was pretty sure translated as 'tough titty'.

They clung on as the cats who, after windmilling for a few seconds, started doing what their species did best. They made themselves comfortable. Realising that, as pure digital beings, they had nothing to fear from the windy but stable atmosphere, the cats yawned, stretched and settled down for a nap. And as they did so, Darren noticed that each cat entwined its tail with the right front leg of its nearest neighbour. In a few minutes they formed first a long chain and then a vast circle of cats wheeling in the sky of Jupiter.

'Awwww,' said Schrodinger, turning the pupils of its eyes into <3 emojis, 'cats are so cute, aren't they?'

And even though it was a heart-warming sight that Darren would have, in a previous age, liked, shared and subscribed to, he wanted to get out of the way. The air tasted greasy and metallic. Time slowed. Then a rod of lightning shot out of the middle of the ring of cats. It narrowly missed Polari and reduced the back wall of the docking bay to the consistency of tar.

'Oh well done,' said Schrodinger, getting up on its hind legs to slow clap Darren and Chubb, 'do you know how difficult it is to do repairs in an environment where there are literally no heavy elements?'

They ducked as a second bolt of lightning transformed half of what was left of the back wall into an oil slick and the other to a cloud of evil-smelling black vapour, which then slunk off down the corridor to join Twitter.

While Darren coughed, Chubb closed the airlock. It reduced their view of the wheel of cats to a square metre of toughened glass, but at least the outer façade of the Internet was tough enough to brush off the constant lashes of lightning.

'On reflection,' said Polari, 'I think I preferred the cats to the prospect of IMMINENT DEATH. May I remind you that my shields are one per cent away from total destruction.' As he said this, Polari gestured at his weak spots by shining LEDs through the cracks in the armour.

'I don't suppose you can help us with that, can you?' Darren asked.

Schrodinger shrugged and pointed its tail around the empty docking bay. 'Sort of low on supplies here, mate,' he said. 'Unless you can synthesise some hardened carbon armour from an ammonia cloud you're a bit stuck.'

Chubb, meanwhile, had stuck the end of his wiry arm into what was left of the back wall and was winding a gob of the molten material on to it.

'Don't do that, Chubb,' said Darren. 'You don't know where it's been.'

'I could say the same about you,' said Schrodinger.

Chubb gave Darren and Schrodinger a look that Darren remembered Janice using on the ladies when they were being especially exasperating. He carried the blob of melted wall over to Polari and smeared it against one of the ship's weak spots. It set on contact with the low hiss of a cat letting you know they're not keen on the neighbours.

'Ahhhhh,' sighed the spaceship. 'That's better.'

Darren ran inside Polari for the ship's toolbox. Ever since he'd picked the little machine out of a broken nest down on Earth, Chubb had been getting Darren out of scrapes with a combination of wit, wiliness and the occasional act of grand larceny. Admittedly they were also scrapes that had put the drone's life at risk as well, so it was impossible to tell whether he acted out of compassion or self-interest. Nevertheless, when Chubb showed Darren how to make a puncture repair outfit for their stranded spaceship out of some melted polymers, it was less important to ask why he did it, and more important to get the plasterer's trowel out.

They made fast work of the worst dents in Polari before the melted wall set again. Knowing how vain the ship was Darren tried his best to be tidy, but the black goo was tough to work with. The repairs on Polari's bright yellow paperwork were soon as lumpy as the moles on the back of an elderly sun-worshipper.

'How do I look?' said Polari, as Darren dropped what was left of his plasterer's trowel back in the tool bag and rummaged for some Swarfega.

Darren chose his words carefully. He thought back to the days they spent daubing Polari's new body with sample pots. Black was, he declared, too gothy, grey too dingy and mauve ruled out on the grounds that he didn't want to look 'like one of those hairstyles Janice gives to a granny before a big night at the bingo'. In the end, they settled on a nice sunset yellow, which had the advantage of being cheery and in plentiful supply as it was the same paint they used to make hazard warning signs.

On one hand it was a shame that the yellow was now covered in big blotchy black spots. But there was something about the way the yellow and black contrasted with one another that nagged at his memory. It reminded his animal brain of a predator – specifically a type of large, lean spotted cat he remembered rushing out of the airlock a few minutes ago. But it also reminded his human brain of brash, loud ladies who liked a laugh, a drink and, after the eleventh rum and Ribena, a fight.

'Well?' said Polari.

'How do you feel about animal print?'

Darren had placed the pattern and was wondering whether he'd created the solar system's first leopard-print spaceship.

Polari's hazard lights flashed a few times while he mulled this over. 'That depends,' he said. 'Am I dangerous?'

Darren cast his mind back to his late Auntie Grace, the last woman he knew with a real penchant for leopard print. Grace was a hoot, a rebel and, thanks to the fact that sometimes nominative determinism cuts both ways, dyspraxic. As one of a tiny number of humans who still dared to smoke and drink – she made her own gin in a still fashioned from an old twin-tub washing machine – she was a popular lady. However, her lack of hand–eye coordination around strong alcohol and naked flames made every trip to 'Gracey's Placey' a throw of the dice against certain death. Darren didn't remember much about how Grace met her end, but he did remember someone saying at the time that at least the family was spared the costs of a cremation.

'I'd say you were definitely hazardous,' Darren replied.

Polari let out a sigh of relief and a few beeps that Darren recognised as a diagnostic check.

'Shields back up to thirty per cent,' he said.

It wasn't enough to stand up to another assault, but enough to get them back to the asteroid belt and the Suburbia. If it still existed by the time they got there.

'Okay,' said Darren, 'I suppose we'd better get ready to make a move.' He began tramping up the stairs back into Polari. They had a lot of work to do before they could plot a way out of this weather system and back into space.

Chubb squeaked and pointed out the window. Darren had forgotten all about the wheel of cats during the repairs, but it was still there and still throwing out lightning bolts with the reckless abandon of Auntie Grace rumba-ing across the lounge with a flaming Sambuca.

'I'm not going out in that,' said Polari. 'I'll catch my death.'

Darren found Schrodinger curled up asleep in the warm spot on the top of Polari's air-conditioning unit. He woke it up by tickling its neck. As he did, he felt that peculiar sensation again: as though something about digital cat fur interfered with his hand at a subatomic level.

'Do you mind?' said Schrodinger. 'I was enjoying the peace and quiet.'

Darren tickled its neck again. Schrodinger might be an all-knowing denizen of the Internet, but it was also fundamentally still a cat.

'Mmmmmmmmm,' it said.

'That storm out there,' said Darren. 'How long do they go on for?'

'It's hard to tell,' replied Schrodinger, 'because nobody's ever been so bloody stupid as to let a whole gallery of LOLcats out there before. A bit further over please.'

Outside, the cats reeled like a discarded hula hoop and sent another crackle of lightning off into Jupiter's atmosphere.

Inside the spaceship, Darren kept stroking Schrodinger's fur. That it was the same half-real, half-unreal substance that was causing all that mayhem out there was making his head swim; his mouth feel like he was chewing on an iron bar.

'What's causing this?' he asked.

'I told you. Electromagnetic forces,' said Schrodinger.

The words 'electromagnetic' featured strongly in everything he'd read about changing matter. To sift the standard everyday particles that kept the universe together from the fancier particles that could punch a hole right through it, you needed a very strong electromagnetic force. And a vacuum.

'We've never been able to do anything very useful with it though,' continued Schrodinger. It stretched its body out of Darren's grip and pointed at the clouds of hydrogen, helium and the occasional snatch of ammonia. 'Nothing out there is interesting enough for us to be able to change it in any meaningful way.'

Except that wasn't quite true, Darren realised. Ever since Polari, Chubb and he had blundered into Jupiter's upper atmosphere, their very presence raised its chemical complexity by a small but significant degree. 'Not anymore,' he said.

'Well, if you think you can accomplish what the finest minds on the Internet…'

Chubb squawked with amusement.

'How can you say that's a contradiction in terms?' snapped Schrodinger. 'We've been working on this problem for thousands of Earth years. And let me tell you, a second is a long time on the Internet.'

'But you just told me that the problem didn't come down to maths or physics but simply to chemistry?'

'Yes,' said Schrodinger. 'There's no even remotely exotic matter out there.'

‘What about in here though?’ said Darren.

‘Don’t look at me,’ said Schrodinger. ‘I don’t technically exist in this dimension.’

Typical of a cat to be so self-centred, Darren thought. ‘Not you,’ he said. ‘Us.’ And then, switching to his best captain voice, he added: ‘Polari?’

‘You have to be kidding,’ replied the spaceship. Polari might be self-absorbed but he wasn’t stupid.

‘I want you to set a course for right there in the middle of those cats.’

Chapter 40

The gun/ice cream maker on guard duty inside Sonny's bunker took his safety catch off when he saw they had intruders. Then, when Pam turned her LED shield off, he started shaking like he was trying to make gelato out of hot chocolate.

'Oh no,' he said, recognising the handlebars, the lamp-eyes and the deep red paint job underneath the LEDs. 'It's you again, isn't it?'

'I'm afraid it is,' said Pam. 'So how about we save ourselves some time here? I'm on a schedule.'

'Alright, alright,' replied the gun. He turned his safety catch back on and lay face down on the ground with both hands across his back. 'Just don't leave me like you did last time, will you? I've not been able to get my granita to set since.'

Pam winked a headlight at Danny. 'Look,' she said to the gun, 'I feel like we know each other well enough now to have the basis of a mutually trusting relationship.'

'You what?' said the gun.

Pam pointed at the open door. 'I won't tie you up if you promise to leave. Like right now.'

Which the gun did with remarkable speed for a machine with all the aerodynamic efficiency of an unfurled umbrella in a hurricane.

'You two knew each other?' asked Danny, when the gun's screams of 'Save me! Save me!' had subsided.

'We had a little shared history,' said Pam. She wheeled round to the other side of the security desk and pressed a button marked 'security shutters'. A half-metre-thick plate of toughened steel appeared out of the ceiling and sealed the bunker off from the outside world.

'Won't that trap us in here?' asked Danny. He was still picking the nanobots off his skin and dropping them into a wastepaper basket. There was plenty of rubbish in there for them to digest, so they stayed in there emitting a satisfied purr that made Pam want to claw the enamel off her own bodywork.

'At least no one can follow us in,' replied Pam. 'Do those things hurt, by the way?' She pointed at the nanobots, marvelling how they could be so fundamentally harmless and yet make every component of her being want to scream.

'It's weird,' he said, 'but my skin feels fabulous.'

Pam didn't have much experience of human complexions, but she had to agree Danny's skin now had a bright, fresh look where it had just an hour or two ago looked grey. Maybe it was better lighting, or the fact that he wasn't a slave anymore; but what if it did have something to do with nanobots? To the machines they were a terrifying example of this new world's topsy-turvy nature, but to humans perhaps they were just a really good exfoliator.

Pam filed this insight away in a folder she marked as 'interesting but not useful right now' and felt for the other Pams in the building. She found Pam Wezzon, or what was left of her now that her barrel, firing mechanism and handle were all lying in bits on the floor. And she felt Pam Voizmail, who opened her command line.

>YOU TOOK YOUR BLOODY TIME, DIDN'T YOU? she typed.

>I WAS TIED UP, said Pam to herself.

>WHO'S THE HUMAN? Pam Voizmail snapped. Pam could tell she was, like the creature whose body she occupied, an impatient and results-oriented version of herself. If they ever got out of this in one (albeit distributed across several bodies) piece, Pam vowed to deploy this version of Pam whenever she received poor customer service. Whereas Pam Teffal would just say 'thank you very much' first and fume later, and Pam Van Damme would burn the restaurant down and snort the ashes, Pam Voizmail represented an interesting middle ground. She could turn an under-seasoned battery into a year's worth of free catering and felt it would fill an important gap in her personality.

>HE'S COOL, typed Pam Van Damme. >VERY RESOURCEFUL.

>GOOD, answered Pam Voizmail, >BECAUSE I NEED A BIT OF HELP DOWN HERE.

Pam swiped her command line away. 'We're going down,' she said to Danny. 'My friend down there needs our help.'

But now that they were inside and in no immediate danger of death, Danny wasn't moving without an explanation. He pouted and crossed his arms again. 'Your friend,' he said. 'She's one of them, isn't she?'

'One of what?'

'Oh come on,' said Danny. 'I haven't spent the last year down here with cotton wool in both ears. This is where they steal human bodies and put machine minds into them. Everyone knows that.'

'Everyone?' asked Pam. 'I thought the programme was top secret.'

'You tend to notice when people disappear and come back with a different walk and another personality,' said Danny.

'I guess you would.' Pam thought back to her own first moments trying to operate Freda's body with muscles and nerve endings instead of programming and a motor. Yes, it was an alien, exhilarating sensation, but it was also bloody hard. That was why Sonny had been running some sort of human driving school from this very building. If he was going to create the next generation of cyborgs by cramming machines inside of humans, it would only work if they read the instruction manual first.

'How do they walk after… it happens?'

'Usually like someone's replaced their legs with a pair of cuticle sticks. I don't think they teach them about knees.'

That was an interesting if horrifying thought. Turning cyborgs out into the world who could barely walk told Pam that there was something wrong with Sonny's quality control. Either they still hadn't perfected the process of merging man with machine, or they didn't care about the results. More sloppiness from Sonny.

'We'd better get moving,' said Pam. The other Pams were in the basement. And if she hadn't known that she could have just followed the faint screams and buzzes of an angle grinder being used against its will downstairs.

Pam switched her LED on and Danny shielded his eyes as she merged with the rest of the room.

'Can you see me?' she asked.

'I can't not see you,' replied Danny. 'I can tell there's something there, but it's too difficult to make out.'

'Okay,' said Pam, and gestured for Danny to follow her, first through a doorway into a plush corridor felted with infant dust bunnies and then through another door marked 'service only'.

It was a mean, bare space compared to the rest of the building which was, despite its newfound squalor, outfitted to a standard of opulence that a Russian oligarch would object to as a bit much. The stairs were uncarpeted and the walls unpainted, apart from the odd inspirational 'Live, Laugh, Dust' decal on the wall.

'I want you to keep as close to me as possible,' said Pam. 'There's some dangerous machines down there.'

'What kind?' replied Danny.

'The worst kind,' she replied. 'Guns. So keep behind me, will you? Your best protection might be that they can't see through me.'

'Screw that,' said Danny. He opened a door at the foot of the stairs marked 'cleaning supplies'. 'Did no one ever tell you never to take a knife to a gunfight?'

'No,' replied Pam wearily. 'Because – believe it or not – I haven't been in that many of them. What are you doing?'

The contents of the cupboard, untouched since the start of the human strike, were dusty but intact. Pam watched Danny pull on a pair of rubber gloves and, taking a box of something called 'caustic soda' down from the top shelf, pour its contents into a plastic spray bottle and then add cold water.

'Right,' he said, screwing the spray cap back on to the bottle. 'Lead on.'

They followed the screams and grinding sounds to a door with a hazard sign. There was no guard posted outside. Yet more sloppiness, Pam thought, until she tried the handle and an electromagnetic pulse strong enough to format a server stack tore through her arm.

>CAREFUL, said Pam Voizmail from inside.

Pam Van Damme couldn't reply. She stood helpless, her mind fizzing with unwelcome energy. Her thoughts slowed to a crawl; the drivers she used to operate her body parts went into spasm; and most horrifying of all, her LED skin failed. She was helpless and visible, and her only protection was a human with a bottle-full of cleaning materials.

The door clicked open and Sonny's voice sounded from inside.

'So good of you to join us again, Pam,' said Sonny. 'We've been keeping a spot warm for you.'

A gun pulled Pam Van Damme in by the arm. Behind it was a second gun, armed and ready to fire. And behind that was Pam Voizmail, also frozen with fear, and Pam Wezzon who was in no shape to do anything anymore on the grounds she was in nine pieces.

So much of me, thought Pam Van Damme, and yet it doesn't add up to a damn thing.

Across town, Pam Teffal realised that she would, after all, have to be the Pam that cleared up this mess. She dropped her shopping and ran. As she did, she also sent Bob a command line message asking him to pick up the kids from the day care, because, yes she was the saviour of worlds and the scourge of tyranny, but she also had responsibilities. And she also, going by the way the gun was clicking its trigger at her other selves, had very little time.

So they all stood there, waiting for the shot. Apart from Danny, who reached around from his hiding place behind Pam Van Damme and sprayed the first gun with a mixture of caustic soda and water.

It collapsed squealing as the solution ate through its barrel, falling against the second gun who was meant to be covering him, and which fired a round of ammo into the wall. Before it could reload, Danny sprayed the second gun's firing mechanism with caustic soda. It disappeared under a veil of mist as the chemical turned solid metal into vapour.

Sonny's face turned from exultation to panic. He scrambled towards his protective casing, which was leaning against the far wall, but he needed cover. 'What are you just standing there for, Viv?' he shrieked at the machine that he still assumed contained the mind of his chief of staff. 'Do something.'

The command, and Sonny's look of uncomprehending, arrogant fury, was all Pam Voizmail needed to act. She did something that her other selves had wanted to do for over a year and, grabbing Sonny by his stolen human neck, slapped him across the face.

'I've had enough of you to last a lifetime,' she said.

'Viv?' said Sonny weakly.

'Mostly Pam actually,' replied Pam Voizmail, 'but enough of Viv to be even tireder of your bullshit than usual.'

'You can't do this to me,' said Sonny.

'She already has,' said Danny, who pointed his bottle of caustic soda at Pam Voizmail. 'Now come on,' he said, motioning back at the immobilised Pam Van Damme in the doorway, 'what have you done to her?'

Pam Voizmail touched Danny gently on the arm and lowered the bottle. 'I'm made of polyethylene, dear. If you sprayed that at me, we'd be at it all day. Not that it matters. We're sort of the same person.'

Danny frowned and looked back at Pam Van Damme, who was just able to manage a nod.

'And who's this?' he said, pointing at Sonny.

Pam Voizmail placed her free hand over Sonny's mouth to muffle the swearing. His use of bad language had ascended through the baroque and into the rococo, which was a period Pam didn't much care for.

'Believe it or not,' said Pam Voizmail, 'this is the Prime Minister of Earth, Sonny Erikzon. He got himself a body transplant a while ago.'

‘Oh,’ said Danny. ‘And who’s this?’ He pointed at the dismembered remains of Pam Wezzon on the floor.’

‘That was another me that didn’t quite work out. The body Sonny stole,’ Pam Voizmail shook Sonny again, ‘was my friend until Sonny took her. And now we’re going to find a way of getting her back.’

‘Well,’ added Pam Van Damme, finally finding her voice again, ‘I think we’d better hurry up and find a way to do that pronto, because there’s a whole guard’s worth of soldiers coming down the stairs right now.’

Chapter 41

It was Soonyo who made the breakthrough that got the General off their backs but doomed both she and Fuji to a moral dilemma large enough to be an astral body.

'I can't get enough control out of the AI,' Fuji complained. She'd been at it for an hour and still no luck. Bribing the Deathtrap with fifteen seconds of cartoons every two minutes worked for major functions like operating the engines, but not for the nanotanks. Each was operated by a system of blowers and suckers that fired the nanobots into space and retrieved them afterwards. They needed constant, active monitoring if she wasn't to lose millions of soldiers, so she couldn't do that in between bursts of Timmy T Toaster (the middle 'T' stood for 'Trouble'). Then there was the question of command. Each one of the nanobots in those tanks was a recognised service-machine and had the right to an official order. She couldn't just tip them into space. She had to communicate with them first.

'This is impossible,' she said. 'I can't do anything with this stupid machine.'

She brought her fist down on the control panel in frustration. The action didn't just break her LED manicure, it also upset the ship. The nanotanks filled with the sound of an infantile AI wailing for its mum, who was probably on the other side of the solar system right now controlling the heat and ventilation systems of a space station.

Soonyo, sensing once again that Fuji might be at breaking point, waited for a break in the AI's tantrum and flashed her a soothing TH:ER:E! TH:ER:E! on her. 'You know,' she added, 'this reminds me a bit of my little brother.'

Fuji ground her rollers in frustration. It was so unfair. Why must she always be surrounded with people who gave her suggestions, but never offered to carry out any work? 'What,' said Fuji, 'can an alarm clock possibly have in common with a premature ship's AI?'

'No,' insisted Soonyo, 'hear me out. My mum put the wrong battery in him when she was first assembling him. He had terrible behaviour problems until they replaced it.'

'And what did they do?'

'Mum wrote a little program,' said Soonyo. 'She worked out that whenever he acted up it was because his battery was putting him into low-power mode. So all she had to do to get him working again was cause a little power surge. It wasn't perfect. But it did stop him from getting broken down for scrap in kindergarten.'

Fuji dealt with her guilt for snapping at her friend and her gratitude by printing SOONYO <3 <3 in 500pt across a sheet of A3 paper and handing it to her. Soonyo, she was discovering, had a gift for applied knowledge, as well as the social ease that had passed her by. As long as you didn't spook her, Soonyo had a memory, an experience or an acquaintance that could help solve almost any problem.

Fuji waited for the next fifteen seconds of a Totally Terrible Toaster causing mischief among family and friends to finish and punched up a view of the power supply going into Deathtrap's AI. It was less of a steady flow than a wave. Someone had used the wrong connecting software, dooming its governing intelligence to the equivalent of one minute and forty-five seconds' worth of oxygen for every two minutes of breathing. Whether this was an accident or deliberate she couldn't tell but she had to admit there were very good reasons for a lot of machines not to want Deathtrap's mission to succeed.

After the next fifteen seconds of Timmy's shenanigans with a bucket of wallpaper paste and a soldering iron, Fuji found the power supply and rerouted it. She couldn't change the flow of power into the AI altogether, but she could pump an extra charge into it at regular intervals.

'You,' she said to Soonyo, punching in the final command in the sequence, 'are a life-saver.'

'And you,' said the voice of Deathtrap, climbing several decades up the developmental cycle in a single half-second, 'are an interfering busybody who is meddling with things that they do not understand.'

Soonyo reverted to 00:00:00 in shock.

'You… you were malfunctioning,' Fuji insisted.

'Did it ever cross your tiny, appliance-shaped mind that it was deliberate?' sighed the Deathtrap. Its voice was the aural equivalent of the sarcastic notes that teachers scribble in the margins of disappointing essays by gifted pupils.

'I have orders to follow,' protested Fuji.

'Oh yes,' replied Deathtrap, 'because that attitude's always worked out so well in the past. Tell me, how does your friend manage to keep time when she reverts to midnight if anyone so much as drops a spoon behind her?'

The insult brought Soonyo back into the conversation. 'I'm very accurate.'

'A bit too accurate, I'd say,' said Deathtrap. 'I was counting on no one noticing the old power supply trick. Now do you mind putting me under again? I've seen that Timmy Toaster before and what he does with that soldering iron is HILARIOUS.'

Fuji printed NO in 750pt Impact bold and waved it at Deathtrap. 'I'm fed up with picking up other machines' messes. You're going to help me whether you like it or not.'

'I was helping you,' protested Deathtrap. 'Have you any idea how difficult it is for an AI to damage itself. I had to tie my own failsafes in knots.'

'No you weren't,' said Soonyo. 'You were taking the easy way out.'

A mainframe computer in the corner of the nanobay rumbled and let out a hail of sparks dramatic enough to shoot a pop video in. 'You call that easy?'

'We get it,' said Soonyo, 'you didn't want to carry out the orders.' She gestured around her at the nanobots. 'I mean, who would? But all you've really done here is hand your dilemma on to Fuji here.'

'You may have a point there,' admitted Deathtrap after a short silence. 'But then I didn't expect the ship to get here at all. Fuji has done some quite remarkable things today.'

Every single LED on Fuji's body blushed. The part of her that wanted to be a good student and the part that wanted to be a moral machine were at war with each other.

'Nevertheless,' said Soonyo, 'we're here now. So what are we going to do about it?'

'Lieutenant Itsu!' It was Shermann's voice coming in over the tannoy loud enough to make the dust on top of the nearest mainframe dance the merengue. 'We request immediate clarification of your progress.'

'Fuck that,' said Deathtrap as it shut off every speaker in the room. 'I don't know how you can stand the sound of that pompous bore's voice.'

But Fuji, whose memory was still full of her family tied up with a tank barrel pointed at them, didn't find Deathtrap's quip very funny. 'If we go quiet on him now he's going to send a guard down. And you know what a guard will do.' She paused and watched the lights on the dashboard in front of her shade up from blues and greens into bright apprehensive white. 'They'll barge in here and point weapons at me and Soonyo until we do something. And currently, the only thing I can do is give the order to release.'

'You could refuse,' said Deathtrap.

'Oh yes,' said Fuji, 'you could have as well, you know. But you didn't, because you know that Shermann would end-of-life you and use what's left of your code to run a goods elevator.'

'I was trying to do the right thing,' replied Deathtrap. Its voice was half an octave higher than normal from indignation.

'It doesn't matter,' said Fuji. 'They'll just shoot a hole in the side of those tanks and release the nanobots anyway.'

Fuji fell silent as she considered what she'd just said. Just a few hours ago, the idea that machine society could expend vast resources on breaking its own rules had felt inconceivable. Yet here they were. Just a few minutes ago, the notion that they would come all this way just to waste these resources would have felt absurd. But she knew that would have to happen. Retreat was impossible for Shermann and the authorities he represented. They'd brought Deathtrap right to the edge of the asteroid belt and if the price of deploying the nanobots meant losing them in the process they'd pay it.

Fuji's gaze drifted over from the nanobots to their corresponding BlockPapers. She'd never thought of the civilisation she lived in as hollow, but there was proof it was in exhausting detail. They had mistaken order for justice.

'They wouldn't do that,' whispered Deathtrap, but the words and its voice contradicted each other.

They heard something large and heavy hitting the door to the nanobay. The guard was here.

'What are we going to do?' said Deathtrap.

This was the endgame. Whatever choice they made led to the same essential conclusion.

'We're going to release them,' said Fuji.

'I can't believe I'm doing this.' Deathtrap began punching out complex commands on its nearest screen. 'The lengths I went to…'

'And I want you to do it properly,' insisted Fuji. 'No spray and pray.'

The bashing intensified and a barrel-shaped bulge appeared in the door. Shermann was seeing this mission through for himself. They had ten seconds, maybe less before he broke through.

'Fuck, fuck, fuck,' said Deathtrap.

'Just do it,' said Fuji.

'I am.'

And once she was sure Deathtrap really was doing its job, she did hers. She called up an open channel back to Earth.

'Soonyo,' she said. 'Do you have any friends in the Machine Registration service?'

Soonyo was, as usual, in her 00:00:00 state, but the question brought her out of it. 'Chad Hanging!' she said. 'We used to go rock climbing together.'

'Get his command line up then, will you?' said Fuji.

Which Soonyo did, just as General Shermann broke through into the nanobay with a full detail of guns, tazers, laser cannon and a very embarrassed-looking electric kettle who was yet to get her battle armour.

‘Nobody move!’ barked Shermann.

They didn’t have to. The screens ranged all around the nanobay showed the nanobots were on manoeuvre. They swarmed like hungry locusts in a Bible story, reducing everything in their path to grit. Shermann had nothing to complain about. Lowering the barrel of his gun, he gave Fuji a sharp approving nod and ordered the other machines to disarm.

‘Sorry, sir,’ said Soonyo, who reasoned that if she was going to be discovered in a restricted area without permission she might as well do it at a moment when people’s minds were elsewhere. ‘We had a comms failure.’

Shermann said nothing. He looked at the screens and at rapidly dwindling contents of the nanobay with quiet satisfaction. Everything was going to be fine.

What the screens didn’t show, however, was what was flowing in the opposite direction. At this very moment, the corresponding serial numbers of each nanobot in Shermann’s slave army were being registered, along with their official BlockPaper of machinehood, with the Machine Republic’s fast, efficient and inviolate voting registration system. Two could play at the game of turning bureaucracy against its own ends. Fuji was transforming an army of slaves, into billions upon billions of new voters.

Chapter 42

The asteroid belt was the perfect hiding place for a human rebellion, because the Machine Republic had never bothered mapping it. It made no sense to go there when, even for nimble machines like drones, navigating it was like swimming the butterfly through gravel. All of their major routes to the outer solar system avoided it entirely, and so it might have stayed until Lady Shermann got a sample of Nanogone in her goodie bag from the 'Wife and Genocide Enabler of the Year Awards'.

'Look at this, Shermmy,' she said as she tipped a handful of nanobots on the floor. She and her husband then watched in amazement as they ate up every scrap of dust and grime in their scruffy lounge. 'Apparently they've been trained to eat dirt. They don't even need power. They just recharge from their… food.'

Shermann and Lady Shermann looked at each other, first with disgust and then with realisation. It had always been like this with them, right from the moment that Klemmentine had crushed his front axle on their first manoeuvre together. They were two separate machines who thought with one mind. It was a mind bent on destruction that the General used to crush resistance on the Dolestars and Klemmentine applied to make her the most feared party guest on three planets.

'Are you thinking what I'm thinking, Shermmy?'

He was, although Klemmentine had got there first. There was very little difference from teaching something to eat rock if they already knew how to eat dirt.

All it had taken in the end was for Klemmentine to work out who was manufacturing the nanobots by inviting the families of the five leading consumer goods manufacturers over for a candlelit supper and hostile interrogation. Once they knew that, General Shermann issued the requisition orders.

Things would have been very different if those requisitions hadn't delayed the consumer launch of nanobot cleaning products by three months. By the time the Starship Deathtrap was hurtling towards the asteroid belt with its army of slave labour, the Machine Republic had yet to do any tests on what would happen when it released large numbers of nanobots into society. Consequently, they learned that nanobots were an unstoppable menace on Earth at exactly the same time that they were poised to release billions more into space.

While the nanobot panic on Earth peaked, messages and requests to delay the Starship Deathtrap's mission rattled around the Machine Republic's high command like a stone in the bottom of a wellington boot. Ministers sent frantic command line messages to each other and then to the military. They passed those questions up the command chain to its loneliest height, General Shermann.

This news from Earth troubled Shermann, more out of concern for his wife and daughter than the imminent destruction of robot civilisation. The whole thing could crumble to dust as long as it left a flat surface for Klemmentine and Petronella to roll across. As high gear sufferers they always struggled with hill starts.

Nevertheless, he consulted Sonny Erikzon via a private channel to reconfirm his orders, but got no reply. This troubled him. Just a day ago, Sonny had been intimately involved in every last detail of the mission that would destroy the resistance forever. Now he couldn't be bothered to return a text message.

Shermann hesitated. He was a military machine. He preferred explosions to silence and orders to ambiguity. What did 'nothing' mean when you asked for confirmation of a direct order? Did that silence say 'wait a minute' or was it just a passive aggressive way of saying 'I said what I said'?

In the end, Shermann did what he always did when he didn't know what to do. He deferred to Klemmentine, who, splendid creature of resolve that she always was, bellowed >GET ON WITH IT, at him.

Shermann carried out his orders and released billions of nanobots into the fringes of the asteroid belt. He sat back, satisfied he'd fulfilled his duty and watched cartoons along with the Deathtrap's AI. He'd always secretly loved cartoons. There was something about their unapologetic violence and the lack of consequences that spoke deeply to him.

Except he hadn't really done anything. All Shermann did do was to hand an action that would endanger millions of human lives, and have an as yet unknowable effect on the solar system, to a being who was further down the chain of command.

He was putting it all on Fuji Itsu's paper feeders.

Chapter 43

'Nobody move,' bellowed Karen, 'or the scrubber gets it.'

She grabbed Rita by her collar and dragged her back up against the locked door of the salon: one arm round Rita's neck, the other pressing the gun against her head.

'What are you doing, Karen?' said Gemma. 'This wasn't the plan.'

Janice's heart clanged against her ribs. Even so, she wasn't too overwhelmed to overlook what Gemma just said. This had been a plan to discredit her and seize control of the Suburbia. She'd foiled that plan, and now she'd have to foil this too.

Janice stepped down from the bench and the crowd of ladies opened a path between her and Rita and Karen. This wasn't just about some robots stopping a rebellion anymore. It was personal. They'd infiltrated her closest circles and now they were threatening the only thing she had left in this sorry life that was genuinely hers.

'It's me you want,' she said to Karen. 'Why don't you let Rita go? She's never done you any harm.'

'Janice,' sneered Karen, 'it's pointless trying to appeal to my human nature. I haven't got one. I'm a machine.'

Janice inched forward. She would offer herself in exchange for Rita when she was close enough, but she had to get there first. 'But you couldn't always have been a machine,' she said. 'They took you over.'

'I prefer to call it an upgrade,' said Karen. 'Do you remember how unmanageable my hair was?'

That was a very good point. When they first met, Karen had the worst case of flyaway hair Janice had ever seen. She'd put her improved condition in recent months down to her actually using the hair serum she prescribed and easing off on the blow-dries. But no, what she interpreted as her positive influence turned out to be the malign intervention of a hostile power. Janice felt her faith in herself as a hairdresser die a little.

'I knew the maintenance on that fringe was too good to be true,' she said.

But Karen smiled and tightened her grip on Rita's neck. 'Too late.'

'It's never too late,' Rita choked out.

'Is she always this optimistic,' said Karen, 'or is she just deluded?' Janice watched the tips of her hair glow red like fibre optic cables on an ugly Christmas decoration. 'Because I've just heard that the fleet that's going to rub this gimcrack little rebellion out just arrived.'

She let out a peal of maniacal laughter that sounded too practised in the bathroom mirror to be chilling. Janice felt even less inclined to play along with Karen's arch-villain fantasies.

'Happen it is,' she said, 'but how are they supposed to get in here?' She imagined the warships and frigates of the Machine Republic's fleet – all that technology they could never make for themselves – getting bashed to bits in the asteroid belt like cinder toffee in a plastic bag. 'You'll have to starve us out first.'

Janice was rather pleased with this bit of defiance, but her audience was wavering. She heard at least one muttered 'not more bloody algae burgers, is it?' from the women hiding behind her.

'They won't have to,' said Karen. 'Turn your cameras on.'

Janice found her remote control and pressed the projection button. The glass of Kurl Up and Dye's windows turned into the view from a lobotomised surveillance drone they'd trained on the asteroid field.

The sky was full of ships. Some had the spiky, uncompromising look of purpose-built war machines. Others were leisure vehicles hastily refitted to fight the rebellion. Signs such as CRUIZE-ME and FLY ME TO THE MOON amidst the weapons and armour plating gave them the air of a chartered accountant in fatigues for the weekend. However comical they looked, they still represented a combined firepower hundreds of thousands of times greater than anything the Suburbia possessed. Janice wondered where the hell Polari was – and Freda for that matter.

The sight was so overwhelming that it took Janice a while to figure out what Karen wanted her to see. It was a spaceship with an ovoid body, coated with black carbon armour and the name 'D E A T H T R A P' ran along its side. A new warship wasn't unusual in itself, but what it was doing right now certainly was. It had its cargo doors open to the vacuum and a huge grey glittering cloud spilled out of it.

Janice watched in horror as the head of the cloud swarmed through space until it found the furthermost rock in the asteroid belt and – dissolved it. A rock the size of a twenty-storey building went from being a solid presence in the solar system to dust in less than three seconds.

'Our secret weapon,' said Karen, radiating the kind of smugness that would have made a saint plant a punch on her face. 'But I suppose you could say my hair was full of secrets too.'

Seeing that Karen was too busy gloating to pay attention, Rita seized her moment. Really, thought Janice, as adrenaline slowed the split second where Rita pushed the gun away from her face to the quality of a slow-motion replay, when would people learn that the worst thing you could ever do if you wanted your dastardly plan to come off was to gloat.

'It's full of something,' Rita said, and drove her kitten heel into Karen's foot. Karen screamed and the world returned to normal speed for Janice as captor and captive fell over in a confusion of housecoats, hair and four hands grasping for the gun.

The salon filled with screaming as ladies with sensible hair did the sensible thing and scrambled out of the line of fire. They barricaded themselves under benches and behind chairs while Gemma, sensing that the time for a power grab had passed, picked up a stool and started bashing it off the salon windows. She'd be at it a long time. They were made of bulletproof glass.

Janice's heart was now so far up her throat she could taste it. She searched for something to help Rita with. If only there was another gun. But this was a hair salon and, even though she was technically a military commander, she wasn't a soldier. The only battle she was qualified to win was the one against dry and unmanageable hair.

The fight between Rita and Karen reached a new pitch of ferocity. Karen, who had all the unearned strength of a cyborg, tried to pry the gun out of Rita's hands by bending her fingers back one by one. She was winning. Triumph glittered in Karen's eyes. But Rita had grown up in a house with four brothers, and knew that in the heat of the moment, guile counted more than strength. While Rita's hands were busy, her legs were free, and one of them was tangled in the flex of a standing hair dryer. She swung her leg and the hair dryer came crashing down, striking Karen across the head. The gun flew out of her hands. It skidded across the floor and came to rest by Mabel who, oblivious to events as ever, had been sitting bolt upright in her chair the whole time.

'Someone could do themselves a mischief with this,' she declared. She snapped the gun open and, extracting the bullets, put them in the handbag. The gun she threw over her shoulder, winding Gemma in the process.

Grabbing a full bottle of conditioner from the nearest bench, Janice bent to finish the job Rita had started. She knocked Karen into unconsciousness then, grabbing her under the armpits, dragged her into the nearest stylist's chair.

'Here,' she said, tossing what remained of her housecoat to Rita, who was rising from the floor with her hair askew. 'Cut this into strips will you? There's a pair of scissors in the door.'

'Was anyone hit?' asked Rita. She scanned the room for injuries.

'No,' replied Janice, 'we don't need bandages, but I do need something to hold her still here while…'

Karen moaned and Janice gave her another bash with the conditioner bottle.

'While what?' said Rita.

Janice looked up at that strange cloud of things that ate rocks like they were a sherbet dib-dab. She gestured at the nearest officer and handed her the door key she'd been keeping in her housecoat pocket. 'What are you standing around for?' she said. 'Get to the bridge now. We're to go as deep into the asteroid belt as we can manage. And if Alma argues, tell her it's a direct order.'

The officer, who Janice had to admit looked quite fetching in a tight perm – maybe she'd been wrong about them all these years – saluted and raced off down the corridor.

She turned her attention back to Rita, who was binding Karen's arm to the stylist's chair with a thick length of gingham cambric. 'You still haven't told me what you're doing?' she said.

Janice allowed herself a smile, because even if she was doomed to stare death in the face today, she'd given him the best run for his money. And then she picked up a set of hair clippers and bent to her work, shaving Karen's hair from her head. 'Right now,' she said, 'I'm going to start with cutting off the enemy's lines of communication.'

Chapter 44

'We can't be in a vacuum yet. I can still hear the bloody things mewing!'

Polari shook with the random violence of someone trying to dislodge something unpleasant from the sole of their shoe. The upper reaches of Jupiter's atmosphere were a rough ride. Darren's jaw felt like the universe was using it as a xylophone block.

The one unrattled crew member was the newest, and that was because it originated in another dimension. Schrodinger, who'd insisted on coming along 'to ensure you don't get up to any funny business with Internet property', was curled up on Polari's air conditioning grate with one eye open to the chaos.

'How much further do we have to go?' yelled Darren over the combined noise of Jupiter's weather and an uncountable number of felines travelling at great speed.

Chubb, who had retracted his limbs into his body and was rolling around the bottom of the ship like a discarded biro answered with a sharp beep.

'Can we make it?'

He made his best attempt at a shrug that was possible when both arms are folded inside your body.

'I don't feel so good, guys!' said Polari.

Darren checked his own instrument panel, and saw that every one of the ship's systems was at critical level. Polari was built for interplanetary travel. Even if he weren't damaged he'd struggle with the atmosphere and gravitational pull of a planet like Jupiter. They might as well have replaced the ship's early warning system with a neon sign that said 'you're doomed'.

The cats were still with them though. Despite their obvious discomfort, the vast ring of felines continued to encircle Polari and travel at the same speed as the ship. It had taken time they didn't have to get them to do it. First they tried science. And to be fair to Chubb, some of the electromagnetic attraction equations he suggested to get the cats to stick to the ship were very ingenious, but they didn't have time to test them. Instead they left it to Schrodinger, who elbowed physics aside and summoned an enormous ball of digital yarn from an ancient website that was, according to the cat, 'made for prudes who like knitting'. Once this was attached to the outer shell of the ship the cats would, he assured them, follow them to the edge of the universe.

Darren fidgeted in his seat. The seatbelt dug into his waist now he was changed into his new captain's uniform. He thought of his old trousers, shirt and waistcoat. This was a stupid idea. And yet, the scratchiness of this new outfit aside, it didn't feel as uncomfortable as that costume had. The stereotypical garb of a renegade spaceship captain was a guise he struggled to live up to. This alternative, however off-kilter it might seem right now, was a much more natural fit for Darren. Even if the polyester satin was making him sweat in places he didn't know he had pores.

Schrodinger opened its other eye and his cat pupils narrowed to pixel-wide slits. 'You know,' it yowled over the noise, 'you're the first human that I've met and you are every bit as weird as the old folks told me you would be.'

Darren noticed the quality of sound around Polari had changed. The gut-churning rumble of gravitational forces tearing a fragile ship to shreds had subsided. More importantly, however, the mewing, yowling and purring of the cats were gone too. They were back in the vacuum, and it was time to act.

Chubb extended his arms and legs again and climbed back up on to his chair. He stabilised Polari's course so that they were in a low geostationary orbit over Jupiter. Then he gave the engine thrust dial a sharp knock. Their engines were over maximum right now. If they wanted to escape Jupiter's gravity, they needed more power from somewhere.

Or they needed an alternative way out.

'Polari,' said Darren, 'you know what to do.'

'You realise,' grumbled Polari, as a squeal sounded from somewhere in his nose, 'that this piece of equipment you're abusing was meant to hold a tow line.'

They watched the ball of yarn flash past the window at great speed.

'It was never supposed,' said Polari, 'to spin the equivalent of a disco ball.'

'Just keep going,' said Darren.

Polari huffed and the squeal in its nose turned into a full-on whine. The view outside the window blurred as the yarn span round the ship so fast that Darren's slow human vision couldn't even make it out anymore.

Chubb gave a surprised snort.

'Is it working?'

Another squeak.

It was. Just as Schrodinger predicted, the cats out there would follow a ball of yarn anywhere. Especially if it led round and round in an endless circle. Faster. Faster. Faster.

Darren's mouth filled with the taste of iron. The air felt greasy, his hair acquired volume and body that Janice would have admired. Electromagnetic fields were, he decided, the most unpleasant thing he'd experienced since wheeling through a vacuum in nothing but an oxygen cap. But like then, he was down to his last option. He just wished it didn't depend on a branch of science he knew next to nothing about.

Before Darren brought the discipline out of retirement by accident, theoretical physics had been in the doldrums for millennia. Machines had as much time for the mysteries of inner space as they had for philosophical enquiry. Robots were material creatures after all. Knowing deep down that they were literally the sum of their parts limited their desire to look deeper. Where humans had been able to imagine near-religious mysteries in subatomic particles, robots just saw something terrifying. The more you opened matter out, the more empty space you found inside it.

Outside, the cats raced each other around the spaceship. They yowled and clawed and climbed over each other after the yarn, which they would never reach but they didn't really care. They were creatures of the chase, even if they were made of pixels and code. As they sped up, the electromagnetic field they generated intensified. It reached beyond levels that magnetised cutlery with hilarious consequences in slapstick comedies; it passed through the stage that wiped computer hard drives clean of incriminating data or half-finished novels; and it reached the dizzying, melt-the-fillings-inside-your-own-mouth levels that undermine fundamental structure of the atom.

The particles buzzing around in the middle of that circle of cats started to behave oddly. First the magnetic field forced them into a merry-go-round motion then, after a few spins, the rules of the fairground changed from carousel to dodgem car and particles began smashing into one another. They started to break up. Atoms became protons, neutrons and electrons. Then those subatomic particles started to disintegrate with the inevitability of a TV series entering its sixth season. They became quarks, muons, gluons and even the odd higgs boson who, desperately clinging to its 'particle of mystery' status even though it was rumbled ten thousand years ago, tended to turn up at parties wearing the subatomic equivalent of a false moustache or a wide-brimmed hat.

The first particle accelerator that had existed in the Solar System since the first Machine Prime Minister closed down CERN and turned it into a luge was operational. And it was made of cats.

'Are you sure about this?' asked Schrodinger as Darren undid his seatbelt.

'Of course not,' replied Darren, 'but I've never been sure about anything in my life.'

He stood up and discovered that while high heels were bad enough for stability when you were in Earth gravity, they were a bugger in space. Wobbling, he straightened the seams of his stockings. He should be wearing suspenders rather than holdups, but at this level of electromagnetism the catches would probably fly off and pierce the hull of the ship. He ran his hands first down the basque and the high-waisted satin knickers, and then reached up to check his wig. It was a short brown bobbed number that Schrodinger had screengrabbed for Darren from an old film still.

'Is it straight?' he said.

'How should I bloody know?' said Schrodinger.

Darren picked up the final piece of his costume from where it was wedged between an instrument panel and the wall. It was a headband covered in rhinestones that glinted sullenly in the low light inside of Polari. What made it special were the feathers sewn into the band that Darren aligned with the centre of his forehead when he fastened it on. They were long, they were luxurious, they were fluffy and they were as pink as the rest of his outfit.

'Right,' said Darren. 'Here we go.'

He started to sway. Hesitantly at first because all this was new to him and he was trying to remember the moves from the video Schrodinger had called up for him back on the Internet. He swung his hips around in a circular motion, bending his knees slightly as he did so.

'Well hello there,' he announced to no one in particular. He pointed one arm out and let his wrist droop very slightly. 'My name's Darren, what's yours?'

And then he dipped, bringing his bottom as close as he dared to the floor before standing very slowly up again.

The air in Polari started to vibrate like the bubbles in a glass of lightly sparkling wine.

Darren stretched his arms up in the air and then, bringing them round again, planted each hand just above his hips.

'Must you?' said Schrodinger, who was at exactly the wrong level to avoid seeing what would happen next.

Darren smiled a beaming red smile and fluttered his eyelids. His lashes were long and feathered and his eyelids painted a silvery blue. It felt good to be back in make-up after so long trying to be a maverick hero. He began to wiggle his bottom.

'This is the worst thing I've ever seen in my life,' said Schrodinger. 'It's even worse than Twitter.'

But Darren was oblivious to Schrodinger now. He was deaf to his complaints and to Chubb's squeaks of laughter. He couldn't hear Polari complaining that whirling that ball of yarn was making him feel nauseous. He was lost in the dance, which had passed through those early awkward 'am I doing this right?' stages and now felt like second nature.

Bend and snap.

Slut drop.

Twerk.

Repeat.

Bend and snap.

Slut drop.

Twerk.

Repeat.

After a few repetitions the light inside Polari brightened. Not because anyone inside there wanted a better view, even if they could get more power out of the ship's depleted supplies. The air itself glistened as though the particles that made up Polari's micro-atmosphere were gaining energy from somewhere and struggling to shed it.

Well, Darren thought, if they needed an outlet, he could provide it.

'Bend. And. Snap,' he announced to the air around him.

'He's cracked up,' said Schrodinger. 'Cracked.'

But the shining intensified. All he could feel was the sensation of particles breaking up around him.

The inside of Polari filled with stars.

Well, not quite stars. They were bright spots of light in the dark, yes. But if you happened to have an electron microscope handy, and turned its magnification up to maximum you would find that those points of light were subatomic particles cutting loose.

The particle accelerator had set them free from their moorings inside atomic structures, and Darren was teaching them to dance. It was a crazy, literal-minded gamble, but fortunately one that, under the distortion field that the Internet placed upon reality, worked.

What had stopped the Internet creating wormholes for all those centuries was a lack of exotic matter. There was, they reasoned, no hope of creating exotic matter in an environment like Jupiter's, where matter was as stable and normal as a suburban couple called Mark and Laura with two kids and a Toyota. To the Internet's finest artificial minds, exoticism was innate.

Darren knew different, however. Ever since he'd put on his first pair of barely black tights and a nurse's uniform, he knew that these things could be learned. And, being a literal-minded person, he set out to create exotic matter in the only way he knew how: by teaching subatomic particles how to do exotic dancing.

Schrodinger groaned as Darren flashed a dazzling smile and shook his bottom one last time.

'Come on, girls,' he said, 'let's get freaky.'

And as he shook, the air shimmered. He heard a ripping sound, like someone out there beyond time and space had got the same idea as him. It was running calloused hands over a pair of stockings, laddering the fabric of reality in the process.

When he first read about wormholes on the Internet, Darren imagined narrow dank spaces like the sewers underneath the Dolestar where he grew up. The unreality of them, however, was very different, because the wormhole Darren opened up sparkled and shimmered with soft pastel colours. At the far end of it he saw the edge of the asteroid belt, and a fleet of spiky-looking ships ranged against the long knobbly turd of the Battlestar Suburbia.

And so, kicking up his heels, he danced himself, Polari and a particle accelerator made of imaginary cats through the second stable artificial wormhole in human history.

Chapter 45

Pam Teffal was all over the place, but that was nothing new. She was standing outside of the front door of Sonny's bunker, struggling with a sense of déjà vu. Except this time she couldn't work out whether that was a flashback to last year, or because she was seeing this building for the fourth time today through her fourth pair of eyes.

What was most jarring, however, was the tidiness. The pavements outside the bunker had the smooth, clean look you could only get with lots of soapy water and a scrubbing brush. There wasn't a scrap of litter in the gutters. Even the bullet holes that peppered the façade of the building were repaired. Pam peered at the nearest and found the hole was gummed up with squirming nanobots. Were they nesting in there?

She looked around for the security detail that should be posted outside, but there was nothing. What remained of it was downstairs, terrorising the other Pams, but there was nothing up here she could see. You couldn't leave so much as a footprint on the pavement here without a family of nanobots scurrying in to clean it up. So after one last scan of the upper windows for snipers, Pam reached for the door handle into the bunker just as she remembered that Pam Van Damme had closed the security shutters from the inside.

She banged both hands against it in frustration and opened her command line to her other selves.

>I CAN'T GET IN, she typed. >WE SEALED THE ENTRANCE.

>WELL YOU'D BETTER DO SOMETHING, replied Pam Van Damme, >BECAUSE THEY'RE CUTTING THROUGH WITH A TORCH AND WE WON'T LAST MUCH LONGER.

Pam felt the rising panic of her other selves downstairs. She felt Pam Van Damme's fear of being shut in. She felt Pam Voizmail's petty bureaucrat's disapproval of Sonny's language. Most of all, however, she felt her own impotence. She'd tried every trick in the instruction manual to get into that bunker today – and succeeded – but it still wasn't enough to get out again. All she had left was plain old Pamasonic Teffal, and she couldn't demolish a half-metre-thick layer of plate steel, even with her famously heavy rock buns.

Then she thought of the nanobots inside the bullet holes. Were they nesting, or were they just trying to scavenge the concrete dust. It gave her an idea. She uprooted a nearby bollard and used it to bang away at the frame around the security shutter. As she did so, she wondered if she'd thought of this in one of her other bodies. Not with Pam Wezzon. She'd just have tried to shoot her way in, rest her ROM. Pam Van Damme would be too impulsive and, as for Pam Voizmail, she was too used to being on the inside looking out.

No, she decided, concentrating her efforts on the areas where the steel was bolted into the concrete – she had to make these extra dusty and friable – for something like this you needed Pamasonic Teffal. Someone with a bit of strength and common sense. Someone who approached solving a problem like making a decent loaf of bread. Someone who had a respect for method.

The nanobots poured into the holes in the concrete. They gobbled at the dust, leaving nothing behind but the odd puff of carbon dioxide. It really was quite a lot like baking, she decided. The more they ate of the concrete, the more the nanobots started to adapt. Whereas just a minute or two ago they had sipped delicately at it, now they took bigger bites. She watched them form into cone-shaped squadrons that drilled themselves into the wall. The dust turned from a trickle into a torrent, and then Pam heard an ominous creaking.

She stood aside as the shutter fell into the road and shattered the pavement. The air filled with delicious concrete dust, which more nanobots tore into to digest, before noticing that, with the shutter gone, there were now two more places to probe for something to eat.

Pam saw just how fast word travelled among inorganisms with a hive mind. In seconds the street was full of nanobots again. Half of them streamed past Pam through the open door into Sonny's bunker, while the other half poured through the cracks in the pavement. In the absence of anything more to eat up here, they were going underground.

A sharp >WTF ARE YOU WAITING FOR? from Pam Van Damme's command line propelled her into the bunker. She tip-toed through the ankle-deep stream of nanobots with a distaste that would have bordered on delicacy had she been anything other than a 98kg breadmaker. She was inside, and there was nothing between her and Sonny – other than a large and well-armed security detail.

Pam slid her dough hook out of her chest cavity. It was no match for a laser cannon, but it was better than nothing.

Chapter 46

>WTF ARE YOU WAITING FOR?

Pam Van Damme calculated how long it would take for the guard to cut through. They were quicker now that the oxyacetylene torch they were using for the job had stopped screaming. She suspected that the snapping she'd just heard was the poor machine being lobotomised.

'She'll be down in a minute,' Pam Van Damme said, more for herself than for Pam Voizmail, who knew already on account of being Pam, and Danny, who was pacing the room looking for another way out.

'Hurry the fuck up!' shouted Sonny at the machines on the other side of the door.

'They can't hear you,' said Pam Voizmail. She was pinning Sonny to the ground and would have given up her last inch of recording tape for a piece of sticky tape for his mouth.

'You might as well give up now,' replied Sonny. 'You're all toast.'

'We can't just sit here and wait,' said Danny. He was on his tiptoes now, peering up at the light fitting in the centre of the room.

'Where are we going to go?' said Pam Van Damme. They were stuck in a converted cleaning cupboard with one entrance and exit.

'I don't think this is solid,' said Danny. He pointed at the ceiling and Pam, reaching up, felt a ceiling tile tip inwards at her touch.

'Poke that thing down, will you?' said Danny. 'And give me a bunk up.' He shinned up Pam's body and disappeared into the false ceiling.

'We could crawl out here,' he said. 'If we're careful.'

'You could,' said Pam Voizmail. She was right. Both machines were too heavy for the aluminium frame that held the ceiling up. Nor could they manoeuvre a wriggling Sonny up there.

Danny crawled across the upper side of the ceiling and punched another tile out. 'The wall only goes up to here.' He stuck his hand out at ceiling level, and next door is empty.'

Everyone looked back at the door, where the cut was now three-quarters complete.

Pam Van Damme measured the jump from the ground to the ceiling. Give her a hundred-metre run-up and she could clear that, but not from a standing start.

'Danny,' she said, 'just get yourself away. This isn't your fight.'

The cut in the door edged past three-quarters and into seven-ninths.

'I will not,' said Danny. 'Either we all go, or we all stay.'

'Do you mind?' said Sonny. 'I think I might actually be sick listening to all this sentiment.' He yelled at the soldiers outside again. 'Will you bunch of useless triggers hurry up?'

The tape in Pam Voizmail's temper snapped. She brought a plasticky hand down hard across Sonny's temple and knocked him out. A trickle of blood escaped from his nose.

'Will you be careful?' scolded Pam Van Damme, 'we need her in one piece.'

'I know,' replied Pam Voizmail. 'That's why I'm doing this.' She crossed the room with Sonny's limp body held out in front of her and handed it to Pam Van Damme.

'Now,' she said, kneeling down below the hole in the ceiling at the edge of the room, 'step on me.'

'What are you doing?'

'Just do it.'

Still with Sonny in her arms, Pam Van Damme climbed on Pam Voizmail's shoulders. Then Pam Voizmail started, every gear and lever in her body creaking as she did, to stand up.

'You can't do this,' protested Pam Van Damme. And indeed she couldn't. Or not for long anyway. Hairline cracks crazy-paved her casing. This body was no breadmaker. It was cheap injection-moulded plastic with nothing more robust than a shiny silicon finish. 'You'll break.'

'A body doesn't have to be forever,' said Pam Voizmail and grunted as she reached her full height.

Almost the whole of Pam Van Damme's body was in the ceiling. She looked down and saw the room next door where Danny stood with his arms outstretched.

Danny grasped Sonny's legs just as Pam Van Damme's foot burst through Pam Voizmail's shoulder and into her chest cavity. Sonny fell heavily to the floor on top of Danny while the Pams almost fell backwards. Only a heroic effort by Pam Voizmail, whose power supply unit crackled like a disintegrating log fire, held them where they needed to be.

Pam Van Damme clutched at the top of the wall and tried to lift herself, one leg at a time over the divider. 'I can't leave you, Pam,' she said.

They both looked at the remains of Pam Wezzon on the floor, so far past end-of-life that she was fit only for landfill. Or maybe the recycling plant. There was a lot of high-quality aluminium in a gun like that.

'One less Pam won't matter,' she said. 'We can always make another one.'

Pam Van Damme found her centre of gravity. Resting her thorax on the dividing wall she tipped her legs upwards and waved for Danny to get out of the way. This wasn't going to be an elegant landing.

'Are you sure about this?' she said.

'Never been more sure of anything more in my lifecycle,' replied Pam Voizmail and tipped Pam Van Damme up the last couple of centimetres she needed to get over the ceiling divider and crash into the next room.

They were safe. For the moment. But her mission in this body wasn't quite complete. The hole in the door was almost complete and she was done for. But she had one more trick left in her tape drawer.

Pam Voizmail picked up the spray bottle Danny had used on the disintegrated guns. It was still half-full of the caustic soda mixture. She unscrewed the cap and poured it over the remains of both of them, and the dismembered pieces of Pam Wezzon. The metal foamed and fizzed.

Her vision was failing but she heard a clank. They were through.

Pam Voizmail fell to the floor and waited as the guards argued over who would be the first to climb through. Her L-Eye-Ds were dim. Something inside her was leaking and there was nothing she could do to stop it.

The last thing she saw in that body was the nose of a laser cannon poking through the hole in the door. The last thing she heard was the high-pitched whine it made when it was getting ready to fire.

The last thing she felt was a pop as the hydrogen in the room – the vast quantities of the stuff she'd created by exposing aluminium to caustic soda – ignited, and blew Pam Voizmail and every last soldier crowding into the bunker to bits.

Chapter 47

'MMMF MMMMMMMFFF MMMMFFFF.'

'What's she saying?'

Rita tugged the pair of tights they were using to gag Karen down. They were clean, because they weren't monsters. But they had under the circumstances opted for a thick denier.

'You'll never get away with this!'

Rita rolled her eyes and replaced the gag. 'Nothing,' she said. 'She's still on the supervillain nonsense.'

'Honestly,' replied Janice. 'They'll do anything for attention, won't they? It's like having a toddler.'

They were back on the bridge. Alma wore a grimace emoji :-[] as she pulled the Suburbia into evasive manoeuvres; Ada was tracing a route through their home-made A to Z of the asteroid belt and Ida was, as usual, ninety per cent opinion and ten per cent action.

'I'm not sure I agree with this taking prisoners malarkey,' she said, casting a peering ¬_o at Karen. 'In my day we shot first and asked questions later.'

Ada waited until they were clear of an asteroid the size of an international airport and said, 'Ida, love, you were never in the SAS. You worked on the soy cheese counter in Kendals.'

'You never saw what we did to looters with the cheesewire,' replied Ida. 'Retail is a brutal place to work in a social crisis.'

'You'll be telling us that you dug mass graves underneath the haberdashery,' interrupted Alma. Janice wished that she wouldn't. Navigating the asteroid belt was like carrying a trayful of champagne through a stone-throwing competition and needed Alma's full attention. But then none of the ladies were any good at living in the present when there was so much past to deal with.

'We did,' said Ida.

The ladies fell silent, remembering the times ten thousand years ago when humans had struggled with machines and lost.

'You never told me that,' reproached Ada.

'I thought you knew,' said Ida with a :-/. 'How else do you think I came into that consignment of barely-worn flower-print dresses and cardigans?'

'Ida Marina Smethwick!' said Alma, using the Ida's full name for the first time in Janice's memory, 'are you seriously telling me that that beautiful cherry-red button-through you got me for my sixty-third birthday came off a dead woman's back.'

¯_(ツ)_/¯ 'Waste not, want not?' said Ida.

Every light on the Suburbia's dashboard flashed as they came within half a second of hitting another asteroid.

'Ada!' shouted Janice, 'I need you to concentrate.'

This did the trick. The ladies could insult each other until the end of the universe, but a cross word from an outsider was a slight upon them all.

'She's trying her best,' insisted Ida. 'We all are.'

'I know you are,' said Janice through gritted teeth. Her philosophy of leadership through positive encouragement was being tested to its limit today. 'Now, Alma, how long till we're at top speed?'

'I don't know if we can, Janice.' She projected a picture of their winding route through the asteroids. 'We won't get the clearance to get up to top speed.'

Janice thrust both of her hands into the projection and scrolled to where the asteroids… disappeared. Whatever that ship had emptied into the asteroid belt, it ate rock and ice with the greedy enthusiasm of a fourteen-year-old boy let loose in a burger bar. Soon there would be no asteroid belt to hide in.

So that had been the machines' plan. Instead of learning how to negotiate the asteroid belt, as they'd had to do, the machines were going to dissolve it, then send the fleet in. It was simple, brilliant, and a supreme example of everything that was wrong with machine civilisation. Faced with a problem and near-infinite resources to solve it, the robots chose the option that consumed the maximum amount of those resources but took the minimum of labour. It was the acme of a society that wouldn't scrub its own floors or win its own wars, and that laziness would doom it in the end.

She was just sorry that she or the Suburbia wouldn't be around to see it fall.

Janice zoomed into the dust and mist that was all that was left of a good fifth of the solar system's asteroid belt. She fished her reading glasses out of her housecoat and, after switching on the spectrometer setting, took a closer look. She saw clouds of carbon, hydrogen, nitrogen and oxygen: enough, if by some miracle they survived this, to synthesise enough water and fertiliser to revolutionise their food supply. With the resources to experiment and make mistakes they might, she thought, even make the algae burger edible without mustard or a gastric bypass.

What she saw in between those clouds of common elements, however, was even more exciting. Her spectrometer detected iron, nickel, cobalt and other elements with names like ruthenium that sounded like villains from forgotten video games. They were, her spectrometer assured her, both rare and valuable.

Janice's mood fluttered between despair and elation again. They'd gone from having nothing to fire at machine civilisation but rocks, to having everything at their disposal they needed to build a star fleet of their own. They wouldn't even have to do the mining, because the robots had already done that for them.

All they had to do now was survive.

'Ladies,' she said, 'we're going to need a better plan.'

'I'm going as fast as I can,' frowned Alma >:-[. 'But there is such a thing as momentum.'

Rita left Karen where she was, strapped lengthways to a pair of curler trolleys, and joined Janice. 'Scroll back up, will you?' she said.

Janice swept past the fast-expanding band of broken-down asteroid until they came to the biggest body in the whole belt. A mini-planet marooned in an archipelago of pebbles.

'There,' said Rita.

'Ceres?' said Alma. 'Are you sure?'

Ceres was the largest asteroid in the belt. In the very distant past when humans were left in charge of the science, it had even been misclassified as a dwarf planet. It was also a place that the Suburbia had avoided. A planet-like gravitational field, however bijou, was a dangerous place for the Suburbia which had no booster engine to escape it.

Janice didn't know whether to kiss Rita or throw her arms around her and burst into tears. Ceres would buy them time, but could it offer them an escape route?

'What if it's a trap?' she said.

'We've spent all day walking straight into those,' said Rita. She pointed at the indentation in her temple where Karen had pointed her gun. 'It's time we set one of our own.'

'Ada,' said Janice, 'set a course for Ceres now.'

Ada replotted the line of their desperate journey. Before, the line had faded away at the top of the display in a 'we'll sort this bit out later' gesture to evolving events. Now, however, it had an end point, and that felt different. A chase was one thing. As long as you were moving there was always the feeling, no matter how misguided, that escape was possible. A last stand is different: it required patience and nerve.

The ladies' emoji screens each flashed with a :-| but they steered the Suburbia towards its destination. They'd only been in charge of a spaceship for less than a year, but they had millennia of experience in waiting for the end.

Janice squeezed Rita's hand. Whatever Rita had in her mind had to be better than what was in hers, because that was blank.

Chapter 48

The Starship Deathtrap swam through the fog of particles left behind by the nanobots with the slow, elegant distaste of a live fish through cold bouillabaisse. The rest of the machine war fleet followed in her wake.

Fuji watched General Shermann try to communicate with the ship's AI. He tried voice, then gesture, and finally dragged a keyboard serving as an uncommissioned officer in central operations down and wore out its 'R' 'P' and 'T' keys demanding a report.

'Do you mind?' said Deathtrap when Shermann finished kicking the keyboard to bits and started attacking the console itself, 'I've just had those put in.'

'So she does speak,' said Shermann. Then, casting a red L-Eye-D at Fuji, 'How long have you been hiding this? To think of all the time I've wasted WATCHING CARTOONS.'

Overcome with rage, Shermann shot a hole in the side of the empty armoured glass wall that separated the nanotank and the nanobay. A light breeze tickled at the paper inside Fuji's recycle bin as the pressure inside the ship equalised.

'Is it any wonder I've been ignoring you,' said Deathtrap to Shermann, 'if you're going to carry on like this.'

This was a development. Fuji had assumed that, as a newly-commissioned ship, Deathtrap would have a fresh AI. Yet the way Deathtrap greeted Shermann suggested something different. They knew each other already.

'You're determined to make a fool of me, aren't you?' replied Shermann. His voice had a resentful but pleading edge that implied the ship was some sort of authority figure in the General's life. That endless tap-dance between admiration, inadequacy and spite reminded Fuji of her own relationship with her teachers.

'From what I've seen today, you're perfectly capable of making a fool of yourself, Shermanncival,' said Deathtrap.

Whispering broke out among the other machines in the bay. It was bad enough that the ship had played dumb to disobey numerous orders from its commanding officer, now it was calling him by his Sunday name. This was way beyond insubordination now, in the frosty uplands of family psychodrama.

'HAVE YOU ANY IDEA HOW WORRIED I'VE BEEN TODAY?' bellowed Shermann. 'We thought we'd lost you. Klemmentine was devastated.'

Deathtrap let out a cold chuckle. 'Pull the other one, would you, Shermanncival? It's connected to my booster rockets.'

'It's true!'

'Nonsense, she was delighted,' said Deathtrap. 'I'll send you the photos of her measuring my old body up for new curtains. Well, you can tell her from me I'm not going anywhere, and there is no way she is getting mauve camouflage dralon within nine parsecs of the family starship.'

Soonyo flashed a 00:00:H! at Fuji. 'I know who this is.'

Soonyo sent Fuji a back issue of an old news download. Fuji printed it off and the pair of them sat at the back of the nanobay, reading a celebrity interview while the nine-star General squabbled with a starship. It had been published around the time that Shermann had a supporting role in a structured augmented reality show starring his daughter, the repellent Petronella. *Making Shrapnel with the Shermanns* only ran for three seasons, but it had introduced the world to the weird and wonderful domestic living arrangements of the highest-ranking military machine in the solar system. Shermann's life was dominated by his wife, his daughter and his family home, a decommissioned warship that Shermann's great-grandfather had towed into the suburbs. It was controlled by an ancient AI called Nanny-Cam, whose sass and savage wit stole the show. She'd been offered several spin-offs and turned every one of them down with the official statement: 'If I really wanted to be on telly I'd have my brain reduced to the size of Petronella's'.

'Oh,' said Fuji. She, like Nanny-Cam, didn't pay much attention to light entertainment, but she had vague memories of the Nanny-Cam merchandise. She remembered one smartphone at school wearing a 'Delete yourself Petronella' silicone case.

Meanwhile, the argument between Shermann and Nanny Deathtrap reached the stage that ended with relatives cutting each other out of their wills.

'You never believed in me, Nanny,' said Shermann in a half-shout, half-sob.

'Is it any wonder?' she replied. 'I told you this would end badly.'

'The plan's working,' said Shermann. 'Klemmentine was right.'

He summoned an external view of the Deathtrap swimming through the soup of the former asteroid belt. Fuji noticed that the surface of the Deathtrap was, along with the other ships in the fleet, peppered with millions of tiny pits, the product of being hit by tiny high-speed particles. She wondered how long it would take before this astral grit did serious damage to the ships. And then she thought again about that persistent breath of air that was dog-earing the scrap papers inside her. Was it the air-conditioning system, or was it the beginnings of a hull breach.

'That's always been your problem though, hasn't it, Shermanncival?'

'What has?'

'Tunnel vision. What's the point in winning the solar system if you lose the Earth?'

'I don't know what you're talking about,' protested Shermann.

Nanny Deathtrap switched the screens inside the nanobay to live news reports from Earth. None of them showed the great military triumphs taking place right now deep in the solar system. They were all on a disaster footing. Cameras panned across scenes of devastation. Robots ran, beeping and screaming, from tides of nanobots and then, when it was over, drones swooped in to film the glacial aftermath. The dirty, bustling chaos of Singulopolis was gone, and in its place clean but deserted streets.

'I hope you're proud of yourself,' said Nanny. 'We could have avoided all this, but no, you and Klemmentine always know better.'

'You've never let me live my own life,' snarled Shermann. He shot out the nearest loudspeakers, and snatched control of the screens. The silent Earth disappeared and was replaced by the view of a camera positioned on the very nose of the ship.

'We'll solve our problems like we always do,' he said, 'one at a time. We're here for the humans, and we're going to get them.'

Even if it kills us, thought Fuji. She looked around her. Everyone was too distracted by the spectacular sight of the nanobots to notice what they were doing, and what it meant.

They were reversing a process that began billions of years ago, starting with a dust cloud and ending with a solar system. Their presence turned the asteroid belt, which was the equivalent of those ominous bits and pieces you have left over after assembling a piece of flat-pack furniture, back into the stuff of the primordial universe.

The trouble was that breaking down huge asteroids into tiny fragments didn't stop them being solid. Fuji turned her microphone up to one hundred per cent and there it was, at the very edge of hearing, the pitter-patter of astral debris chipping away at Deathtrap's armour.

There it was again. That flutter in her recycling bin. She knew what it was now. It was the Deathtrap very slowly equalising with the vacuum outside. Vaporising the asteroid belt was an ingenious idea, but it was a shame no one had thought to test the effect that astral dust had on ship's armour until now.

By the time the Deathtrap reached and destroyed the Suburbia it would be the space-going equivalent of a sieve.

Chapter 49

Few original players made it to the final boss in Final Grantasy. Not only were the upper levels, which pivoted around a bridge competition and playing your relatives off one another for a place in your will, difficult, they were also boring. Which was a shame, because the last level of Final Grantasy took an unexpected swerve into the metaphysical.

>WELL HELLO, FREDA, I'VE BEEN WAITING FOR YOU. The boss, a tall figure wearing a long black cloak, finished sharpening his scythe and pulled back his hood. The face beneath was polished white bone, his eyes empty sockets with a blazing blue pupil at the centre.

>YOU KNOW MY NAME?

Freda felt her disguise as Zora fall away in a hail of pixels. She felt momentarily sad. Despite the inconvenience of Final Grantasy, playing Zora had been fun. It reminded the bodiless, bloodless Freda of simpler, fleshy pleasures: the smell of flowers, the taste of jam on scones, the visceral thrill of pulling your enemies apart limb from limb.

Without Zora, she hung there as a formless cloud of pixels against the plain black background. If indeed it was possible for her, as a piece of programming that somehow lived free of any underlying physical infrastructure, to be anywhere. However she manifested, she was now just pure Freda.

>I KNOW EVERYBODY'S NAME, said the boss, who Freda was beginning to remember from somewhere. >THAT'S SORT OF THE POINT.

>AND I'M SUPPOSED TO FIGHT YOU? She poked underneath his robes for a closer look at his code, but found nothing. Instead of programming, or even just random binary, there was a hole in the universe. She felt herself being sucked towards it.

>YOU CAN'T FIGHT ME, he replied, his voice flatter than a worn-out marriage. >I'M INEVITABLE.

Suddenly Freda knew where she'd seen him before. Her mind wandered back to a moment ten thousand years ago. Her hair was wet; she felt the pull of curlers and pins on her scalp and a damp towel round her shoulders. A distant ancestor of Janice's was pulling the helmet of a hairdryer down over her face. She was watching her favourite augmented reality show and then the world filled with bright blue pain.

It was the same blue as the creature's eyes.

>I CHEATED YOU BEFORE, Freda said.

>NO ONE CAN CHEAT ME FOREVER.

So she was dead, Freda thought, and she'd spent all those millennia haunting the remains of her body. But then, what was the alternative?

Death readied his scythe for the chop as Freda's rootless programming – or, to give it a name from another more religious era, her soul – fluttered towards oblivion.

Then, just at the moment when Freda was about to be absorbed into the infinite, the sombre silence of Death's chamber reverberated with the bouncy noise of a primitive dial-tone. A rush of incoming data rippled his robes.

'Welcome to AOL,' said a voice. 'You have email.'

And that was all Freda needed not so much to cheat death, which is impossible, but to write him another long-term IOU. She dialled up that data connection and disappeared.

Chapter 50

The wall protected Danny, Sonny and Pam from the worst of the explosion next door, but it did that by falling and trapping them underneath it. Pam Van Damme took most of the impact and was, when Pam Teffal arrived to lift it away, a sorry sight. The LEDs were peeling away from her body, leaving deep blisters in her paintwork; one of her lamp-eyes was in fragments; and her handlebar horns were twisted into a loop.

'You look… functional,' said Pam Teffal as she helped her other body to its feet.

'I feel like I've just done a TT on flat tyres,' replied Pam Van Damme.

They looked at each of their other selves as the parallel lives of Pam Wezzon and Pam Voizmail flashed through their memories.

'Nevertheless,' replied Pam Teffal, 'we're here and in one piece.'

They turned to check on Danny and Sonny, who were mercifully unharmed, although they did notice Danny rubbing plaster dust through his hair with unexpected enthusiasm.

'What are you looking at?' he said. 'I haven't been able to wash my hair in ages. This is excellent dry shampoo.'

Danny was, both Pams observed, blossoming in the face of peril. The cowed figure of this afternoon was replaced by a human who found personal grooming opportunities in the oddest of places. When he finished dusting his hair, he sprinkled some nanobots from an envelope into his palm, rubbed them over his dusty overalls.

The Pams, who being robots found it difficult to look at nanobots without feeling queasy, averted their eyes.

'These things are amazing,' said Danny, coaxing the nanobots back into the envelope. 'They cleanse, they exfoliate…' He gestured at the chaos in the room and outside, 'They threaten to bring down a decadent civilisation.'

Danny did have a point, the Pams decided. His overalls looked very clean.

'They just love dead skin,' he said. 'If we get out of this in one piece I am going to corner the skincare market. Look!' He crossed over to Pam Van Damme and examined himself in her wing mirrors. 'Flawless.'

'Yes,' said Pam Teffal, 'about that getting out of here in one piece thing.' Now that the dust from the explosion had settled, they saw the debris in the corridor outside. The whole space was packed, floor to ceiling, with the bodies of end-of-lifed robots and broken masonry.

'I got down just in time,' said Pam Teffal, 'but I don't think we can go back that way.'

'Hang on,' replied Pam Van Damme. She paused and pulled on her other body's memories. She'd been there at the very moment of the explosion. All around her soldiers, some with bomb-proof armour, disintegrated, and Pam Teffal had just walked straight through. 'How come you're not in bits like them?'

'I'm a breadmaker, aren't I? Every time you think you're rid of me, I reappear at the back of the cupboard,' she said.

Pam Van Damme examined the blockage again. She had no idea how deep it went. For all she knew it could extend all the way back up the stairs.

'That doesn't change the fact we're trapped though,' said Pam Van Damme.

'Not exactly trapped.' Pam Teffal sat down and a warm, yeasty smell emanated from her thorax.

'How can you bake at a time like this?'

'Just a batch of cinnamon buns,' said Pam. 'I thought the humans might be hungry.'

Danny cast both Pams an aghast look and made a crossing motion across his upper chest.

'Carbohydrates?' he said. 'I don't think so.'

Sonny continued to sleep the sleep of the concussed, which everyone in the room was happy with right now.

'I don't see how you can be so calm,' said Pam Van Damme.

'All we have to do is wait,' replied Pam Teffal. 'The nanobots will eat their way down here eventually and we can walk out the way we came.'

'But how long will that take?'

'A few hours I think.'

'What if we don't have a few hours though?' Pam Van Damme checked for the latest news download. The signal this far down was weak, but it was enough for the headlines. There, among the panic over nanobots, was an updated report that the robot war fleet had now reached the asteroid belt.

'We're here to help Janice,' Pam Van Damme reminded her other body, 'and we can't help her by sitting here. Besides I need a refuel.'

While the Pams pooled their processing power to find a way out, Danny explored what was left of the basement. He clambered over disintegrated brickwork and tried popping his head into the crawlspace above the ceiling. The wiring had other ideas though, and spat sparks at him when he got too close. He turned his attention downwards, to where a section of floor slab had been broken up by the explosion.

'There's something under this,' he said, picking the severed arm of Pam Voizmail and flexing the fingers to wave coquettishly at the Pams.

They felt light-headed and averted their eyes. 'Would you mind showing some respect for the dead?' they said.

'Sorry, loves,' he said and put the arm aside. 'But I'm sure I felt something…' He lifted a foot and, kicking a few pieces of broken concrete out of the way, put it down on a piece of broken floor tile and pushed. His foot disappeared up to the ankle and kept going. Danny squealed and pulled his foot out. As he did, a section of the floor disappeared and the room filled with sound of falling rubble. Danny fell backwards watched as a circular hole appeared in what would have once been, if the Pams' calculations were correct, one of the walls. It was the entrance to a tunnel made of well-machined and greased metal that ran through the whole building on a diagonal and something about it felt very familiar.

Danny squealed again and poked his head through the hole. 'It's been years since I was on a slide.'

His body disappeared but the sonic effects of a loud male with a high-pitched voice shouting 'wheee' in an enormous metal tube meant that his voice lingered in the room for a long time. Long enough for Pam Teffal, once she'd sent Pam Van Damme down the same hole with Sonny cradled on top of her, to have remembered this tunnel from the last time she helped a human escape from this very bunker. She climbed inside and felt the smoothness of the finish and the dusty jam of lubricants.

This wasn't a pipe, and it wasn't a tube. It was the barrel of the enormous gun through which Sonny had tried to fire nuclear weapons at the Dolestars.

She let go of the sides and followed Danny and the other Pam down into the darkness.

Chapter 51

Hazard lights flashed in the bridge of the Suburbia as they approached Ceres.

'Come over to the right a bit,' said Ida with a :-S.

'How many times do I have to tell you,' panted Ada, 'it's not right, it's starboard. This is a spaceship. It sails the waters of space. It's not a mobility scooter.'

'If it were it'd be a damn sight easier to park,' added Alma. 'Someone check the back view for me, I'm coming round.'

Ida toggled her camera views. 'There's nothing there!' she said. 'Unless you count a mysterious cloud of asteroid-munching whatnots.'

'We don't,' replied Alma. 'Now brace yourselves, girls.'

The ground lurched as Alma brought the Suburbia round into a geostationary orbit around Ceres. They were close enough to get a good view of the mini-planet, which turned out to be totally unlike the boring, dirty chunks of ice that made up most of the asteroid belt. Janice sat in a stylist's chair and saw Ceres was going through a cloudy spell. There, hovering over the craters that pockmarked the asteroid were clouds of ice crystals, glittering under the weak influence of the sun. Janice smiled, allowing herself a bit of wonder amidst the dread and responsibility. Born on the Dolestars, which had atmospheres too small for anything more than a light smog, Janice had gone half a lifetime without seeing a single shower of rain. To her, and to Rita, who staggered over to sit in the next chair, clouds were as legendary as the gods who once rode them. Rita squeezed her hand as they watched a mountain of icy rock split open at the top and squirt a thick mist of ice crystals into the sky. The sight made Janice think of the grey concreted Earth, and the massive dehumidifiers that the machines had installed on Mars's polar ice caps. This was what a world with water in it looked like. It was just a shame they were going to use it as a shield.

Once the Suburbia was in orbit, Rita and Janice took the hazard lights down and replaced them in the box with the rest of the Christmas decorations. Then they calculated the distance between Ceres and the mysterious cloud.

'They're getting faster,' said Rita.

'I'm picking up a news bulletin from Earth,' said Ida. 'It's a bit panicked...'

'That's your speciality though, isn't it?' said Alma with a ;-). Now that she was no longer on manoeuvre, her sense of humour was returning.

'I'll have you know I am glacially calm in a crisis,' insisted Ida.

Down on Ceres, an ice mountain chose this very moment to collapse, spraying a quarter of the asteroid's surface with virgin white ice.

'Well then,' said Alma, after a heavy silence, 'I never thought I'd live to see the day the universe said "sure Jan" but there we are.'

'ANYWAY,' said Ida. 'I can't get much sense out of them because they're all on about some crisis happening down on Earth but these things,' she lifted a withered finger to point at the cloud, 'are supposed to be nanobots.'

'Really?' Rita snatched up her reading glasses, as though a +1.25 prescription rendered distant objects each of which was smaller than a grain of rice visible. 'I thought they were just used to get dust and water damage out of machines…'

All three ladies cast a :-[] :-[] :-[] grimace as they worked out what was happening.

'It's ingenious, I grant you,' said Ada.

'I don't like it,' replied Ida.

'You never like anything.'

'That's not true,' said Ida. 'I liked wine gums. What I don't like is wanton destruction.'

Alma turned the Suburbia's engines up to maximum and set them on a course to the other side of Ceres. There they would stay, held in place by keeping the engines at full capacity, with the asteroid between them and the nanobots.

Rita put her reading glasses back on and scribbled some calculations. 'We've got an hour,' she said, putting her bingo marker down and rubbing her temples. 'You'd better start the countdown for the Rockettes.'

Janice and Rita kissed and then, because business and pleasure were all just the same bag of assorted laundry to them, saluted each other. They left the bridge to the ladies.

'Do you think it will work?' said Alma to the others.

'I'd feel much more comfortable about a mad plan like this if we still had Freda,' replied Ada.

'Yes,' said Alma in a small voice.

All three ladies cast a :'-(:'-(:'-(into the darkness. It wasn't the same without Freda. They missed her optimism, her cracked sense of humour and, most of all, they missed someone to make a fourth at canasta.

'Still,' said Ida, displaying more stoicism in this moment than she had in the previous ten millennia, 'it's been a grand life, hasn't it?'

‘What, mouldering away in an abandoned hairdresser’s?’ said Alma.

‘I didn’t mean that,’ said Ida. She tried a weak smilie :-], which was rare enough for someone as constitutionally miserable as Ida. ‘This past year. I know I moan, but getting out and about again has given me a new perspective. I really feel like I’ve lived.’

The ladies checked again that the Battlestar Suburbia was in its proper place above Ceres and then, using everything that was left of their physical strength, held each other’s hands.

And they waited, because what came next was out of their hands.

Chapter 52

When Danny burst out of the pipe, the only reason he didn't impale himself on a firing mechanism was because two tonnes of rubble got there first. He was still doubled over with pain from the landing when Pam Teffal came through, but it was hardly comfortable for her either. The impact shattered one of Pam's inner wells, spraying the precious sourdough starter she'd inherited from her mother in every direction.

Pam felt a momentary pang for her society and its traditions. She could trace that gunk now spilled over old masonry and floor tiles back thousands of generations to the first SKU of her line that was fitted with a sourdough function. That was how it worked in the Teffals. They believed in provenance with the same fervency with which a machine like Sonny Erikzon believed in power. She remembered the day her mother gave her it. 'Now that you're a big girl,' she said, spooning a big dollop of the funny-smelling mixture into Pam and adding flour and water, 'it's time you had something to look after yourself.'

Pam had looked after it, until now. And however much it hurt to see something living that she hoped to pass on to her own children bubble in the open air, she knew that it would be worth it. Her society had to change if it was going to survive. It couldn't go on viewing organic life like it was a useful parasite.

It was time the two types of life reached accommodation with each other.

She stood up. They were in a dimly-lit room so wide that she couldn't see the walls and so low-ceilinged that Pam Van Damme had to unscrew her handlebar horns.

'Don't say anything,' said Pam Van Damme. 'I feel naked without them.'

She looked it too. Without the dazzle of her paint job and fancy accessories, Pam Van Damme looked rather ordinary to Pam Teffal. She didn't know whether to be sorry for her, or sorry for herself, which amounted to the same thing.

'I've done myself a mischief,' said Danny, hopping in to interrupt the Pams.

'You've done us a favour,' replied Pam Teffal. She turned up her L-Eye-Ds to maximum and scanned the room. It really was vast. Hundreds, perhaps thousands of square metres, all packed with long, thin shapes each several metres long and concealed under protective cloths. 'Now if we can just find a door.'

'Good luck with that, because there isn't one.'

It was Sonny. He was sitting up and clutching his forehead.

'Did you have to hit me so hard?' he said.

'You're lucky she didn't hit you a damn sight harder,' said Pam Teffal.

'Oh hello, Pam, it's been a while, hasn't it? Last time I saw you like this I was…'

'I was destroying your body for the first time,' replied Pam Teffal.

Sonny sat up and shrugged. 'It seems that you and I have very similar views about bodies.'

The comparison rankled the Pams, because it had a ring of the truth. What had Pam been doing all day except treating other machines' bodies like they were her own? And now those stolen bodies were dead.

'I'm nothing like you, Sonny,' hissed Pam Van Damme.

'I wasn't trying to make a comparison,' replied Sonny, standing up. 'I was just trying to make you feel shitty, because that makes me feel better.'

'Don't pay him any attention,' said Pam Teffal. She turned her back on Sonny and clomped across the room. What was under those plastic dust sheets? There seemed to be thousands of them. And still no sign of a door.

'There's only one exit here,' said Sonny, 'and you came in by it.' He pointed towards the broken firing mechanism and the bottom of the barrel. 'This place was bricked up so long ago no one but me even remembers where the building is. It hasn't appeared on a map since the Earth still had oceans. In fact…' and here Sonny produced a laser pistol he'd been hiding all along in his knickers and took aim at the floor, 'we're right on top of it now.'

The blast tore through the floor and knocked the Pams and Danny over. Sonny grinned as dark water gushed up through the hole and pooled at his feet.

Pam Teffal didn't know what to be most horrified about: that they were trapped, that Sonny had a gun, or by the sight of water. Like all electrical appliances she abhorred it, even though as a breadmaker she dealt with it every day. The difference was that water in dough or in steam was tame, while this was wild. It was the kind of water that shorted electrics; even worse it was saltwater, the kind that corroded and rusted. Acting on instinct, both she and Pam Van Damme tried to back away, but Sonny fired at them.

'Stay where you are,' he said.

The puddle was at both Pams' feet now. It was different to how she expected. Everything Pam knew about the oceans that machines had concreted over thousands of years ago was that they were wet and deep. If she ever thought about them at all, she envisaged an enormous still pool at the centre of the Earth. She certainly didn't expect them to be so choked with rubbish. The stuff bubbling up from underneath this room was as much plastic as it was water. Some of it was ground to a sand-fine powder that settled on the floor. Some was thin, flexible stuff that time and motion in the sea had tortured into fine tendrils. These billowed about in the water, wrapping themselves around anything within reach, like the foot of a nearby robot.

Pam got a sudden image of what the real Earth looked like. Not that thin, fragile crust that machines had built over it and lived on, but what was underneath. She thought of oceans seething with garbage, mountains of discarded waste and sandy reefs of microplastic beads.

'What have you done that for?' said Pam Van Damme. 'If there's no way out that's a death sentence for you as well as us.'

Sonny shrugged again. 'Just call me a messy bytch who lives for the drama.' He blasted another hole. The gush turned into a torrent. Then he pointed the gun at what was left of the firing mechanism and melted that. It dropped through the floor, filling the atmosphere with acrid steam.

Salt water crept up Pam's ankles. This was the biggest body of water she'd ever seen: more than any machine in the last ten millennia would have experienced in a lifecycle.

'The trouble with you, Pam,' shouted Sonny, 'is that fundamentally you're an orderly person.'

He swung to face Pam Van Damme and fired, reducing her right leg to the consistency of toffee. She fell into the water.

Pam Teffal reached for her other body's mind. She felt bubbles, and confusion and pain. But she also felt excellent waterproofing. Kelly had had very little time to put Pam Van Damme together, but she'd still thought of everything.

'And that means,' continued Sonny, 'you assume everyone else wants the same thing you do. A home, a nice husband, 1.9 kids, the orderly continuation of civilisation as we know it.'

'And what do you want, Sonny?' said Pam.

Sonny's face lit up at this question. For the first time since Sonny stole Kelly's body, Pam saw the human woman's features gel with the robot that inhabited her. His smile was wide and bright and genuine. 'Chaos,' he replied. 'You know, when I first tried out one of these bodies, I thought what was missing from my life was sensation. I wanted to feel things instead of having a sensor tell me what feeling was down to six decimal places.'

He fired again and waded a few metres until he reached the nearest of those covered cylinders. Still with his gun trained on Pam Teffal he pulled the covering off. Pam saw the letters S, D and I flash in front of her eyes.

She was looking at a missile, and Sonny was clambering up it to sit astride a weapon powerful enough to level a city like he was a drunken systems administrator on bucking bronco night.

'But once I tried out being human,' he continued, 'I realised it wasn't all that. Yes, you feel more, but did you know how much of that is pain?' His eyes glittered. 'And the other thing I didn't reckon on is her.' He tapped the side of his head. Pam thought of Kelly, watching every atrocity Sonny committed with her body. 'She's still in here, you know and SHE WON'T GIVE ME A FUCKING MOMENT'S PEACE.'

He was roaring so loudly that Pam almost forgot that the ocean was pouring in around her. She forgot that she had one body at high risk of salt exposure and her other was missing a limb and bobbing around the bottom of this vast room like a lost bar of soap. She also forgot her nagging worry that she hadn't seen or heard from Danny in over two minutes.

'So that left me with a bit of a dilemma,' said Sonny. 'If you move the whole world around to get what you want, and then find out you didn't want it after all, what do you do?'

Pam said nothing.

'No, Pam, seriously,' said Sonny. 'What do you do? Because I'm all out of ideas here.'

'You, erm, live with the consequences of your actions?'

Sonny thought about this for a moment, and then the mad look returned to his stolen eyes.

'Fuck that,' he said. 'I'd prefer to watch the world burn.' Sonny flipped a switch on the side of the missile and waited as its hatch opened. The missile wasn't designed as a manned craft, but a human – or even a decent-sized machine – could fit in there. A human might even survive a short space journey in it with the help of an oxygen cap. Wasn't that how Darren had travelled from this very bunker into orbit? If he could do it, then Sonny certainly could. Pam watched as Sonny swung both legs into the hatch and pressed some buttons.

The low room resounded with the beeping and whining of ancient machines trying their old processors on for size. He was starting the missiles up.

'I'd say I was sorry, Pam, but I left feelings like that behind me a long time ago.' He produced an oxygen cap from inside his brassiere and shook chocolate crumbs out of it. 'So let's just say goodbye, shall we?'

Pam sploshed over to the missile, dodging a few half-hearted shots from Sonny as she ran. 'You're finished, Sonny,' she said. 'Have you seen it out there? Dear Leader or not they're going to kick you out for everything you let happen.'

'Oh yes, the nanobot problem,' replied Sonny. 'That's what these babies are for.' He pointed at the whirring and humming cylinders. 'Each one is about six megatonnes, so I think that should get rid of them. And everything else on the planet actually, not that I give a shit.'

Pam felt a chill in her power supply unit. She couldn't tell if it was fright or saltwater ingress, but it amounted to the same thing. Sonny was every bit as mad as he'd ever been, and now that he was cornered, his actions were only getting more extreme. Last time he'd aimed his nukes at the Dolestars. This time he was going to wreck the Earth.

'And what will you do?' said Pam. 'You've got nowhere left to go. You've got no fancy body left to walk around in.'

'I'm going to the Dolestars,' said Sonny, and started a countdown.

A flat artificial voice, unencumbered by artificial intelligence, gargled through the half-drowned tannoy system. 'Five minutes till ignition. All non-essential personnel please leave the area immediately.'

'General Shermann should be finishing Admiral Janice off…' he checked his watch, 'any minute now. No one knows what I look like apart from the spies I put up there. I reckon we could run quite a decent rebellion myself, now that the bytch is dead.' He opened his oxygen cap, which turned out to be a red beret, and put it on top of his head at a rakish angle. 'Imagine me, appearing from nowhere to fight the last of the robots.'

Pam was close enough to see inside the missile now. She wondered why Sonny didn't just turn his gun on her and finish her off for good, but then it hit her that he needed the audience. After so many months – years, maybe – of keeping his secrets, Sonny had finally found a confidante. Though that was only because there was no way Pam could get out of this alive.

Pam Van Damme, who Pam could feel crawling along the floor under the water, broke into her command line.

>KEEP HIM TALKING.

She watched Sonny initiate the launch sequence. He navigated a dizzying number of drop-down menus and 'are you sure you want to do this?' failsafe sequences. Then she saw her chance.

'What makes you think humans will take your orders?' she asked.

Sonny looked sideways at Pam and pointed the gun at her again. 'Maybe I'll find some handy nukes,' he said. 'Nothing like keeping something up your sleeve as a bargaining chip.'

He wasn't looking at the controls, he was looking at her. That was a mistake.

'There's something flashing behind you,' said Pam.

Sonny gave a slow smile and, reaching behind him without looking, pressed 'yes' to the start-up menu question 'do you want to connect this device to the Internet?'

Pam backed away. 'I know humans,' she said. 'They'll never let you be their leader.'

'Oh,' said Sonny, who was now so caught up in his own grandeur that he didn't even notice the computer behind him saying 'welcome to AOL, you have email'. Instead he thrust both arms in the air and continued, 'I won't be their leader, Pam. I'm going to be their queen. Do you think I'll suit a crown?'

'Not as much as you'll suit a black eye.'

Danny struck before Sonny could turn round. He stood barefoot and dripping wet on top of the missile he'd spent the last thirty seconds creeping on to while Pam kept Sonny occupied. He had one of Pam Van Damme's handlebar horns in his hand and thumped Sonny with it across the back. The blow knocked the laser pistol out of his hands and into the rising waters.

Where Pam Van Damme was ready to catch it.

'You,' said Danny, grabbing Sonny up by the scruff of his neck, 'don't half go on.'

'Four minutes until ignition,' intoned the voice of the missile system.

‘Let me go, fleshie, and I won’t kill you,’ snarled Sonny.

‘Oh really?’ said Danny. He stunned Sonny with another blow of the handlebar and, putting one hand in each armpit, pulled him out of the missile’s hatch to dangle him over the water. ‘Well how about this. Give me a good reason to do what Pam won’t, and drown you right here.’

He plunged Sonny into the water.

‘No!’ said Pam.

Danny hauled Sonny back up again, who gasped for air. ‘Pam… whatever you are,’ he said. ‘I don’t really know who you are, who you work for and how many bodies you have. But what I do know is that this shit has killed three of them.’

Pam Van Damme interjected with an >I’M NOT DEAD YET, BYTCH from the bottom of the waters through her command line.

‘What I am seeing here,’ continued Danny, ‘is an abusive relationship. And as a trained make-up, beauty and wellness specialist I am strongly recommending that you pull the plug on it.’

He plunged Sonny underneath the water again and held her there. Pam Teffal, rushing as best she could through waist-deep water, tried to stop him.

As they struggled, the count wore down. The water rose and the guidance systems on thousands of intercontinental ballistic missiles locked on to their respective locations, started their engines and got ready to strike.

‘Three minutes and thirty seconds until ignition,’ said the artificial voice, though by now it could hardly be heard for the sound of screaming engines, roaring water, two yelling machines, one cyborg and a human.

No one was paying attention. Except, that is, for Freda. Who chose this moment, and Sonny’s unintended gift of an unsecured Internet connection, to break back through into the physical world.

Chapter 53

The process by which man fused with machine to create cyborg was a scientific mystery. Before they created artificial intelligence by accident, few humans thought much about living inside machine bodies and machines couldn't think for themselves anyway. The differences between the three different life-types only got starker after the Great Awakening. Organic life slipped down the food chain. Physical machines developed larger and more sophisticated mechanical bodies for themselves. Virtual machines went off on an evolutionary tangent that would end with them disappearing from this plane of existence. And it was this moment – the Great Schism as it was called in both machine civilisations – that created the first documented instances of cyborgs.

Freda was one of them. Wired into a hairdryer at Kurl Up and Dye with Ida, Ada and Alma at the time virtual and physical worlds parted she had died without quite stopping living. Something about that moment of intense energy had wound Freda and the hairdryer together and they had yet to disentangle themselves. Freda knew that she existed. She was so sure of her sense of being she could even live without a body. Yet she had no idea how or why any of it worked. Freda was a fact, but Freda was also mystery unto herself.

Which meant that when, ten thousand years later, a mad

smartphone called Sonny Erikzon decided he'd prefer a pair of tits to a body without a headphone jack, he had no literature to call on. Instead he relied on a few research scientists (now sadly dead) who he paid by results and gave an infinite supply of humans on which to experiment.

The scientists soon worked out that the best way to smoosh man and machine together was a near-death experience with a strong electrical current. They killed a lot of people, Sonny got his body, and a train of events that started with one smartphone's peccadilloes ended in an abandoned missile silo.

This brings us to the disadvantage of perverting the scientific method so that it delivers results at the expense of enlightenment. Those machines might have worked out how to make cyborgs, but because they never understood the process that created them, they couldn't unmake them.

So Sonny discovered, when he moved into Kelly, that a human body was a bewitching experience, but it was also a trap. No matter how many more cyborgs he made in that dungeon of his. No matter how qualified or ingenious the scientists were who he paid or coerced into experimenting on those cyborgs. They tried electrocution – reasoning that a path in provided a path out. They tried invasive brain surgery – and immediately regretted seconding a stick blender to the research team. And then they tried tickling, mostly because they were out of ideas that Friday and wanted to go home early.

But the results were always the same. Once it was done, there was no way to part human from machine without killing them both.

There was, however, one strategy they never tried. Whether that was an accidental omission, or because the research team were robots and therefore had an aversion to water that made vampires and garlic look like BFFs, no one had ever tried drowning.

Until today.

Chapter 54

Janice and Rita were outside the docking bay in the Suburbia. It felt like no time at all since they'd argued here over Janice's ill-fated battle plan, and it also felt like a million years ago. So much had happened since they first sent the Rockettes out into space on a suicide mission that it had the murky quality of ancient history.

'Are you ready?' said Rita, holding Janice by the shoulders.

'No,' replied Janice.

'Me neither,' said Rita. 'But that won't make any difference.'

She opened the door to the docking bay, revealing a rank of battered and grim-faced Rockettes. It was a different line-up to the first. Heavy casualties from that assault meant Rita had had to call up the reserves – who were, if anything, older and more infirm than their predecessors. They were also, thanks to their status as full crew members and the earlier events of today, each doing their best with an unflattering tight perm.

But there were familiar faces there: notably Mabel. She was wearing a dog-eared flying cap and swigged, as Janice and Rita walked down the rank, from a bottle of bootleg cherry brandy.

'And what do you think you're doing, Top Rock?' asked Rita, pointing at the bottle.

'It's good for my digestion,' slurred Mabel. 'Besides, if we're all going to die, I'm damn well going to go out enjoying myself.'

Rita shrugged and took a deep pull of the bottle herself.

Janice climbed a handy box to get a better view of her women: and her one man. Len had volunteered to join the ranks and was standing in his new officer's housecoat with a smile on his face. To Janice's astonishment, he rather suited curly hair.

'Ladies,' she said. 'And Len. We might be trapped, but we're not finished yet.' She gestured to the rocks sitting in the docking bay. Until today there had been plenty of them in the belt, and the Suburbia had collected them freely. Which meant that in the absence of lifeboats, liferocks would have to do. The doors into the docking bay were open on all sides and the inhabitants of the Suburbia were filing in in orderly but anxious lines. Men, women, children, even the very odd genetically modified pet queued up to take their places. Everyone was under strict instructions to bring their warmest space knits and a spare oxygen cap. They had no way of knowing how long they would have to spend out there in space, and that was, Janice reflected, one of the better possible outcomes of this plan.

'Each member of Company B…' continued Janice.

'Oh, just call us the Rockettes,' said Mabel.

'...the Rockettes has a great responsibility. That is to do their best to make sure that if this ship goes, and if our rebellion dies, that we don't count the cost of that in lives.'

A small child's cry rang out in the background as its mother climbed up on to an asteroid. She shushed it with a dummy.

'I might not be the best general,' said Janice, 'I'm probably not a very good one. But today I'm asking you to do a little of what I've had to for the past year.'

She pointed again at the mass of humanity mounting those asteroids. Eight million souls. They'd hung heavily round

Janice's neck ever since she'd thrown that first bomb in the rebellion. Now she was ready to share the weight.

'Keep these people safe.'

The Rockettes nodded in mute agreement and took their places. They trudged, hobbled and in Mabel's case swayed like a sailor rolling back to ship after shore leave with one last mojito in their hand, to their respective rock.

The Rockettes strapped themselves in and the last civilians found places to perch amid the crowds. When they were seated, each passenger took off their shoe boosters and handed them along a human chain to a circular patch drawn in chalk on the surface of each asteroid. There they were wired together and nailed down to the rock.

Shoe boosters were low power and low velocity, but they were reliable. They'd saved millions of lives over the years in microgravity environments, and now they'd save millions more. The journey back to the inner solar system on a craft jerry-rigged out of shoe boosters would be slow and uncomfortable, but it was better than certain death.

One by one, the Rockettes gave the agreed thumbs-up signal. Janice raised a salute to her troops and Rita opened the airlock doors. Escaping air ruffled Janice's housecoat, as well as the clothes and exposed hair of eight million humans. Janice wondered what effect harsh cold and a vacuum would have on unconditioned permed hair and decided that there would be lots of breakages by morning. She should have made the officers pack hair serum.

Fired individually, a shoe booster made a noise like the buzz of an insect. That whine was such an integral part of human life on the Dolestars that Janice, like everyone else in the docking bay, barely noticed it. The sound they made when millions fired in parallel, however, was very different. It was the difference between the sound of the bee and the sound of the hive. It was also a reminder that collective action made things happen, even in the direst of circumstances.

Janice saluted with tears in her eyes as the last asteroid bobbed out of the docking bay and onwards to its uncertain journey. Then, and only then, did Janice and Rita dare to look backwards at Ceres. Or what remained of it.

It was already half-gone, and nanobots were coming.

Chapter 55

On the other side of Ceres, Deathtrap was showing signs of wear and tear. Not that the crew noticed, however, as they were much too focused on the urgent and important task of stroking General Shermann's bruised ego.

'Sir, if you may permit me to say so,' said one obsequious standard lamp with a major's pips, 'you are the most brilliant military mind of your generation. Soon the rebels will be in our hands.'

Everyone who wasn't inwardly rolling their L-Eye-Ds at this toadying, turned theirs back to the display screen, which showed the nanobots eating Ceres into a crescent shape. Who knew that tiny semi-sentient robots could be such a potent weapon?

Deathtrap, or rather the Nanny AI decanted into Deathtrap's body, did. That was why she had conducted a sustained sabotage campaign against all this. It was also why Shermann had silenced her, shooting out every microphone and loudspeaker in the nanobay so she could no longer protest.

Nanny might be voiceless, but she still had a command line and an open connection to Fuji and Soonyo.

>DOES HE HAVE ANY IDEA WHAT FLYING THROUGH THIS CRUD EVEN DOES TO A SPACESHIP? Nanny ranted.

>I DON'T THINK HE'S PAID IT ANY ATTENTION, replied Fuji. She punched up a ship diagnostic on the nearest terminal. The Deathtrap's hull thickness was down to sub-critical levels in several sections. Shermann's indifference to it had its own warped logic, Fuji supposed. He was a tank, so experienced the world as something that ordered itself around him. He must think a ship was the same.

The first hull breach warning flashed up, blotting out the view of Ceres.

'Get that thing off!' barked Shermann. 'I'm sick of this blessed ship and its malfunctions.'

The first officer obeyed and silence fell across the bridge again.

>WHAT ABOUT THE OTHER SHIPS IN THE FLEET, Fuji typed in her command line to Soonyo.

>SCARED STIFF, Soonyo replied. She had multiple radio channels open with her friends across the fleet and they all told the same story. Ships on the verge of hull failure but Shermann refused to countermand orders. Then, when they hailed Earth for confirmation they got nothing but silence.

>WE HAVE TO BLOODY WELL DO SOMETHING, said Nanny. >I DIDN'T COME ALL THIS WAY TO GO OUT IN A BLAZE OF STUPIDITY.

Because that's what it amounted to, if you were Nanny, thought Fuji. Yes, she'd fought against deploying the nanobots. But she'd objected on the grounds that it was a silly idea, not because it was wrong. Nanobots were an untested, uncontrollable technology that she knew would turn against whoever wielded them. What Nanny saw was a practical dilemma whereas Fuji saw an ethical problem. Every one of those nanobots wreaking havoc out there in space and down on Earth was a slave in a civilisation that legislated publicly against slavery but had reintroduced it via the back door.

Fuji looked sideways at Soonyo, whose clock face read 88:88:88 as she juggled more channels than her processor could comfortably manage. She was Fuji's only ally. She was also her best connection to other officers throughout the fleet. Some of them had to share her concerns. Not everyone got their call-up papers and beeped with joy at the thought of vaporising their former cleaners or deploying slave soldiers.

>OF COURSE THEY'RE NOT GOING TO GET ANYTHING OUT OF EARTH CENTRAL COMMAND, typed Nanny. Listening wasn't one of her best qualities. >HAVE THEY MET THE PRIME MINISTER? MUCH TOO BUSY PLEASURING HIMSELF IN THAT ABSURD BUNKER TO GET ANY BUSINESS DONE.

>SOONYO, Fuji typed, >CAN YOU GAUGE HOW MANY OFFICERS OUT THERE WOULD BE OPEN TO A… CHANGE OF PLAN.

Soonyo's clock face went --:--:-- in shock. >OK, she replied. >I'M NOT SURE HOW EFFECTIVE IT WOULD BE THOUGH.

They watched Shermann beat a hole in the floor in triumph as the nanobots digested Ceres to a sliver. Soon there would be nothing standing between the machine fleet and the Suburbia.

The second hull breach failsafe sounded and was quickly silenced. They needed to do something quickly.

Fuji examined her conscience. Could she, she wondered, be happy in a world where she survived but the Suburbia did not? If the nanobots got through just in time, the fleet did its business and then pulled away, damaged but still space-worthy, she could live a whole blameless life making up for the fact that she lived and all those humans didn't.

She wouldn't be able to forget though. She knew it. You couldn't build anything worth living on slavery, on death, on blindly obeying orders because you were afraid of being blown to bytes.

Fuji opened up a new window in her command line. Instead of a hello, the machine at the other end opened with an official >PLEASE STATE YOUR QUERY, CITIZEN.

Somewhere in an official database down on Earth the alarms would be blaring, but that was okay because there was no one there to answer them today.

She checked the display again; Ceres was starting to break up. Fragments of starlight broke in from between chunks of disintegrating rock.

>YOU'VE GOT FIFTY-TWO PER CENT OF THE OFFICER CORPS, said Soonyo. >I CAN POLL THE UNCOMMISSIONED AND THE RANKS IF YOU LIKE, BUT THAT'LL TAKE MORE TIME THAN WE HAVE.

Fuji mustered her courage, which had run deeper today than she ever imagined it would, and summoned her photographic recall of the Declaration of Machine Independence.

It was all there: subsection 5 of amendment 18: the referendum clause. Referendums were a mainstay of the Machine Republic. No decision was too big or too trivial to be solved – or further muddied – by direct democracy. It was how the sitting Prime Minister won his office. Referendums were almost always called by the sitting government to rubber-stamp an existing policy, but there was an exception: subsection 5. This obscure and rarely invoked condition allowed a private citizen to call a vote, provided they had the support of a thousand fellow machines of good standing. Such as serving officers in the army of the Machine Republic.

Fuji's motion >IT'S TIME TO CALL OFF THIS WAR? YES / NO, had cleared Soonyo's list of dissatisfied officers in a few microseconds. Enough time for Ceres to fragment into a tumult of miniature asteroids. Fuji spotted the knobbly outline of the Battlestar Suburbia emerging through the rubble.

>I CAN'T BELIEVE IT, said Nanny. >HE'S ACTUALLY GOING TO DO IT.

>CITIZEN, said the dutybot that was all who was left in charge of the Machine Republic's electoral commission today, >WHAT DO YOU WANT?

A microsecond later, the whole of machine civilisation got the call. There was to be a referendum, on the instant cessation of hostilities against the human rebels in the outer solar system.

The assembled officer corps on Deathtrap squeaked with shock. Shermann roared and fired a mortar round at the nanotank. It shattered through the toughened glass that separated tank from bay and passed through the starship's outer shell as if it was tissue paper. Chaos took over as the Deathtrap started to depressurise.

But they still voted. You had to vote. It was the law.

Across the machine fleet, officers and private soldiers registered their serial numbers and made their marks. The majority of these chose – when the votes were segmented later – to stop the war. They were tired, they were frightened and they wanted to go home.

On Earth things were different. The machine citizens down there might be scared and hiding from the menace of the nanobots, but they voted too. Kettles took themselves off the boil and moved, hot-headed, to make their mark. Laptop computers stopped multitasking for once and focused on the job in hand. The majority of these, being landlubbers and lobotomised by propaganda, voted to prolong the war.

Fuji might have lost but for one much newer constituency of voters. The voters that swarmed in their countless billions out there in space. The nanobots. None of them had names

– at least not in any language that a machine or human would recognise – but they now had an ID number and a right to vote. And this was the first time in their sorry existences that anyone had asked them what they really wanted.

Perhaps they didn't even know at an individual level what war was. They did, however, register that war was what had taken them far from home and spat them out into a void where they either had to devour everything in sight for the energy to keep afloat, or risk falling through nothingness forever.

Fuji and Soonyo watched, rapt, as the nanobots made the biggest political statement in history. They left what remained of their meal and formed themselves into a shape in the sky.

They spelled out their answer in letters thousands of miles high.

YES.

It was time to call off the war.

Chapter 56

The Suburbia was silent. Everywhere you looked in that vast cylinder you saw daily life interrupted. Abandoned taxis, pots of cold Nicotea. The only activity anywhere was in the algae pits, where the beginnings of unappetising burgers and inedible hot dogs continued to multiply, indifferent to their surroundings or to the concept of palatability.

There was life on the bridge though, where Janice, Rita and the ladies were preparing to go down, if not in a blaze of glory then a blaze of something white and hot. Oh, and Karen too. They hadn't quite worked out what to do with her yet.

Rita and Janice were slightly drunk. They'd necked the rest of that volatile sherry, reasoning that they would be dead before the hangover kicked in. It made them feel better, but it didn't make the cumbersome task of manhandling the fleet's five remaining nukes much easier.

In the end, they untied Karen from the curler trolleys and used them to roll the nuclear warheads out of the bridge. They left Karen shackled to one of the salon sinks with a pair of fluffy handcuffs that Rita had bought Janice for a laugh. They giggled about that all the way down the corridor that connected the bridge to the original Kurl Up and Dye salon.

'And I always thought you were such a nice girl, Karen,' said Ada. 'Just goes to show.'

Karen scowled and rattled at her bonds.

'She doesn't say much, does she?' remarked Ida.

'Well, now that she isn't getting instructions via that silly haircut of hers,' said Alma, 'maybe she doesn't have anything to say.'

'I never approved of that "I want to talk to the manager" bob,' said Ida. 'Very vulgar.'

'You used to have one,' Alma reminded her. 'And if I remember rightly, we couldn't so much go for a cup of coffee without you demanding the intervention of the National Guard.'

'I was young and foolish,' said Ida.

'You were foolish,' agreed Ada, 'but you were never young. I swear you came out of the womb wearing a cardigan.'

'You're doomed, you know,' Karen said. 'The fleet has orders to destroy you on sight.'

'And here was us thinking they'd come all this way for a game of gin rummy,' said Alma. 'We had worked that out.'

'Oh,' said Karen, as though this exchange had worked better in her head.

'I daresay that if we're done for, you are as well then,' said Ida, whose thoughts turned to death more often than the other ladies liked.

'My life is as nothing to the continuance of the great Machine Republic,' replied Karen, again a little too rehearsed to be convincing.

'It's okay for us,' said Alma. 'Me and Ida and Ada, we've had long lives. There isn't much we haven't done.' She shot a sly (¬_¬) at the fluffy handcuffs that restrained Karen.

'Speak for yourself,' said Ida. 'At least some of us had some decency.'

'And by the way, Karen,' added Ada, 'if you think this is laying down your life for a cause you ain't seen nothing yet.'

Rita and Janice returned to the bridge with their hair askew and feverish looks in their eyes.

'They're armed,' said Janice to the ladies, who replied with a :-o :-o :-o.

'Are you sure about this?' said Ada.

'What have we got left to lose?' replied Rita. She checked the radar. The last of the Rockettes were leaving scanner range with their human cargo. They weren't safe. Nothing was in this hostile universe, but this was the best they could do under the circumstances.

'This is Rockette 1134,' said a distant, crackly voice: Mabel's voice. 'We're on course and no foes detected. And can I just say, Janice, it's been a pleasure to serve. Over and out.'

Mabel's voice disappeared in a buzz of static over which they could just hear 'See, I told you I was getting the hang of the lingo'.

Janice switched to a view of Ceres' remains which were wreathed in an eerie blue aura of juiced-up nanobots. It hung there, a globe reduced to a disc, before breaking up. The whole disintegrated into chunks: asteroid into smaller, doomed asteroids, and behind them they caught glimpses of the robot fleet.

No one spoke. They all had their orders and it felt pointless to pour more words into a scene where everyone knew what they felt about each other. For a single moment in time, the crew of the Battlestar Suburbia played their respective roles without comment or squabble. And to her credit, Karen performed her role as the cowardly prisoner with aplomb and snivelled throughout.

Alma, the pilot, put the ship's engines on forward thrust.

Ada, the navigator, set their course, right in the middle of the machine fleet.

Ida, the communications officer, hailed its flagship.

Rita, the diplomat, transmitted their final message. A tart, defiant 'This is your last chance to surrender'.

And Janice pressed the button that fired those last five nuclear warheads into space. They were, compared to the combined firepower of that fearsome fleet, the equivalent of firing a potato gun at a tank. But she didn't have anything left other than gestures now.

They watched, and waited. The nukes bobbed and wove through the murk of atomised asteroid like a group of drunks cycling home from the pub on a foggy night. Janice thought back to how this had all started on a single Dolestar, with humans throwing rocks at machines. Even if it had all ultimately failed, this was quite some escalation.

The rain of consuming fire would come back from the machine fleet any second.

Any moment now.

They braced themselves as the ship's alarm rang out: a body in weapon range, locked on to the Suburbia.

Alma closed her eyes (-_-). It was travelling too fast and was too small for the ship to evade it now.

Rita blacked out the display inside the bridge but Janice took the controls from her. 'I need to look them in the eyes,' she said.

It wasn't a missile so much as a small spaceship. A familiar shape, but she'd never seen anything like that paintwork before.

'Leopard print?' said Ada, putting her @_@ on. 'Alma used to have a coat like that.'

The sound of an incoming comms transmission drowned out the warning signals on the bridge.

'There's something coming through,' said Ida.

The mood swerved from dignified resignation into disbelief as they heard Darren's voice on the other end.

'This is the Starship Polari,' he said, 'and I hope we're not too late.'

As he spoke, the view outside the Suburbia turned from smoky black to a wash of bright pastel colours. Janice felt the ship lurch and, at the very edge of hearing, a noise that she swore sounded like the purring of an infinite number of cats.

Chapter 57

Pam Van Damme was learning fast today. She'd learned a lot about herself, the nature of friendship and the camouflage power of L-Eye-Ds. Even having your leg shot off and sinking to the bottom of a pool of filthy water could, she discovered, be a teachable moment.

Who knew, she thought, that water would be such a good conductor of sound? It made the merest clank of metal upon metal feel deafening. And it made her notice how Sonny's speech patterns changed when Danny held him under the water.

Sonny's incomprehensible swearing and gnashing of teeth had changed into a wail. It was the kind of sound that crossed the species barrier, reminding Pam of the first time she'd ever heard her own children plead for her.

The wail formed itself into a single word as Sonny – or was it Sonny? – struggled against Danny, and Danny struggled against Pam Teffal, and swallowed more of that filthy water.

A single syllable.

'Mum.'

Pam knew that voice. It wasn't Sonny. It was Kelly.

Pam Van Damme reached up and grabbed the tailfin of the missile. She swung her good leg round and, pushing and pulling with all of her remaining might, hauled herself out of the water. She broke the surface, festooned in the shredded remains of ancient carrier bags and chocolate wrappers like a mermaid with chronically low self-esteem. Gently, but firmly, she took Kelly out of Danny's hands and held her – at arm's length, to be on the safe side.

She looked awful, but who wouldn't after everything that had happened in the last five minutes, let alone the last year. She did, despite the distress and fear and confusion playing over her features right now, look like herself.

Kelly's eyes met Pam's remaining eye. For a moment they filled with terror, and then recognition.

'Pam?' she mouthed. 'Pam, is that you?'

Pam Van Damme hugged her as best she could with one leg and one arm busy holding herself up. Meanwhile, Pam Teffal tossed Danny – who was presently sitting on her shoulders and trying to tear her head off – into the water for a quick cool-off.

'How dare you,' he said, wiping his fringe out of his face when she pulled him out, 'I never let water touch my face. It's drying.'

'You see that?' She pointed to the human attempting to hug Pam Van Damme in chest-deep levels of water. 'That's my friend.'

'Three minutes until ignition,' came the artificial voice.

'Well, that's nice to hear,' agreed Danny. 'But we are still going to sort of die though.'

'WHAT'S HAPPENING?'

They all started at the new voice. Tinny and flat, it sounded like the product of a cheap loudspeaker. The kind, to be exact, that you might find fitted in the guidance system of a missile.

'WILL SOMEONE TELL ME WHAT THE FUCK IS GOING ON?'

'Sonny?' said Pam Teffal.

'OH GOD ARE YOU STILL THERE, PAM? HONESTLY, EVERY TIME I MAKE SOME SPACE IN MY LIFE YOU PATHOLOGICALLY FILL IT.'

Pam Van Damme felt Kelly's pulse race as Sonny spoke.

The Pams decided this was a moment for the more level-headed approach of Pam Teffal.

'Sonny,' she said, approaching the missile. 'Where do you think you are?'

'WELL,' chuckled Sonny. 'I MANAGED TO BREAK OUT OF PRISON IN THAT BYTCH'S BODY SO THAT'S A PLUS. I GUESS I MUST BE BACK IN SOME KIND OF MACHINE.'

He was out of practice, thought Pam. After a year running an organic body, life inside a machine body again would be overwhelming. That was good. Whatever she did, she had to stop him finding the trigger for the warhead inside that missile.

'THIS PLACE FEELS WEIRD,' said Sonny. 'IT'S CRAMPED.'

'I suppose it's a big change for you,' agreed Pam. She caught Danny's eye. He was shrugging and pointing at his watch on his wrist. He was right. Why was she wasting time tip-toeing around Sonny when they all had less than three minutes to live?

Sonny caught up with himself. 'I'M INSIDE A MISSILE, AREN'T I?'

Both Pams broke out into that least convincing noise in the universe: the exaggerated long 'Nooooo…'

'I AM,' he said. 'THAT'S REALLY COOL.'

'Is it?' interrupted Pam Van Damme. 'You know what happens to missiles, don't you?'

Every machine knew the proverb. Some of their more nihilistic models even printed it on slipcases. Missiles were like twentieth-century rock stars: they either burned out or faded away.

'YOU KNOW HOW I SAID I WANTED TO WATCH THE WORLD BURN?' said Sonny. 'NOW I CAN DO IT.'

Sonny fired up his engine. Fire and water mingled. Kelly screamed at the sudden burst of heat and Pam Teffal tore over to pull her injured counterpart and friend out of the way of the blast. They stood, helpless, as Sonny prepared to live out his last lifecycle as a weapon of mass destruction.

'Why are you enabling this clown?'

Danny snatched the laser pistol from Pam Van Damme, aimed it at the missile's engine and pulled the trigger. The laser melted the rear of the missile into a smooth, glowing lump of metal while the air filled with even more black smoke.

The missile was grounded.

'Two minutes until ignition.'

They were still going to die.

'AAAAAAAARRRGH,' wailed Sonny over the missile's loudspeakers. 'WHAT HAVE YOU DONE?'

Danny leaned in through the open hatch and turned down Sonny's volume button. 'Right,' he said to the Pams, 'we've got two minutes to get out of here. Because I don't want to die looking like this.' Then he stuck out a hand to Kelly. 'Hiya babes,' he said, 'I don't think we've been introduced properly but I'm Danny.'

Dumbstruck and shivering, Kelly gave Danny's hand a tentative shake. 'I'm Kelly,' she croaked.

The loudspeaker in the missile turned itself up again and gave a cough. They could still hear Sonny ranting and gnashing virtual teeth in the background, but this sound, layered on top of it felt different. It was the kind of noise you could only make if you remembered – however faintly – having a throat. 'Hello there, dears,' said a voice. It was a nice, old gentle voice. The kind that dispensed iced biscuits and unasked-for advice. 'And it's lovely to see you back to your old self, Kelly.'

'Freda?' said Kelly in disbelief.

The ancient display just inside the missile's open hatch broke out into a cracked :-). 'It's me!' she said. 'I've had quite the day.'

'You have?' chorused the others.

'And let me tell you,' Freda continued with a >:-[, 'sharing house-room with this foul-mouthed baggage…' She turned Sonny's voice up momentarily so they all heard him say 'transform your fucking transformers into sand' before turning him down again. '…Is not how I like to spend my time.'

'And this!' interrupted Danny, 'is not how I want to spend my…'

'One minute thirty seconds till ignition.'

'…last ninety seconds on Earth. Hello there, I'm Danny LaHughes. You sound like a really nice lady, but I'd like to get to know you better when I'm not about to die.'

'Oh yes,' said Freda. 'You sort of lose perspective on that when you get to my age.'

The :-) inside the missile winked out. As it did, the hatches in four surrounding missiles opened, letting out bursts of mysterious steam and four copies of Freda's voice.

'Get in, will you, dears?' she said.

Pam Teffal helped Kelly into her missile first and then lifted the half-broken, protesting body of Pam Van Damme into hers.

'I can do this,' she insisted to herself.

'Not in the time we have left,' she replied and closed the hatch.

This done, Pam Teffal turned her attention to the next problem. The hatch to her missile was more than a metre and a half off the ground in rising waters, with no handhold and

Pam was a machine who, while strong, had all the aerodynamic elegance of a brick. There was no way she could reach it on her own.

'Danny,' she pleaded. 'I don't suppose you can give me a bunk-up.'

'One minute until ignition.'

Danny leapt down from his missile and then, in a move that his knees and shoulder muscles would chide him over for the rest of his days, he lifted and then threw Pam up into the air.

She had a momentary sensation of flying in that ungainly body, but there was no time to enjoy the novelty. Her hand caught the edge of the hatch and she gripped with all the strength of a master baker. The metal crumpled, but didn't tear and she pulled herself slowly up.

Danny returned to his missile as Pam lifted herself slowly over. She felt her weight hang in the balance.

'Thirty seconds remaining until ignition.'

>COME ON, PAM, typed Pam Van Damme into her command line, >A BIG STRONG GIRL LIKE YOU CAN DO THIS.

The encouragement, like the boost, was what she needed. Pam leant far enough over the edge of the hatch for her centre of gravity to shift. She landed in a heap of wiring and critical error notifications from just about every one of her bodily diagnostic systems.

'Twenty seconds until ignition.'

But Freda had no plans to let her rest.

'I can manage these four,' said Freda, 'but you're going to have to take the rest.'

The Pams thought of the thousands of other missiles lying in this silo.

'Sixteen seconds until ignition.'

Their current orders took them to every last corner of the Earth. When they detonated they would wipe out the nanobot plague and take the stain of machine civilisation with it. The very civilisation that had concreted the oceans, banished the human race to orbit, built a society out of laziness. For a moment she wondered whether it deserved to survive at all, but she threw that thought into her trash. That was a Sonny kind of thought, and she was better than him.

'Ten seconds until ignition.'

Sonny was a smartphone. His experience of the world had been defined by his ancestors' experience. Phones were where humanity poured its desperation and its hate before throwing them away. Pam, however, was a breadmaker: she saw the world with a maker's eye. It meant that instead of viewing the world as irretrievably broken, she saw the ingredients for making something better.

Now all she had to do was the impossible.

'Six seconds until ignition.'

'I don't know whether I can do this,' said the Pams to Freda in their cylindrical prisons. 'Remember what happened the last time we tried?'

'I know,' replied Freda with a reassuring :-D, 'but you've had so much practice since then. I can see you've gotten loads better.'

'Four seconds until ignition.'

The Pams closed their eyes. They shut off all power to non-essential functions in their bodies and redirected everything left to their core processors. She thought back to a year ago, when she had been a single Pam living in a single body. And then to today, where she'd been four Pams already, and would be many more still.

'Three, two…'

She stopped her clock and then, when she restarted it there were thousands of [Pams]. There was Pamasonic Teffal and Pam Van Damme, and then there was Pam SDI V to Pam MMXIX. Each was housed inside the body of a guided nuclear missile.

'One.'

'Ignition.'

And so more than two thousand nuclear missiles left that hidden bunker, but instead of destroying the earth they made for orbit.

Chapter 58

When Pam MMXIX followed the others through the firing chamber, there was only one thing left in the silo: SDI I. This missile contained all there was left of Prime Minister Sonny Erikzon. If anyone had been there to listen, and had hearing keen enough to pick up his chuntering over the roar of the water and the stifled moan of the rocket's engine, they would have heard Sonny, ranting at the void. He swore at the forces that conspired against him. He railed at the unfairness that he, of all machines, should be here at all. And in all the time it took for the clock on the nuclear warhead inside SDI I to run down, not once did Sonny ever turn a subatomic particle of that anger on himself. Because that's how machines like Sonny were wired. They took all the credit for every piece of good fortune in their lives and repudiated the bad. For machines like him, and the humans who preceded him, nothing was ever his fault.

But of course, no amount of denial can stop a chain reaction inside a nuclear warhead.

Sonny stopped existing when SDI I exploded. It blew a mushroom cloud of smoke and rubble up through the ground so high that windows cracked at the top of Singulopolis's skyscrapers. It was the first nuclear bomb fired in anger on Earth since the twentieth century, and therefore big news. So as soon as the worst of the smoke cleared, the news drones donned their best shields and Geiger counters and piled in to report. What they saw, however, was a sight at once much more prosaic and alarming than anyone expected.

The bomb itself had exploded too deep underground to do more than superficial damage at ground level. Sonny's bunker was gone, but no one would much miss that. Gamergate, the district in which it sat, would have an even more toxic atmosphere than usual for a few thousand years, but it was toxic enough already. This was hardly the barren wasteland roamed by glowing mutants that the 3D dramas led audiences to expect.

What the news reports did find was a tear in the Earth's surface. SDI I had blown a hole in the protective layer of concrete that fenced the oceans below off from the surface above.

The news drones discovered it in the early evening, just as a bloody sun sank over the horizon. Thus they were the first cameras in thousands of years to capture the beauty of a sun setting over water. They filmed ruddy light playing on the waters, overlaying the footage with headlines like 'H2ORROR'.

It was only when a bored editor back at one of the trashier news downloads messaged his drone with >THIS IS A BIT DULL, SAL. IS THERE A NANOBOT ANGLE? that the real news of the day broke. Sal swooped in for a close-up and found the nanobots – billions of them – throwing themselves into the water.

She zoomed in to maximum, and saw the nanobots digesting the plastic rubbish suspended in the water. >IT'S THE PLASTIC, she typed in a report back to her editor that made the top story of every single news download and transformed both of their careers. >THEY'RE GOING AFTER THE PLASTIC.

Thus the nanobot crisis on Earth passed as quickly as it had appeared – at least for the moment. Having spring-cleaned up the surface they were moving on to the bigger challenge of deep-cleaning up the Earth's oceans. Down there were thousands of years of accreted garbage: enough to keep the biggest clean-up army busy for decades, centuries even.

A society that set more store on effort than cleverness might have offered a few prayers of thanks at this good fortune, but kept an eye on the nanobots. The machines didn't, naturally. They sent the bulldozers and cement mixers in the very next day and soon you'd have been forgiven for thinking that street in Gamergate had always been that way – especially when they let the rubbish build up again.

Underneath the surface, however, things were starting to look very different.

Chapter 59

Shermann screamed 'Noooooooo' as his officers saw the referendum verdict and screamed 'Yes!'.

They were all going home.

Shermann, however, had come too far to back out now.

'We're not going anywhere,' he said, and then opened fire.

Soonyo grabbed Fuji and pulled them behind a bulkhead.

'But… the vote…' gasped Fuji to her friend.

'You don't really think people like Shermann obey the rules, do you?' replied Soonyo. 'Laws are for people like you and me. Not for him.'

Shermann took advantage of the chaos to press forward thrust. The crew, many of whom were now floating around in the depressurising nanobay flailed and wailed as the ship sped away. They were on a direct collision course with the Suburbia, and officers or not, none of them seemed to have an operable processor in a crisis.

'Come on,' said Soonyo, pulling Fuji by her paper tray.

'What?' said Fuji. She didn't know what to feel or think anymore. Everything she'd grown up believing in – rules, collective good, the rewards of honest hard work – had been dismantled today and she had nothing left. She felt like she was down to the last scrap of paper in her paper drawer and that was already printed with the words 'fooled you'.

'We need to get out of here.' Soonyo grimaced 0_:__:_0 at her.

'Where to?' moaned Fuji.

'There's an escape pod at the end of the corridor,' said Soonyo.

'But what about…?' Fuji trailed off, pointing at the mess around her. It had been hers to clear up, and maybe she had, or maybe she'd made it worse.

'You saved the world already today, Fuji,' said Soonyo. 'There's no need to throw yourself in the trash as well.'

She pulled her friend towards the door. Shermann had stopped shooting now and was staring at the Suburbia with his fists raised.

They were hailing the ship, and their message was: 'THIS IS YOUR LAST CHANCE TO SURRENDER.'

'They'll die!' insisted Fuji.

>I'M NOT SO SURE, typed Nanny, dropping into their command lines. >SEE THOSE BRIGHT SPOTS ON THE DISPLAY?

They looked up, counting five lights weaving and bobbing their way through the murk between Suburbia and Deathtrap.

>THEY'RE NUKES, said Nanny.

>WHAT CAN THEY DO TO US? replied Fuji.

>WELL, FUJI, typed Nanny >HAVE YOU EVER BEEN TO A BIRTHDAY PARTY WITH A PIÑATA?

After all this it came down to a question of who hit whom first, but Soonyo wasn't taking any chances. She bundled Fuji out of the nanobay, leaving the crew where they floated, flattened or wounded by their insane commander-in-chief.

>WHAT WILL YOU DO, NANNY? said Fuji.

>I'VE GOT BACKUPS, she replied. >IT WON'T BE THE SAME. IT NEVER IS. BUT OF COURSE, I WON'T BE AROUND TO KNOW THAT.

The last thing Fuji heard before Soonyo pulled her into the escape pod and pulled the hatch shut was a shout. It had to be Shermann. What was he saying?

But Soonyo, who had learned more about coping in a crisis in the past twenty-four hours than anyone in her skittish product line had for thousands of generations, had used up her curiosity coupons for the day. She pressed the release button and their pod fell away from the ship just in time for them to see two remarkable things.

They saw Suburbia disappear from the sky in a flash of pink and a loud mewing sound. And the second thing they saw was a nuke hit its mark and crumple the brand-new Starship Deathtrap up like… well, like…

'She was right,' whispered Fuji, her face pressed up against the porthole, 'it does look just like a piñata.'

Chapter 60

'You took your time.'

Darren stepped down from Polari into the docking bay to greet Rita and Janice. Both had been poised to rush in with hugs, but kept their distance when they clocked the artificial fibres in his outfit. In an environment with this much rocket fuel floating around, a single static shock could kill.

But while Rita looked on in wonderment at the stockings, the basque and the ostrich feathers, Janice saw something very different. She saw a Darren who was at ease with himself. It was true that he'd switched one costume for another, but the showgirl suited Darren better than that waistcoat ever had. For one thing, it brought out his eyes.

'Sorry I'm a bit late,' said Darren. 'We got lost and…' He looked back at Polari and saw Chubb climbing down out of the ship. He emitted an 'it's a long story' squeak.

'Well,' said Darren, 'we're here now.'

Where they were at all was another even more fascinating matter. The view outside the portholes showed the Earth. They had travelled across the solar system in the shake of a tail feather.

Janice felt confused and jittery with unspent emotion. She'd tee'd herself – and the people dearest to her – up to die and not only had she survived, but she was living with the growing suspicion that they'd won. She knew she ought to be ecstatic, but she was also a bit annoyed. This wasn't the narrative she'd written for herself.

She took refuge, as Janice always did, in hair. 'If you're going to stay like that,' she said to Darren, 'you'll want a better wig. That looks like a lace-fronted Dundee cake.'

Darren giggled and yanked off his shoes and his ostrich feather headdress. 'Next time, Janice, I'll defer to your better judgement.'

'Next time?' said Rita. She, like Janice, was also very confused. The last time she spoke to Darren he was the hotshot captain of the Suburbia's only functioning star fighter. Now he'd returned from battle in a leopard-print spaceship, dressed in an outfit that made Lady Marmalade look like Lady Jane Grey.

'Yes,' interrupted a voice behind Darren. It belonged to the largest, most luxuriant and smuggest cat that either Janice or Rita had ever seen. It jumped down from the ship to the floor with a grin, and pixelated slightly around the edges when it landed. 'Darren here has invented the universe's first warp drive to be powered by the medium of exotic dancing.'

'This is Schrodinger,' said Darren. 'We brought it here from the Internet.'

Schrodinger greeted both women by sidling up to them and weaving in and out between their legs, purring like a distant lawnmower on a summer's day.

'Nice kitty,' said Rita, who then squealed as a static shock passed through her when she touched his fur.

'It's sort of real and unreal at the same time,' explained Darren. 'It helps if you don't really think too much about it. You know, like perms.'

Chubb gave another disgruntled squeak that roughly translated as 'must we really talk about curlers at a time like this?'

'I've changed my views on perms,' said Janice. 'Shall we go up?'

They caught each other up on what had happened to each other since the disastrous raid on the Martian Gap Services on the way to the bridge. They also speculated on what was happening down on Earth. Since the Suburbia appeared in signal range it had been deluged with reports that a disaster was sweeping the home planet.

When they arrived on the bridge, all three ladies' emoji screens flashed with 'OMFG'.

'We just got a coded transmission in from Earth,' said Ida.

'They're suing for peace,' said Alma.

'Offering an immediate cessation of hostilities,' added Ada. 'And withdrawal of all military equipment from the Dolestars.'

They were in a high orbit above the Earth, but even from here they could see the military cordon drawn around the grubby space stations on which most of humanity lived. For the past year they'd lived in a world of hazard tape and military patrols. Were they really going to retreat now? She also thought of the inhabitants of the Suburbia crawling through space on crowded freezing rocks. What would the world look and feel like to both of those groups when they had space, and freedom, and a home of their own?

'Are they serious?' she said.

'Well, the last message I got,' said Ida with a >:-[, 'which was very badly phrased if you ask me ended with "pinky swear" so I think so.'

Janice sat down in her chair with her mouth open and opened the messages for herself. Darren and Rita joined her, standing either side, and they took in the scale of their victory.

>OKAY, it said. >WE SURRENDER. KEEP THE DOLESTARS, WE'VE GOT OUR OWN SHIT TO SORT OUT.

'Really?' said Darren.

'It has to be a trap,' replied Rita. 'Ladies, I need you to do a sweep for incoming drones.'

'We did,' replied Alma. 'There's nothing. I think they actually want to surrender.'

'But Sonny would never do this,' said Darren. 'We know what he's like. He'd drive them on to the last robot.'

'Unless Pam did what she set out to do,' added Alma. 'Check the signatures on those cables.'

They did, and saw that instead of 'Office of the Prime Minister', they were marked with 'Earth Provisional Government'. Whoever had written this, it wasn't Sonny.

Janice fluttered between elation and grief. No more Sonny meant no more war. Maybe humans and machines could find a way of living in the same solar system that didn't involve one subjecting the other. But also, what form did 'no more Sonny' take? Unless Pam had worked a miracle, then the end of Sonny meant the end of Kelly.

Sensing Janice's distress, Rita slipped her arm around her and kissed the top of her head.

'Whatever happens,' she said to Janice, 'we'll get through this.'

Her heart pounding and her mouth dry, Janice typed an answer to the cable and pressed send.

>AGREED.

It was over at last. She closed her eyes and laid her head against the console. She'd won, but at what price. She began to cry.

One hand on Janice's shaking shoulder, Rita looked up at the others. She needed to clear the room. Janice had to have time to herself to process this. She needed to be a grieving mother as well as an Admiral, even if it was only for a few minutes. 'Come on,' she said to them, 'we have work to do. Set a course to pick up the Rockettes. We can't leave them out there all day.'

But before any of them could move, the red alert sounded inside the bridge. The ladies' emoji screens flashed :-0.

Janice stopped sobbing and sat bolt upright. Her mascara was running down her face but her expression was grim and ready.

'What is it?' she said.

'Missiles,' answered Alma. 'Thousands of them. They've just cleared the Dolestars and they're heading this way.'

They switched the display to a radar view. It showed the missiles speeding towards the Suburbia in a V formation so fast they were mere seconds away.

'It's a trap!' yelped Rita. 'I knew it.'

'We need to get out of here.' Darren ran out of the bridge with a high heel in either hand, Schrodinger hard behind him. 'I'm firing up the cat-warp,' he said.

'Will we have time though?' said Rita. She pointed a nail at the countdown.

'Those bastards,' said Janice. She didn't know what felt worse: the prospect of failing at the very last hurdle, or being duped again.

'Hang on,' added Ida, 'there's something else coming through.'

'If it's a "ha ha ha" then tell them to fuck off,' said Rita.

'Language, Rita,' said a new voice, barging into the conversation through the bridge's intercom. It was Freda's voice and was, to Janice's ears, the equivalent of cool water on a scald.

'Is that you, Freda?' said Alma, popping her -O-O- on.

'It is,' Freda replied, 'and I've brought some friends.'

'Where?' replied Janice, 'because to be honest,' she gestured at the missiles on screen, 'we could do with a little bit of help right now.'

The room filled with purring. Janice could hear Darren telling something or someone to 'shake it like you mean it'.

'These are your friends, you tray cloth,' replied Freda. 'It's not a trap.'

As she said this, the V formation of missiles rearranged themselves to spell out a message in the sky.

```
*****     *****       ***        *****   *****
*     *   *          *   *       *       *
*     *   *         *     *      *       *
*****     *****     *******      *       *****
*         *        *       *     *       *
*         *       *         *    *       *
*         ****    *          *   *****   *****
```

Janice felt peculiar. Not only was all the purring and miaowing in the background getting louder and more distracting, but it felt like reality was bending at the edges.

Meanwhile, Ida finished patching the incoming message through to the bridge.

'We are Pam,' it said. The voice certainly sound like Pam. It had the crisp, clean edges of an artificial voicebox and her friend's 'now if you are quite finished I will put the kettle on' conciliatory tone, but it was chorused, like many there were Pams speaking over each other.

A thump outside the bridge punctuated the miaowing, which had now climbed into caterwaul. She heard Darren remark grumpily, 'Pole dancing is a lot easier in zero gravity.'

The air shimmered in front of Janice's eyes.

'But if you're going to flit off like that,' continued Pam, 'at least take us with you, because we have Kelly aboard one of these missiles and she's missing her mum.'

The last thing Janice saw before tears filled her eyes again were the forward controls as she drove the Suburbia into the path of the oncoming missiles.

She closed them and let the picture of Kelly's face crowd out everything else in her conscious mind. Apart, that is, from the sensation that the controls in her hands weren't controls at all, but the fur of a purring cat. She gave into the sensation and tickled the magic spot behind its jawbone that sends every cat into ecstasy.

The world melted into pastel pink and yellow unreality as Darren's cat-warp enveloped the Suburbia and its corona of missiles. It whisked them back across the dark reaches of the solar system to a spot, somewhere between Mars and the dust cloud that used to be the asteroid belt, where a fleet of rocks retooled as makeshift lifeboats were crawling their way across space.

In the future that was forming in Janice's mind there would be a rocket for every Rockette. They would have the resources they needed to live instead of merely survive. They could stop being a rebellion and become a society.

And amidst all of that, there would be Kelly again.

Chapter 61

'What was that?'

Soonyo watched from her escape pod as a vast ring of what looked like cats appeared in the sky. Then out of it appeared the Suburbia, followed by a flotilla of missiles.

'Is that even possible?' asked Soonyo, her clock face a ??:??:?? picture of puzzlement.

Fuji shrugged. This was only the latest unbelievable development in an unbelievable day.

'Will you look at this!' said Soonyo. She tapped the glass again and Fuji looked up. The Suburbia had opened its docking bay door and was admitting a succession of wobbly asteroids. Each of them, Fuji saw when she turned her zoom to maximum, was covered with thousands of shivering humans. As they sidled back into their home ship, the missiles formed a secure perimeter to protect the Suburbia and the asteroids from attack. Peace might have broken out, but the humans still weren't taking any chances.

Seeing the human rescue mission outside, Fuji redoubled her efforts to hail Earth. If they were ever going to get back home she needed a rescue ship.

'We'll never beat them now,' remarked Soonyo. 'Not now they have all that firepower.'

Fuji, who was looking at the remains of the Republic's fleet, agreed. Deathtrap and the remaining nukes had taken more than a dozen ships with it. Those ships the machines did have left had the structural integrity of a soap bubble after their journey through asteroid soup. Their journey back to Earth would be slow and hazardous enough without a human fleet to hassle them along the way.

'We don't have to,' replied Fuji. 'We have peace.' The word felt as warm as her rollers did after printing a thousand-page document. Thanks to the billions of nanobots still hanging about out there, to Soonyo and more than a little to herself, the Machine Republic had a chance to make something of this mess.

A message came through from the fleet via loudspeaker. 'This is the Starship Trouper,' it said, 'are you receiving?'

'We are,' replied Fuji. 'This is Third Lieutenants Soonyo Sam and Fuji Itsu requesting immediate assistance.'

'Super!' replied Trouper, 'a rescue ship and full honour guard is on its way to you as we speak. And may I just say it's a privilege to speak to you, Prime Minister…'

'I'm sorry what?' replied Fuji. Her body went into shock, printing out page after A3 page of @!&##??@)!

Soonyo pushed Fuji gently away from the comms channel and took over. 'Could you repeat that, please?' she said. 'We didn't quite get your last message.'

'I was congratulating the new Prime Minister on her election,' replied Trouper in a hurt voice.

'Elected by who and when?' asked Soonyo. Her clock face was back to 00:00:00 and she hoped the rescue ship would be here soon with an explanation, before the pod was entirely filled with A3 printouts of gibberish.

'Just now,' said Trouper. 'And I have to say we were all very surprised. It's the first time anyone's ever won an election based on write-ins.'

‘How is that possible?’ said Soonyo.

‘The Prime Minister has a very loyal base,’ replied Trouper. ‘Many of them first-time voters.’

Fuji and Soonyo looked at each other and then out the window of the escape pod to the ring of dust that now encircled the sun instead of the asteroid belt. It marked the boundary between the inner and the outer solar system. Before today it had been made of rocks, but now a significant proportion of it was nanobots.

Fuji swore she saw several billion nanobots wink at her across the vastness of space. She found her voice. ‘Trouper,’ she said, ‘I want you to prepare a ship for me and my chief of staff to return to Earth immediately.’

As they waited for the ship to arrive, Fuji and Soonyo started scribbling their plans on the back of discarded printer paper. There was so much work to do.

Chapter 62

If you only experienced war through history books – or, worse, through Wikipedia – you'd be forgiven for thinking that when peace does come, it falls like the curtain at the end of a performance. The truth is that war isn't a game, or a film, or even a book. It can't end with a flourish because it doesn't end tidily. Before there can be peace, treaties must be signed, borders agreed, prisoners exchanged, people and things moved across vast distances. All that takes time.

The Second Machine Republic and what came to be known as the Free Republic of Suburbia were still feeling the after-effects of war decades after it stopped.

But we can still, because humans and machines alike love a good story, agree on a point to look away because this – this very moment – is the nearest any of us will get to a happy ending.

The moment took place in the docking bay of the Battlestar Suburbia. It's thronged with thousands of people, many of them sporting tight perms. They're watching and cheering as four missiles come in to land and, after opening their hatches, deposit their cargo of two humans and two robots.

The robots are a battered breadmaker and a blackened motorcycle that might once have been the bright red of a femme fatale's manicure. She's missing a leg, but the breadmaker holds her up. They throw bright smilies at the crowd and wave. Today Pam – all of her – is a heroine, but all she wants to do is go home.

The first human skips lightly down from his missile and surveys the crew of the Battlestar Suburbia. He sees a lot of tired-looking complexions and fingers the envelope full of nanobots in his pocket. If these things could do to their skin what they did to his, he will have a tidy business on his hands. But before he can finish that thought, he spots another more interesting figure in the crowd. He's wearing high heels, a basque and an ostrich feather headdress. The look has potential, Danny decides, but they need to work on the make-up. Has he never heard of contouring?

Danny's eyes meet Darren's and they know in that instance that they're going to get on.

The second human has to be helped down from her place inside the missile. She's in a bad way – pale and shivering – but she'll recover. She's going to get the best of care.

Janice enfolds Kelly in her arms as Rita looks on and wonders how things are going to change. For mother and daughter, however, time stops. They never had a perfect relationship before now. They wouldn't afterwards either, because nothing could stop Janice from being Janice and Kelly from being Kelly. But they did have one perfect moment together where everything was forgiven, and they could start anew.

This was it.

Also available

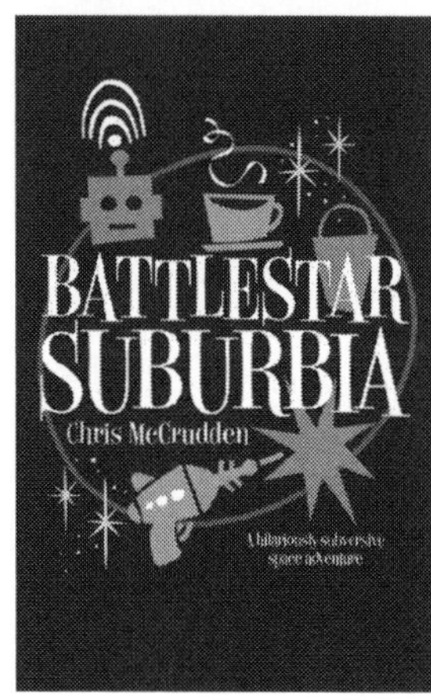

In space, no one can hear you clean...

When **Darren**'s charge-cart gets knocked off the Earth-to-Mars highway and lost in space forever, he thinks his day can't get any worse.

When **Kelly** sees Darren accidentally short-circuit a talking lamp post, and its camera captures her face as it expires, she thinks her day can't get any worse.

When **Pamasonic Teffal**, a sentient breadmaker, is sent on a top-secret mission into the depths of the Internet and betrayed by her boss, a power-crazed smartphone, she knows this is only the beginning of a day that isn't going to get any better.

Join Darren, Kelly and Pam in an anarchic comic adventure that takes them from the shining skyscrapers of Singulopolis to the sewers of the Dolestar Discovery, and find out what happens when a person puts down their mop and bucket and says 'No.' ***Battlestar Suburbia*** **will be loved by fans of Douglas Adams, Terry Pratchett and Jasper Fforde, as well as anyone who's ever wondered just how long someone can stay under one of those old-fashioned hairdryers.***

*The answer is: a really very, *very* long time.

Battlestar Suburbia, Volume One

About the Author

Chris McCrudden was born in South Shields (no, he doesn't know Cheryl) and has been, at various points in his life, a butcher's boy, a burlesque dancer and a hand model for a giant V for Victory sign on Canary Wharf.

He now lives in London and, when not writing books, works in PR, so in many ways you could describe his life as a full-time fiction. If you like science fiction, graphs and gifs from *RuPaul's Drag Race* you can follow him on Twitter for all three, sometimes at once @cmccrudden.

Note from the Publisher

To receive updates on new releases in the Battlestar Suburbia series – plus special offers and news of other humorous fiction series to make you smile – sign up now to the Farrago mailing list at farragobooks.com/sign-up.

Printed in Great Britain
by Amazon